HALLOWED GROUND

WARHAMMER
AGE OF SIGMAR

HALLOWED GROUND

RICHARD STRACHAN

BLACK LIBRARY

A BLACK LIBRARY PUBLICATION

First published in 2022.
This edition published in Great Britain in 2022 by
Black Library, Games Workshop Ltd., Willow Road,
Nottingham, NG7 2WS, UK.

Represented by: Games Workshop Limited – Irish branch,
Unit 3, Lower Liffey Street, Dublin 1,
D01 K199, Ireland.

10 9 8 7 6 5 4 3 2 1

Produced by Games Workshop in Nottingham.
Cover illustration by Lorenzo Mastroianni.

A CIP record for this book is available from the British Library.

ISBN 13: 978 1 80026 221 8

See Black Library on the internet at

blacklibrary.com

Find out more about Games Workshop
and the worlds of Warhammer at

games-workshop.com

Printed and bound by CPI Group (UK) Ltd, Croydon, CR0 4YY

The Mortal Realms have been despoiled. Ravaged by the followers of the Chaos Gods, they stand on the brink of utter destruction.

The fortress-cities of Sigmar are islands of light in a sea of darkness. Constantly besieged, their walls are assailed by maniacal hordes and monstrous beasts. The bones of good men are littered thick outside the gates. These bulwarks of Order are embattled within as well as without, for the lure of Chaos beguiles the citizens with promises of power.

Still the champions of Order fight on. At the break of dawn, the Crusader's Bell rings and a new expedition departs. Storm-forged knights march shoulder to shoulder with resolute militia, stoic duardin and slender aelves. Bedecked in the splendour of war, the Dawnbringer Crusades venture out to found civilisations anew. These grim pioneers take with them the fires of hope. Yet they go forth into a hellish wasteland.

Out in the wilds, hardy colonists restore order to a crumbling world. Haunted eyes scan the horizon for tyrannical reavers as they build upon the bones of ancient empires, eking out a meagre existence from cursed soil and ice-cold seas. By their valour, the fate of the Mortal Realms will be decided.

The ravening terrors that prey upon these settlers take a thousand forms. Cannibal barbarians and deranged murderers crawl from hidden lairs. Martial hosts clad in black steel march from skull-strewn castles. The savage hordes of Destruction batter the frontier towns until no stone stands atop another. In the dead of night come howling throngs of the undead, hungry to feast upon the living.

Against such foes, courage is the truest defence and the most effective weapon. It is something that Sigmar's chosen do not lack. But they are not always strong enough to prevail, and even in victory, each new battle saps their souls a little more.

This is the time of turmoil. This is the era of war.

This is the Age of Sigmar.

PROLOGUE

The sun was on its long decline as the scavenger came across the dead. Spears of light lanced down from the far horizon and stabbed into the littered plain. The afternoon drowsed into dusk, coloured by all the bold shades of Ghur: purple and scarlet, orange and gold. It would be a long night, the scavenger thought. You could never really tell in this realm; even the nights seemed possessed of their own volatile and irrepressible will. They lasted as long as they pleased.

He waited above the plain for a little while, crouched by an outcrop of rock until the light had further dimmed. Around him, tough sprigs of thorn grass wavered in the breeze. He tapped his fingers lightly against the flank of his cart and gazed down on the spread of corpses a hundred yards away. Orruks mostly, he thought. An ogor or two, perhaps. Stragglers from the great armies that had marched this way a season ago, heading to the city on the Coast of Tusks – Excelsis, proud bastion of Sigmar's domain. Fell tales had drifted along the trade routes since then, weaving their way through the wilderness. Awful stories of slaughter and dread, mayhem and violence. The walls of the city had been breached, some said. The populace had been drowned in their own blood. The hosts of Destruction had given no quarter, and they had feasted well that night.

Kragnos...

The scavenger shivered. He had heard the rumours. Some said a god had burst forth from the mountains of Ghur, a beast fit to trample entire empires into the dust. A new god or a very old one, no one could quite say. Whether Excelsis had survived or not was hardly his business, but he doubted any mortal stronghold could have held back such violence. The ground had shuddered for days with the passing of the host, but the scavenger had not been foolish enough to try and lay eyes on it. Better to wait, he had thought. Better to skulk about in the mountains and keep your head down, emerging only when the air had ceased to tremble with rage.

Whether these orruks and ogors on the plain below him had died at their own hands or at the hands of their enemies was not the scavenger's business either. They were a brutish, violent breed, and it would have come as no surprise if they had all torn themselves apart over some slight or insult, or just for the sheer pleasure of fighting. No matter. He only cared that they had left a goodly spread of bodies for him to pick over. Weapons, scraps of armour, trinkets – all would fetch a decent price in any of the frontier towns on the other side of the plains. Some young bloods would trade all they had for orruk teeth as well; a handful of those in your pocket and you could pretend to any maid you fancied that you had torn them from the beast's jaw with your own hands. The scavenger chuckled to himself. There was hardly a thing in the Mortal Realms you couldn't put a price to one way or the other, or that someone, somewhere, wouldn't be willing to pay for.

When the dusk had deepened a little further, he dragged his cart down the dusty incline towards the dead, rolling it over the stones and thorn grass. The smell from the bodies was atrocious, but it was nothing the scavenger hadn't experienced before. He dragged his scarf up over his mouth and nose, and hefted the tools on his belt: pliers for teeth, a bone saw to cut rings from fingers, hammer and chisel in case he was lucky enough to find any jewels embedded in shields or breastplates. He hummed mildly to himself as he got to work, ignoring the slick, mouldering flesh under his hands; the cold dead eyes that stared up in milky blindness at the spread of night, its gaudy weave of stars. Battered pauldrons, iron belt buckles, earrings and teeth – all of it went into his cart.

He had been working for perhaps an hour when he heard the footsteps. The night was still and cool now, broken only by the distant roar of the Hellspeak Mountains grinding themselves together, the hooting call of some plains-bird scurrying across the dust. But then he heard them, steady and firm, crunching across the ground ahead of him, and… something else. A shuffling, stumbling tread; a quiet, eerie moan that raised the hairs on the back of his neck.

The scavenger stopped where he was, crouched by the stinking corpse of an orruk, its eyes frozen in shock at whatever blow had killed it. He gripped his shears and carefully drew his cloak around his shoulders, hoping the darkness would be enough to hide him. Damn it, he'd fight if he had to, but he muttered a prayer to Sigmar, Alarielle, Nagash and any other god he could think of all the same. Kragnos, even.

Kragnos protect me…

The footsteps came closer. The sound of that faint shuffle weaved itself around and through them, a dragging scuffle against the dirt. The scavenger raised his head and risked a glance from the shadows of his hood. There, skirting the spread of corpses, was a dark figure wrapped in a black cloak, holding an obsidian staff. He walked confidently but without haste, and at his side there moved… *something*.

Gods, the scavenger thought, *is that… is that a child?* The scavenger peered into the shadows, and as he did so the spheres above were unveiled of cloud, and the scene was lit for a moment by a pale and trembling light.

'I seek the way to Excelsis, friend,' the figure said.

He stopped no more than twenty yards away, on the edge of the charnel ground. His voice rang out like a bell in the stillness of the night. By his side, the child – if that's what it was – stumbled to a halt. The scavenger could see its pallid face, thin and drawn, the dark eyes under a hooded brow. The figure reached out and carefully gathered the child into the folds of his cloak.

'Am I on the right track?' he said.

There was no longer any point in hiding. The scavenger slowly stood, his shears still gripped in his hand. Wrenching his eyes away from the child, he said, 'Close enough, sir. You're maybe a week away from it, on foot, if it's on foot you'll be going.'

'It is.'

The scavenger swallowed. The stranger was slight, his face veiled by the shadows. He had no weapons, as far as the scavenger could see, but in all his long years on the plains of Ghur, he didn't think he'd ever come across someone who radiated such a feeling of danger and threat. It came off him like an aura. The very rays of the dying sun seemed to fear him.

'I'm honour bound to say,' the scavenger stuttered, 'that you might not find Excelsis in quite the state you were hoping.'

'How so?'

'A big battle,' he said, 'not a season past. Terrible destruction, from what I heard. The walls thrown down, people slaughtered in the streets. Sure, it's said the city doesn't even stand no more.'

The smile that broke across the figure's face was terrible. The scavenger looked away. His legs were shaking, he realised. He wanted more than anything to run, but intuition told him that to do so would only be to invite disaster.

'I can assure you otherwise,' the figure said. 'The city stands, and I would go there.' He looked around at the corpses at their feet, tangled and rotting. 'I see you have no fear of the dead,' he said.

'No, lord,' the scavenger said, wringing his hands. 'What's ceased to live can't hurt no one now, can it?'

The dark figure laughed. The child at his side began to tremble, making a horrible choking sound in its throat. Its hands shook, the jaw champed open and closed. Immediately the man crouched and wrapped his arm around its shoulders, hushing it, whispering in a soft and gentle voice.

'There now,' he said. 'Peace, my son, peace.'

The scavenger felt he was going to scream. No corpse he had come across, no matter how ravaged and mutilated, had ever seemed as awful as that blank-faced child trembling in its father's arms.

When the boy had calmed down, the dark figure stood and drew his cloak tight around him.

'To Excelsis, then,' he said. He smiled and gave a courteous nod. The scavenger averted his eyes.

He watched them walk off into the shadows, heading deeper into the night. Eventually, all he could hear of them were those flat, patient footsteps and that shuffling tread as it broke against the dusty plains, and the further they went, the better the scavenger began to feel. It was like a cold, clammy blanket had been taken from his shoulders.

He wiped the sweat from his brow and sagged against the side of his cart.

Gods be praised, he thought as he reached for his flask. *Sigmar,*

Alarielle, or whichever one of you kept your eye on me then, thanks be unto you for keeping me safe!

He tipped the flask to his mouth and drank deep, the firewater burning a channel of courage all the way down his chest and into his stomach. As he pushed the cork back into the bottle he glanced at the bodies at his feet, steeling himself to get back to work. He clipped the shears to his belt and unhooked the pliers, kneeling down in the dirt and tugging open the jaw of the nearest orruk. The stench of its rotten mouth was appalling, but with a lighter heart he began to prise and probe, tapping the pliers against one of the creature's massive tusks.

It took him a moment to realise that the orruk was looking at him. They all were – each of them staring at him through the milky pupils of their cold, dead eyes.

PART ONE

INTO THE WILD

CHAPTER ONE

THE THREAD
OF MEMORY

In the darkness, hands shaking, the girl hushed her breath and tried not to scream. There was a gap in front of her, a line of light to which she pressed her face. She peered through into the shadowed room beyond. The crackle of flame from elsewhere in the house, the stench of smoke, the reek of blood. On the floor lay her mother's body, arms and legs twisted at impossible angles, her face turned away. The rent in her throat, blood pulsing onto the floorboards, the loaded crossbow at her side. She could see this. She could see everything. Her bed, the blankets tossed aside. Her dolls slumped on the sideboard. Her books. Her mother's corpse.

She peered through the crack onto the ruin of her life.

'Little girl...' came the voice from deeper in the house. A woman's voice, mocking and amused, sharp with pleasure. 'Little girl, I can smell you... Come out, little girl, come out and play!'

Breath like a bellows now, rattling inside the darkness of the wardrobe where she had hidden herself. The girl clamped one hand over her mouth and reached with the other for the pendant around her neck. She squeezed it so tightly it broke the skin on her palm. The twin-tailed comet. Sigmar's sign. Her mother's final gift.

'Sigmar protect me!' she whispered. 'Father, protect me.'

'Child, don't be so shy,' the voice laughed. It was getting closer. The girl could hear the whisper of silk, the rustle of the woman's gown. She could smell her corpse-scent beneath the stink of spilled blood. 'If you're waiting for your father to join us, then I'm afraid I have some bad news for you.'

The girl's heart lurched in her chest. She sobbed, and the woman laughed to hear it. She was near now, very near.

'Oh, don't worry,' the woman said. Her voice was like red wine, like velvet. 'He's still alive, for now. Although, I imagine it will be a long while before he can walk again…'

The girl crouched in the darkness, tears burning in her eyes. Smoke was drifting into the room now, creeping in frills and tendrils across the floorboards. Her mother's blood as black as oil, smouldering in the light of the aether-lamp.

'What did you think would happen?' the woman said. 'For your parents to come after me like this, to try in their blundering way to hunt me down, like an animal…' She snarled suddenly and the girl felt the blood in her veins curdle. 'Like an animal!'

There was no way out. She would die here, die like her mother at the hands of this thing. And then her father would die, and his strong and gentle light would be taken from the world forever, snuffed out in agony and humiliation. The girl cried, no longer trying to muffle the sound. The tears burned down her face. In her hand the pendant felt like a circle of fire, but as the woman laughed, the girl felt something far beyond the pain and sorrow begin to take hold of her. Something stronger, and infinitely more powerful than grief or

16

the love she felt for her parents. Something more fervent even than her fear of Sigmar.

The girl began to hate, and her hatred was like a cool, clear flame burning in the darkness. It was inextinguishable. Even if she died here now, the girl knew that her hatred would live on. It would never die. Even from the Underworlds it would shine out to her, like a beacon calling her home, until she had had her revenge.

She pressed her fingers to the wardrobe door, inching it open. The crossbow was on the ground at her mother's side, the wooden bolt sharp as a dagger, anointed with holy oils and carved with the names of Sigmar's saints. She pushed the door open another inch, and another. The woman's voice drifted like a winter breeze, dusted with frost and ashes.

'Oh, yes, little girl… that's right. That's good, I wholeheartedly approve. Don't die like a rat in a trap, shivering in the dark. Come out into the light, little girl. Stand your ground…' She laughed again, and the sound was like a broken bell pealing across a graveyard. 'Come out, and embrace your mother one last time…'

The girl looked at her mother's body, lying there as torn and twisted as a rag doll. She pushed the door open yet another inch, and as she slowly stepped out into the light of the aether-lamp, the corpse began to twitch.

The arms flopped against the floorboards. The broken neck jerked around. The eyes, cold white coins pressed into her mother's frozen face, blinked and swivelled in their sockets. And as the dark laughter rang out against the night, her mother slowly grinned and slumped forward, her head lolling backwards, mouth hissing, her arms twisting as she hauled herself to her feet. Stumbling forward, straightening, she looked down at her daughter with the cruel and malicious gaze of the undead.

Her dress was drenched in blood, but the savage wound in her neck had already healed. Her blonde hair was as pale as snow, and under her skin the girl could see the pulsing traceries of her veins, black with unlife. Her mother reached out her arms. When she spoke, her voice was like the creak of a rusting cemetery gate.

'Doralia,' she said. 'Doralia, my darling. Come to mother. Let me kiss you, my child, do not be afraid...'

The girl stooped to pick up the crossbow. The thing that looked out of those cloudy, cataracted eyes was not her mother. She knew this, and yet all the same the crossbow wavered in her hands.

'Put that down, my darling,' the corpse said. She smiled, and her teeth were as yellow as old ivory, as sharp as blades. 'Let me hold you, my love. Don't cry, there's no need for tears. I have something for you... Let me show you... A gift...'

A sound like tearing lace, the stench of death and the brush of cold shadows against her skin. Doralia screamed and pulled the trigger – but then what filled her vision wasn't the creature that used to be her mother, but something infinitely worse. Red wings swept out towards her like a fan of blades, heavy with the stink of rotting violets, a cloying musk that choked her... And then Sentanus, the White Reaper, was screaming in rage as he was torn to pieces, and the hall around them was a kaleidoscope of blood and broken mirrors, her father groaning as he raised his pistol.

The Talon and the Voice...

'Doralia! Shoot it, shoot it for Sigmar's sake!' her father screamed.

In the blazing shadows her mother's dead face faded to a pale smear, and the dark laughter trickled across her skin like melting ice.

She snapped awake, choking, her face a mask of sweat. She gasped and rolled onto her side, snatching up her blade. Frantically she scanned the shadows, hands shaking, the sword stretched out in front of her. She fumbled at her belt for a pistol, but as the embers of her campfire stuttered in the breeze, casting a feeble glow against the scrubland, she knew that she was alone. Instincts from a lifetime of violence had made the sense of danger as clear to her as any sight or sound or taste; nothing had crept up on her while she slept.

Just a dream, she thought as she sheathed her blade. Her breath was ragged. *Just the old dream, and...*

The Talon and the Voice...

Doralia ven Denst shivered and squeezed her eyes shut, clamping a hand to the back of her neck. Fear buffeted through her like a wave, like a black cloud shutting out the light, but after a moment the feeling was gone and she could open her eyes again. She wiped the sweat from her face with a hand that wouldn't stop shaking. Sitting back down beside her campfire, she looked at the hand as if it belonged to someone else. The fingers trembled. She felt cold.

'Damn it all,' she muttered.

She dug about in her kitbag until she found the bottle, pulling out the cork with her teeth and tipping a good swallow into her mouth. She gulped the firewater down, drank again, eyes burning and chest aflame. After one more drink her hand stopped shaking. Her heartbeat slowed, her breathing calmed down. She ran her fingers through the cropped bob of her lank blonde hair. The campfire fizzed and popped before her, and she tossed on a few more sticks to keep it going. Beyond the narrow circle of its light, the wilds of Ghur slumbered in the dark, deep in their uneasy dreams of violence and destruction.

What brought you out here, father? she wondered.

She sighed and glanced again at the bottle of firewater. She wrapped herself in her duster and tried to settle down on the stony ground, the campfire painting a flickering amber light against her grim, unsmiling face.

What are you looking for out here? What do you hope to find?

* * *

19

She had realised her father was missing when she had woken early a few days before, tumbling from her straw mattress with a vicious hangover and a livid bruise against her cheek. Groping for a bottle, Doralia had sat on the edge of the bed and swallowed down the dregs until her vision cleared and she could make out the bleak contents of her garret room: the simple cot, a wooden chair, a plain wardrobe where she hung her coat and stored her weapons. Her wide-brimmed hat had been tossed into a corner, the crown squashed, and there was a scattering of crossbow bolts and nullstone cartridges across the dusty floor. Light fell in a thin stream through the grubby window, and she could hear the chanted calls of the beggars and panhandlers on the streets of the Veins outside, the glimmer-addicts hustling for a shard.

There was the furious percussion of rebuilding as well, hammers and saws and the blunt commands of the stonemasons as they tried to knock the district back into shape. Excelsis had been smashed to pieces during the siege, but the citizens had come together practically the next day to try and rebuild it. Not out of civic pride, she was quite sure, but out of simple fear. The armies of Kragnos and the daemons of Slaanesh had nearly torn the place apart, but only a fool would think the danger had passed. Excelsis was a diamond glistening on the shore, a spear of Sigmar's power planted on the Coast of Tusks. It was a target for everything in the realm that hated peace and order and decency, and it always would be. The siege had taught them that, if nothing else.

The light from outside was sickly and bright. She pressed her fingers carefully against the bruise on her cheek, wondering how it had got there. Last night was a blur to her. She remembered a tavern somewhere, a dark corner where she could nurse her ale, but other than that the evening was a blank. Her knuckles hurt, so she must have punched someone at some point. Always a safe bet... So many of her nights were like this now. Drinking too much, losing herself in low taverns and their masking shadows, her hat brim pulled down to block out the world, as if the bottom of a glass were as far as she wanted to see.

She tipped the bottle to her lips again but it was empty. She flung it into a corner of the room, where it shattered against the wall.

Downstairs, in the plain hallway, she had found a note nailed to the inside of the front door. Her father's handwriting, the cramped flourish of his signature, as if she could have mistaken the terse instructions as coming from anybody else. She plucked the note free and read it, and it took her a moment to make sense of the words.

Doralia, I will return if I can. Forgive me, and don't follow. Galen ven Denst.

Again, as if living through it one more time, she saw her father screaming at her to shoot, the daemons sliding across the skin of reality, broken mirrors splashed with blood. The White Reaper, Sentanus of the Knights Excelsior, his arm ripped from his torso... Those creatures flitting from the void, their black eyes and glistening mouths, the reek of spoiled flowers. And then the crossbow bolt slamming home, the daemon erupting into a cloud of rotting butterflies that stank of iris and musk...

She swore and tried not to be sick as she crumpled the note in her fist. Ever since the siege he had been plunged into this strange gloom, as if their impossible victory had instead been a defeat. He had been withdrawn, distracted, only half there.

Damn him! As if I'm no more than a child or a piece of luggage to be left behind! What does he think he's doing, the old fool?

The hangover seemed to slide off her then, burned away by her anger. Her head felt clear. She checked his room, knowing before she opened the door that his kitbag would be gone, his swords and pistols, his cracked leather coat. She smiled as she gathered her own kit, sheathing the bolts in her quiver, filling her ammunition pouches and dragging a cloth quickly down the length of her blade. She flung on her blood-red leather duster and snatched up her hat from the floor, punching out the crown and carefully placing it on her head. There was no mirror in her room – she had thrown it away after the siege – but she knew the grim figure she must cut.

Very well, father, she thought, as she pushed her way out into the clamour of Excelsis. *The hunt is on.*

Doralia lay beside the fire now and watched the light expand, the fierce dawn of Ghur. Blazing sheets of red and gold erupted against the skyline, a wash of colour that tempered the land like steel. The plains stretched away from her, a rugged landscape of boulders and scrub a hundred leagues across. Far off to the north and west she could see the jagged sweep of the Krondspines, pale in the morning light, a vast, inverted crescent that sheltered the inland sea of Lake Everglut. The Great Excelsis Road to Izalend curved off a few miles away on her right, stretching east and then north along the coast, on its slow journey towards the Icefangs. Her way did not lie in that direction, though. It had taken only two or three intimidating visits to their usual snitches and informants to find out the truth: her father had been seen buying up some supplies and leaving by the west gate. He had turned away from the road in the direction of the Glossom Crevasse, it seemed. She would find him to the north-west. And when she found him, she would demand answers.

As she packed away her camp, she thought back to the dream that had woken her during the night – the nightmare that always flitted about her subconscious when she settled down to sleep. The darkness of that wardrobe, her mother's body twitching on the floorboards. That sinuous, mocking voice, snaking up the stairs; the sound of dark laughter… Twenty years had passed, and it was still something she thought about every day. And now this as well, a new scene intruding on the old: the last moments of the siege, the Slaaneshi daemons birthing themselves from unreality, the city howling in distress around them. The edge of madness and horror in her father's voice as he screamed at her to shoot, the shards of broken mirror glass that seemed to reflect from every angle Doralia's own defeated gaze...

What's the point? she remembered thinking, for just the briefest of moments. The crossbow had wavered in her hands. *There will never be an end to the dangers we face.*

She shook her head, tried to throw off the weight that had settled on her since those days. She stowed the firewater bottle deep in her pack and hefted it to her shoulder, drawing her hat brim down against the thunderous sun as it burned against the horizon. The plains simmered under the sunlight, trembling underfoot as if impatient to transform themselves into something else. Ghur was never still, she knew. She wondered how small a figure she must seem as she set off across its skin. How insignificant.

CHAPTER TWO

BLACK DOG

The great sheet of the burning sky pressed its weight upon her. She scanned the ground as she moved, her crossbow shouldered on its strap so she could keep her hands free. Every now and then she stooped to run her fingers over the displaced dirt, to see in the discoloured edge of a tumbled stone a sign that someone had recently passed. On the border of a stretch of thorny scrub she found a couple of broken stems. Further on, along the line of a slight depression, she found what could have been a footprint from a pair of hard-worn leather boots.

Doralia stopped for a moment, crouching down and pivoting on her heel to take in the landscape around her. She tipped her hat back and scanned the horizon, interrogating the plains the way she would interrogate a prisoner: with clear-eyed and unyielding certainty. She could see the ground dipping slightly as it flowed on towards the west. Further to the north, fifty miles away perhaps, were the low foothills that eventually led up into the mighty jaws of the Krondspines. To her right, she could see the meandering track of the Great Excelsis Road as it swept off towards the coast. Beyond that, a hundred miles or so now, she could see the steel gleam of the distant sea.

The land was empty around her. It felt as if the whole of Ghur had been drained of its inhabitants over the last few months, as if every orruk and ogor and gargant had been swept up and pointed in one direction only: towards Excelsis, where they had all met their squalid end in the streets of the ravaged city. Even the beasts that called this place home, the monsters and megafauna, seemed to be hiding themselves. As she gave the horizon a last full-circle scan, she couldn't see so much as a puff of dust from a passing predator, out on the prowl. The sky itself was clear of birds. All of Ghur seemed to be holding its breath.

She swept off her hat and wiped a handkerchief across her face, her dirty blonde hair dark with sweat. Her head was pounding with the heat, but at least she'd thought to bring more than just firewater with her. As she drank from her water flask she wondered how her father could possibly be managing in these conditions; he certainly wasn't getting any younger. During the siege there had been more than one desperate moment when Doralia's greatest fear had been for his safety rather than her own. With a twist of her heart she called to mind his greying skin, his thinning white hair, the slack look of exhaustion on his face as they had both run for the Conclave Hall. She saw again his look of dread and horror as Sentanus was torn apart in front of them by the daemon Dexcessa, for if not even Stormcast Eternals were safe from these things, then what chance did they have? What chance did any of them have when the gods themselves went to war?

She pushed her hat back onto her head. Not for the first time, she admitted that her greatest fear was finding her father's body out here in the wilds, his bones picked clean by the scavenger birds. He had always seemed as tough as old boot leather to her when she was growing up, and even her mother's death had carved no more than a faint frown on that stony brow. But now, as she herself felt the pain and stress of the job beginning to drag her down, she could only begin to imagine how much worse it must be for him. He had been doing this for decades. There was a good reason why so few agents of the Order of Azyr made it to old age.

If they could have talked about it, perhaps things would have been different. Their fears, the sickening weight of their experiences. She could have told him how much she loved him, how much she worried that he was heading for no more than a miserable death in the line of duty. Surely, for Sigmar's sake, he had done more than enough for the order? He deserved some peace, a measure of contentment, not this relentless stalking from one hellish disaster to the next, risking his body and his sanity as both declined with age.

Doralia gave a bitter laugh. No, it was impossible to imagine such a scenario. Since she was a child, she had been a pupil to him as much as a daughter, and it was no easier to imagine a heartfelt conversation between them than it was to imagine Galen ven Denst happily packing away his weapons and putting his feet up. A witch hunter of the Order of Azyr had no comfortable retirement plan. The blade would never be hung above the fireplace, a source of old war stories made more pleasant by the passage of time. A witch hunter shouldered this burden because no one else could. Death was the only retirement they would get. Death was their duty, in the end.

A surly breeze kicked up amongst the scrub, sending a trail of grit clattering against her coat. She clenched her jaw and shouldered her crossbow, chiding herself for moping about it all.

Press on, she thought. *Always forwards, into the teeth of whatever's waiting for you. What other choice is there?*

* * *

A mile further on, as the plains began to dip towards the line of a distant river that sparkled in the heat haze, she found a cluster of stones and the burnt remains of a campfire. It was hard to tell how long they had been lying there – three days, four perhaps? At the edge of the campfire, as she trawled her fingers through the ash, she found the chewed stub of a cigar. She raised it to her nose and inhaled the scent, and immediately she had her father in mind, sitting in his room, lost in a fug of smoke as he brooded on his troubles. The rich, loamy tobacco that only grew in Ghyran, his one indulgence. Doralia smiled. There was a liquor store halfway up the Pilgrim's Way where he bought them. She hoped he'd stocked up.

She flicked the stub back into the ashes and sat for a while, sipping at her firewater, watching the long drop of the evening sun as it smouldered against the rough peaks of the Krondspines away to the north-west. The sky above her was as vast as the sea, a deep oceanic blue threaded now with streaks of scarlet and orange. Burnt clouds toiled and frayed, unravelling as they met the horizon. The evening breeze lifted for a moment from the skin of the plains, dancing up to ruffle her hair and pluck at the wings of her coat. From somewhere far away she could hear the grinding thrum of the realm as it buckled and shouldered itself into new configurations. Mountains would be stretching wide their stony maws and swallowing down the forests, the rivers bending and thrashing like coiled serpents. Promontories would surge into the boiling seas like spear points, and whole continents would strain to tear apart their rivals on the other side of vast and impassable gulfs. Ghur was never still. It was a place of restless appetites, of hunters and prey.

Which was she? She had always thought herself a hunter, one of the order's most implacable agents, but if the last few months had taught her anything, it was that the roles of hunter and prey were defined merely by the matter of scale. There was always something out there more dangerous than yourself.

She passed a fitful night by the remains of her father's fire, her dreams a troubled spectacle of blood and screaming. When she woke early in the morning, as exhausted as when she had first gone to sleep, the plains ahead of her were speckled with dew. It was as if the scrub grass and the spiny thorns were all draped with a million crystals, dazzling and bright, and she had to pull down the brim of her hat as she walked to shade her eyes.

As the morning advanced, the dew was burned off by the sun into a swirling mist that cast a veil over the scrubland. She paused, unsure whether to go on or to wait until it had cleared. For the most part she trusted her sense of direction, but she was wary of missing any signs that might point to her father's passing, and it was hard now to see more than a few yards in front. She glanced up, trying to find the sun, but the light was so pale that she couldn't place it with any confidence. Still the mist drifted and curled around her, flattening all sound, making her feel as if she had stumbled into some non-place between the realms, where all the strife and matter of existence had fallen away into this airy nothingness. A poised silence descended. All of a sudden her breath sounded impossibly loud in her ears. The slightest shift in her weight from one foot to the other was deafening.

She heard the figure approaching before she saw it: the slow crunch of footsteps over the hard-packed ground, a huffing growl that raised the hairs on the back of her neck. Slowly, with infinite care and patience, Doralia tucked the stock of her crossbow into her stomach and drew back the cord. The nullstone bolt shone with a faint blue glow as it nestled in the groove. She raised the weapon to her shoulder, sweeping it from side to side, scanning the mists ahead of her.

There – a shadow was drifting near. Two shadows in fact, one tall and willowy, the other dense and low to the ground. The footsteps came closer, the sound refracted by the mist until it seemed as if they were coming from all around her.

'That's far enough,' she called out. 'I've a bolt aimed at your heart. Now let's each state our business and be on our way.'

Slowly the first figure cohered. Doralia stepped forward, cautiously, her crossbow never wavering in its aim.

It was a man, at least a head taller than her. He was painfully thin, naked save for a leather kilt, and his skin was caked in dried clay or mud. His head was shaved, his scalp blistered with the heat of the plains. His jaw hung slack. She peered into the deep blue of his eyes, but they were calcified and opaque, as if he were blind. He stared off as if focusing on a sight a thousand miles away. Doralia almost pulled the trigger, but she was sure the man wasn't possessed, and the rise and fall of his laboured breathing proved that he wasn't one of the undead. Flakes of clay drifted off his skin like scrofulous snow. His feet were bleeding, she saw, little better than scraps of torn skin. He had left a trail of blood behind him.

Beside him, hunkered to the ground, its bull neck coiled with muscle, was a massive black dog. Its head reached up to the man's waist, and it peered at her with burning red eyes, the long slab of its tongue lolling out of its mouth and dripping spit into the dirt. Slowly, she drew the aim of her crossbow towards the monstrous hound, but it made no move to attack. There was a length of cord around its neck, the other end loosely wrapped around the man's fist. The two strange figures stood there, silent, the dog watching her, the man staring off into the infinite distance.

'My name is Doralia ven Denst,' she said cautiously. 'I'm an agent of the Order of Azyr. I'm looking for a man, Galen ven

Denst, my father. He would have passed this way, perhaps four days ago. Have you seen him?'

I'm worried about him, she wanted to say. *He's not in his right mind. He's been crushed by what happened to us, and my love and fear for him is strong enough to choke me.*

The man said nothing. He swayed on his feet. The dog, mouth dripping with slaver, cocked its head slightly to the side. The breeze turned and thickened, and the mist was gathered up into billowing clouds that wove their way around them. When the man spoke at last, his jaw loosely mumbling over the words, Doralia had the horrible feeling that it was the dog speaking to her through him. Its red eyes never left her face, and as the man spoke it huffed and growled as if concentrating on the words he was saying.

'Sigmar's servant,' the man said in a dry, papery voice. 'Far and round your path must lie, from Secret to Secret. A tide will rise of the resurrected, and the child will be killed before the father is free. Servant of Sigmar, go on. Heed not the Talon and the Voice. Seek what you have lost, or the spear will be broken. Seek what you have lost, or Excelsis will fall.'

The man blinked his vibrant blue eyes, and a tear rolled slowly through the cracked mud on his face. The monstrous dog bared its teeth in a silent snarl, and then the man took a faltering step forward. Slowly he shuffled past her and headed on across the misty plains, the dog at his side. Neither man nor dog looked back, but Doralia kept her crossbow trained on them all the same. They vanished into the creamy fog, and before too long even their footsteps had faded, leaving her standing there in the anxious silence alone.

...or Excelsis will fall.

She turned to go, troubled by his words, by the deep strangeness of the creature at his side. A priest, she told herself. Some wandering mendicant of a forgotten religion, lost in the wilds, driven

31

mad by sorrow and isolation. She looked back as the mist began to rise, but there was no sign of them. She stowed her crossbow, and for a moment her fingers yearned for the bottle in her kitbag.

The child will be killed before the father is free…

CHAPTER THREE

SIGMAR'S JUSTICE

The town was called Fortune, but she couldn't see anything fortunate about it. Its name was painted in faded letters on a brittle plank of wood, at the head of a track that led down towards its flimsy timber walls. On the far side, the town was bordered by a jagged flank of grey rock about a hundred feet high, a spur perhaps of the distant Krondspines breaking through the earth at the very limits of their range. On the other sides, the walls protected the town as best they could from the wide-open scrubland that surrounded it, a desert place of dust and rock, the dun spray of cactus and thorn. Approaching from the south, Doralia had come to the top of a slight rise about a mile away and gazed down over those walls at the town's close, hard-packed central square, the spread of two-storey wooden houses, the drifting smoke that rose from a dozen chimneys. She could see a handful of figures moving quickly across the square, and even from this distance she could sense a buzz in the air, a feeling of feverish activity.

She hefted her kitbag and followed the beaten track towards the town, her boots kicking up a plume of dust behind her. These frontier settlements were all the same, no matter where in the realms you went. Hardscrabble little places, founded with great industry and enthusiasm, and then left to sink or swim depending on the drive and talents of their settlers. Some had been set up as staging posts for pilgrims or traders, while others were founded with furious zeal by the faithful, who had set out from their parent city with prayers to Sigmar on their lips. They were all planted in the most hostile territory imaginable, and it was on the flip of a coin whether any of them survived much longer than a season. Fortune looked as if it had been around for a while at least. Either it was so far off the raiding paths it had been overlooked by Ghur's more belligerent inhabitants, or the people who lived here were tougher than they seemed. Doralia hoped it was the former but had the feeling it might be the latter. She loosened the pistol in her belt all the same.

There was a gate set into the eastern wall, but it was unlocked and open, and there was nobody guarding it. She passed through, stepping into the dusty, ochreous acre of the town square. Directly ahead of her, on the other side of the square, was a Sigmarite temple and what looked like the town gaol, with a cast iron door and bars on the windows. On either side were dry goods stores, an ironmongers. The buildings were all squat, brick-and-plasterboard places, the kind of plain and functional structures that could be thrown up over the course of a long afternoon. On the northern edge of the square there was a three-storey tavern, the Good Fortune, its windows wide open and a dozen men and women gathered on the veranda outside with tankards in their hands. All of them were staring at her as she walked slowly across the dusty square. She thought she may as well start with the tavern; if there was news of Galen to be had, that's where it would be found.

And, she admitted to herself, she'd pay any price they asked for a decent ale right about now…

Two men flitted across the square ahead of her and disappeared into the gaol, slamming the great iron door shut behind them. Doralia looked up and around, and she could see that most of the windows in the surrounding houses were open. She had a glimpse of faces peering around shutters, twitching curtains, folk watching her. Some of the people standing in front of the tavern slipped back inside. She took a careful glance over her shoulder. There were two men slowly following her. One was young and jittery, his hand resting on a knife that was tucked into his belt. The other, older, hard-faced, with a black bandana tied around his neck, peered at her through narrow, squinting eyes. He had an axe in his hand, she saw. She allowed her own hand to rest lightly on the butt of her pistol. She pushed back her hat brim, and as she glanced again to her left she saw what looked like some gallows far over in the corner of the square, raised up above the rusty ground on a wooden platform. The noose hung empty.

Doralia stopped in front of the Good Fortune, a smile on her face that had made more dangerous men than these plead for mercy. Of the half a dozen or so who were left on the veranda, none could meet her eye. They stared into their tankards, one or two hiding their faces by taking a deep drink and swallowing nervously. She could hear that the two men who were following her had stopped as well. She left her hand resting on her pistol and made a show of loosening the greatsword in the scabbard across her back.

'Good morning,' she said to the men on the veranda. She let the smile die on her face. She must look as cold and unyielding as the grave, she thought. She almost felt sorry for them. 'My name is Doralia ven Denst. I am an agent of the Order of Azyr. I'm looking for a man, Galen ven Denst, my father. He may have passed here a few days back. An older man, white hair, thick moustache. A duster, much like mine.'

The men exchanged glances. One, a rangy fellow with lank black hair, jutted his chin at her.

'Where you come from then? Excelsis?'

'That's right.'

'Heard Excelsis was no more,' another one of them said, a tubby middle-aged man in a faded, patterned waistcoat, his face twisted by a long scar against his cheek. 'Orruks tore it down, the Ironjawz. Them and the gargants, and some god-creature born out of a mountain near the Crashing Gulf, so they say. Can't figure it right myself, but all the same you can't be from Excelsis, I reckon. It's gone.'

'The city stands,' Doralia told them, and so hard was her voice that there could be no gainsaying it. 'Excelsis was besieged, it's true, but it was victorious. All the scum of Ghur threw themselves against its walls, and they were cut down in its streets. Excelsis is bloody but unbowed, I guarantee it.'

There was much excited murmuring at this, but before she could press on with her questions, there was a shout from the other side of the square, a crash of iron as the gaol door was thrown back and a scuffle as a mob dragged someone out into the dust.

'Here we go, boys!' the rangy man said from the veranda. He tossed back his drink and called through the open door into the tavern. 'Fun's about to start, folks – that's them bringing Harrow out now!'

The men dashed off across the square, followed by another dozen men and women from the confines of the tavern, clattering down the wooden steps from the veranda and crunching across the dirt. They barely gave Doralia a second glance. She stood there with her hands on her hips, watching them gather around the stage of the gallows, chattering and excitable, as if waiting for a performance. There were folk leaning out of windows now, resting their crossed arms on the sills. The sun blazed overhead, baking the earth around them.

With much cursing and jeering, the mob hauled the condemned towards the gallows. It was a young man, Doralia saw, with a mop of black hair, a droll smile on his unshaven face. She caught his eye, briefly, before he disappeared into the press of bodies. He nodded as if they were merely passing in the street on a pleasant afternoon.

Striding from the gaol behind them was a tall man with a shaved head and round spectacles that caught the light, reflecting it back as twin white circles, so that it looked as if he had coins for eyes. He was wearing a long, black leather coat, much like Doralia's, and a neat calfskin waistcoat with gold buttons. He pointed off towards the gallows and the mob redoubled its efforts. The young, dark-haired man stumbled and rolled in the dust. He was dragged back to his feet with a flurry of blows.

She stepped across the veranda into the shade of the tavern, a wide, rectangular room with a horseshoe bar at the other end, a dozen tables scattered around. All the chairs had been roughly thrown back, and the tables were covered with half-empty glasses and tankards. The floorboards underfoot were dark, polished mahogany, and there was an incongruously beautiful chandelier hanging from the ceiling, a dripping cascade of cut crystal that glinted with pink and blue. She flinched and turned away as she saw it. She took off her hat and wiped a line of sweat from her forehead.

The nullstone bolt striking true, the frail glissando of the mirror as it cracked. The stench of those butterflies...

Doralia passed a hand over her eyes and approached the bar, where the innkeeper was drawing a dirty cloth over the surface. He was a big man, soft, with a studied blankness to his face – an expression no doubt honed by years of having to wrangle drunkards every night. As the witch hunter set down her hat, though, she could see the faint tremble in his bottom lip, the bob of his throat as he swallowed.

No matter where you went, she knew, people would always recognise who – and *what* – you were. They might be glad of you sometimes, when the dark things that stalked the realms had to be dealt with. The rest of the time? They hated your guts.

'Can I help you there, miss?' the innkeeper said, mustering as much false cheer as he could manage. His drooping moustache quivered on his lip. He placed both hands on the polished bar, and then after a moment folded his arms instead. Doralia looked at him. He unfolded his arms and let them hang slack at his sides.

'Ale,' she said. 'A duardin brew, if you have any.'

The innkeeper blustered, wringing his cloth in his hands. 'Sorry to disappoint, miss, but we're a bit off the main trade routes, if you know what I mean. The good duardin stuff don't make it quite as far as Fortune, but I've several perfectly respectable brews I can offer you instead? Local ales, brewed right here.'

'Fine,' she said. She slipped her kitbag from her shoulder and took out her empty bottle, clunking it down on the surface of the bar. 'Fill this with whatever firewater you might have while you're at it. Oh, and if you call me "miss" one more time, I'm going to rip that moustache off your face and make you eat it.'

The innkeeper's face flushed and his mouth went slack. With downcast eyes and muttered apologies, he bumbled about filling the bottle and drawing the pint. Doralia sat herself down at one of the tables near the open door, where she could keep an eye on the gallows, about sixty yards away across the square. She could hear the rise and fall of the crowd's voices baying for blood, the strident call of someone making a no-doubt self-righteous speech before the main event. The gallows were crowded by spectators, some waving their hats in the air, others standing with their arms folded. The tavern was quiet around her, drowsing in the empty afternoon. Light from the chandelier was smeared in many colours across the table in front of her. Dust motes sparkled in their silent drift, burning up as they passed through the sunbeams that fell across the floor from the doorway. She could see the young man with the dark hair standing at the side of the gallows, his arms tied in front of him. Too far to see if he was still smiling, though she doubted it. Bravado only took you so far. When you found yourself standing in the shadow of the noose, all of a sudden it didn't seem quite so funny...

The innkeeper brought over her drinks, bowing and scraping, standing there wiping his hands on his apron. She tossed a couple of realmstone shards on the table, fragments of Bones of Amber, and stowed the firewater in her kitbag. The ale was cool, much better than she had been expecting, and as she took her first swallow she felt it threading through her veins, smoothing her out, wiping the dust of the journey from her soul. She closed her eyes, luxuriating in it. On one of the only occasions her father had brought up her drinking in the last few weeks, he'd told her that the booze wouldn't make her feel any different. *I know,* she'd said. *I don't drink to feel different. I drink to feel normal.*

'Having yourselves a hanging then,' she said, nodding at the open door. 'What's the crime?'

'Oh, most grievous, mi– I mean, your worship. Vampirism, no less!' The innkeeper's eyes were wide, as if he couldn't imagine such horrors in a genteel place like Fortune. 'Caspar Harrow, the young fellow's name is. Drifter of some sort, not from these parts. Turned up a few days ago, and then he killed all three members of the Hoffmann family – terrible nice folk, not like they deserved it in the slightest. Drained their blood, they say...' He shuddered.

'Who says?' Doralia demanded.

'Well,' the innkeeper stammered, 'the law in these parts. Hektor Vogel, you probably seen him just now leading the young fellow out. Tall, spectacles. He got them imported from Hammerhal, it's said. He's one of your lot,' the innkeeper said. 'You know – from the order. Least, that's what he says.'

'Vogel? And how long's he been here?'

'A good few months,' the innkeeper offered. There was a crafty look in his eye all of a sudden. He lowered his voice. 'Always thought it strange myself, what with one thing and another, that a witch hunter would spend so much time in an out-of-the-way place like Fortune...'

Doralia sighed. She gazed into her tankard, the trembling meniscus of golden ale, its fringe of creamy foam. All of a sudden she felt exhausted. That young man was no vampire, even an idiot could see it. And Vogel was certainly no agent.

She'd heard of it before, in backwater places like this where the locals didn't know any better. They'd have heard of witch hunters all right, but the order's agents were fewer in number than it cared to admit, and it was highly unlikely any of them had actually met a real one before. There was plenty of scope for the unscrupulous to step in and claim an authority they didn't have. Extortion, robbery, or just for the simple pleasure of exercising power – and she had a feeling it was the last of the three that motivated this Hektor Vogel. From the looks of things, it certainly wasn't gold that had brought him to Fortune.

Still, at least it told her something: her father definitely hadn't passed through this town. If he had, there was no way he would have let an impostor like Hektor Vogel live.

She drank down the rest of her ale and clacked the pot to the table. Her mother's pendant felt cold against her skin suddenly. Clenching her jaw, she stood up and drew the pistol from her belt, ramming her hat onto her head. The innkeeper backed off, hands raised.

'Now, we don't want no trouble, not if it can be helped!' he cried.

'Don't worry,' Doralia said as she headed for the door. 'This will be no trouble at all.'

* * *

They'd dragged the young man up to the noose by the time she crossed the square. His face was pale, his lip trembling, but he was still trying to keep up his front of amused indifference. The smile was sickly and strained, and he couldn't stop his hands from shaking, but he would go to his grave without giving them the satisfaction of a breakdown at least. She admired that. There weren't many who could look upon death with indifference, but how you faced it was one of the few real choices you had in life. You could go out with your head held high, or crying on your knees. That was it.

The tall man, Vogel, was standing with his back to the condemned. He had his arms raised as if intoning a sermon, and as Doralia approached she caught a snatch of his speech.

'Sigmar's justice has caught up with this foul creature, denizen of the darkness!' he cried. 'No more to weave his evil about the good folk of this town, to sneak into their homes and drink the very lifeblood from their veins!'

Idiot, she thought. She raised her pistol into the air and fired, and she took a small pleasure in seeing the crowd jump.

All eyes turned towards her. Calmly, without haste, she reloaded the gun. Nullstone shot, designed to dispel rogue magics and predatory spells, each bullet probably worth more than half the value of this town. Still, when a demonstration needed to be made, there was little more effective than a black-powder weapon.

'If he's a vampire,' she called out, 'then why in the name of Sigmar are you hanging him? He'll dance a jig on the end of that rope and he'll still be undead when you cut him down. You'd better off burning him.'

'I'd really prefer it if you didn't!' the young man said, his head in the noose.

A voice came out of the crowd. 'We'll hang him, and *then* we'll burn him!'

'Burn him first!' someone else cried. 'Burn him at the stake!'

'Burning's too good for him! Hanging's what he wants, that scum!'

'Hanging and quartering!'

With her other hand, Doralia drew the greatsword from the scabbard on her back, and the crowd fell into a deathly silence. The consecrated blade smouldered in the light with a dull and brooding power.

'No one will be hanged until I have had a chance to examine the bodies of the victims,' she said. 'If I deem they were killed by a vampire, then this man will be set free, for he could not have done it. He is no more a vampire than any of us standing here. He is a man, for good and ill.'

'I concur!' the young man called out. Something of his earlier insouciance had returned to him. 'And I thank you. A witch hunter, are you? I'm in your debt.'

'Don't thank me yet,' she said. 'If I deem those bodies were killed by any other means, then this town can have its hanging.' She looked at him and smiled. 'I'm sure you're guilty of something.'

'By what authority do you dare interfere with Sigmar's justice?' the tall man called out. He pushed his way towards her. She could see the fear in his eyes immediately, the realisation that he was suddenly far out of his depth when confronted with the real thing: a true agent of the order, and not the facsimile he had been presenting. She could see the calculations he was making too. If he was going to get away with this, then he needed to get the mob on his side, and fast. He pushed his spectacles back up the bridge of his nose. 'The good people of Fortune have suffered under the depredations of this dark villain, and they will see him punished for his crimes!'

He turned to the crowd, which had parted to let him through, relishing their murmur of assent. He pointed at one woman who stood on the edge of the crowd, her head covered in a black shawl of mourning.

'Emilaine, the Hoffmanns were cousins of yours, is that not the case? Would you see their killer set free on the whim of this... this wanderer from the wilds? She is no true agent of Azyr, it's obvious!'

The woman shook her head vigorously, her eyes staring at the ground.

'And you,' Vogel said to a young man, a dirty bandage wrapped around his head. 'Young Mikael, injured as you bravely tried to apprehend this killer – would you see him turned loose, free to kill again?'

'No sir, Master Vogel, sir,' the young man said. His lip trembled but his face was set. He reached up to touch the bandage, as if reminding himself of the wound.

Vogel turned to the crowd at large, raising his hands in pious exclamation. He had thrown back the wing of his coat and Doralia could see a blade sheathed on his hip. Duardin-made, a decent sword. She wondered how fast he was with it.

'Since first I came to Fortune, I have done my best to keep you all safe,' he called out. 'I have done my *duty* to Sigmar, as all of you have done in your own way, through obedience, and industry. Whose word will you take?' he asked them. 'Mine? A servant of the hammer and the throne, dedicated to rooting out evil wherever it rears its ugly head? Or this... this *woman*, who strides into our town as if she owns the place, claiming an authority she clearly does not possess!'

There was a rolling mutter of agreement across the crowd, and not a few of them turned towards her with hard eyes, their hands drifting to the knives in their belts. She glanced up at Caspar Harrow, standing there with his head in the noose, and his expression was suddenly a whole lot less certain than it had been before.

'That's an interesting interpretation of events,' she said. She rested her blade against her shoulder and addressed the crowd. 'Now let me tell you all what's really going on here. Master Vogel is no agent of the Order of Azyr. He's an impostor, a confidence man playing on your fears. Let me guess,' she said, looking him in the eye. Vogel's gaze flickered and fell away; he could not meet the weight of all Doralia had seen in her long and violent career. 'You drifted from Excelsis, after burning a few too many bridges. Found yourself out here, where the good folk didn't know any better and might be impressed by a decent blade and a firm attitude. Before long, you had them dancing to your tune, and you had comfortable lodgings and a decent wage from people who could ill afford it.' She looked over her shoulder at the tavern on the other side of the square. The innkeeper stood on the veranda, clutching his apron, watching the scene. 'And no doubt you never had to put your hand in your purse for an ale or two of an evening. I'm impressed,' she said. 'It's a nice little set-up you have here. But here's where it ends.'

Vogel's face was twisted with rage and fear. 'How dare you,' he snarled. 'You mock Sigmar himself with these baseless accusations!'

She pressed on, pointing at the man on the gallows.

'I've no doubt you've all suffered some losses recently, and this drifter will have made as good a scapegoat as anyone else. Serves another purpose too, shows you the reach of Vogel's authority. He points a finger, and up goes the scaffold. Keeps you all in line, reminds you of who's in charge.' She looked up at Caspar. 'What brings you to these parts anyway, drifter?'

Caspar Harrow shrugged. 'My career takes me to many out-of-the-way places.' He smiled. 'I'm always finding myself on the move.'

'That doesn't exactly fill me with confidence that you're a reputable character,' she said.

Caspar laughed. 'Shrewdly guessed,' he said. 'But I'm no villain, I assure you.'

'We'll see about that.'

Vogel had clearly had enough. He gripped the hilt of his blade.

'This farce ends now,' he sneered. 'I demand to see your credentials. And let me warn you, if they fail to satisfy then I'll see you up there with your head in a noose beside him!'

'My credentials?' Doralia said. She smiled. 'Let me show you my credentials.'

She raised her pistol and shot him through the heart.

CHAPTER FOUR

ON THE TRAIL

The line of light in the darkness, her face pressed against it, staring, seeing, her breath as ragged as an autumn breeze. Her mother's body, twisted and flung carelessly to the ground. Her mother, who had held her, who had nurtured her and cared for her, lying now in the slick crescent of blood, black as oil in the aether-lamp's hesitant glow. And the voice purling through the house, rising above the crackle of the flames, laughing, taunting...

The voice of Jael Morgane...

She tore herself from the dream, the ice of that voice lingering like an illness. The vampire who had killed her mother, who had *turned* her... She remembered the grip of the crossbow in her hand, almost too heavy for her to lift. Her father, dragging himself through the flames on his shattered legs, screaming, *'Shoot it!'*

Or was that the siege, the madness of the Conclave Hall? She saw again her father's face, grim with pain and fatigue, the greater daemons revelling in the tortured siren song of their rapturous followers. She saw Synessa's conjured mirror sweeping across the hall towards Sentanus, held in the grip of some monstrous disembodied hand. The White Reaper bellowing prayers to Sigmar as he readied his warding lantern, and then Doralia taking careful aim with her crossbow and shattering the mirror with a well-placed nullstone bolt. The smell of that place, the awful, mind-bending horror...

It was as if all her traumas had melted into one, since the siege. The sight of her mother's broken body jerking back to life, her dead eyes, her mouthful of rending teeth, hunkered in her mind alongside the mayhem of Excelsis, squatting there like a toad. She saw again the skaven bursting from their gnawholes and skittering through the streets; the orruks hammering their way through the city's defences; the daemons capering in the ruins, shards of madness. All the sick horrors that she had spent her life fighting against.

In the darkness, she rolled onto her side to face the campfire. Caspar Harrow crouched there, his narrow face lit by the flames, tending the rabbit as it crackled on the spit. He tapped the meat with the point of his knife.

'Something to eat?' he said. He pushed his black hair out of his eyes. 'I can't vouch for the quality of my cooking, but at least it's hot and fresh? Well...' He looked down at the meat and squinted. 'Fresh-ish.'

She sat up and shook her head, then fumbled in her kitbag for the firewater. As she took a long pull on the bottle Caspar's eyes lit up, but when she was finished she stowed it away again. The crestfallen look on his face almost made up for her anger at allowing herself to fall asleep. He might not have been a vampire, but no one made their way through the wilds of Ghur alone unless they were at least halfway dangerous. He could easily have put that knife in her throat while she slept.

Getting careless, she thought. She felt the firewater burning in her chest. *Or too drunk to care any more.*

They had camped in a hollow on the crown of a slight rise, a low hill that was fringed with scrub and vast, misshapen boulders. In the darkness they looked like the deformed heads of huge, monstrous creatures peering down at them. The night air was tense and sultry, and lightning prowled against the line of the horizon off to the west, great blades and sharp flickers of white strobing in the darkness. A storm, moving east. With any luck it would pass them by.

'Suit yourself,' Caspar said. 'More for me.' He grinned and plucked the rabbit from the spit, laying it out on a pewter plate. The smell turned her stomach. Or maybe that was just the firewater. She couldn't remember when she had last eaten cooked food. 'You're sure I can't tempt you?'

She relented. 'Who am I to turn down gourmet cooking in such pleasant surroundings,' she said. Caspar cut a shank and passed it to her, and she forced herself to eat. She had to admit, she felt better for it.

When he'd finished eating, Caspar sat back and gave a contented sigh.

'Storm coming,' he said. He peered at the horizon. 'We can miss it if we're heading east for a spell. By the time we turn north again it should have moved on.'

'I'll take your word for it.'

'If your father's gone that way, then it should be easy enough to pick up his trail. The land's changeable as we pass around the eastern flank of the Krondspines, and there's a river that's hard to cross, but I know a few routes through.'

'We'll set off at first light,' she said. She had told him enough about her father so he could be useful in helping to find him, but no more than that. Nothing about her fears for his state of mind, the black depression that had seemed to settle on him in the weeks after the siege. She told him only what he needed to know.

Caspar wrapped himself in Hektor Vogel's coat and stared off towards the flicker of the lightning. He was wearing Vogel's boots and he had Vogel's sword by his side as well. All in all, Doralia thought, smiling to herself, for a man who was about to be hanged that morning, everything had turned out pretty well for him.

No one had moved when she had shot Vogel down. His legs had kicked in the dirt once, twice, and then with a great puff of exhaled breath he was still. Doralia had tensed, the blade still up on her shoulder, but the expression on her face must have convinced the crowd that *this* was what a real agent of the order looked like. And no doubt they were all more than a little relieved to see the end of him.

Uncertain, unsettled, the crowd milled about the gallows while the innkeeper took her to see the bodies of the dead, the Hoffmann family, now laid out in the cold cellar of the town gaol. Caspar Harrow still stood there with his head in the noose, but he had seemed quietly confident as she set off across the square.

'I promise you I'm innocent!' he had cried cheerfully. 'I've never even set eyes on the Hoffmanns.'

The innkeeper led her across the rusty dirt, tugging open the iron door when they reached the gaol.

'Not to speak ill of the dead,' he muttered as they passed into the bare and austere office, 'but I do wish someone had confronted Master Vogel in just such a permanent way a while back...'

'It's fair to say he had few friends then?' Doralia said.

'Not as such,' the innkeeper smiled, his moustache bristling. 'But after all, who would dare stand up to the Order of Azyr?'

'No one,' she admitted. 'Not if they know what's good for them.'

Some of the crowd had trailed after them, including the two

men who had stalked her from the gate, along with a few of those who had dragged Caspar from the gaol not twenty minutes before. Natural followers, the witch hunter thought. They changed with the wind, and the breeze in Fortune was now distinctly cool.

They took the stairs down to the basement. The cellar was a long, narrow room, the walls bare and clammy, and it was empty save for a few bookcases stuffed with scrolls and ledgers. The corpses were laid out in the middle of the floor. They'd been covered with a bloody sheet. Doralia nodded to the innkeeper and he stepped forward to snap the sheet aside. An older man and woman; a youth not far off eighteen. Their skin was waxy, and by the smell it seemed they were starting to turn. Their eyes were as cold as glass, clouded, unseeing.

'Why haven't they been buried yet?' she asked.

'Hasn't been the time. They were only found late last night.'

'Where?'

'In their house,' the innkeeper said. 'Off by the other side of the Good Fortune, if you please. Gave me quite a turn to think of them being killed so near. First thing Vogel did was to have that drifter dragged out of his bed right here in the tavern and thrown in the cells.'

He made the sign of the comet against his chest.

Doralia crouched to examine them, although the cause of death was obvious. Each had had their throat torn away, and in the jumbled ruin of windpipe and artery, she could clearly see the marks of fangs. She reached for the man and lifted his arm, pressing her fingers into his skin. No bruising, just a soft, doughy resistance. There was barely any blood left in their bodies. Killed a few days back, probably.

'Vampires then?' the innkeeper said. He stood back by the doorway, his apron lifted up to his mouth.

'One vampire, at least,' she said. She drew the sheet across the bodies. She wondered which of them had died first, and which had been forced to watch.

'Sigmar preserve us,' the innkeeper wailed. He took a step back. 'What dark times we live in. Truth to tell I'd almost been hoping it *was* just that drifter who was responsible.'

'Caspar Harrow didn't do this,' she said. She stood up from the bodies. 'No human did.'

'What should we do? They say vampires have to be beheaded and buried at a crossroads, but...' He looked almost like he was going to cry. 'Well, we don't have any crossroads in Fortune, do we.'

'That's nothing but a primitive superstition,' Doralia told him. 'Garlic, the sign of the comet, even sunlight doesn't really hurt them.'

She tried to disguise the impatience in her voice; a lifetime fighting creatures like these could make her complacent about the way other people saw them. To the ordinary citizens of Sigmar's domain such monsters were the stuff of nightmares. Fell shadows in the dark, the resurrected dead charged with a new and implacable evil.

A tide will rise of the resurrected...

The pale man and the black dog in the wilderness. Was this what he had meant? Was this why her father was out here? But then why go alone, why not take her with him if the threat was so great? And surely this was the work of just one vampire, not a tide?

She gritted her teeth and turned to go. None of it made any sense.

Damn you, Galen ven Denst, you old fool. What are you doing out here?

As she stalked back across the square, the innkeeper scuttled at her side, tugging on his moustache. There was still a crowd around the gallows, patiently waiting to see what would happen next. This had turned into quite the interesting day for them.

'But what about the bodies, the poor Hoffmanns?' the innkeeper said. 'What if they turn, what if they... *come back?*'

'They won't. They were no more than food and sustenance to the creature that killed them.' *Her limbs twitching on the floorboards. Her broken neck snapping round, the glare of those lifeless doll's eyes.* 'A vampire has to fill its victims with its essence to resurrect them in its unholy image. The Hoffmanns have found Sigmar's peace, at least. See that they are decently buried. That's all you can do for them now.'

'Well?' Caspar Harrow called from the noose. 'Am I innocent?'

The crowd turned towards her as she stopped before the gallows. She stood there with her hands on her hips, her wide-brimmed hat shading her eyes. Hektor Vogel's body was slumped lifelessly on the ground at her feet.

'Career takes you to many out-of-the-way places, you say?' she asked.

'Indeed so.'

'You know the lands around here well enough, then?'

'Well enough,' he said. 'I've travelled back and forth around these parts.' He frowned. 'Why?'

'I'm looking for someone, a man who may have passed near here a few days ago. I'd have use of a scout.'

'I'd be delighted to help,' Caspar said, grinning. 'I'm in your debt after all.'

'Cut him down,' Doralia called, and immediately half a dozen of the townsfolk scrambled to free him. Caspar, rubbing his neck where the noose had chafed, dropped down from the edge of the gallows and approached her cautiously. His shirt was ragged on his back, and he wasn't wearing any shoes.

'Congratulations, Mr Harrow,' she had said, turning to collect her bags and her crossbow from the tavern. 'You've just been deputised into the Order of Azyr.'

The fire was burning low, but Caspar's eyes caught the flames now as he gave Doralia a shrewd look from under his black fringe.

'So,' he said. 'The siege. Excelsis. Was it as bad as they say?'

Doralia didn't look at him. At first she didn't answer. The words wouldn't come, and she couldn't think of any way to frame it so he would understand. How could you understand something like that, if you hadn't lived through it? And if you had lived through it, why would you want anyone else to understand it in the first place? Better to keep them innocent of such horrors.

'Depends what they say,' she said.

Caspar shrugged. 'You get all sorts of rumours at second-hand out here, but anyone with eyes in their head or a nose to smell the breeze could tell what was heading towards the city. I've never seen this part of Ghur so empty. Didn't seem like anything could survive that, but then I heard tales that the city had won. Didn't seem possible.'

'I don't know if "won" is quite the word I'd use,' Doralia said. 'But we survived. We're still standing, and they're not.'

'Are you?' He stirred the embers with his knife. 'If you don't mind me saying it, you look more like someone who's running from a defeat.'

Doralia fixed him in her gaze, her face blank.

'I've a length of rope in that kitbag, you know. It's not too late to fix ourselves another hanging.'

Caspar held his hands up as if in surrender, his smile as droll as when he'd been led to the gallows in the first place.

'Point taken.' He was silent for a moment, and the only sound was the far-off rumble of the thunder from the storm that was passing east. 'What about the vampire though, the one that killed the Hoffmanns back in Fortune?'

'What about it?'

'They were dead not one day before they were found. What if the vampire's still there, back in town?'

54

'Worried for the townsfolk, are you? I'm surprised to hear you've got such warm feelings about the place.'

'You know what I mean,' Caspar protested. 'Just seems like bad strategy to leave something like that behind us.'

She stretched out on the ground and closed her eyes.

'That thing will be long gone,' she said. 'If it wanted Fortune as its personal larder it wouldn't have left the bodies to be so easily discovered. The Hoffmanns were a quick meal on the go, nothing more.'

'I don't know, these are dark times. You hear things, rumours… The dead rising from their graves… Shouldn't you be hunting it down?' Caspar asked. 'I thought that's what you people did?'

'You'd be willing to lend a hand, would you?' she said. Caspar looked away. 'Thought not. So don't tell me my business. I have a higher priority right now, and I swear, if I'd known that deputising you into the order was going to be such a pain in my rear end, I would have left you on the gallows.'

Caspar nodded and lowered his gaze. 'You're the boss,' he said as he rolled onto his back. 'See you at first light, then.'

A higher priority, she thought bitterly. She pictured the bodies in the cellar, the bloody sheet. *I will hold this against you too, father…*

CHAPTER FIVE

THE CROSSING

'Hold it higher,' he said. 'The stock firm against your shoulder, the bolt pointing straight. As you know full well, your life will depend on it.'

'It's heavy, father,' she said.

'So is the weight of our duty, yet we bear it all the same. Now,' he snapped. 'Higher! Straight!'

He hobbled back on his walking sticks and slowly lowered himself onto the bench. His face was twisted and shrunken with pain. He was still weak, but he was getting stronger every day. Doralia wished she could say the same; they had been training for weeks now, and there wasn't a muscle in her body that didn't ache. She raised her mother's crossbow and aimed at the target fifty yards down the meadow. The breeze stuttered across the dry grass. She blinked away the tears and pulled the trigger, feeling the stock smack back into her shoulder. She remembered the look on her mother's face as the bolt went in.

It whipped through the air like a thunderbolt, clipping the edge of the target. She glanced over at her father. His expression was grave. 'Not good enough,' he said. 'Again. Again, until you get it right.'

They found another burnt-out campfire not half a mile from where they had spent the night. Another stub of her father's cigars, a trail of bruised grass which led off towards the north-west. They were on the right track. Doralia felt her heart lift. Since Fortune, she was worried that they had missed him, that he had doubled back or that they had been turned aside and lost the signs that would have pointed them in the right direction. But here he was – still going, still stalking the territory to who knew what end.

They headed on towards the silver line of a river in the distance, where Caspar said there was a bridge that would take them into the grasslands by the foothills of the mountains. The landscape was beginning to change around them. Not with the normally sudden and ferocious rapidity of Ghur, but with a milder shift from the desolation of the plains. Soon there was grass underfoot, and the thorny scrub gave way to green brushland, to groves of woe trees moaning in the breeze. From the barren flats of the plains, they entered a land of shallow valleys and low hills, of long, windswept meadows speckled with stands of garnet-berries. She felt herself ease slightly, but still she didn't lower her guard. At one point, crossing a rolling sward of tall grasses, they stumbled across a small herd of grazing yethars. Doralia snatched up her crossbow at once, but the great beasts proved timid and turned their bifurcated horns in the other direction, thundering off across the grass until they were out of sight. *You always have to assume,* she reminded herself, *that everything in Ghur wants to kill you...*

Caspar walked at ease by her side. If he was intimidated by the witch hunter he gave no sign of it, and more than anything this signalled to Doralia that her new companion was a man used to dangerous company. He was a few inches shorter than Hektor Vogel, and the dead man's coat trailed in the grass at his feet, but he had slung the sword onto his hip as if practised to it. As they walked, he scanned the ground ahead with his keen blue eyes, always brushing the lock of black hair out of his face. He was a lean and handsome fellow; and what was worse, he knew it. He smiled when he saw her looking at him.

'A mote for your thoughts,' he said.

'Not sure they're worth that much.'

She paced on, slightly ahead of him. They had come to a faint, beaten pathway that snaked between stands of tall mahoganies, the trees' branches frothing out high above them and casting a welcome shade onto the ground. She could hear the track of running water somewhere a mile or two ahead.

'Dark, no doubt, and full of brooding vengeance,' Caspar offered. He plucked a stalk of grass from the ground and idly began to chew it.

'What makes you say that?'

Caspar raised an eyebrow and looked her up and down.

'Forgive me,' he said. 'I mistook you for a witch hunter, when clearly you're a merry player from a travelling company of circus folk.' He gave her a dazzling smile. 'Brooding and vengeance do rather seem to go with the territory for your sort.'

'Hard to argue,' she said. She took off her hat to wipe the sweat from her forehead. 'And what about this territory? You've been this way before, in this cryptic career of yours?'

'Now and then,' Caspar said. 'I know the bridge well, at least.'

'And what is this career, exactly?'

'Oh,' Caspar sighed, waving his hand airily. 'This and that. Imports, exports. Logistics, moving goods from one locale to another. Dealings in financial matters, gemstones, investments, that sort of thing.'

'You're a bandit,' she said. 'You steal things.'

Caspar huffed in mock affront. 'I repudiate such accusations!' he said. 'Ghur is a very dangerous place at the best of times, and sometimes shipments go awry for perfectly innocent reasons...'

'Other times for less innocent reasons, I'm sure.'

Caspar gave her a strained laugh. 'I wasn't aware your remit stretched to petty larceny, witch hunter!'

'I dispense Sigmar's justice wherever it's warranted,' she said. Out of the corner of her eye she could see the sickly expression on his face, as he wondered whether or not to run.

Cruel, she thought. *But you have to take your pleasure where you can find it.*

'Don't worry,' she told him. 'As long as you're useful, you're safe. There's a base human motive to your crimes, at least. I'm more concerned with the inhuman.'

He brightened and strode ahead of her, calling back over his shoulder. 'Then let's get you to that bridge! I'll show you just how useful I can be.'

The river was a pounding cataract, a rolling avenue of foam and thunder near half a mile wide. Spray kicked off from its surface and spattered onto their coats. Doralia could see tree trunks and the corpses of animals tumbling in its sway, big aurochs from off the mountains caught in its fury and swept away as easily as if they were rats. If there had been a bridge here once, there was no sign of it now. She doubted if even duardin engineering would have had much chance against this.

She turned to Caspar, who stood beside her with his arms folded and a bemused look on his face.

'I swear,' he said, spreading his hands, 'there was a bridge here not one week ago!'

'And what do you suggest we do now?' she said. 'Swim?'

They both looked at the torrent as it hammered past. The water was so fast and chill it had turned the air by the bank cold. A thick mat of grass leaned over the river, shaking in its passage.

'I… wouldn't recommend it,' Caspar said.

Doralia stared upstream. The river would only narrow the closer it got to its source, and that would be many miles away in the foothills of the mountains. The Krondspines loomed there in the bleary distance off to the west, a jawbone of ragged teeth gnawing on the pastel sky. Downstream would be the better bet, but who knew how long they would have to go out of their way before they could cross to the other side. She scanned the further bank, made dim and vaporous by the spray. If her father was over there, then he was receding further by the hour. Had he crossed the bridge before it fell? Or had he destroyed it himself, to prevent anyone from following?

'There's a ferry a few miles to the east,' Caspar said. 'We could cross there. I haven't been down to those parts for some time, but I'd bet it still stands.'

'Like the bridge still stands, you mean?' she said dryly. 'And a *ferry*? We'd need a bloody galleon to cross this thing. Do you reckon there are a few Scourge Privateers camping nearby, perhaps we could ask them?'

'You just need to have faith, Doralia,' Caspar said, brushing his hair from his eyes. He gave her his brightest smile, and it was all she could do not to smack it off his face.

'Don't talk to me about faith,' she said. 'I've seen the Holy City in Azyr, I know what faith means.' She turned to head downstream. 'And don't call me Doralia,' she called over her shoulder. 'Only my friends call me that.'

'What friends?' he said.

'Exactly.'

* * *

It took half the day to track downstream, walking along the length of the chill riverbank in the shade of the mahogany trees. By their side, the river rolled and churned, brute evidence of Ghur's relentless power. They could see clouds massing off to the north, far away beyond the river's further bank: a dark, roiling tide that smothered the horizon. Ahead of them, glimpsed now and then through the trees, was the distant smudge of the Icefangs on the coast, three hundred miles away at least.

Eventually, as the light began to fade into the late afternoon, the river calmed its fury. The distance between the banks began to widen, and the water gushed between them with a gentler flow, rich and brown, sluggish as it turned a shoulder of ground and headed on towards the coast. Doralia saw the crossing point half a mile further on, nestled at the side of the bank: a straight pier heavily reinforced, with a low wooden hut beside it. A boat bobbed and swayed on the water, and a long rope stretched out across the surface of the river, tied to a similar pier on the other side.

'There!' Caspar cried, pointing. His relief was palpable. 'Didn't I tell you?'

The ferryman stood by the door of the hut as they approached, a long, leaf-bladed paddle in his hand. He was old, with a long white beard that he'd tucked into his belt, but he looked as tough and sinewy as sun-dried leather. He was barefoot and dressed in a ragged green tunic, and as they got closer, Doralia realised it wasn't a paddle he was holding, but a wide-bladed spear. A sensible precaution for anyone who plied their trade in the wilds.

'That's far enough,' he called out in a quavering voice. He hefted the spear. 'Saw you coming up the trail a mile back. Now, are you here to rob me or to cross the river? 'Cos if it's the former, well... let's just say it'll cost you more than you're likely to get in return. If it's the latter, it'll cost you too, but no more than what you can afford, you have my word. And I can't say fairer than that.'

Doralia and Caspar paused at the head of the track that led down to the crossing, their hands raised. On their right, the woe trees buckled in the breeze from off the water, whispering their sad songs. The river thrummed on the other side, surging ever onwards, utterly indifferent to the people who stood on its banks.

'We're here to cross, old man,' Doralia said. 'Nothing more, you have my word in return.'

'Witch hunter, eh?' he said, peering at her. She stepped closer, reaching into her pouch. 'Well, that's good enough for me, I reckon. If you're Sigmar's servant, then step aboard and I'll have you over in no time. "Faithless is the man who refuses aid," isn't that right? Well... aid at a good price, anyway!'

'*Intimations of the Comet*,' she said. 'You know your scripture.'

'Not much else to do in the wilderness but forage for my food and contemplate the Word of Sigmar,' he cackled.

Doralia pulled a small phial of Aqua Ghyranis from the pouch, the precious waters of the Realm of Life. She tossed it over to him and the ferryman snatched it from the air, grinning a toothless smile through his beard. He stowed the phial in his shirt pocket and ushered them down to the jetty.

'Now,' he said, capering about behind them. 'I don't know if you're much in the way of seafaring folk, but if you're more of the landlubber type then you might want to hold on to the rail...'

It was more of a raft than a boat, she saw. Ten square feet of wooden planks roughly hammered together and caulked with tar, it lurched underfoot as she stepped aboard and almost tipped her into the water.

'Gods above and below!' Caspar groaned, clutching the rail and sinking to his knees. 'Let's make this quick, for pity's sake. What I wouldn't give for that bridge to have stood instead.'

'Bridge out, eh?' the ferryman said. He snorted. 'Well, there's no surprise. Don't see why those folks keep rebuilding it. You can't ever rely on this here river to keep to its banks, not in Ghur, and it bursts them more often than not. Ferry's good enough for me, don't see why it ain't good enough for others.'

'What folks?' she asked him. The ferryman had untied the hitch on the guide post and slowly began to drag the raft along the rope that stretched over to the other bank. It was a thick ship's cable, she saw, clamped and tightly woven, and more than enough to stand up to the rigours of the surging water.

'Them folks up at Raven's Hollow,' he said. 'Biggest town in these parts, up the hills there. Seem to think the bridge is their business.' He huffed his scorn at the idea. 'Ferry's my business anyways, not theirs. I figured Raven's Hollow was where you were heading.'

His wiry arms showed no strain as he pulled on the rope. Slowly, the raft began to slide out into the body of the river, swaying slightly, dipping to the tide. Caspar groaned again and clutched the rail, but Doralia found she could keep her footing if she adjusted to the rhythm of the craft. The far bank seemed to rise up out of the hazy spray ahead of them. She could see the silhouettes of trees, the suggestion of rugged grasslands beyond. The air was cold around them, shivering in the passage of the water.

'You been to this Raven's Hollow?' she asked Caspar. His face was green, mouth open and panting lightly. He looked like he was trying not to be sick. 'Sigmar's sake, man,' she said. 'We've barely been on the water for half a minute.'

'I'm not a great sailor,' he whined. 'It's not natural.' He glanced over the side of the raft. 'It's less the motion than the thought of the... *things* that live in it.'

'I'd advise staying away from Excelsis Harbour then,' she said. 'There are *things* in those waters that would turn your black hair white.'

'Sigmar save me,' he muttered. 'But as for Raven's Hollow, then yes, you could say I've been there... It's bigger than Fortune, much bigger. Sits tucked away on a hilltop at the far curve of the Krondspines, in the foothills there. High walls, decent defensive position – it's more like a fort than anything.'

She thought for a moment. If it was as big and prominent as Caspar claimed, then she was sure her father would have stopped there, for supplies if nothing else. Perhaps that was where he had been heading all along. If they could get there quickly, she would finally catch up with him, finally get the answers she had been looking for.

She turned back to the ferryman as he dragged on the rope. His hands must be like steel, she realised. 'Why did you think we were heading there?' she asked him.

'On account of the dead,' he said. 'Or, better to say, the missing. Witch hunter and all, seemed like it might be your business.'

Doralia gave him a sharp look. 'What do you mean? What missing?'

'The dead, in the cemetery,' he said. 'Even out here I heard the tale.' He took a hand from the rope to make the sign of the comet against his chest. 'Grim tidings, anyway. Seems one morning the folks of Raven's Hollow woke up and found the cemetery completely empty. All the graves dug up, or...'

'What?'

'Well, not *dug up*, exactly.' He grimaced. 'More like the dead had dug themselves out, if you know what I mean.'

Caspar looked at her, his lean face dark and serious.

'Could be what your father was investigating?' he said.

'Could be.'

Doralia chewed her bottom lip. She felt the tug of the firewater in her chest, almost reached for the bottle there and then.

'You seen anyone else coming this way over the last week?' she asked him. 'An older man, coat much like mine, white hair, moustache.'

'Another witch hunter?' the ferryman said. 'Can't say I have, but if there's two of you out here then times must be bad. Oh,' he sighed, shaking his bald head, still pulling hand over hand on the rope. The far bank was only a hundred yards away now. 'These are fell days indeed. There's more besides that I've heard, strange stories on the breeze. Some say there's a shadow stalking the wilds, waylaying travellers and drinking their blood in the dead of night. Others heard tell of a black dog that talks with the voice of Sigmar himself, making prophecy and whatnot, foretelling the future. And a dead child that walks across the plains at night, carrying its father with it, sobbing for mercy. Oh, Sigmar save us all! Alas, as if the fall of Excelsis wasn't enough to try us in these dark times.'

'Excelsis stands,' Doralia said. Her voice was like stone. 'Take my word for it. Now get us across this river a touch faster and you'll have twice the payment for your trouble. I've got work to do.'

CHAPTER SIX

RAVEN'S HOLLOW

The trail rolled and twisted through the foothills, curving back around the rugged flanks of boulders and rocks and climbing on through a rough country of sweet herbs and sorrel. Here and there from the side of the path loomed boxy shrubs of Hysh-flower, their berries glowing in the darkness as bright and clear as Hysh itself. The Realm of Light drifted gracefully through the aether above them on its long parabola across the night. It was so bright, it cast their shadows in front of them on the trail, even in the darkness – blots of ink that surged ahead as Doralia and Caspar hacked their way up the incline. If this was the only path into Raven's Hollow, she thought, then no wonder Caspar had called it more of a fort than a town. Even an army as powerful as Kragnos' would have had a hell of a time broaching this position.

The hordes that had besieged Excelsis had only done so after an insane rampage along the southern borders of Thondia, and towns like Fortune and Raven's Hollow to the north and west had been spared the destruction that was rained down upon the city.

To them, the hordes of Kragnos were a hair-raising rumour, a blur of smoke in the distance, and the fate of Excelsis only a dark tale that grew with the telling. She couldn't help feeling bitter as she climbed the path towards the town. What did they know of the sacrifices that had been made by the city? They were lucky, blessed by their ignorance. They hadn't suffered, not as Excelsis had suffered. Not as she had suffered.

It's not their fault, she thought. She grabbed the twisted trunk of a salt pine and pulled herself further up the slope. *And if the tales the ferryman told were true, they have their own darkness to contend with now...*

'That's it,' Caspar groaned beside her, his face dark with sweat. He flung himself to the ground. He had taken off Vogel's coat and wore it bundled across his back like a bedding roll. 'My legs are like rubber, I can't go on another step.'

'These look like wild hills to me,' Doralia said, staring down at him. 'Could be orruks around. Could be grots, beastmen even. I'd be happy to leave you here, of course...'

She looked back the way they had come, down the trail as it snaked towards the grasslands far below. The foothills tumbled away on either side, humped barrows and knolls rolling into the deeper mountains that rose above them. Even in the growing darkness she could see the white line of the river twenty miles away, surging across the landscape like a silver arrow. If she concentrated, she was sure she could even hear it. There was a fragrant smell in the air from all the herbs and grasses that thrived in the rocky ground of the hills. It was sharp and musky, and made her think for a moment of the marketplace in Excelsis, in Starbank Square on the edge of the Veins.

Gone now, of course, she thought. *Shattered, torn asunder. They'll rebuild, but... it will never be the same.*

On the ground beside her, Caspar rubbed his calves and rolled onto his hands and knees. With effort, his face contorted, he dragged himself to his feet again.

'You're a hard taskmaster, witch hunter,' he muttered. He scowled and looked up at the town, still half a mile distant. The trail looped and curled away ahead of them, east to west and back again. The darkness thickened. Raven's Hollow loomed high above, the walls spread out on either side like the wings of the bird that gave the town its name. It was nestled into a wide and natural depression, and a shelf of rock jutted out from the hill behind it like a protective hood. On its wall, a dozen lamps flickered and glowed with the promise of a warm fire and hot food. 'Truth to tell,' Caspar said, 'it's been a while since I've been here.' He rubbed his jaw thoughtfully.

'Why do I have the feeling that you hope you won't be remembered?' she said. She leaned on the stock of her crossbow. The climb had been tougher than she wanted to admit, and her heart was thumping in her chest like a broken aether-endrin.

Caspar grinned nervously. 'I'm sure it'll be fine,' he said. 'It was a long time ago. And,' he said brightly, as if just remembering, 'I was wearing a mask as well, there's no way they'll recognise me.'

'I'll keep my fingers crossed,' she said.

It was another hour of hard climbing, but at last the gates of Raven's Hollow came into view. The walls were at least a dozen feet high, and it took her a moment to realise that they weren't made out of wood, but of some kind of black, reinforced bone.

'Thunderwyrm bone,' Caspar said. 'There are huge flocks of them in the Krondspines, and sometimes they come this far east. Rumour has it the town even trades with the Bonesplitterz for bone as well. Keeps them safe enough, I guess.'

The gates were twin wooden doors that were barred against them, with a squat gate tower on the left-hand side, where a guard looked down from a crenellated wall. The trail reached across a narrow, rocky promontory towards the gate, and on either side of it there was a sharp fall towards a defensive ditch about twenty feet below. Doralia stopped before the promontory and took her hat from her head, her crossbow shouldered. Caspar leaned beside her, hands on his knees as he panted for breath. She could see movement up on the gate tower, the guards wondering whether to challenge them or just to see them on their way with a well-placed arrow or two. The bone walls seemed to glow faintly in the darkness, reflecting the light of the aether-lamps.

'I'm an agent of the Order of Azyr,' she called out. 'My name is Doralia ven Denst. We seek only food and lodgings for the night, and I would speak with your arbiter, if you have one.'

There was silence, but she could sense the muffled conversation going on somewhere above her in the gate tower.

'Gods, I really hope they haven't recognised me,' Caspar muttered at her elbow. 'Perhaps, just to be on the safe side, we should be on our way?'

'If you're keen to hike all the way back down that trail in the dark, then be my guest,' she said in a low voice. 'What exactly did you get up to here anyway?'

He shifted his weight from one foot to the other. 'I may have robbed a certain… prominent citizen,' he said apologetically. 'Like the arbiter, for example.'

She looked at him.

'Broke into his house while he was asleep,' Caspar went on. 'Lifted a pretty decent haul of gemstones and gold, I have to admit. Pawned them for a tidy sum in Bilgeport, more than I was expecting. Alas, he seems to be a light sleeper though, and not well disposed to those he finds creeping about his house at night…'

She shook her head. 'Gods, I hope for your sake it was a decent mask.'

'More of a bandana, to be honest.' He shrugged. 'I didn't really have time to plan anything else. Fortune favours the bold, and all that. Still, I managed to escape by the skin of my teeth.'

He brushed his hair out of his eyes, and then, as if reconsidering, quickly dragged it forward into a lank curtain that swept down across his forehead.

Doralia sighed. 'I really wish I'd let them hang you back in Fortune...'

There was a grinding creak as the doors swung slowly open. A lamp was raised high on the walls then, and a voice called out of the darkness.

'Enter, witch hunter,' it cried. 'Raven's Hollow has need of you!'

The inn was called The Beak, and the zephyrwine they kept behind the bar was some of the best she had tasted since before the siege. She raised the pewter goblet to her lips with reverence and took a deep draught, closing her eyes as the golden liquid slipped down. It was as if every cell in her body had suddenly come alive, and even the prospect of empty graves and the living dead was no more than a mild inconvenience to her. She sat back in her creaking wooden chair and sighed with what she could have been forced to admit was contentment.

The inn was a small place, compact and well appointed, sitting at the juncture between the town's two main streets. The walls were panelled in rich aspen, and behind the bar a stuffed orruk's head had been mounted on a brass board, the monstrous greenskin glaring down at the warm, low-ceilinged room with an outraged expression on its snarling face. A fire crackled in the grate behind them, warming the chill from their bones. Doralia sighed and drank again. There were half a dozen tables set up in the inn's front room, but apart from themselves and the barkeeper, the place was empty. Raven's Hollow itself seemed half deserted.

After they had passed through the gate, the guard waving them on their way, they had walked along a street that was wreathed in the shadows cast by guttering aether-lamps, a narrow avenue bordered on each side by tall, single-fronted wooden tenements made of the same thunderwyrm bone as the wall. Most of the buildings were dark and quiet, and few lights shone in the small, lead-framed windows. The town was silent, and in the air around them there was a sense of hushed expectancy.

Caspar sat next to her at their fireside table, turning slightly away so that he was only presenting his profile to the man who sat there with them: Argen Schmidt, the arbiter of Raven's Hollow. The bandit dragged his fringe further across his face and rested his palm against his cheek as he leaned on the table. He looked deeply, deeply uncomfortable. She only wished she could stretch out her stay in the town to prolong his agony as much as possible.

'I hope the rooms will be to your satisfaction,' Schmidt said. 'And of course, any supplies you need will be provided at the town's expense – we are dedicated servants of Sigmar here.'

He was a big man with a boiled red face, and the collar of his mauve doublet strained against his fleshy neck. His sparse blond hair was scraped back across his scalp, and when he leaned forward, his hands clutched together as if beseeching them, she could smell the cloying floral scent of his pomade. She finished her wine, slamming down the goblet and nodding to the barkeeper to bring another.

'We didn't come here to see about your dead,' Doralia told him. 'First I heard of it was from the ferryman when we crossed the river.'

Schmidt looked crestfallen. He dropped his hands into his lap. The barkeeper came over with Doralia's wine, and for a moment she thought the arbiter might snatch it from her grasp.

'I have to confess,' he said, 'that is not the answer I was hoping for. Your colleague said more pressing matters drew his attention to the north, but when you arrived at our gates I assumed you were following up on his investigation. Things have been desperate here since... since the incident with the cemetery.'

She leaned forward, pushing her goblet aside.

'This colleague of mine – an older man, white hair, moustache?'

'Indeed so,' Schmidt said. He lowered his eyes. 'Not a day past, he was here. I tried to argue that he should stay and help us, but, if you don't mind me saying, he was quite the forceful fellow. Not to be gainsaid, if you understand.'

'That sounds like him, all right.' She gave a tight smile. 'His name is Galen ven Denst. He's my father. I've been looking for him.'

Schmidt shook his head. 'Well, whatever took precedence over our troubles here must be serious indeed,' he said. 'He didn't even examine the graveyard, stopping only to resupply before trekking on into the mountains. There is a small outpost up there, a village called Hollowcrest. That seemed to be where he was heading, although he did not confide in me as to his reasons.'

Schmidt glanced at Caspar, who was still half turned away from him. The big man slowly frowned and narrowed his eyes, rubbed his hand thoughtfully across his jaw. Caspar squirmed in his seat.

'What exactly happened here?' Doralia asked him. Schmidt drew his attention away from Caspar and clasped his hands together again.

'I'm not sure I can even put it into words,' he said. 'Certainly, nothing like it has ever happened before, and it is far outside my experience. We contend with raids from the greenskins in the hills, of course, but Raven's Hollow sits in a well-defended location, as you can see.' He looked anxiously at her. 'We've rarely worried about an attack from outside, but for something like this to come from within... Well, you can understand why so many people have left since it happened. No one feels safe here any more.'

She finished her wine. 'I think it best if I see this for myself,' she said.

CHAPTER SEVEN

THE RESTLESS DEAD

Schmidt, accompanied by two guards armed with gleaming bill-hooks and wearing polished-bone breastplates, led them through the quiet evening streets towards the southern edge of town. Doralia looked for the light of candle flames or lamps in the windows, but most of them were still dark. Their footsteps rang out on the rough stone roads, and there was no sign of anyone abroad in Raven's Hollow. It was as near to a ghost town as she had seen in these parts.

The street they were following began to slope downwards, and as they reached the end they came to a tall, wrought iron gate that had been wreathed in heavy chains. On either side of the gate was a crumbling stone wall smothered in moss. Schmidt signalled to one of the guards, who stepped forward with a long iron key and unlatched the padlock. The chains fell away with a slithering rattle, and with a gaunt look on his face the guard slowly pushed the gate open.

They emerged into a rough oval of enclosed ground perhaps

a hundred yards from end to end, descending the natural slope of the hills and enclosed by the bones of the city walls on either side. On the left as they came through the gate was a small stone house with an arched slate roof. Its door was sealed with a heavy padlock and the windows had been boarded up. On the other side, a twisted woe tree mumbled in the silence, its black branches quivering. A faint mist lingered across the ground, creeping like bindweed around the bars of the iron gate.

'Welcome,' Argen Schmidt said in a hushed voice, 'to the cemetery of Raven's Hollow.'

The cemetery was a ruined field, a stretch of ground littered with broken gravestones and tumbled sculptures. Tomb chests lay fractured, and the gate of one mausoleum had been roughly torn aside and cast to the ground. The graves themselves were hollow pits of disturbed earth, the grass around them greasy and black. There was a cold smell in the air, the dusty reek of the dead. Here was where Raven's Hollow had buried its loved ones for generations, for as long as there had been people living in the hills.

'You always bring me to the most charming places,' Caspar muttered. 'Such a lovely location for a moonlit stroll...'

Doralia ignored him. She walked between the open graves, peering down into the earth, occasionally crouching to examine the soil. In some of the graves she could see shattered coffins, while others held only ragged grave shrouds. Schmidt followed at one side, Caspar at the other. The two guards stayed by the gate, their billhooks in hand.

'Near every single grave has emptied, as far as we can tell,' Schmidt said. 'Of course, you'll forgive us if no one has looked too closely. This is not the sort of thing we are used to here.'

'When did this happen?' she asked. She stooped to pick up a mouldering length of bone: a finger, its joints still held together by desiccated cartilage and sinew.

'Perhaps a week ago, near enough,' Schmidt said. 'Although it feels like longer.'

She tossed the finger bone back into the dirt. She crossed over to a small mausoleum, a marble structure topped by a carving of Sigmar reaching to the heavens with Ghal Maraz. The gate had been wrenched and twisted, and when she ducked her head inside she could see a coffin in the gloom, the lid smashed on the ground amidst a scattering of dead leaves from the woe tree.

'Tell me exactly what happened,' she said to Schmidt. 'Everything. Leave out no detail.'

As they moved between the graves, Doralia pausing every now and then to examine the ground, the arbiter gave her an outline of the dark events that had gripped the town.

'It was at the time of Ulgu Ascendant,' he said, 'not ten days back. The town was preparing for the festival, but then reports came in from the southern quarter that someone had broken into the cemetery and had destroyed some of the headstones. One old woman who lived near the cemetery made a ridiculous claim that her recently buried husband had reappeared in her bed one morning, quite as if he had never died in the first place! She had run screaming into the streets, but when the guards accompanied her back home there was no sign of the dead man at all.'

'You didn't believe her story?' Doralia asked.

'It seemed so absurd, scarcely worth crediting. But then,' Schmidt said, his face drawn, 'one night we were all awoken by these terrible noises coming from the cemetery. The broken stones, the awful moaning, the stench that drifted through the streets...'

He made the sign of the comet against his chest and passed a handkerchief across his brow.

'You saw them?' she asked. 'The dead?'

'Yes, Sigmar save me!' Schmidt wailed. 'We all did. Hundreds of corpses, stumbling through the graveyard, their eyes unseeing, lifeless. The terrible sounds they made… By Sigmar, I don't think I'll ever have a good night's sleep again. They tore their way through the gate there and staggered out into the streets.'

'Was anyone attacked? Anyone bitten by them?'

'No,' Schmidt said. He was making a visible effort to control himself. 'It was as if we, the living, barely existed to them. They shuffled through the streets towards the town gates, and we threw the gates wide to let them out. Sigmar alone knows where they went after that, and none of us were minded to follow. Into the hills, for all I know. It is a sight I will never be able to scrub from my mind, I fear – living corpses, staggering through the moonlight, while good folk locked themselves in their homes in terror.'

Doralia stood there in the middle of the graveyard with her hands on her hips. She looked down at the open graves, at the cemetery gate, at the streets beyond. The mist drifted across the disturbed earth, and suddenly it felt colder in the quiet town. None of it made any sense to her. The dead did not rise of their own accord, and to have risen in these numbers would have taken the exercise of real power. She thought of the vampire in Fortune, but a vampire could not have done this. They had some degree of control over the dead, but not sufficient to raise corpses in those numbers, to drive them on in that way, enthralled. And why did her father not see fit to investigate something so serious? What could possibly have drawn him onwards, instead of staying behind to help? What was happening?

She turned to Schmidt. 'Have you had anyone from the town go missing lately?'

Schmidt shook his head, confused. 'Not to my knowledge,' he said. He shrugged. 'People come and go all the time, of course, but nothing has been reported.'

'No sudden, inexplicable deaths?'

'No.'

'A black dog,' she said. She thought back to the ferryman's words. 'A child and its father, walking the wilds? Nothing like that has come to your attention?'

'I should say not,' Schmidt said. He looked confused. 'Are these things linked to us, in some way? Azyr help us if so…'

'I confess I don't know,' she said. 'My father, Galen, he said nothing about any of this?'

'Not a thing,' Schmidt told her. 'As I said, he stopped long enough only for more supplies, and then headed further on into the hills. The village I mentioned, Hollowcrest, that seemed to be where he was heading.'

'And what's at Hollowcrest?' she asked him.

Schmidt spread his hands. 'Very little. A staging post more than anything, for the road that leads on through the Krondspines to Lake Everglut. But he seemed determined that that's where he needed to go.'

Then that's where I need to go too, she thought.

Caspar looked at her and she nodded. He swallowed, his mouth turned down; this was more than he was expecting, she was sure. Being a thief was one thing, but tangling with the undead was quite another.

She was deciding what to do next, whether to head back to the inn for the night or to press on immediately for Hollowcrest, when a sound in the corner of the graveyard drew all of their attention. It was like a spade striking soil, but when she turned to look there was nothing there. Just the mist brewing in the hollows of the cemetery, a lank spread of weeds, the unsettled earth. She heard it again, louder this time.

No, not like someone digging into the soil at all, she thought. It was like something digging its way out.

'Witch hunter?' Caspar said. 'Please tell me that's not what I think it is…'

He drew his sword with a scrape of steel. The guards at the gate hurried forward to flank the arbiter, while Doralia calmly loaded her crossbow from the quiver on her hip.

'Oh, gods above and below,' Schmidt fretted. He backed off. 'Quick, to the gates!'

'Wait,' she said sharply. She held out a hand to stay them. 'Just… wait.'

The deadwalker, an ancient thing of scraps and brittle bone, long buried in the deeps of the cemetery, took an age to claw its way from the ground. From a tangled, forgotten corner strewn with weeds, it drew itself up from its long sleep. Doralia stood sentinel and watched it lever itself from the dirt, jaw clacking, the frail skull broken and packed with mud. Eventually it gained its feet and staggered forward on frail, bony legs across the grass. A grave shroud trailed behind it. The breeze that flowed down from the hills seemed suddenly very cold.

The guards stepped forward, levelling their billhooks, but she gestured them aside as the dead thing advanced.

'Don't touch it,' she said. 'Just watch.'

She backed off, her crossbow still raised to cover the thing. Caspar darted behind her, while Schmidt sought the safety of his guards. The deadwalker staggered onwards, jaw opening and closing, rags trailing along behind it like ivy. It was little more than a skeleton, and a faint smell came off it of ancient decay. It must have been one of the very first people from the town to have been buried there, she thought. Centuries back perhaps, and each year seeing another harvest of the dead buried on top of it. It had taken that long to claw its way free.

They watched it stumble its way across the cemetery, heading with some mute instinct towards the gate. It paid them no heed at all.

'Witch hunter!' Schmidt beseeched her. 'Do something, you can't let it out into the streets!'

If she'd had the time, if her father hadn't led her on this inscrutable chase across the wilds of Ghur, she might have let it continue towards whatever destination drew it. She would get to the bottom of all this, she would find answers to these questions before it was too late…

The dead thing clawed at the gate, rattling the bars. Slowly, more by accident than design, it managed to draw them open, staggering backwards as the hinge swung.

'If you're going to do something, do it now,' Caspar muttered. He held his sword out in front of him, darting a glance around the darkened cemetery in case anything else was trying to sneak up on them.

If she had the time…

She raised her crossbow and fired, and the nullstone bolt plucked those bones from the grip of whatever fell magic held them together.

CHAPTER EIGHT

GALEN VEN DENST

'The thing that killed your mother was a vampire,' he said.

In front of him was a battered iron box, waist high. There was a door at the front of it, secured by a solid metal bolt. He ran his gloved hand across its surface. Slowly he began to walk around it. He had no need of the walking sticks now.

'Do you know what a vampire is?' he asked.

'Yes, father.'

'Tell me.'

'They are lords of the undead,' Doralia said. 'Powerful, immortal, strong... They retain their will and the memories of their experiences, and they are without mercy.'

They stood in a low and gloomy chamber, the walls painted with a dirty whitewash. The ceiling dripped with damp. A torch hissed on the far wall. In the corner of the room, an iron door stood open.

'Indeed so,' her father said. 'Most of them...' He paused, standing there silent and grave, staring down at her without expression. Since that day, she noticed, his hair had begun to turn white. 'What else?'

She glanced at him, swallowed, tilted her head back.

'I'm not...'

'What else!'

She jumped, ransacking her thoughts for what he had taught her. She thought of her mother.

'They... they reproduce by draining the blood of their victims, and on the cusp of death feeding them their own blood. It is how new vampires are made. A dark communion.'

Her father nodded, staring into the distance. His face was a mask. He stood by the side of the iron box. She could feel something in there, brooding, plotting, stoking a dreadful malice.

'That is what happened to your mother, to... to my wife,' her father said. 'The vampire that turned her did so only as a cruel jest, a form of torture to make our own deaths more unpleasant to us. The creature's name was Jael Morgane. Jael Morgane... Never forget that name,' he said sternly. 'Never!'

'I won't, father,' she said. She would never forget that voice, dripping through the burning house, coiling its way up the stairs towards her. She would never forget the sight of her mother, broken on the floorboards, and then coming dreadfully to life once more.

Her father stood before her. He towered over her. She was nine years old.

'You are inducted into the most holy Order of Azyr,' he said. 'Our sacred duty is to protect Sigmar's empire from enemies within and enemies without, by whatever means necessary. I have taught you much over these last few months, Doralia, but your true training begins now.'

He reached out as if to touch her shoulder, but at the last moment drew his hand away. He passed her a silver stake, razor sharp at the point. He looked her in the eyes, and Doralia saw the pain and anger there, the rage. He turned away and stalked towards the door in the corner of the room. As he passed the iron box he drew the bolt *free from the lock. He reached the door in the corner of the room, and he didn't look back as he closed it behind him.*

Doralia held out the stake in front of her, her eyes wide, her breath shuddering through her body. She stood her ground.

And then the door of the iron box flew open.

Against her better instincts, she decided to head into the hills at once. Pausing only to restock with food and water, she gathered up her kitbag and weapons from the tavern and headed for the town gates, Caspar trailing at her side.

'But you will return?' Schmidt protested as he hurried to keep up with them. He mopped his brow with his handkerchief. 'Please, I'm begging you. Raven's Hollow needs answers, we need to be protected!'

'You're as safe as you can be,' Doralia called over her shoulder as she strode down the narrow street. Her footsteps echoed against the bone walls of the buildings, the black tenements looming on either side of her, as sad and dark and empty as the graves in the cemetery. Most of the folk who had lived here had left now, too terrified of the dead. They had taken their chances on the road to Izalend or Bilgeport, maybe even to Excelsis. She loaded her crossbow, checked over her pistol and ammunition pouches, her knives, the sword on her back. She pulled the hat brim down low, her blood-red coat billowing out behind her. The night sky above Raven's Hollow was bruised, lit by the passing spheres. It would be a long night, but she couldn't afford to waste any more time.

'The dead that rose from your cemetery were answering a distant call, a locus of power that they wouldn't have understood in any case,' she said. Schmidt scurried up beside her. 'I don't believe the citizens here were ever in any real danger, and what danger there was has now passed.'

'How can you be sure?' Schmidt cried.

The town gates were ahead of them now, tall and narrow, the

guards on the watch tower looking down at the arbiter for instructions. She came to a halt and turned on her heel to face him.

'I'm sorry,' she said. 'For what it's worth. But there is something larger at stake here, something that I don't yet understand. There are dark rumours abroad in these lands, whispers on the wind, strange tales and portents. I believe my father may have the answers that I seek. I need to find him immediately.'

She felt the smallest pricking of her conscience then, seeing how frightened the arbiter really was. He stood there trembling before her, a head taller but as diminished and insignificant as a child.

'We will discover the truth,' she told him gently. 'And we will find whoever is responsible. They will have Sigmar's justice, this I promise you.'

Schmidt sighed wearily. He signalled to the guards and the gates slowly creaked open.

'Then I wish you good fortune,' he said as he waved them on their way. 'And may Sigmar go with you, witch hunter.'

They hiked the trail in darkness for a few miles, the track winding back and forth as it snaked its way along the flanks of the hills, heading ever higher. Down below, she could see the dim glow of Raven's Hollow sheltered in its nook. She thought of the tavern, that damned good zephyrwine they had behind the bar... At least she'd remembered to refill her bottle of firewater. She absently reached round to pat her kitbag, where the bottle was safely nestled. Thank Sigmar for small mercies.

The air turned cooler after a while, the grass on either side of the trail giving way to bare rock littered with stones and pebbles. She could see her breath ghosting out in front of her. Now and then they came across a gnarled salt pine lurking at the side of the path, but other than that there were no trees, no real shelter from the wind as it began to strengthen. Snowflakes drifted erratically around them, a light dusting that melted as soon as it hit the ground. She peered up the trail, but she could see no sign of Hollowcrest. Tucked into a fold of the land, a valley sheltered from the wind, it was hidden from them yet.

'I'm not much use to you as a scout any more,' Caspar said wearily. He had buttoned Hektor Vogel's coat up to the neck and staggered up the rough incline behind her, scrambling for handholds amongst the rocks as they came to a flatter stretch of ground. 'This is further than I've ever been in these parts.'

'We'll find a use for you yet,' she said. 'Many are the tools that Sigmar can turn to his purpose.'

'I have to admit, I've never exactly seen myself as one of Sigmar's most loyal servants.'

'I'm sure there'll be a chance for you to prove your faith before too long.'

Suddenly, Caspar grabbed her elbow and turned her around. Doralia bristled at his touch. She was about to reproach him, when she saw just how troubled he clearly was. His black hair whipped in the wind, and underneath it his face was pale and drawn. Even his cocky insouciance seemed to have left him since Raven's Hollow. He had looked more cheerful with a noose around his neck.

'I know I'm in your debt,' he said. 'And I've tried to repay it, but all this… Vampires, the very dead rising from their graves… I'm sorry, but this is far more than I expected. I'm out of my depth here. I'm not even that much of a thief, truth be told. Bravado gets you a long way, but like I said back in Fortune, I'm no villain.'

She looked at the stretch of flat ground they had reached, a narrow cleft of rough hillside at the side of the trail. It was sheltered from the worst of the wind by a spur of rock, and on the other side there was a long, sloping copse of salt pines that tumbled down towards the lower flanks of the hills. She still couldn't see Hollowcrest above them. Half a day's journey, Argen Schmidt had said, but the night was deep now. They would risk too much by going on.

'Let's set up for the night here,' she said. 'We're not going to reach Hollowcrest before morning as it is.'

'And in the morning?'

'I'm going on regardless,' she said. 'As for you? Well, I guess we'll see.'

They set up camp with the spur of rock behind them, shielding their campfire not only from the wind but from anyone who might be watching down below. Caspar stoked the fire and unpacked some of his provisions: salt meat, dried fruit and a few herbs he'd picked up in Raven's Hollow. He boiled it all with some water from his bottle in a cook pot that he'd stolen in Fortune. As meagre as the ingredients were, she thought the smell was appetising. She just hoped nothing else could smell it up here as well.

She took the firewater from her bag and drank down a long swallow. After a moment, relenting, she passed the bottle to Caspar and the young man took a grateful drink. In the firelight he'd regained some of his colour, and the firewater gave him back a touch of his old confidence. Doralia watched him as he stoked the pot. He was handsome, she had to admit. Even that wryness and arrogance had a certain appeal. Maybe, she thought, if the circumstances had been different…

She shook her head and smiled bleakly to herself. What was she thinking? It was an absurd idea, sentimental. Her life had no space in it for anything but duty. Even a moment's comfort couldn't come from anything but the bottle she cradled in her arms. *If the circumstances had been different…* The only way they could ever have been different would be if she'd never joined the order in the first place. Such a concept was beyond her. She couldn't imagine what her life would have been like without it.

She could see that Caspar was agitated, though. He couldn't

settle, and even the gulp of firewater couldn't stop his hands from trembling. He had been shaken by what they'd seen down in Raven's Hollow, it was obvious. Probably nothing in the realms more disturbing to an ordinary person than seeing the dead come back to life, she thought. There was something uniquely sickening about it, stabbing to the heart of what folk felt was most sacred. The dead should have peace, if nothing else.

She recognised in Caspar the need to talk after something terrible had happened. She had felt it often enough herself, and knew all too well the cost of keeping your fears contained.

'You've never seen anything like that before then?' she said. 'The cemetery back there?'

'Gods no,' he said. He closed his eyes, as if fearing to see it again. 'That... *thing* pulling itself from the dirt, staggering across the dead grass... How is something like that even possible?'

'Dark magics,' she said. 'Powerful magics, very dangerous in the wrong hands.'

'I imagine it's a fairly mundane sight for someone like you?'

'I've seen worse,' she said. She drank from the bottle. 'After a while, a lone deadwalker stumbling about a cemetery counts as a quiet day. In Shyish, the dead are legion, but I have to admit – it's not something you see much of anywhere else.'

Caspar shuddered. He decanted the stew into two pewter bowls and passed her a wooden spoon. Doralia ate, and the warmth that spread through her was cleaner and more wholesome than the warmth from her bottle. She should quit drinking, she thought. Talk, perhaps, like Caspar was talking. See what difference that made. Talk to her father...

'I dread to think of what you would call a hard day's work,' he said, blowing the steam from his stew. 'How in the name of Sigmar did you get into this line of business anyway? It doesn't seem like the kind of thing someone would actually choose to do.'

She ate in silence for a moment. How to explain it to him? How to give him some idea of the roads she had walked in all the long years she had been doing this, and what put her on the path in the first place? Behind her, on the other side of the trail, the salt pines rustled and whispered in the wind, and the lonely hills brooded in the darkness around them. The flames of their campfire buckled. Embers sparked like fireflies in the night.

'My father,' she said at last. 'He inducted me into the order.'

'How old were you?'

'Nearly ten,' she said.

The iron box, the door springing wide. The smell of the vampire mouldering in the dark, its ravenous jaws, the hate in its red eyes. Not Jael Morgane, though. Not her.

'Gods save me…' Caspar muttered. 'What did your mother have to say about that?'

'My mother?' she said. She stared into the flames. 'She was in the order too. She… she was killed.'

'I'm sorry,' he said quietly. 'That must have been difficult for you.'

'It was,' Doralia said. 'I killed her.'

'What?'

She gave him an ironic smile. 'She'd been murdered by a vampire,' she said. 'Turned into a vampire herself. I… I didn't have much of a choice. Shot her through the heart. Shot her with her own crossbow.'

Caspar's eyes drifted to the crossbow at Doralia's side. He said nothing.

'After that,' Doralia said, 'didn't seem like I had much of a chance at a normal life, whatever that is. The order saved me, gave me purpose.' She drank from the bottle, tried to keep the bitterness out of her voice. 'My father saved me.'

'I suppose you could call it that…'

'What about you?' she said sharply. 'Like you say, you're not much of a villain. What drew you to an outlaw's life?'

Caspar shrugged. He finished off his stew and lay back with his head on his pack.

'No one plans it, I suppose,' he said. 'Just something I fell into. My parents died when I was young, and I grew up on the streets, poorer than you can imagine. Damn, I was eight years old before I'd even worn a pair of shoes... You steal to survive there, or...' He smiled. 'Or you don't survive.'

'You're from Excelsis?' Doralia asked.

'Izalend,' he said. 'The lowest possible level, down by the Pauper's Wall. I don't know if you've been there, but if you have you'll have seen the Everflame.' He grimaced. 'Always hated that damned thing. Seemed too much like a prison wall to me, keeping everyone in. And even with the Everflame, Izalend is *cold*. First chance I got to leave, I took it.'

Doralia nodded and leaned back. She had some idea of what he meant. The sense of restlessness, of always moving forward. Life in the order was like that, in some way. There was always a threat to investigate, an enemy to fight. A risk that had to be taken, though your life might be forfeit. Standing still, dealing with all your doubts and fears – that was the hard part.

Her eyes felt heavy and her legs ached from the climb. They had been going flat out for days now, hiking through brush and scrub, cutting across the plains and clambering through these tumbled hills. She wondered what awaited them at Hollowcrest and doubted it was a warm bed and a good night's rest. That was tomorrow's problem though. *Enjoy the fire*, she told herself. *Enjoy the food in your belly, for tomorrow you might be dead.*

'I don't know if you've quite got what it takes for my line of work,' she said, 'but if you ever tire of stealing jewels from provincial arbiters, you could do a lot worse.'

'Join the order?' Caspar scoffed. 'Are you mad! I don't actually have a death wish, you know.'

Doralia laughed: a light sound there in the darkness, one that she hadn't heard herself make for months.

'I never said that, exactly. But the war we wage has many fronts, and many ways to serve. You know this part of Ghur well, we can always use informants or scouts. You would be doing good, in the wider scheme of things. I promise you.'

Caspar gave a dismissive sigh. 'The wider scheme of things has always been a little out of my league. When you have to scavenge food from what rich folk throw away, you don't tend to care that much about "Sigmar's domain", it has to be said. Doesn't seem like much of your business.'

Doralia closed her eyes. 'I've always found,' she said, 'that if you don't pay attention to the wider scheme of things, sooner or later it starts paying attention to you…'

It was a smell on the breeze at first, sharp and rank, the sickly scent of decay. Doralia snapped her eyes open and reached for her crossbow. She sat up, eyes scanning the darkness on the other side of the trail. Caspar was bolt upright too, hand lingering on his sword hilt.

'What is it?' he whispered.

A crackle of broken twigs, the sound of branches roughly pushed aside.

'Doralia?'

She raised her crossbow and shot on instinct, the bolt skimming into the shadows where the salt pines stood, pulling her pistol in the same motion and firing blindly. She heard the smack of the bullet hitting flesh and drew her blade from the scabbard on her back.

'Oh, gods save us!' Caspar wailed.

'Stay behind me!' she shouted. She tossed the empty pistol to the ground; there was no time to reload.

From the shadows and the brush at the side of the path and

from further up the slope came a mob of deadwalkers, a wave of corpses that staggered and stumbled towards the campfire. Broken teeth grinned from rotten gums, lips black with necrosis. Dead, milky eyes glared from fractured skulls, scraps of parchment skin fluttering in the breeze. Some of the corpses tumbled over the edge of the path, falling down the jagged slope and splitting to pieces on the rocks below. Others tripped on the uneven ground and were crushed under the feet of those who came behind them, still trying to claw their way forwards on broken bones. The deadwalkers surged on, their numbers impossible to judge in the shadows that masked them. The stench was nauseating: the cloying stink of rotting flesh; the dry, powdery scent of old, disinterred bones.

'Arm yourself!' Doralia cried. She darted forward, sweeping her sword like a club to smash the first line of corpses to the ground. Scraps of flesh were scattered across the path. She cut down and cleaved the jawbone from one zombie, kicking out to send it flying back into the darkness. In the corner of her eye she could see Caspar leaping backwards, scrambling to escape the grasping hands of the dead.

'At least we know where the dead of Raven's Hollow went,' he yelled.

There were too many of them. Every wound she inflicted was simply ignored. She cut brutal tranches in their flesh, hacked arms off at the shoulder, cut one deadwalker almost in half in a great, two-handed blow, but every parry and riposte she made only gave the rest of them a chance to lumber forwards. Pale, decomposing fingers scrabbled at the hem of her coat. Stinking corpse-breath poured from mouths that dribbled a foul black ichor. She saw Caspar sweep the head from one zombie's shoulders with a frenzied blow, but then the weight of the undead pushed him back towards the spur of rock. Doralia dodged aside, leapt over the stuttering flames of the campfire and speared a corpse through the back of the head with her sword. Caspar flailed out with the flat of his blade and knocked another one aside, stamping down with his boot on its head until the skull cracked.

'For Sigmar's sake,' he cried, 'we need to get out of here! We don't stand a chance!'

They were hemmed in, surrounded on all sides, their backs against the spur of rock. Behind them was only the steep fall down the side of the hill, the barbed rocks as deadly as any blade. Doralia snatched up a burning brand from the campfire and stabbed it into a deadwalker's face, almost vomiting at the stench of scorched flesh as the branch pierced its skull. She raised her sword, blade back against her shoulder, ready to strike.

'Come on then,' she snarled. 'And may Sigmar damn your dead bones!'

There was a sharp crack of flame, and dark blood was dashed into her face. One of the deadwalkers hit the ground, a slop of brains spattering over Caspar's boots. Doralia hacked down with her blade, taking the head off another one as it staggered towards her. A second shot rang out, sharp as a whipcrack, blasting more brains into the darkness.

Caspar turned and vomited, the sword trembling in his hands. Doralia snatched up her crossbow and quickly reloaded, aiming at the other side of the trail. The salt pines gathered their shadows beneath them, their branches whispering in the cold wind like parchment. A tall figure emerged from the night.

'Father!'

Galen ven Denst stepped into the wavering light of the campfire, a smoking pistol in each hand. His face was dark, and his white hair was ruffled by the breeze. He looked at his daughter.

'Should have known you'd find me,' he said. 'You always were the better tracker. Now, if you don't mind taking advice from an old man – run!'

CHAPTER NINE

SHADOWS
OF THE PAST

For the best part of an hour they hiked and doubled-back along the path, clambering up into the rocks that overhung the northern flank, snaking through the gorse bushes, doing everything they could to throw the deadwalkers off their trail. It was impossible to tell how many of them there were, but Doralia guessed it must be a hundred at least. Whenever one noticed them, the others seemed to swivel their malign attention towards them too. Caspar started pushing rocks down the slope and clattering pebbles far off onto the other side of the trail, and eventually the corpses took the bait. Following the sounds, they staggered off back into the darkness, and only when the grave-stink had slackened on the breeze did Doralia give herself a chance to relax. They hiked on up the slope, deeper into the hills, until they found a sheltered spot to set up camp.

Now, they sat there brooding by a sparse little campfire, neither of them able to meet the other's eye. Doralia cracked a few sticks in her hands and threw them into the flames, watching the fire bend and flurry in the breeze. The night was wide and deep around them, slipping down the hills with not a hint of the dawn behind it. She reached into her kitbag for the bottle, glancing up to see her father's disapproving stare. She ignored it. The firewater burned deep, flushing the exhaustion from her. Galen looked away, staring off to where Caspar, twenty yards further down the trail, was keeping an eye out for the dead.

'Where did you find him?' Galen asked. His voice was low, gravelly from all the cigars he smoked. He unclasped the armoured gorget at his throat and rubbed his neck. There were dark circles under his eyes and his face was heavily lined. He looked old, she thought. He looked like a wind-dried husk of wood, as if all that was keeping him together were the straps of his weapons and the great double-breasted coat he had wrapped around himself against the cold.

'Caspar?' she said. 'Found him in Fortune, not too far from Excelsis. Knew the land, thought he might be of use.'

'He made it this far,' Galen said, grudgingly. 'For a pretty boy, I suppose he's tougher than he looks.'

Doralia looked over at him. Caspar lay there, flat against the rocks, peering down the slope. She could see him trembling from here.

'I guess you could say that…' She looked back at her father. 'You didn't make it to Fortune,' she said. 'Didn't find a trace of you anyway. Figured you must have cut up straight to the north instead.'

Galen nodded. 'Bridge was still standing then, although I heard it was swept away not a day later. How did you cross?'

'Ferry further down,' she said. She drank again from the bottle, hissing with satisfaction. 'Caspar there knew of it, found a trail we could follow. Heard some strange tales from the ferryman. Saw some strange things in Fortune, as it happens.'

She looked at him, but his face gave nothing away.

'Killed a man there,' she said. 'Went by the name of Hektor Vogel. Claimed he was an agent. Had the coat for it at least, same one Caspar's wearing now.'

'Takes more than a coat,' Galen said.

'That it does.'

'I'm impressed you caught up with me so quickly,' he said. 'Had to double back a couple of times myself, must have left a muddy trail to follow.'

'Never thought I'd find myself tracking my own father.'

'Thought I'd left a note telling you not to,' he said.

'Must have missed it…'

The subject sat there between them, squatting on their talk, a weight neither of them could shift. All the miles she had been travelling, and not once had she thought of what it would be like when she finally caught up with him. She could have rehearsed any number of questions and demands, but when she was face to face with him it was like she was a child again. He spoke, she listened. That was the way it had always been. That was all there was to it.

The silence grew until it was unbearable, but Galen was the first to break it. He pinched the bridge of his nose and squeezed his eyes shut, and when he opened them again they were tired and watery. His skin looked grey in the firelight.

'I'm sorry I left,' he said. His mouth twisted under the pressure of the words. 'Without telling you. I didn't want you to come.'

Doralia leaned forward. She thought about reaching for his hand.

'Why not?' she said. 'What are you *doing* out here?'

Galen shook his head. 'The siege,' he muttered. 'The battle for Excelsis… There was a moment near the end, when the White

Reaper was leading us through the streets to the Conclave Hall. I thought that was it. Just a small moment, but out of everything that happened during the fight, it was that moment I remember most. We'd failed. We were going to die.' He looked at her. 'You were going to die.'

She tried to remember the mayhem of that furious hour, but it was a blur. Her arm aching from the weight of her sword, pausing whenever she could to reload her crossbow, the orruks capering through the streets, the skaven and their chittering yellow teeth. The White Reaper's monstrous calm as he smashed them aside, and the dreadful sound of his voice as he intoned prayers to Sigmar – more terrifying in its way than the blood and death that surrounded them.

Galen, seeing her confusion, said, 'You didn't notice. The fight was swirling around us as we cut up the Pilgrim's Way. Bodies in the streets, rubble cascading from the buildings as they collapsed. I turned and saw you hack one skaven down, and then… There was another one behind you, its blade raised, ready to stab you in the back.'

He set his jaw, jabbed at the flames with the point of his knife.

'There was nothing I could do,' he said. 'I couldn't reach you in time. I was too slow. Too old, too weak. I'd been doing this too long, and this was the worst I had ever seen. And then you were going to die in front of me, and there was nothing I could do.'

'Sigmar must have been watching over me then,' she said. 'Last time I checked, I was still in one piece.'

Galen smiled bitterly. 'The White Reaper was watching over you. Sentanus took the head off that rat without breaking a stride. We went on, the moment had passed, but… it's still there with me. I was so close to losing you.'

'And then the Conclave Hall,' she muttered.

'Aye… The hall of mirrors… and the Talon and the Voice… But

out of everything I saw that day, all those nightmares, it was the sight of you so close to death that has marked me the most. I see it in my dreams, Doralia. You dying in front of me...'

'But we did it,' she urged. 'We won, we saved the city!' She reached out and grabbed his gloved hand, holding it tightly.

'All I have felt since then is shame,' Galen said. He pulled his hand away. 'Shame and guilt. That I had put my own daughter in the way of such horror, that I had condemned you to a vicious and miserable death, one way or the other. If you survived the siege, then it was only to die in another fight we couldn't possibly win.'

'There's no fight we can't win,' she protested. 'We're Sigmar's right hand in the Mortal Realms.'

'Are we?' Galen said. 'We're in the middle of a war that has spiralled totally out of our grasp. The very gods themselves battle in the streets of our cities now. Kragnos, Morathi... What next? What can mortal men and women do in the face of such power? We're no more than ants scrabbling about beneath them. Sometimes...' he said.

He glanced up at her and held her gaze.

'Sometimes I wish I had never recruited you into the order,' he said.

It was like a blow to the heart. She reeled back from the campfire, her mind blank, stunned by his words. But then slowly, almost against her will, it was filled with dark flashes of the past. The long days and nights of her training. Her arms aching with the weight of sword and crossbow. The iron box in that dank chamber, and the sound of her father closing the door behind him.

The sight of her mother's broken body slowly twitching back to life.

The look on her face as Doralia shot her through the heart.

'It's a bit late for that,' she whispered.

Her voice shook. She couldn't trust herself to say any more. She turned away, hiding her face from him. She could see Caspar sitting on the ground back along the trail, still idly casting pebbles down the slope. The night sky was a fume of white stars above him. He wasn't stupid, she thought. He knew that she needed space to be alone with her father.

Not quite the happy reunion I expected...

'So that's why you left me behind,' she murmured, still with her back to him. The campfire fizzed and crackled under her words, almost drowning them out her voice was so low. 'You thought you were keeping me safe.' She gave a cynical laugh and reached for the bottle. 'Well, danger found me all the same. And it still doesn't explain what you're doing out here.'

'Suppose it doesn't,' Galen said. He sighed from the depths of his lungs, and it was like every last ounce of his energy went with it. Doralia faced him again. She offered him the firewater, but he shook his head.

'What do you remember,' he said, 'about the night your mother died?'

He told her then all the details that he had never been able to share with her before.

'Morgane had been terrorising settlements deep in the Amber Princedoms for months,' Galen said. 'She had no pity, no mercy – none at all. Sigmar knows where she'd come from, but I'd rarely encountered a vampire more sadistic than her. None were safe from her predations. She killed whole families, tortured people for days before she put them out of their misery. The folk that lived in those parts were terrified, and they turned to those they thought could help them... The Order of Azyr. Your mother and I were assigned to the case. Fool that I was, I thought it would be simple, routine, no more than another quick kill. I was so sure of myself back then, so arrogant... I was wrong.'

He passed a hand across his face, pinched the bridge of his nose again.

'Morgane was much wilier than I gave her credit for, and more ruthless,' he said. 'I was complacent, we both were. I was following up a lead while Marie stayed behind with you at our lodgings. Little did I realise that Morgane had lured me away with a false trail, that she… that she had broken into our house and murdered Marie while I was gone. She turned your mother, converted her into her own disgusting kind. I think her plan was for Marie to then kill us both…'

He bowed his head as he told the story, staring into the depths of the flames. Doralia felt the anger in her solidify, a cold stone buried in her heart.

'I returned early,' Galen said. 'Had an inkling something wasn't right, but when I got back I didn't realise Morgane was already there. She quickly overpowered me, beat me half to death, broke both my legs as easily as we would breathe. Left me lying there helpless while she went looking for you. Your mother must have told you to hide, confronted Morgane to give you time. I don't know how I did it, what strength Sigmar lent me in that moment, but I managed to drag myself across the burning floor towards your room. I could hear her stalking her way towards you, and all I wanted in that moment was to kill the monster that had destroyed my family. That had killed my wife.'

'I remember,' she said, although her mind lurched away from it. The line of light as she peered through the crack in the wardrobe door. The woman who was looking for her, strange and alluring, her velvet voice, the cascade of her ebony hair.

She looked up into the night sky, flecked with its pinprick stars, the wheeling spheres of the cosmos. Flakes of snow fell slowly in a gentle rain, fizzing as they met the flames.

'I was near crippled, but not disarmed,' Galen said. 'I blacked out once or twice, but when I came to I had crawled as far as your bedroom door. I saw Marie... and Jael Morgane, standing there in triumph. You fired, giving your mother Sigmar's peace with her own crossbow. And before Morgane could react I shot her in the back of the head with my own.'

'Then Morgane died in that room?' she said. 'But all these years, I thought...'

Galen shook his head, his face lined with sorrow.

'You know better than that, daughter. It takes more than a bolt to the head to kill a vampire. Though she was badly wounded, she escaped. And now,' he said, 'Jael Morgane has returned.'

CHAPTER TEN

HOLLOWCREST

The air thinned as they climbed higher, the milky dawn gradually bleeding out into a steely blue. Slowly the shadows of the night lifted from the hills, leaving behind only a faint, cold mist that lingered in dell and hollow. The track stretched on away from them, sweeping off towards the north and then curving around as it passed between a rocky defile fringed with flowering yellow gorse. Above them, hazy in the dawn light, and now no more than a mile distant, were a few scattered buildings: stocky, two-storey things built from local stone, hunkered there on the hilltops like the rough-hewn forts and crude bastions of ancient days.

She turned and looked back down the trail, where Caspar Harrow was struggling to keep up. He had drawn his sword and was using it as a walking stick to gain purchase on the rough shale track, his pale face puffed and red and his black hair plastered to his forehead with sweat. Although the hills they had been climbing were low-slung, brooding things, nowhere near as steep as the mighty Krondspines that towered over them in the distance, the winding track and its sudden, unexpected inclines had taken it out of all of them. Doralia paused for a moment with her hands on her hips, regaining her breath. The view was spectacular. She could see far down towards the plains, a crumpled spread of olive green that stretched off towards the distant coast, where the steel line of the ocean was like a sword thrust between land and sky. She turned and looked up the track, where her father forged on ahead, unyielding.

'Things didn't seem to go too well with him last night,' Caspar said as he caught up with her.

'You noticed then?'

'I do have eyes in my head. I wasn't exactly expecting warm hugs and weepy sentiment, but in the end neither of you seemed too pleased to find each other.'

'I wouldn't call ours an affectionate relationship at the best of times.'

'I suppose I wouldn't know,' Caspar said. She caught the hint of rebuke in his tone. 'I wasn't lucky enough to grow up with a father. Or a mother either, for that matter.'

'I knew my mother for barely nine years before she was taken away from me,' Doralia said.

'Nine years is more than some get. Haven't you ever wondered what it would have been like if she'd lived? I wonder what you'd be doing now?'

She rounded on him. 'You overstep the mark, thief,' she said sourly. 'I have the feeling your charms may have let you slip the noose more than once, but don't go assuming we're friends. We're not that familiar.'

Caspar grinned widely, wiping his hair back from his face. He rested the duardin-forged sword against his shoulder.

'So...' he said, raising an eyebrow. 'You think I'm charming then?'

Doralia sighed. 'Sigmar certainly loves a trier, it's said...'

They pressed on, trying to catch up with Galen. The old man hiked the path as if running towards a fortune, not to a confrontation with one of the most dangerous creatures in the realms. She shook her head again at her father's revelation last night.

Jael Morgane, like a nightmare made real, stepping out of the mists of the past…

Jael Morgane has returned…

It was incredible. Not the desperate fights in the streets of Excelsis or the confrontation with the daemons in the Conclave Hall had struck her with as much simple terror as those words. Fear, an emotion she had virtually mastered in all the long years of her duty as an agent, had come crashing back and hit her like ice water dashed into her face. For one horrible, dislocating moment, she was a child again, hiding in the darkness as the thing that had killed her mother and crippled her father stalked through a burning house to find her.

Jael Morgane…

A name she had held close for twenty years. And now this.

From Galen's web of informants, the spies and confidants he had placed in practically every town and city in Ghur, had come word of a vampire matching Jael's description. She had been seen in Izalend, it was said. Bodies drained of blood had been found in Bilgeport. Flitting through the rough country, she had then disappeared in the wilderness. Galen had wasted no time, setting off at once and leaving Doralia behind. He had followed Morgane's trail, cutting back and forth as she tried to avoid him, doubling back to the edge of Fortune, pushing on towards Raven's Hollow. And now at last, the vengeance he had brooded on for twenty years was almost in his grasp.

She spat in the dirt, stopping to take a slug of water from her flask. The weight of her weapons dragged against her shoulder. She thought back to their conversation the night before.

Damn him, she thought. If he had never wanted her in the order in the first place, then what on earth had her life been for? What had been the point of all the violence and horror she had experienced, the battles she had fought? What the hell gave him the right?

She had tried to talk about the strange things she had seen and heard on her journey to track him down: the dead rising in Raven's Hollow, the bodies in Fortune, the black dog and the prophecy spoken by the man who followed it. The ferryman had said that the dog spoke with Sigmar's voice. Could that even be true? She had never heard the like before, but then the realm felt twisted out of sorts these days, and nothing would have surprised her. Or perhaps it was just another of these strange rumours that were stalking the land, weird omens and dark portents? Galen had dismissed it though. Even the attack by the deadwalkers the previous night only served to confirm his suspicions. It was all Jael Morgane's doing, he had claimed. Kill her, take her down at last, and everything would be solved. Doralia wasn't so sure. More than a hundred zombies had stumbled across them on the hillside, and that took more than the power of one vampire. She knew it. She felt it in her bones, but her father had been immovable. She had argued that they should follow the deadwalker horde, that they needed to investigate exactly what was going on, but Galen had shaken his head.

'What if they go on to Excelsis, what if there's more of them, what–'

'A handful of corpses aren't going to trouble the gates of Excelsis,' he said.

'We need answers!'

'I have my answers,' he had snapped. 'Morgane is throwing everything she has at us, but it won't be enough. I'm going on to Hollowcrest and I'll do it alone if I have to. The choice is yours, daughter, if you want to follow and avenge your mother.'

Doralia had felt crushed beneath the weight of that choice, but in the end it was no choice at all. If there was even a chance that Morgane was here, she needed to take it. Although she could barely admit it to herself, she needed revenge as much as her father did.

They headed on. The ground was beginning to get hard underfoot. It sparkled with frost, and further up Doralia could see thin patches of snow strewn on either side of the path. The sharp blue sky was beginning to fade, although it was still early. Dark banks of cloud were massing over the Krondspines far to the north-west, sending out exploratory tendrils towards the hills. It would snow again before the day was out, she was sure. Perfect conditions to finally run their prey to ground…

'You know, one thing strikes me,' Caspar said, reaching for the water bottle. Doralia passed it to him and he took a long swallow. 'He may not be demonstrative about it, but in his way your father's done everything he could to keep you safe. That's got to be worth something.'

She looked at him in amazement. 'Keep me safe? You do realise what I do for a living, don't you?'

Caspar passed her back the bottle and sheathed his blade. 'Exactly. Think about it,' he said. He spread his hands wide. 'Just look at the world we live in, the dangers even the lowest citizen of the realm has to face. In the last two days alone I've seen more corpses than I ever have before in my life, and most of them were trying to kill me. Have you any idea what that's like for someone who isn't used to it? I don't think I'm going to sleep soundly again… At least your father gave you the tools you need to survive in a world like this. He could have sheltered you from it, tried to hide you away so you never had to think about the horrors that exist out here. And then what?'

She turned and looked up the path. Her father was about a hundred yards away now.

'The horrors would have found me all the same,' she said quietly.

'And you would have been helpless to do anything about it,' Caspar said. 'It looks to me like Galen ven Denst, miserable old sod that he might be, knew exactly what he was doing. He trained you, he gave you what you needed to fight back, to defend yourself. He kept you safe, and he did it by throwing you into danger every day of your life.'

'That why you're still here?' she said. She inclined her head towards the squat buildings of Hollowcrest, closer now, the grey stone leaden and dull in the lowering day. 'Figure it's safer striding towards danger than heading away from it, as long as you're by our side?'

Caspar strode on ahead of her, patting her shoulder as he passed. 'Oh, absolutely. I'm not stupid, believe me. Confronting a ruthless vampire is the last thing I want to do, but right now I reckon the safest place from here to Excelsis is between two witch hunters as they go about their business.'

Galen ven Denst slumped to the ground on the cusp of Hollowcrest and drank from his water bottle. His hands were shaking. There were black spots dancing in his eyes. Pain, dark and insistent, shot through his bones. His legs ached with the climb, and there was a sharp, searing throb in his lower back. He ignored it. *Tamp the pain down,* he thought, gritting his teeth. *Press on.* He was no stranger to it. He'd been carrying pain with him a long time now. It was his closest friend.

There was a flank of rock at the edge of the trail as it ascended into the village, masked by a withered stand of gorse. He sheltered in its lee and peered around it to take in the first few houses just ahead. Hollowcrest looked like a two-street town, and he was sure it was quiet at the best of times. Now, it looked dead. There were two stocky wooden huts on either side of the track about twenty yards in front of him, their doors hanging open on broken hinges. The track passed between them, arrow straight. Beyond, he could see a long stretch of dirt road with stone houses on either side. Mist lingered in the street, curling up against the walls of those plain, unadorned places. There was a smell in the air of stale smoke and decay.

Some of the buildings had rough signs hammered above their lintels. He couldn't read them from here, but he was sure they were advertising goods stores, taverns, trading posts. There was even what looked like a temple towards the end of the road, with the sign of the comet emblazoned on its door. He took some comfort in that. Hollowcrest was no more than a place you stopped in on the way to somewhere else, but if there was anyone left in the town then they would have taken refuge in the temple. As for Jael Morgane, there was no telling where she might be hiding.

No matter. Whatever had drawn her into the wilds outside Excelsis, it ended now. He had tracked her this far, always on her trail, relentless. In the breeze as it flowed across the plains, he had sensed her growing fear, her disbelief that at every turn he was only one step behind her. She had physical strength and fell powers, and the dread immortality of her kind. She was ruthless and cruel, one of the most terrible creatures in all creation. But she was a child compared to Galen ven Denst when it came to the strength of his hatred. Her will was as brittle as winter grass compared to his own. He would never stop. She would die at his hand.

He checked his weapons again, cocking his pistols, loosening his sword in its scabbard on his back. He patted the silver stakes in his belt and stretched the cramps from his legs. Glancing back down the trail he saw Doralia and the young fellow, Harrow, flitting closer as they moved from rock to rock. Doralia had her crossbow in her hands and a look on her face that he recognised. Determined, implacable.

He sighed, a bone-deep shudder that went right through him. She'd been a happy child once, he remembered. A bright and inquisitive girl, irrepressible. He looked at her now, and her face was the charge sheet he laid against himself, the visible evidence of all his failures as a father and a man. She was gaunt, haggard, as grim as a Sigmarite priest looking over an empty congregation. When they'd sat by the fire the night before, the smell of drink coming off her was unmistakable, and not just from the bottle of firewater she had in her kitbag. She'd been marinating in it for weeks. Stumbling home at all hours from the taverns in the Veins, puking in her room, waking up with crashing hangovers that she could only shift with another bottle. Ever since the siege…

He turned back towards Hollowcrest, a bleak expression on his face. It was something else he could blame himself for.

I wish I had never recruited you into the order…

Damn it, why had he said that! It wasn't what he meant, and she'd taken it the wrong way too quickly for him to explain. She was more than capable – though she didn't realise it, Doralia was close to being the best agent in the order. She was tenacious, an exceptional tracker, skilled with her weapons. She was the best shot with that crossbow he had ever seen, and the engraved null-stone bolts she had made during a sojourn in Hysh were things of great art and power. But every day for the last twenty years he had worried that his decision to recruit her had condemned her to nothing more than pain and misery. What kind of father would choose to watch his daughter risk her life and her sanity every day? And what kind of father couldn't even protect her when she needed it most?

Well, he had tried to protect her now, when it was too late to make a difference. When word reached him that Jael Morgane had been seen far out at Izalend, he had been determined to track her down alone. While Doralia drank away her sorrows in whatever low tavern or ale house she'd found, he had gathered his supplies and set off from Excelsis, taking the hard road into the wilds. He would do it alone, if he could. He wouldn't inflict this awful task on her, not if he could help it.

It lived in him always, that dark memory. The flames around them, the girl standing in her room with her mother's undead corpse unfurling from the ground. The crossbow in her hand. Her father, helpless as he crawled towards her, with the mocking figure of Jael Morgane between them. And now, once more, Doralia would have to come face to face with her mother's killer. Another failure.

His daughter came up to him now, Harrow trailing behind her as they took refuge behind the outcrop of rock beside him. The young man looked blown out, as if the hike up the path had utterly exhausted him. His face was strained, his jaw twitching with nerves, and he clutched the hilt of his sheathed sword with a white-knuckled grip. Galen looked on him with disdain. The fight with the deadwalkers had nearly ended him, it seemed.

'Sure you're up for this, son?' he said. 'Have to say, you look like the sort who'd be more comfortable in a tavern with a lute in your hand, rather than a blade.'

Harrow mustered a cocky smile as he gained his breath. He tugged the sword from the scabbard.

'Guilty as charged,' he said. 'Wouldn't you rather have some sweet music and fine ale before you, instead of this?'

Galen grunted. He supposed the young lad was Doralia's problem, although Sigmar knew why she had dragged him along.

'Can't say the lute's an instrument I've ever turned my hand to,' he said. 'Mind you, maybe you'll come in handy. Always good to have some bait for a decent trap, after all...'

Doralia checked her crossbow and stared off up the lonely street. The two huts on the edge of town looked like dead eyes blankly staring at them. Beyond, Hollowcrest seemed a cold and deserted place, the ground like iron under the frost.

'Morgane,' she said. 'You're sure she's in there?'

'As I can be,' Galen said. 'She meant to rest a while in Raven's Hollow, I'm sure of it, but moved on as soon as I arrived. This is the last stop before the long trail into the Krondspines and Lake Everglut beyond. There's nothing on that side of the mountains for her.'

'Lucky for the folk at Raven's Hollow she didn't stay,' Doralia said. She glanced at him. 'What's left of them, anyway. The rest lit out when the dead began to rise.'

'More of Morgane's doings,' he said. 'Hoped to distract us, keep us fighting them off so she could escape, no doubt.'

If Morgane had raised them, then it was only to slow him down, and he hadn't taken the bait. Same with the bodies of that family she'd killed in Fortune, he reckoned.

You won't get away from me that easily, he thought. *Your life is numbered in hours and minutes now, nothing more…*

'Come on,' he said. 'Daylight won't stop her, but it will slow her down some. We need to move while we still have the light.'

He hauled himself to his feet, grimacing against the pain in his legs. He took the path into Hollowcrest without waiting to see if the others were following him.

'Not long now, Morgane,' he hissed to himself. He squeezed the handle of his pistol. 'By sundown, you'll be ashes. I swear it.'

CHAPTER ELEVEN

HUNTING THE DEAD

Three greasy crows took wing when they hit the street, rising from the Hollowcrest signpost like scraps of tattered cloth. They each cawed once, a discordant chorus, and flapped off towards the west. The breeze was like a knife blade, sharp and clear.

Galen, for the fourth time, checked the hammer on his pistol. He walked down the centre of the narrow road, boots crunching on the frosty ground, scanning the empty windows of the buildings on either side. Dry goods, an ironmonger, a money lender. Even a realmstone dealer, for those lucky enough to have panned for Bones of Amber deep in the Krondspines. All were shut. Not a lamp to be seen, not a single smoking chimney. He doubted Hollowcrest was much of a place at the best of times, but it was desolate now. A trading post, they'd said down in Raven's Hollow. It was a hard climb through the hills, and no one had thought to improve the track for folk transporting goods, but it was quicker than the three-hundred-mile detour around the mountains. Didn't look like much was going to be traded there again, though.

What a place to end up, he thought. *What a place to die.*

The street was little more than a rumpled, muddy track, glazed here and there with frozen puddles. A few of the buildings were only stone to waist height, the rest of the structure finished off with a flaking, greyish hardwood. There were no pavements to walk along, just a warped duckboard or stoop in front of the larger stores. There was rubbish in the street, scraps of parchment, a few phials of glimmerings, broken glass. Somewhere a sign was creaking above a door, a rusty wheeze that put his nerves on edge. He moved the pistol back and forth, covering the road from one side to the other as he paced its length. Doralia was behind him and to his right, crossbow drawn. Harrow, for all the use he was likely to be, was on his left, sword out in what Galen figured he thought was a fencing pose. The young fellow would find out the hard way what use that was going to be. With the long black duster and the duardin blade, the young man looked like an up-and-coming actor performing the role of a witch hunter on stage.

'Over here,' Doralia said as they reached the crossroads. She jogged to the corner and crouched by a bundle of rags. 'A body,' she called. 'Dead a few hours, at least.'

Galen joined her, eyes flicking across the street before risking a glance down at the corpse. A young man, little more than a boy. His throat had been ripped out, and one of his arms had been near torn off at the socket. Blood formed a frozen puddle around him. His eyes were open. Judging by the expression on his face, he hadn't much liked what he'd seen before he died. Few did.

'Not been turned,' he said. 'Not been tortured much, either.'

'Killed while trying to escape, maybe,' Doralia said.

'Morgane,' Galen muttered.

'You're certain?' she said. 'Far as I can see, you've not even set eyes on her yet. Rumours, reports, but where's the proof?'

'We'll have the proof soon enough. I feel this in my bones, daughter. I know it's her.'

'Maybe,' she said. 'But I'm worried that you *want* it to be her, and damn the consequences.'

Doralia stood up and looked down at the boy. Galen thought he saw her mumble a prayer, but he said nothing. In the order, he knew, you didn't much feel the need to ask for Sigmar's intercession. You *were* Sigmar's intercession.

'Can I retract my previous statement?' Harrow said. He was trembling, although if Galen was feeling charitable he would have said it was because of the cold.

'Which was?' Doralia said.

'Being between two witch hunters as they go about their business perhaps isn't the safest place in the realms to be.' He tried to laugh. 'Maybe the palace of the High Arbiter in Excelsis instead. All those guards to keep you safe...'

Galen looked at him. 'One of the last High Arbiters turned out to be an agent of Chaos. Few years back,' he said. 'Colleague of mine spent a lot of time and effort tracking him down after he tried to seize the city. Lot of people killed. Bad business.'

'Then I would like to retract that statement as well,' Harrow said. His sword drooped to the ground.

'Be my guest.'

'Place is empty,' Doralia said. 'Looks like everyone cleared out.'

Galen shrugged. If circumstances were different he might have reached for a cigar, but he'd run out some time back when he was crossing the plains. Knew he shouldn't have been so miserly when he was putting his supplies together. Damn fool habit anyway. Just another crutch for an old man to help him get up in the morning.

'No sign of them down in Raven's Hollow, if so,' he said. 'Either they ran in the wrong direction, or they never got the chance.' He turned to Harrow. 'My daughter says you're something of a scout. You know this place? How many folk would you expect to find here?'

Harrow shook his head. 'I've never been this high in the hills,' he said. 'But from what I've heard, there'd be at least a hundred people here at any one time. Store owners, innkeepers, folk passing through. And that would be on a quiet day.'

Doralia gave Galen a sharp look. 'Where are they, then? If they're all dead, maybe we're looking at more than one vampire,' she said. Galen nodded.

'She might have company,' he admitted.

'Should have brought more help. Jelsen Darrock maybe, he was always handy in a tight spot wherever vampires were concerned.'

Galen frowned. 'That man is a disgrace,' he muttered. 'He was expelled from the order for a good reason, and I wouldn't trust him at my back no matter the cost. If we're doing this, we're doing it alone.'

The crossroads was ahead of them. In the middle there was a rough stone statue of Sigmar, stern of brow, glaring up at the heavens as if they'd done him an injustice. There was a tavern diagonally opposite, its double doors closed, one of its windows broken. The temple was on the other side of the street from the tavern – a nice juxtaposition, Galen had to admit. He could imagine the pious and the impure alike, each going into their places of worship and casting frosty glances at the other.

There was a lot more litter in the streets, dozens of crumpled sheets of parchment that danced and fluttered in the breeze. One blew near and he snatched it from the air. He unfolded it and began to read.

'"Blessed be those in Sigmar's name who do smite the unjust and cause the unjust to be smited. And though age fail them and their strength be bowed, yet Sigmar's grace will give them the power to continue."'

'That's from *Intimations of the Comet*,' Doralia said. 'These must be pages torn from the book.'

'Strangely apposite,' Caspar Harrow muttered. Galen crumpled up the paper and dropped it to the ground.

'The temple,' he growled. 'She's desecrated it. That's where she'll be hiding.'

There was a crash from the other side of the street, the sound of breaking glass. All of them turned their heads, Galen bringing up the pistol while Doralia aimed at the tavern doors. A short silence, then another, quieter tinkle of glass.

'Someone's in there,' she said.

'I thought vampires only drank blood?' Caspar offered.

Galen checked his pistol. 'I'll tell you one thing, son. If you can make jokes at a time like this, then there's hope for you yet...'

He jogged across the road while Doralia covered him with the crossbow. The pain thrummed in his legs, shooting up into his hips, but he ignored it. He reached the stoop, which was no more than half a dozen planks of wood set haphazardly in the mud. He aimed at the broken window while keeping his eye on the doors, and beckoned his daughter over, Harrow scurrying along behind her.

Doralia didn't pause. She charged straight across the stoop and booted the doors wide open, the sound crashing through the empty town. Crossbow in a tight grip, she barrelled into the tavern, Galen quick to follow. Harrow, hanging back, crept in after them.

'Sigmar save us...' Doralia whispered.

The room was gloomy, the lamps unlit, and little light had forced its way through the broken windows. It was an undistinguished place, like any other small-town tavern you might find in the realms: a short bar against the far wall; a few shelves of bottles and a couple of casks of ale; a handful of tables; bare, whitewashed walls. A spit-and-sawdust kind of place, Galen thought. Spit, and sawdust, and blood…

An old man and an old woman sat at one of the tables. Both of them had been beheaded, their eyes gouged out. The ground around the table was soaked in gore. The heads lay on the table in front of them, placed next to each other, their faces distorted with the agony of their murder while the bodies sat there, rigid and upright.

Caspar Harrow staggered back, one hand covering his face, the other thrown out to support himself against the wall. Galen was sure he was going to run, but to his credit the young fellow stayed.

Who could run from something like this? he thought. *Who wouldn't want to stay, and visit the most appalling vengeance on those responsible?*

'In the name of the gods,' Caspar shuddered, hanging back. 'What sick monster would do such a thing?'

'There's not much sicker than a vampire,' Doralia said, grimacing.

Galen slowly crossed the floor towards the table. His boots crunched on the broken glass. The gore was slippery underfoot – still fresh. These folks had been killed within the last hour or so, probably while the witch hunters were still on the trail up to Hollowcrest.

'It's a welcome party,' he muttered. The air was rich with the coppery tang of blood. 'Here to show us what we're up against.'

'Don't flatter yourself, old man,' a voice called from the shadows.

Galen snapped up his pistol while Doralia pivoted on her heel, crossbow out. A young man with sandy hair and a dusting of blond stubble stood behind the bar, a tall glass in his hand. His face was almost spectrally pale, threaded with fine purple veins, and his red-rimmed eyes were little more than black pinpricks. When he smiled, Galen saw the savage fangs, like knife blades, crowded in his mouth. He raised the glass and took a long, luxurious drink. The glass was brimful of blood.

'These fine people here,' the vampire said, 'aren't for your benefit. Happens that these are my parents.' The creature grinned widely, red-stained teeth gleaming. 'Do you want to know their names? They knew mine. They kept calling it as I killed them, funnily enough. Over and over and over, just calling my name...'

He laughed, a sickening gurgle in that dark, dead place. His eyes had no more life to them than a couple of glass beads.

'Jael Morgane's getting desperate,' Galen said. He didn't take his eyes off the creature. 'She used to be more the aristocratic type. If she's turning rustic scum like you into her kind, then she's lost her touch.'

The vampire hissed at them, face twisted with hatred, the glass shattering in its hand. Faster than the eye could see, it vaulted the bar in one smooth motion and leapt towards them.

The witch hunters both fired at once, but so swift and fierce was the vampire's attack that their shots went wide. Doralia's bolt shattered a bottle behind the bar, while Galen's pistol shot clanged neatly against an iron bell on the countertop. It chimed like the call to prayer from a Sigmarite temple, high and clear.

Doralia brought the stock of her crossbow up, but the creature snarled and lashed out with a backhand that sent her sprawling off into the corner. She crashed into a table and tumbled clear over the other side. Galen dropped his pistol and snatched one of the silver stakes from his belt, dragging his sword free with his other hand. He just had time to parry, bringing the blade up to block the vampire's hand as it whipped towards him, the claws rusty with blood. Two of the creature's fingers dropped to the ground. The vampire snatched its hand back with a shriek, eyes blazing with lust and madness. Caspar dropped his sword, and out of the corner of his eye Galen saw him scurry under a table.

'Any time you want to join in, son,' he muttered, 'you just let me know.'

He tried to swing back with the sword, hoping to catch the vampire off balance so he could plunge the silver stake into its chest, but the creature was even quicker than he'd realised. It side-stepped the blade and threw itself into Galen's open guard, bloody hands scrabbling at his chest, those gleaming yellow fangs inches from his face.

'You remind me of my father, old man,' the creature hissed with its stinking breath. 'Shall I have your head as a table ornament too?'

'Can't say it's in the best condition,' he gasped. He reared back and snapped his head forward, catching the vampire a savage blow on the bridge of its nose. 'Only one careful owner too.'

As the vampire staggered backwards, blood pouring down its face, Doralia hacked in from behind, swinging her sword high above her head and slicing down from shoulder to sternum. The creature near split in half, a gout of blood sheeting out and drenching the floorboards. It screamed, a horrible, wailing screech that suddenly cut off and gurgled out of its slopping lungs. Caspar, too late to make much of a difference, snatched up his sword and darted in to cut the vampire's other arm clean off at the elbow.

The creature flopped to the ground, twitching, eyes wild, and in its undead madness still trying to scrabble towards them. Galen stamped down on its face with the heel of his heavy boot, smashing an eye back into its skull, stamping again and again until its face was a wheezing pulp. Its brains had spilled out onto the floorboards. Caspar daintily stepped away from them, covering his mouth.

'Hammer and throne!' he retched. 'It's still alive!'

The lad was right, Galen saw. Slowly, very slowly, like a web knitting itself back together, the creature's flesh was regenerating. Bloody bubbles popped and spat in its ruined face. It looked more like a butcher's yard than a living thing, but given enough time and enough blood it would be able to make itself whole again.

'Takes more than that to kill a vampire,' Galen said. His forehead buzzed with pain from where he'd headbutted it. He wiped his boot against the creature's clothes. 'One thing guaranteed to put them down permanently, though.'

He knelt beside it while Doralia reloaded her crossbow. He reached into the bloody wound his daughter had hacked into its chest and strained to crack the ribcage aside. In the open cavity, like a jewel in offal, he could see its unbeating, chambered heart. Galen placed the point of his silver stake against it.

There – just on the edge of its awareness, the vampire knew that death was near. It shuddered, and it felt afraid. Its soul was now a plaything for Nagash, and who knew what fell delights Old Bones would take in it.

'I hope this hurts,' Galen whispered.

He pushed down, and the stake slid smoothly in.

CHAPTER TWELVE

AFTERMATH

Caspar found a rag behind the bar and wiped his blade clean, and then searched amongst the debris until he chanced across a bottle of Ferncrawle Porter. He plucked the cork free and gulped the ale down until his eyes were streaming.

'Gods, there's the good stuff,' he said, sighing. 'Brew this in the Ferncrawle Swamps, didn't think to see any of it this far north.'

He tossed the bottle over to Doralia, who snatched it out of the air. She sniffed the contents suspiciously, raising an eyebrow, but took an experimental drink all the same. There was a peaty richness to it, dark and spicy. She felt it stoking a warm glow in her belly, which slowly spread into her chest and down her arms and seemed to chase some of the chill away. It *was* good stuff, she thought. She made a mental note to check which taverns might sell it when she got back home.

If we ever do get back to Excelsis...

'What's this?' Galen said. 'A damn drinking party?'

Caspar gave a bitter laugh and swept his hand at the corpses around the table, the ravaged body on the floor.

'Forgive me if I'm not exactly taking this in my stride,' he protested.

Galen snorted dismissively. 'Some outlaw you turned out to be, son.'

Doralia stepped over to the bar and passed the bottle back.

'First time for everything, Harrow,' she said. 'You did better than I would have expected, but I'm getting the feeling you're less of a renegade than you want folk to think.'

He shrugged defensively, turning his gaze away from the corpses on the ground.

'Like I said, a little bravado goes a long way. I may have exaggerated my exploits somewhat.'

'I'll say. Heading out of Fortune, I thought you quite the dangerous character.'

'Folk tend not to bother you if they think you're deadly,' Caspar said, shrugging. 'Figure it's easier to cheat someone out of their money than fight them. And anyway, it takes skill, finesse, *precision* to be a decent thief. I don't just go blundering in waving a blade around and hoping for the best.'

'In the end, blundering in and waving a blade around is all any of us can really do,' Galen said. He sheathed his sword and stood over the bodies at the table, looking down without emotion at the row of severed heads. 'Three more,' he said softly. 'The folks here, and the boy who killed them. Three more to lay at her door.'

Doralia checked her own weapons and peered out of the broken window. The dingy crossroads was quiet, the scraps of holy writ still blowing sadly in the breeze. The statue of Sigmar looked like something you'd find in an abandoned ancient settlement, left over from the Age of Myth. There was no one abroad, nothing, and yet she knew Jael Morgane was out there somewhere. Watching them, waiting. She'd run this far, but it was the end of the road now.

Her right hand began to tremble and she grasped it quickly with her left, squeezing her fingers until the shaking stopped. Ever since her father had told her Morgane was back, she'd tried to push the thought of this moment from her mind. What would it be like to see her again, to stand bathed in the dreadful heat of that murderous gaze? She thought of the iron box in that squalid chamber, all those years ago. Her father pulling the bolt back and leaving the room, the feel of the silver stake in her hand. She hadn't known what to do then either. The hatred and madness radiating from the creature inside, the lust for death and blood... It had only been some half-starved creature dragged out of the swamps, a degenerate vampire Galen had captured for just that moment.

I was only a child... A little training exercise to see if I had what it took to join the order.

She remembered the door flying open, the thing leaping out at her, the stench that preceded it like a wave. A tangle of desiccated flesh and sinew, its teeth knocked out, although she hadn't known that at the time. She had not had the least idea what to expect, but then something like a buried instinct had kicked in, as it had when her mother uncoiled from the burning floor in front of her.

Fight. Fight or die.

Her father gathered up a cloth from behind the bar and threw it over the bodies of the vampire's murdered parents. The weakness she had seen in him last night, the exhaustion, seemed to have burned away in the heat of the fight. He didn't look human, all of a sudden. He was an automaton, vengeance made flesh. He would do this until he dropped dead. There was some faint reflection of her own fate there, she was sure. If she didn't die in the line of duty, she would live long enough only to become as fierce and hollowed out as her father. She looked at the shapes of the dead couple under the white cloth.

Worse things to become, I suppose, she thought.

'Something still doesn't sit right,' she said. She turned away from the window and looked at her father. 'Jael Morgane. Why's she running like this? Why pause long enough to turn this young lad into one of her own?'

'What are you saying?' Galen asked.

'There's more going on here than we understand. What about the bodies down in Raven's Hollow, the corpses that attacked us on the trail?'

Galen was dismissive. He stalked over to the window and glared out at the street. Doralia grabbed his shoulder and turned him around to face her. For a moment, he couldn't meet her eyes.

'We saw the cemetery, heard the story the arbiter gave us. Every grave there was empty. You saw how many attacked us. Takes more, *far more,* than a vampire's capabilities to raise those kind of numbers.'

'Rumours too,' Caspar said. He still stood behind the bar, hands spread on its surface quite like he owned the place. 'All along the Coast of Tusks, there's tales of resurrection, of some strange figure moving through the wilderness, raising the dead.'

'Heard that from the arbiter as well, did you?' Galen scorned. 'Schmidt, down in Raven's Hollow? Man probably calls an emergency conclave if he misses his lunch. I wouldn't put too much store in his opinions.'

Caspar looked faintly embarrassed. 'From the ferryman, actually.'

Galen laughed: a short, cruel bark, not a trace of humour in it.

'The ferryman?' he said. 'Let me guess, some half-mad yokel in the wilderness? Not exactly the kind of report I'd trouble my superiors with.'

'You don't even believe this yourself,' Doralia said. 'How many years have you been doing this, and have you ever turned away from even the faintest rumour if there was a chance to pass Sigmar's judgement at the end of it?'

He met her eyes then, and it was her turn to look away. If anything had been keeping him going all these long months since the siege, it was this. It was all he had left.

'This is what we do,' she said. 'We investigate, we hunt, we track down and destroy anything that could threaten the realm. *Anything*. We don't… we don't let ourselves get swayed by our own concerns. By vengeance. What if something important is slipping by us while we're sidetracked here?'

'The only rumour I'm interested in,' Galen said through gritted teeth, 'is the one that's put Jael Morgane in my sights after twenty years. Not Sigmar himself could stop me from killing her now.'

'You think she's just been running from you?' Doralia pressed him. 'No offence, father, but you're not that good. You put a vampire and a witch hunter alone in the wilderness, and I know which one my money would be on. She's faster, stronger, and there's hardly anything that can kill her outright.'

'Doralia's right,' Caspar said, as he came out from behind the bar. 'I may not have the experience, and the thought of you on my trail doesn't exactly give me warm feelings, but from what I've seen of vampires it takes more than just one witch hunter to bring them down. If this Jael Morgane is as fearsome as you make out, then maybe she's not been running. Maybe she's been luring you here.'

'Can't see how it's your business, boy,' Galen spat. 'I'm sure if you rifle through these folks' pockets you'll find something worth stealing, though, if that's your main line of work.'

'Damn it, I want to help!' he shouted. To Doralia, he said, 'I've made it this far, haven't I? And I remember your words – doing good, in the wider scheme of things. Maybe it's about time I started.'

Doralia nodded, a faint smile on her lips. Strange, she thought. You could never picture the exact moment, but there always seemed to come a time when a person had to make the choice. Do good, or let someone else do good for you.

'Fight or die,' she mumbled.

'Well,' Galen growled. 'Let's hope it's not the latter...'

The silence was torn then by wild, skirling laughter – a screech that was tinged with cruelty and madness. It shattered through the streets and trailed away into an eerie cry.

Galen leaned against the window again and stared out into the street, eyes scanning the shadows, the doorways, the rooftops. Doralia crept to the door, her heart thumping in her chest, and gingerly pulled it open. She peered out through the gap.

'She's near,' she said, then swallowed. Her voice was shaking, and she took a moment to get it under control. 'Coming from the temple, sounds like.'

She looked at the temple across the road: an austere, white-washed stone building with a blunt spire on its roof and two stained-glass windows in its frontage. The windows were dark, but much of the stained glass had been smashed out and littered the road, a swatch of blue and red and green.

'Galen...' a voice called from outside. It was high and clear, slicing through the silence like a razor. Doralia felt the adrenaline flooding into her system. She had never thought to hear that voice again, as long as she lived. 'Galen ven Denst!'

Laughter again, whispering through the streets. Galen dashed out the last few shards of glass in the window with the butt of his pistol and leaned out.

'End of the road, Morgane!' he cried. 'Nowhere left for you to run. May as well make it easy on yourself. If you don't, I promise you, dying is going to be hard!'

'Oh, but Galen...' the voice sang. 'What happened to you? So old, so old… Twenty years is such a long time for your kind, isn't it?'

'Not long enough for me to forget!' Galen shouted into the street. He looked over at Doralia and held up a finger. There was a blunt, fearsome look in his eyes. She tilted her chin at Caspar.

'Come on, bandit of the badlands,' she murmured. 'Time to do some good.'

She held up her hand: three fingers extended, then two, then one. Together, they burst through the door and ran across the road, boots hammering on the frozen ground. Doralia had her crossbow up, aimed at the blank temple windows. Pages of the holy book crackled underfoot like dead leaves.

'Go left when we get inside!' she cried, and she didn't stop to see if Caspar had understood. Straight on, head down, no thought in her mind but the job at hand, Doralia crashed through the temple door.

CHAPTER THIRTEEN

JAEL MORGANE

He saw his daughter smash the doors aside, the young lad Caspar close behind. Galen jogged across the road and followed, pistol out and pointing into the shadows, that mocking laughter loud in his ears. Doralia broke right as she entered the temple, Galen behind her, staying his shot, waiting those precious seconds for his eyes to adjust to the gloom. Every nerve in his body was jangling. He crouched behind the first row of benches, scanning the length of the building down to the chancel, the lone altar at the far end. A beam of light fell through the broken windows and struck the altar with its enervating flame.

Sigmar sees all, he thought. *Sigmar as witness, I will end this today.*

The temple was a long hall with two blocks of benches on either side of a central nave. The peaked ceiling disappeared into the shadows of the open rafters above. The walls were panelled in dark wood, illuminated here and there with rough frescoes of Sigmar, illustrating his journey through the cosmos and the discovery of the Mortal Realms. Some of these frescoes had been crudely defaced, the plaster torn away, and the benches down the nave were skewed as if hastily thrown aside by a congregation desperate to escape. There was a sharp grave-reek in the air. More pages of the holy texts littered the ground like so much refuse. He could see that the very altar itself had been desecrated, the lectern from where the priest would read from the *Intimations* at the beginning of every service cast to the ground and broken, the altar smeared in blood and filth.

This wouldn't have been Morgane's work, he knew. She was a monster all right, but she was above such petty vandalism. While she would have mocked the worship of any god but Nagash, she would not have wasted her time by taunting the faithful in this way. Her pet back in the tavern was the more likely candidate: a rebellious young local, no doubt, who had resented the authority of his priest and the services he was forced to attend.

Immortal beings, he thought, *but in so many ways they are little more than children, enslaved to their base desires. There's no barrier between a thought and its expression with this kind.*

Doralia was over in the right-hand corner, crouched down and scanning the hall. Caspar was over on the left, his sword drawn. There was a bit more grit in his expression at least, Galen thought. If it came down to it, maybe the lad would prove himself useful, although in Galen's experience an extra sword was a positive disadvantage in a fight if the wielder didn't know how to use it.

There was no time to worry about such things now, though. He raised his hand and gestured Doralia forward while he covered her, watching as his daughter crept down the right-hand wall. Her boots crunched over the broken plaster from the shattered frescoes.

'Now there's a surprise...' the voice called out. It laughed, a sound like breaking glass. 'Is that really you, my dear? Doralia ven Denst, as I live and breathe...'

Soft and beguiling, the voice seemed to slither from every corner of the hall at once. Galen slowly got to his feet and stalked forward down the central nave, Caspar mirroring Doralia's motions and advancing along the line of the left-hand wall.

'You don't live,' Doralia called out. 'And you certainly don't breathe, Morgane.'

She swept her crossbow to cover the far corner of the hall. Galen watched her closely, his stomach tight and his jaw clenched. He knew he could trust her not to take the bait, but this was unknown territory for both of them. This creature was the author of their worst trauma, and she knew it. There was nothing Jael Morgane would not do to make this experience more distressing for them.

'My, you have grown up, my dear,' Morgane said. 'The years certainly have been hard on you, child... Such a soft-faced, gentle thing when you were young. Now look at you... You make your father seem positively cheerful.'

He aimed up at the rafters but he could see nothing. He saw Doralia halt and beckon Caspar to cross the room towards her, while she cut over to the other side, swapping places with him. Galen continued towards the veined marble block of the desecrated altar, peering down the line of benches as he went, pistol at the ready. Reflexively he felt for the silver stakes in his belt, reassuring himself for the tenth time that they were still there.

Getting jumpy in my old age, he thought. *Time was, I would have gone charging in, all guns blazing.*

'So many years...' Morgane called out. 'You were such a bold and compelling figure back then, Galen. Dark and masterful, and now look at you. Grey and tired, and creeping about this miserable temple as if afraid Sigmar will strike you down for your timidity. As for you, Doralia, last time I saw you, you were crying for your mother. So very sad. Shall I tell you what she tasted like?'

Doralia's face was like ice. She said nothing.

'Fear makes the blood sing,' the vampire chuckled. 'Like age with a fine wine, it deepens the flavour. Gives it… *bite*. And your mother was very, very afraid at the end.'

'All you do is prolong your own agony, Morgane!' Galen called out. His voice boomed across the empty hall. He was ten feet from the altar now. He could see scraps of flesh and bone desecrating its surface, and his rage was like a high whine ringing in his ears. 'You have only moments to live. Make your peace with your dark master and prepare yourself for your final death.'

'How are your legs, Galen?' Morgane asked, with mock sincerity. The voice seemed to echo from everywhere at once: from the shadows at the other end of the nave, from the space behind the altar, from the dust-shrouded rafters above them. 'Do they ache when the wind turns chill? Does every throb of pain still remind you of that night?'

'They've got me this far,' Galen called. 'On your trail, every step of the way. We killed your young friend in the tavern, and we'll kill you now.'

The vampire laughed again, high and piercing. 'Poor young Dickon. He was a faithful pet. But I see you have one of your own now too! And *my*, isn't he handsome… Is he yours, Doralia? I'm sure you won't mind sharing him…'

Caspar looked sick. He glanced over at Doralia for reassurance, but she shook her head. Galen had reached the altar now. He readied his pistol and darted around the side of the great marble block, but there was nothing there. He met his daughter's eyes and together they scanned the hall. Doralia raised an index finger and pointed at the rafters. Galen nodded.

'Raise as many of the dead as you like,' he shouted, 'and it still won't stop me. The cemetery of Raven's Hollow didn't turn me aside, and any more of your pets we'll just put in the ground.'

Jael Morgane's laughter then was a shrieking, hysterical thing, tearing through the stillness of the temple.

'You fools!' she cried. 'Did you think that was me?' Her voice

134

dripped with scorn. 'As if I would waste my time with the scraps of old corpses, even if I did have the power to raise them. Two witch hunters from the much-vaunted Order of Azyr, and you have no idea what's really happening here, do you? You're just blundering in the dark, you idiots. Nothing more.'

It was something he rarely allowed himself to experience in the line of his duty, but Galen felt doubt creep its way into his mind then. His daughter, her eyes wide, looked at him with what may have been reproval. He tightened his grip on his pistol and stepped back from the altar, staring up into the shadows of the rafters above, the fine rain of dust that trickled down from them. There was nowhere else she could be.

Wary, he said, 'You claim innocence of this then? Of raising the dead?'

'I'm guilty of many things, ven Denst,' Morgane's voice hissed, 'but if you knew the truth of this then you would curse yourself for your incompetence.'

Suddenly her breath, like ice, caressed the back of his neck.

'And in your ignorance, you curse the very city you are sworn to save...'

Galen spun round as the pistol was knocked from his hand. He heard Doralia grunt with pain, and then all he saw was the vampire's ink-black hair, the burning embers of her red eyes, the flash of razor teeth. All the breath was knocked from him and he reeled backwards, crashing into the first row of benches.

Jael was on him in moments, clawing at his chest, lifting him effortlessly from the wreckage and tossing him further down the nave. Galen gasped as he hit the ground, rolling with the throw and coming up to his knees, his vision black at the edges. He plucked a stake from his belt and whipped it end over end like a throwing knife towards her, but the vampire swatted it from the air with ease. She stood there, a mockery of Sigmar's grace in this holy temple, a dark vision in red velvet, her skin paper pale and marbled with blue veins. The ink-black hair tumbled to her shoulders, and the red eyes burned with all the leering hatred of her kind. She was beautiful – and she was the most disgusting thing he had ever seen.

'Galen, my darling,' Morgane said, grinning at him. Her teeth gleamed in the dim light. 'It feels so good to have my hands on you again, after all these years. Perhaps this time I will break more than your legs...'

'And perhaps this time,' Galen grunted, 'I'll do more than just shoot you in the back of the head.'

Doralia came sweeping in from behind the altar with her sword, screaming with rage. Morgane sidestepped the first swing, and as Doralia tried to catch her on the backswing, the vampire snapped out a hand and caught the weapon's cross guard. She turned and pulled, twisting Doralia's wrist to the side, pushing her down to her knees so that she had either to drop the sword or have her wrist broken.

Doralia spat in her face. As Morgane blinked, she snatched a knife from her belt and stabbed the vampire in the gut.

Galen was up, lurching down the nave, shaking his head clear as he ran towards them. He had another stake in his hand. Morgane screamed with rage, clutching her stomach. She lashed out and sent Doralia flying backwards into the altar.

Where the hell's the boy? Galen thought. *Could use that sword right about now, whether he knows what he's doing with it or not...*

Galen launched himself at the vampire, stabbing down with the stake and trying to catch her square in the chest. Morgane was too fast though, skipping aside, the stake plunging down into the meat of her shoulder. Her claws slashed out, cutting across Galen's face and spattering blood onto the stone floor. As he fell backwards, the pain searing through him, the vampire caught him by the throat and began to squeeze.

'I've led you on quite the merry dance, haven't I, witch hunter?' she hissed, her face only inches from his own. 'Well, it ends now. I thought it would be amusing to stoke your fervour, to raise your hopes that my death was finally in your grasp, but in the end you have only proved as boring as you ever were. No style, Galen. No finesse. Just brute dedication, like an animal too stupid to know it's blundering towards disaster.'

Her fingers were like iron around his throat, her grip so tight he couldn't even begin to prise them loose. He couldn't breathe – the world around him was a black haze, and it was getting darker. His impatience, his recklessness – all the years he had spent waiting for this moment and it was on the edge of slipping away forever.

Doralia, he thought as the darkness crept nearer. *Harrow, damn you, help!*

'Prepare yourself, ven Denst,' she whispered. 'Soon you will see your wife again...'

The sword point lunged from the vampire's chest in a spray of blood. Jael gasped in shock, dropping Galen to the ground as she grasped the steel that had run right through her. Galen choked and spluttered, clutching his throat.

'Caspar!' he tried to call, but his voice was raw. He saw the young man slide the sword out of Morgane's back, stumbling away, as if he was horrified at what he'd done. Doralia knelt by the altar, desperately trying to reload her crossbow. 'Run, boy!'

His pistol. It had clattered under the benches where Morgane had thrown him, and by some stroke of good fortune the hammer was still cocked. *Sigmar protects,* Galen thought. He scrambled across the stone floor on his hands and knees, sliding under the benches to grab it while the vampire rounded on Harrow. Caspar stood there as if frozen, unable to tear his gaze away. The sword dropped from his hand. Jael dipped her fingers to the wound in her chest and slowly smeared the blood across his face.

'Please...' Caspar said.

'I wish we had had more time, my boy,' Jael said softly. 'Oh, the delights I would have taken in one so beautiful...'

'Caspar!' Doralia cried.

The vampire's hand whipped out and Harrow's throat split from side to side, torn open by her claws. His horrified cry turned into a choked gurgle as the blood poured down his chest.

Galen grabbed the stock of his pistol from under the bench, turning and firing from the ground. The bullet caught Morgane in the ribs, blowing clean out the other side of her chest and splattering the altar in blood. At the same time, Doralia fired with her crossbow. Galen saw the bolt smack into the vampire's shoulder and throw her off her feet. She crashed to the ground, screaming, red eyes ablaze. The nullstone hissed and boiled in the wound, a weapon of the purest, anti-theurgical properties. Slowly, it burned away the sorcery that cleaved her to her dark unlife.

Galen staggered to his feet, clutching on to the temple benches for balance. He saw Doralia hastily reloading her crossbow and aiming it at the writhing form of the vampire as the nullstone surged through her. He holstered his pistol and drew one of the silver stakes from his belt. Doralia came around the side of the altar. Together, cautiously, they approached Jael Morgane as she thrashed and screamed on the floor.

'Take it out!' she howled. 'For pity's sake, damn you both, take it out!'

The vampire clawed at the bolt in her shoulder. Blood was spilling across the stone floor from the wound in her chest where Galen had shot her. The nullstone was slowly peeling away the necromantic magics that kept her alive and the wound was not healing. She wouldn't regenerate in time.

She's dying... he thought.

He stood over her, the stake in his hand. Doralia shouldered her crossbow and drew her sword. Morgane, weaker by the moment, scrabbled at Galen's boots, her mad eyes flickering with fear.

'Damn you, ven Denst,' she choked. She spat blood, bared her savage teeth. 'How I wish I had broken more than just your legs all those years ago!'

'You would have crippled me and my daughter,' he said, his voice trembling, 'forced us to lie there while my own wife devoured us. Your cruelty was your undoing.'

Morgane laughed, spraying blood across her chin. The contrast of the rich, arterial blood with her deathless white skin was grotesque.

'Mere sentiment on my part,' she said. 'Always my besetting flaw…'

'Your flaw runs through every vein and sinew in your body,' Doralia said. 'There is nothing that can redeem you.'

There was no self-pity in Doralia's voice, no anger. Her face looked carved out of stone. Galen was almost shocked, although he did not show it. This was what he had done to her, after all. This was what Jael Morgane had done to her.

'Nothing?' the vampire gurgled, grinning at them. Her eyes were becoming unfocused. The blood still dripped from the gunshot wound in her chest. 'Can I not even… trade my life for… information? Isn't that… the traditional method?'

'There is no information you could give us that would be worth your life, scum,' Galen spat. 'My only regret is that your death will come too quickly. You deserve an eternity of torment for what you have done.'

'How noble of you, ven Denst,' she coughed. 'But haven't you wondered… about the risen dead from Raven's Hollow? About this dark figure… wandering the wilds? Don't you know what is happening here, right under your noses? Amateurs… blundering in the shadows.'

He saw his daughter glance quickly at him from the corner of his eye.

'Lies,' he said. He pressed the toe of his boot against the vampire's shoulder, where the bolt had sunk deep into the meat. He pressed down, and Jael gasped in agony. 'Every word that drips from your mouth is a lie.'

He kneeled down beside her, ignoring the pain that stabbed into his hips. He raised the stake in his right hand.

'I swear it!' Jael babbled. She tried to clutch at his coat, but her grip was too weak. 'Kill me now and you will never know... and the greatest defeat of your pathetic lives will soon be on you!'

'It's a small satisfaction,' Galen said quietly, 'to see you bargain for your existence with such fear in your eyes... Here, in Sigmar's temple.'

He raised the stake high above his head.

'Listen, damn you!' she screamed. Blood sprayed up into Galen's face. 'You would have had him if you'd only followed the dead. So blinded by your need for revenge, you idiots... His name is Briomedes! His name is Briomedes, and I can help you stop him! If I die, then Excelsis falls, I swear it!'

Galen shook his head. Truth or lies, it made no difference to him now. Would he do this, even if Excelsis was the price?

Yes... he thought. *Though the world would end, I would kill this thing for all it has done to me...*

'Father?' Doralia said.

He ignored her. Unbidden, his mind conjured an image of Marie as she had been, in the days when they first met. The most beautiful woman in the Amber Princedoms. The woman he was meant to be with for the rest of his life... The sort of person so decent and kind she could even look at a man like Galen ven Denst and find something of worth there.

He saw his daughter, their child, pulling the trigger of the crossbow. He heard Jael Morgane laugh.

He brought the stake plunging down.

CHAPTER FOURTEEN

THE BARGAIN

'Stop!'

At the last moment, Doralia grabbed her father's wrist, the gleaming point of the stake only a few inches from the vampire's chest.

Morgane was fading fast; soon, she would be no more than a husk, a smear of ashes on the temple floor. Galen turned his face to her and Doralia recoiled. He looked almost as inhuman as the creature writhing on the ground beneath him.

'What if she's telling the truth?' she said. 'If Excelsis itself is at risk, then we need to hear what she has to say!'

Galen snarled and snatched his hand away.

'Truth died in this thing a long time ago,' he cried. 'You'd spare its life on its *word*? It speaks lies as easily as we breathe air, don't listen to it!'

Doralia dragged him to his feet, the stake like a dagger between them.

'Do you not think I want to see her suffer for all she has done to us?' Her throat was thick with emotion. She saw the pain, the suffering, etched onto her father's face, like lines carved into an ancient sculpture. 'She killed my mother. I would see her burn in the fires of eternal torment for her crimes.'

She released his arm.

'But we are sworn agents of the most holy Order of Azyr,' she said. She looked at Caspar's body, lying there on the ground, his throat a bloody ruin. 'What we feel does not matter. Only the struggle matters. Only duty.'

Her father looked as if the choice would tear him apart. He clutched the stake with both hands, and it was like he was waging a war inside himself against anguish and rage, against the strictures of his sworn oath as an agent, and the brute sorrows of his need for vengeance. He glared down at the vampire on the temple floor, the fading flow of blood that leaked from her ribs, the red eyes dimmed in their sunken sockets, the parchment skin drawn back from the bared teeth. She was almost gone.

'You know we stand on the edge of something bigger,' Doralia said. 'Something is happening here and we must get to the bottom of it before it's too late.'

'But at what cost?' Galen whispered. He looked a broken man, a bag of bones in a leather coat.

'If Excelsis falls,' she said softly, 'then what was the point of all that suffering in the siege? We owe it to those who survived that they do not have to risk their lives again.'

'And our lives?'

Doralia gave him a mirthless laugh. 'They have always been forfeit to the cause, father. You taught me that.'

He seemed to deflate then, as if all the fight had gone out of him. He dropped the stake and it clattered to the ground.

Quickly, she bent down and pulled the nullstone bolt from Jael's shoulder.

The vampire's scream was loud enough to have been heard all the way down in Raven's Hollow.

Doralia, sitting on one of the benches, turned away in disgust. It was all she could do not to retch, or to snatch up her crossbow and put a bolt in Morgane's chest.

The vampire crouched over Caspar's corpse and lapped up the blood that still dripped from his neck. With every hurried gulp, a little colour flowed back into her. Her hair darkened and grew thicker, and those dreadful pinprick eyes deepened to a richer shade. Doralia could see the blood thrumming under her skin, surging through the thin blue capillaries and veins. The gunshot wound in her ribs was healing over, although her red velvet gown was ruined. She was almost whole again.

Doralia looked over to where her father stood by the altar, his back to the hall. He had wiped it clean as much as he could, and he stared up now at the broken stained glass above it, his hands behind his back. He could not look on the vampire healing herself. He could not stand to see the consequences of his actions, of what he had allowed to happen.

Jael sat up and wiped her mouth with the back of her hand, smearing blood over her chin. She licked her fingers, a look of satiated ecstasy on her face. Opening those smouldering red eyes, she glanced at Doralia and smiled.

'Forgive me,' she said. 'But if I'm to be any use to you then it's better that I'm whole, rather than a husk, surely?'

Doralia grimaced. 'I always thought your kind couldn't drink the blood of the dead.'

'It's not advisable,' the vampire said as she got to her feet. 'But needs must. Think of it as the difference between drinking cheap rotgut wine, compared to a fine vintage. I'm sure you'd know all about that...' She held a hand to her stomach and winced. 'No, don't worry – I'll pay for this in the morning, I'm quite sure.'

'Not nearly enough.'

Doralia looked at Caspar's lifeless body, slumped there on the flagstones, his head twisted round. Drained now of that which had kept him alive, which had kept him so vital. She thought of his smile, his bluff insouciance. He had lived a charmed life, she thought. But all charms must fade in the end.

'I'm sorry,' she whispered. She had never hated herself more than in that moment. She hoped his shade could hear her, wherever it was. And if he could, she hoped he would understand.

The wider scheme of things indeed...

Jael stretched luxuriantly. 'Don't be too upset, my girl,' she said. 'He did his bit, didn't he? It's a shame to waste such a nice piece, but I'm sure Sigmar will gather his soul to his mighty bosom with honour and gladness. Maybe he can become one of those mindless golden automatons you Sigmarites love so much. The lightning-borne.' She grinned. 'He's a true hero after all.'

Galen turned from the altar, and in silence stalked over to punch the vampire square in the mouth.

Jael staggered to the side and sprawled into the benches, her lip split. She dabbed the blood with her fingers and licked them clean. As Galen stood there over her, the cut began to heal. She laughed, mirthlessly.

'Do not speak of him again,' Galen said. 'Do not speak of Sigmar or his holy warriors. Do not speak at all, unless it is in answer to a direct question.'

He cocked his head towards his daughter. Doralia was aiming her crossbow directly at Jael's heart.

Just say the word, she thought. *Give me the signal, and she's just ashes on the breeze.*

'If you speak out of turn,' Galen said, 'you die. If you do not answer my questions, you die. If I do not like what you have to say, you die. You live on sufferance, monster, and the very moment I feel you have outlived your usefulness to us... you die.'

The vampire knew she had pushed it as far as she could. She looked on Galen with wary eyes, and Doralia tightened her finger on the trigger. Slowly, Jael regained her feet. Not breaking Galen's gaze, she inclined her head and the smile she gave him was ice cold.

'Do not delude yourself, ven Denst,' she said. 'It is both our good fortunes, perhaps, that our paths stretch in the same direction, but I do not live to serve the likes of you. You will make no demands of me while I have information to bargain with, remember that, and I am not so stupid as to empty my purse in front of you and not keep some jewels back to trade. I will tell you as much as you need to know, nothing more.'

'Very well,' Galen said. His eyes were like shards of stone. He paced back to the altar while Jael sat down on the bench. Doralia did not take her eyes off the vampire, and her aim was unwavering. 'Now tell me then, this Briomedes. Who is he? What does he want? And what risk does he pose to Excelsis?'

The light was fading as Jael Morgane began her tale. The temple's broken windows darkened, and the breeze outside sang a cold and lonely song through the empty streets of Hollowcrest. They would have to camp here tonight, Doralia knew. Even the prospect of a half-decent bed and a roof over their heads didn't seem that enticing, if the price they had to pay was Morgane's company. Neither she nor her father would get any sleep tonight, she was quite sure. As for the vampire, who knew how much rest those things really needed.

Jael sat and steepled her hands on the back of the bench in front, a gesture almost of prayer or contemplation. Doralia wondered if she were subtly mocking them. It mattered little. She rested the crossbow against her knee, still with the bolt pointing at the vampire's chest. Her father stood by the altar, his hand resting on the grip of his pistol. She had no doubt that he would shoot Morgane down if he suspected her of playing for time, or of being even marginally less than sincere.

That it should come to this, she thought. *The city's safety balanced on the edge of a vampire's word…*

She felt tainted, sickened by the fact that she was even sharing a moment of this creature's company. If there was one thing her long career had taught her, though, it was that the execution of one's duty was rarely a pleasant experience. If Excelsis was at risk, then the burden fell on them to wade through the mire until it could be saved, no matter how filthy they got. That was the job, and they did it so others could stay clean.

'Briomedes is one of the greatest natural necromancers I have ever seen,' Jael told them. 'Many gain their strength in the magical arts through long study, through the acquisition of great artefacts and so on, but Briomedes is one of those rare souls who just innately has the gift. It burns in him like a cold flame, inextinguishable.'

'Then it is to his eternal shame that he uses this gift in the service of evil,' Galen said. 'Necromancy is an abomination, an insult to Sigmar.'

'Our talents can take us in strange directions, as I'm sure you know,' Jael replied. 'But regardless of his motives, he has talent in abundance. I have never met a human so accomplished in the art.' She grinned at Doralia, and in the gloom her red eyes glowed like a cat's. 'He's younger than you, my dear. How old are you now? Twenty-eight? Twenty-nine? Briomedes has achieved so much in such a comparatively short time.'

Galen gathered up some candles from the floor and arranged

them on the altar. He lit them from his tinderbox, and the growing flames illuminated Caspar's body on the flagstones, hidden now under an altar cloth.

'Where does he come from? What brings him here? What does he want?' Galen said.

'Straight to the point as always, ven Denst,' Jael said. 'He is from Shyish originally, although more than that I cannot say. Some claim he first appeared in the Nightlands, where he began his experiments in necromancy. No better place to practise, of course. He made his way to Ghur after the Great Work, it is said.'

'Great Work?' Doralia asked.

'The Necroquake, Nagash's crowning glory. In any case, regardless of where he comes from, Ghur is where we first crossed paths – far, far over in the west of Rondhol, many thousands of miles from here... He was content to work in out-of-the-way places, to explore the deepest recesses of his art undisturbed. His research took him in strange directions. I believe he was experimenting on the resurrection of this realm's more impressive physical specimens. Thunderwyrms, gargants, ogors, megafauna of all kinds. He was of an academic mind, back then, and wanted only to continue his work undisturbed.'

'Unusual,' Doralia said. She looked at her father for confirmation. 'Most of the necromancers I've come across tend more towards what you might call a megalomaniacal frame of mind, to say the least.'

Galen agreed. 'Their dark arts are aimed in one direction only. Once dominion of the dead begins to pale, they tend to want to dominate the living as well.'

'Let me disabuse you of your preconceptions here,' Jael said. She leaned forward, and her mocking insincerity seemed to fade away. 'If you picture a high adept of the necromantic arts, then I assume you're picturing some dusty and ossified old wizard, half corpse himself, creeping around graveyards and charnel houses. Am I correct?'

Doralia shrugged. 'Surprisingly accurate picture, in my experience,' she said.

'Briomedes was not like that,' Jael continued. 'There was such passion in him, a spirit, a questing sense of purpose, that he was almost like an artist. For him, the mystery of death was only a means of gaining a greater understanding of life.' She dropped her eyes, and her voice faltered. 'I could feel it,' she said. 'The moment I met him – his lust for knowledge, the intensity of his vision. I found myself...' She sneered. 'At first, I did anything he asked. I thought we were partners, that... But then, slowly, I began to realise the scale of his deceit. Like one enslaved, I realised that I was not following him as an equal, but as a servant. I was little more than an enforcer, a tool in his hands to enact his purposes, a subject of his experiments. Me!' she howled. 'Jael Morgane reduced to such a degraded state! Such was the power of his art that I could not resist...'

'Your self-pity interests me less than the information you can provide about his purposes,' Galen said.

Jael looked at him with murderous hatred.

'You understand nothing, witch hunter. You have no idea what it is like to find your will utterly subsumed by another's. It is a humiliation unparalleled. I spent years as Briomedes' plaything. He... he tortured me as he saw fit, trying to find the limits of my own sense of self. He destroyed my companions, my family, to measure the effect their deaths would have on me...'

'Your family?' Galen sneered. 'Feeble lackeys not unlike the poor boy we executed in the tavern, I shouldn't wonder. I wouldn't have expected such pathetic sentiment from you, Morgane, to weep over the deaths of those you had already killed. By Sigmar's grace,' he spat, 'the irony is too disgusting for me to take.'

The vampire bared her teeth in a feral snarl. Galen pulled the pistol from his belt.

'Just give me the excuse,' he growled. 'You have no idea how much I yearn for it.'

Jael laughed softly. All the savagery faded in her, and she became again a vision of seductive beauty, a daemon in red velvet. Galen holstered the pistol. Doralia felt a line of sweat trickle down her temple.

'I wouldn't expect you to understand,' she said. 'There are many reasons a vampire creates another in their image, but sometimes it is for something like companionship. Like… like love.'

'An emotion I have no doubt is utterly alien to you,' Galen stated.

'You know so little of our kind, witch hunter,' the vampire said. 'For all your professed expertise, you're like a child peering at a map, not realising that it points to a wider territory outside your window. We are capable of more than you think, the Vampire Lords. Not even the drumbeat of Nagash is as powerful as you imagine inside us…'

Doralia interrupted before either of them could go any further. If Morgane had genuine information, then she couldn't pass it on with Galen's stake through her heart.

'From what you've told us so far,' she said, 'this Briomedes seems content to ply his trade in obscurity. What threat is he to Excelsis?'

'He has a son,' Jael said. 'A young boy, Timon. Had a son, I should say.'

'He died?' Doralia asked.

'Yes,' Jael smiled. 'And of the most mundane illness as well, a disorder of the blood common in Rondhol. I believe the lad scratched himself on a thorn, and the disease took root from there. Sad…'

'A tragedy,' Galen murmured. 'For a father to outlive his child…'

'Indeed so,' Jael said. 'But it is not in Briomedes' nature to allow death the final say in any matter.'

'Sigmar's blood…' Doralia whispered. 'He resurrected the boy?'

She blanched. Grief could be a pitiless master, as she well knew, but to be so deranged by it that you would force a dread unlife onto your only child… It was unimaginable.

'Timon was more than a son to him,' Jael explained. 'For Briomedes he was like an heir, a student, a sense of the future. He was something vital and alive, and he gave him purpose. To be snatched away like that by some ridiculous accident was more than Briomedes could stand. At the very least, though, he was so maddened by his grief that it gave me the chance to escape his control. I seized it and ran, but I have dreamt of my revenge since.'

'Surely,' Galen said, 'even one so steeped in horror as a necromancer could see that what he had inflicted on his son was worse than a natural death? Why not let the lad rest in peace, his soul commended to the Underworlds?'

Jael shook her head. 'You misunderstand. Briomedes resurrected Timon only as a temporary measure. In Excelsis, he believes he can find a way to cheat death altogether and bring him back for good.'

'Nothing can cheat death,' Galen said. 'Not true death in any case. And I can think of nothing in Excelsis with that kind of power.'

The vampire was enjoying this, Doralia thought. Seeing them blundering about, always one step behind. For all the network of spies and informants Galen had employed, he had been so focused on tracking down Jael Morgane that this threat had utterly passed them by.

'Can't you?' the vampire said. She sighed with mock regret. 'You're looking at this problem with all the plodding literalism I would expect of you, ven Denst. No creativity, no flair…'

'Speak, monster,' he said. 'You come dangerously close to breaking the conditions of our agreement.'

Jael held up her hands. 'An agreement I choose to honour for as long as it serves my purpose. What Briomedes seeks sits in the centre of Excelsis Harbour,' she said. 'No less than the Spear of Mallus itself.'

Doralia frowned. Galen showed an equal confusion. If she had expected anything from the vampire, it certainly wasn't this.

'I don't understand,' Galen said, scowling.

'Why doesn't that surprise me…'

'The Spear of Mallus is a source of prophecy,' he said, 'not necromantic power. If this Briomedes hopes to restore his son to life using a handful of glimmerings then he will be sorely disappointed.'

'Gods, even now you can't lift your imagination more than an inch off the ground, can you, ven Denst?' Jael scorned. 'Briomedes isn't going to bet his son's life on a few shards of glimmerings. He is going to seize the Spear of Mallus.' She spoke as if to a child. 'The *entire* Spear of Mallus.'

Galen looked baffled. 'But… but what could he possibly hope to achieve?'

'He is an artist,' Jael said. She seemed delighted. 'A wizard of extraordinary abilities. He will use the greatest source of prophetic power in the Mortal Realms to rewrite the skeins of fate and wrench reality itself back to a point where Timon had never died in the first place. That is his plan. He is going to rewrite existence, to save his son.'

There was a moment of stunned silence, and then Galen actually laughed. Doralia couldn't have been more shocked if he'd started crying. He roared and pressed the back of his wrist to his eyes, reaching for the altar for balance.

'Daughter,' he said, his chest shaking. 'Kill this thing and let's be on our way.'

'Damn you, I'm telling the truth,' Jael hissed. 'He will do this, believe me!'

'Really?' Galen mocked her. 'Even if such a thing were possible, how on earth would he do it? The Spear is guarded by the Floating Towers of the Collegiate Arcane, by the Scourge Privateers in the harbour, by every Freeguild soldier in the city. The Stormcast Eternals themselves stand sentinel over it! We may have taken a damned good beating in the siege, but we're still standing. He would need...'

Galen's face fell.

'He would need...' he said.

The mirth died on his lips. His eyes stared into some unimaginable distance, where all they saw was madness and hate reflected back at them.

'Sigmar's blood...' he said.

'Now you're beginning to understand,' Jael said, and grinned. 'Now you see how badly you have failed, Galen ven Denst.'

'What?' Doralia demanded. She stood up, the crossbow pointing at Jael Morgane's face. 'Tell me!'

'He would need an army,' Galen murmured. His voice was as dry as parchment.

'And he'll have one,' Jael said. She leaned back and crossed her arms behind her head. 'Remind me, Doralia, how many were killed in the siege altogether, do you think? Men and women, duardin, aelves, orruks, ogors, gargants, skaven, grots?'

Doralia's mind reeled. 'Thousands,' she muttered. 'Tens of thousands. *Hundreds...*'

'Precisely,' the vampire said. 'All of them mouldering in mass graves both outside and inside the city limits. *All* of them. Briomedes will have his army, all right.'

She smiled, as if the thought were too wonderful to contemplate.

'And it will be the greatest army that Ghur has ever seen.'

Old Lisbeth had to admit, the man in room nine was a strange one. A creepy fellow, she would have said, especially for one so young, but then the times being what they were, and the Cracked Casket being what it was, it didn't do to cast any aspersions on your guests. Every coin counted when you barely had any guests at the best of times, and since the siege the Casket had been quieter than the grave. So little trade passing through, she thought, and they were tucked away in such an out-of-the-way spot on the other side of the Ironweld armouries, with that awful sulphur stink hanging over the streets. And then that grand cemetery on the other side, St Thelemar's – it was no wonder nobody wanted to spend the night here. Not for the first time, Old Lisbeth cursed her husband's name, Sigmar bless his soul. It had all been Geren's idea, starting a tavern in the first place. She'd left it all up to him, and now look where she was – barely two motes to rub together.

Old Lisbeth sighed and took the creaking stairs up to the second landing, bearing a tray of hot soup and a jug of red wine. She paused outside the door of number nine. Gods, but he was a creepy one, him and that boy of his. Never a word from the lad, always sitting quiet in a corner, head down and his little white hands in his lap. And the father standing there, smiling, pale, but the smile just that little too wide and sitting there just a little too long on his lips. Odd fellow, but then it wasn't her place to say anything. Lisbeth was a Sigmar-fearing woman, and she knew it took all sorts to make the God-King's empire.

She balanced the tray in one hand and knocked on the door. There was no answer.

'Sir?' she called. 'I've your supper here for you, same as usual? Shall I leave it out here by the door then, sir?'

She tried the handle and the door swung open. Lisbeth shuffled inside, peering into the gloom.

'Are you there, sir?'

The bed was still made, and the little cot at the side for the boy was empty. The table in the middle of the room was covered by a map, weighted down at the corners. She shuffled near, thinking to lay the tray on top of it. Looked like a map of the city, she thought as she peered down at it. Yes, definitely Excelsis – there was the Consecralium, and the Ardent Parkland, the High Arbiter's Palace...

'Can I help you, Mrs Sauer?' a cold voice said.

Lisbeth nearly dropped the tray, she was so startled. She laid it down on the map and then bustled around the table to the door. The young man stood there in his black cloak, like a streak of midnight, the boy huddled into his side.

'Oh, do forgive me, sir, I didn't realise you weren't in,' she said. 'Just bringing your supper, like you asked.'

'Thank you, Mrs Sauer,' he said. He drew the boy into the room and spoke quietly to him, arranging him to sit on the edge of the cot. He stroked his hand down the side of the child's face, smoothed down his hair and gently kissed him on the forehead.

'Will the lad want nothing to eat then?' she asked. 'Poor mite looks like he could do with a feed.'

'He will be fine, thank you.'

There was mud on his cloak, Lisbeth saw, dried mud around the hem.

'I could wash that for you, sir?' she said. She pointed at the cloak. 'Only three motes and it'll be done by tomorrow morning, quick as you like.'

'There's really no need,' the young man said.

He stood there in the centre of the room, smiling at her – so still, nothing of him but the long black cloak and the pale face, his dark hair receding slightly at the temples. And the boy just sitting there, staring straight ahead, those black eyes… Lisbeth shivered.

'Goodnight, Mrs Sauer,' the young man said as he saw her to the door. 'We will be leaving in the morning. So much to do, you see,' he said. 'So much work to be done.'

PART TWO

INTO THE
STREETS

CHAPTER FIFTEEN

EXCELSIS

The journey from Hollowcrest was a torment. Every step of the way, Doralia had to force herself not to plunge a dagger into the vampire's eye, not to riddle her with nullstone bolts from her crossbow, or take her sword and hack that grinning, malicious head from her shoulders. To be in her presence was an insult.

They camped that first night in the temple, stretching out on the benches as best they could. Galen had been reluctant to spend the night in one of the empty houses; at least in the temple's narrow hall he could keep an eye on the vampire. None of them slept, as Doralia had predicted. In the morning, before they left, she had stood by Caspar's drained body, her hat in her hands, and prayed for his soul.

'I should have let you leave when you wanted to,' she murmured. 'If you can hear me now, Caspar Harrow, then forgive me. Your death will not be in vain, I swear it.'

They marched across the country as if the hordes of the dead were already at their heels. Bypassing Raven's Hollow, they scrambled down the hillside path onto the plains and made for the ferry across the river, hiking in a strained silence so tense that Doralia began to wish they would be attacked by deadwalkers again just to break it. Galen strode on ahead of them, untiring, his eyes focused only on the distant prospect of Excelsis. If he felt any pain or exhaustion, he kept it hidden. He barely even ate when they made their infrequent stops to rest.

Doralia was forced to keep pace with Jael, who seemed drained by the sun overhead. At one point, as they crossed a rough patch of thorny scrubland, the vampire collapsed, her skin scorched and flaking, a drowsy, unfocused look in her eyes.

'I can't go on like this,' she muttered. 'Curse you, witch hunter – if you would make any use of me in Excelsis, then see that I actually get there in one piece! I need the darkness.'

'The better to mask your evil, no doubt,' Galen had said sternly, as he stood over her. 'Surely that above all things must be a sign to you of your true condition, vampire? Only the impure fear the light.'

'Pure or impure, what difference does it make?' she snarled. 'I'll be little better than a sack of bones by the time we reach the city!'

Galen had thought for a moment, and then given a curt nod. After that they moved only at night. As soon as the light began to fail and the dusk swept over the dry and dusty plains, they would rise from the shadows of whatever shelter they had managed to find – a gnarled tree or a boulder, some shallow depression thick with gorse – and head on.

'You know,' Jael said, as they came near the trail to Fortune, 'I haven't eaten in such a long time...' She looked hungrily at the distant town, its rickety walls, the half acre of dusty square. 'Such a pleasant meal I had the last time I was there...'

'We keep moving,' Galen said. 'I know your kind well enough that you can go years without feeding if you must.'

'And in this situation I must, then?' Jael questioned him. 'If I'd known there were going to be such strict conditions attached to this venture, I doubt I would have agreed to come...'

Doralia knew that the vampire was only travelling with them out of some perverse desire for revenge, and because she needed their help as much as they needed hers. Briomedes had wronged her, but she feared the necromancer as well. Though she might deny it, in the hierarchy of the undead Briomedes was far above her. She knew what he was capable of, and she needed to keep her distance or risk her will being enslaved to his own once more. In her mind she had condemned him to death, but she needed the witch hunters to carry out the sentence.

'These companions of yours,' Doralia asked her, as they sheltered from the sun in a copse of buckthorn near the outskirts of the city. They were only a day's travel from its walls now, and she could see the looming silhouette of the Spear of Mallus in the distance, rising above the city far to the east, crackling with corposant energies from the Floating Towers that surrounded it. 'You said Briomedes killed them, an experiment of some kind?'

Jael gave an imperceptible nod. She sat back as if she were lounging on a bolster, rather than in the rough undergrowth beneath the trees. The dying light dappled her face from the swaying canopy overhead.

'Davin and Ursula,' she said. 'Those were their names. They were brother and sister when I found them. Sneak thieves and card sharps, pickpockets. They thought me a mark they could rob as easily as any other in the backstreets of Izalend. When they realised their mistake, it was too late for them. Nevertheless, I admired their spirit. They didn't beg, and they fought to the end. They had fire in them.'

She smiled gently, but then snapped her gaze to Doralia's, as if fearful she was being mocked.

'I don't expect you to understand,' she said. 'You think all we can hear is the echo of Nagash's command, but we are richer in spirit than you can possibly imagine. Like calls to like sometimes, and I recognised something of myself in them. A defiance I had when I was a mortal, perhaps, a sense of the world just sitting there waiting for me to take what I wanted from it.' She stared up into the branches of the trees. 'Immortality is a gift that mortals cannot begin to grasp, but it can be a trial as well. Sometimes,' she said, 'it is a trial that is better shared.'

Doralia was disgusted by her wistful tone. She was talking about two young people she had murdered, and that she had cursed with an appalling unlife that damned them in the eyes of gods and mortals alike. And yet here she was, speaking of them as boon companions, comrades in arms, family even.

'Briomedes took control of their will as easily as you would stoop to pick up something from the ground,' Jael continued. 'The undead are mindless things, you see, mere corpses propelled by an imperative they do not understand. But our kind, vampire-kind, have always been different. I think Briomedes wanted to test the limits of our capacity for emotion. Do we leave it behind when we become what we are? Are we truly soulless, as so many believe, or does some faint imprint of the soul remain, transmuted into something else?'

Her hands, Doralia had noticed, scratched and plucked at each other as she turned over the memories. The vampire was afraid, she realised. She dwelled once more in terrible traumas that had marked her, perhaps more than she cared to admit.

'His conclusion?' Doralia asked.

Jael's face looked wrenched for a moment, a spasm of pain or sorrow passing across it.

'What does it matter, witch hunter?' she sneered. 'Ask him yourself, before you kill him. That's what you're going to do, isn't it? Kill him?'

'If we must,' Galen said. He was sitting with his back up against a tree trunk, idly stripping the veins from a fallen leaf. 'If he truly threatens the city, as you claim, then he will face Sigmar's justice.'

'And that's rough justice indeed, from what I understand,' Jael laughed. 'How rare it seems that Sigmar tends towards clemency...'

'Clemency is a mercy,' Galen said, staring at her. 'Mercy is a luxury.'

Doralia saw the vampire's eyes flicker, and then, like a predator facing a greater rival, she looked away.

'It matters not to me,' she said. 'I will even light a candle in Sigmar's honour as long as you put the necromancer down. And as long as I am there to see it.'

'Then let us move,' Galen said. He tried to mask his groans as he got to his feet. 'Excelsis is near. Our battle is about to begin.'

Dusk, and the lamps were being lit along the Pilgrim's Way. Doralia watched the lamplighters strolling between them, wooden poles resting on their shoulders, the ends aglow with soft green aether-flame. Soon, the sky above the city was lost in the radiance of the lamps, and the gloomy streets took on new life in their misty, emerald shine. As they went about their business, the lamplighters called out for news to the costermongers and barrow boys who were packing up their stalls, and made ribald comments to the young women who strutted the cobblestones on their way home. Ale houses were opening their doors. Workmen were downing tools for the day and taking their thirsts into the taverns for the night. Buskers set up on street corners and strummed their lutes. Hawkers took their trays around the tavern crowds and tried to flog their cut-price wares – shoddy children's toys, matchsticks, bootlaces. Here and there she could see a glimmer addict shiftily crossing the street and disappearing into a dosshouse on the corner of Stellir Lane.

Night fell slowly, and the city came alive. Even the scars of the siege were beginning to heal over. The celestial magics the Seraphon had used to repair the worst of the damage was one thing, but here at street level it was the hard work and elbow grease of the common people that made the real difference. The city had been shattered, but slowly, very slowly, it was coming back together.

But for how much longer? she thought. *How much longer do these people have, before even worse is visited upon them?*

She hefted her kitbag onto her shoulder as she headed home. Their lodgings had been much as they were when she'd left in search of her father, which meant there was nothing worth eating in the cupboards and hardly a stick of wood for the fire. She'd headed out to pick up some cheap cuts of meat, a loaf of bread, a dozen apples and a couple of bottles of ale. She had her father's cigars in one pocket and a bottle of firewater in another, and as she crossed the street and headed deeper into the Veins, she resisted the urge to uncork the latter and take a swig. Galen didn't approve, she knew. He hadn't said anything to her, but he was more than aware of her drinking.

Hell, she thought, *even* I'm *aware of my drinking.* She wondered if she should make a bargain with the old man. *I'll stop drinking when you stop puffing on these damned Ghyranian cheroots…*

Doralia pulled her hat brim down and tried not to make eye contact with anyone as she crossed the street. She didn't want to ruin somebody's evening before it had even begun. Even so, she was aware of the looks she got as she moved on down the avenue, the way easy conversations faltered and died as she passed, and the remarkable number of folk who felt the need to cross the road when they saw her coming. It was ever the fate of a witch hunter, to be feared and despised by those you were sworn to protect. It was all part of the deal. You were an outcast in many ways, but in exchange you gained intimate knowledge of all the myriad threats and dangers to civilisation. And, more to the point, you could actually do something about them.

But can we do anything about this?

Even if Briomedes possessed half the power the vampire claimed he did, then the city was in terrible danger. After the siege, the dead were one thing Excelsis had in abundance, and the grave pits groaned with the corpses of every savage tribe in Ghur. As for the plot to seize control of the Spear of Mallus… it was too incredible to contemplate. But if Briomedes even made the attempt, with an army of undead orruks and ogors, gargants, skaven and grots at his back, then the destruction he could rain down on a city that had barely recovered from its last ordeal would be horrific. It would be the end of Excelsis, she knew. The survivors that she passed as she cut through the streets of the Veins might seem carefree and untroubled, but it was a veneer over an abyss. They had suffered terribly, and they could not be made to suffer again.

She reached the door of their lodgings, a bare, two-storey residence down a quiet side street that had been remarkably untouched by the violence of the siege. The passage was narrow and dark, and it was overshadowed by the tall, black tenements on the other side of the road. A few lamps shone in shuttered windows, but most of the buildings were empty now. Their inhabitants had either been killed in the fighting, or had taken up their meagre possessions and headed out to colonise the wilds, on the crusades to set up new villages and towns in the swamps and scrubland outside the city. The only other light in the street came from the aether-lamps that marched in an erratic procession down the pavements, casting their circles of pale, seafoam green onto the cobblestones. It was a cold and dank place to live at the best of times, but it was perfect for two witch hunters of the

Order of Azyr. Austere and inconspicuous, it was the ideal base from which to plan and launch their assaults upon the enemies of the city.

Or it was, she thought as she reached the door, *when it was just the two of us...*

She hadn't exactly expected an atmosphere of quiet industry when she returned, but the frosty silence that had descended on their lodgings was almost palpable. She passed through the gloomy passage from the front door and into the parlour, a bare and undecorated room at the front of the house with an oval wooden table and a few chairs at its centre. The walls were painted in a drab whitewash, and there were no paintings, no pictures or icons to decorate them. The shutters were closed, and a brace of candles sputtered on the mantelpiece, casting a funereal glow on the scene. The grate was cold, the fireplace covered in a thin layer of grey ash.

Her father sat at the table with a lamp turned down low at his side, a map of the city in front of him. His coat had been slung over one of the chairs, but his sword was in easy reach. A pistol lay before him on the table, weighing the map down, the hammer cocked. He frowned down at the grid of streets, the great sweep of the ornamental gardens, the semicircle of the harbour to the east where the vast monolith of the Spear of Mallus was safely anchored. His finger was slowly tapping on the Consecralium, the imposing fortress of the Knights Excelsior on the edge of the city, perched on a bluff that overlooked the harbour.

Doralia placed her kitbag on the other end of the table and unpacked the supplies, fishing in her pocket for Galen's cheroots. He murmured his thanks, not looking up from the map as he lit one of them. The rich, fragrant smoke drifted across the room. She pointedly clunked her bottle of firewater down on the table, but Galen said nothing.

There was a cough in the corner of the room by the shuttered window, so startling that her hand darted for her knife. Jael Morgane stood there in the shadows, her red eyes shining, the suggestion of white teeth bared in the darkness. Doralia felt again that instinctive shiver of hatred and disgust whenever she looked on the vampire. That it should be standing *here,* in their very home, was almost more than she could bear.

'If I'd known I'd be exposed to your vile cigar smoke, ven Denst,' Jael Morgane said in a honeyed voice, 'I never would have agreed to come.' She looked around the bare room and sighed. 'Never let it be said that I can't slum it when needs must, but really… This is too much. How can you possibly manage in such a grim little place?'

'Scented pillows, fine wines and the tears of your victims are luxuries you will have to go without, vampire,' Galen said. He opened the bottle of ale Doralia placed before him and took a contemplative sip. 'We have work to do, and frills and amenities only distract from the job at hand.'

'So needlessly austere, witch hunter,' Jael said. She emerged from the shadows and sat at the opposite end of the table, her arms folded. She was wearing a dress of black lace now, which she had looted from one of the houses in Hollowcrest. Her hair was piled on top of her head, apart from a single lock that snaked down and framed the side of her face. 'Be careful you don't enjoy that ale too much, or you might have to flagellate yourself later to make up for it.'

Galen, still not looking up from the map, pointedly reached for his pistol. Jael raised her hands in surrender, a tight smile on her face.

Doralia sat down at the table opposite the vampire and craned her neck to look at the map. She saw where her father was pointing: the Consecralium.

'The Knights Excelsior?' she said. 'It took them long enough to respond last time we asked for their help.'

She remembered approaching that forbidding black fortress with her father in those desperate hours before the siege. Her mind had been racing with the mad visions implanted there by the Seraphon, dreadful, half-seen shards of destruction and violence.

'It was less our words that changed the White Reaper's mind than the sight of the skaven scuttling through the streets when they came up from the sewers.'

'Agreed,' Galen said. 'Sigmar's holy warriors are our last, best hope, but… it's true that sometimes they need to see the evidence with their own eyes before they act. We would only waste time by going to them first, and although new Stormhosts have arrived to bolster the city's defences, their numbers are pitifully low.'

'Same with the Freeguild,' Doralia said. 'I passed by the west bastion again earlier, and it was defended by a fraction of the numbers it should be. The bastion wall is a shadow of its former self.'

'All regiments are at half strength, at best,' Galen said. 'I can send word by messenger to prepare, but for now we're thrown back on our own resources.'

He tore a hunk of bread from the loaf and chewed carefully, running the tip of his finger through the streets on the map.

Jael leaned forward and tapped the map with a razor-sharp nail. 'For once I agree,' she said. 'Our best bet is to find Briomedes as quickly as possible and kill him without hesitation. The moment he begins to raise the dead is the moment the city falls.'

'Do not pretend any concern for the city,' Galen said. 'You seek to destroy someone who has humiliated you. You act out of a sense of vengeance alone.'

'And what was your mindless pursuit of me across the wilds of Ghur, ven Denst?' Jael sneered. 'Altruism?'

Galen glanced up at her with hooded eyes. 'Altruism towards

your future victims, vampire. A chance to kill you, so that uncounted innocents might live.'

Jael cackled wildly. 'I don't know what sickens me more, witch hunter. Your self-righteousness or your hypocrisy.'

'Enough!' Doralia shouted. She slammed her fist down on the table. Galen's bottle jumped, but he caught it before it could topple over. 'Let none of us pretend this is a perfect union, but we need to work together if we're going to stop this necromancer. This petty bickering undoes all of us.'

She pushed herself away from the table in disgust and stood by the window, where she drew back one wing of the shutters. The street outside was quiet, a stretch of shadowed cobblestones and gently flaring aether-lamps, the tall tenements on the other side no more than a dark cliff face devoid of people. It was a bleak, miserable sight; just another grey corner of Excelsis, in the moments before a conflagration.

'We have come a long way,' she said, her back to the room. 'Just a little further, and the job will be done.'

Galen watched his daughter as she stood by the window. She was right of course; if they didn't work together the city was already lost, and if Briomedes was as powerful as Morgane claimed, then the vampire would be a valuable ally in the fight against him. And yet her very presence in his lodgings was an offence. The dry, dead-flower scent of her, the unnerving stillness as she sat there at the table was a provocation. He wanted nothing more than to snatch up his pistol and shoot her through the eye, and, while she was still reeling, to sweep his sword from its scabbard and hack her into a bloody ruin. He would water the ground with her blood, he would mount her mangled head on a spike at his door, he would–

The ale bottle creaked in his fist, on the verge of breaking.

Galen calmed himself and took a careful sip. Morgane was staring into some dead zone that only she could see, lost in her vampire dreams. When she wasn't moving, she looked like a waxwork or a cadaver dressed for its funeral. There were some sects in the Amber Princedoms, he remembered, who preserved the bodies of dead relatives and arranged them around their dwellings like decorations, or like still-living members of the family. They dressed them every day, sat them down at the dinner table, poured them drinks that lay untouched all evening. He tried to imagine what it would be like to share a home with this… this *thing*.

Morgane's red eyes flicked to his. A sliver of teeth, the rustle of lace. Always that slight gulp of air before she spoke, he had noticed. Vampires did not breathe, and so had to force the air from their lungs to render speech. Everything about them was a dark facsimile of human life, a mocking performance.

Like moths to our butterflies, he thought. *A night bloom compared to a simple daylight flower.*

It was repulsive.

'Well?' Morgane said. 'Are we going to do something then, or just sit here squabbling like children? I hate to agree with either of you, but your daughter has it right.'

How quickly could he kill her? he wondered. How slow? He tapped his finger against his chin, lost in thought. Chain her up and pare away a little piece at a time. Watch it regrow, then cut it off again… Or hack her into as many pieces as possible and see how long it took her to reform. Was that even possible? If he cut her in half and left each part at either end of the city, what would happen? Could she regenerate after such an appalling wound? And if so, which half would regrow? What would happen to the other half? How much pain would she be in while it happened?

And how much would I relish it?

'Ven Denst!' the vampire said. Galen came back. He looked down at the map of Excelsis. Doralia had turned from the window.

'Here,' he said. He stabbed his finger onto the parchment, to a patch of land not a mile distant from their lodgings. 'St Solicus Cemetery, near the western gate. It's an old patch, one of the oldest in the city, and if he was coming from the same direction we did, then this is where he'd start.'

Doralia came over to stand by his side and stared down at the map. She rubbed her chin thoughtfully.

'Makes sense,' she said. 'There must have been thousands of bodies buried there over the years.' She drew her finger along the route from the cemetery to the wall. 'And if he raises the dead there, then he'll have a clear run at the western bastion from the inside. That'll give him a foothold while he tackles the grave pits out in the western scrub, make it easier for him to funnel his forces into the city.'

'The vampire and I will head there now and investigate,' Galen said. He recoiled at the prospect, but it was the only plan that made sense. 'Doralia, go ahead of us, hit the taverns, the ale houses around the Veins, see if you can pick up any information. Sightings, strange occurrences, anything that could point to the necromancer's location, or if he's even here in the first place.' He folded up the map. 'We may have been lucky and reached here before him, but the sooner we know exactly where he is, the better.'

'He's here,' Morgane said. The vampire bared her teeth. 'I can feel it...'

'The confirmation will put my mind at rest, at least,' Galen said.

They checked their weapons and gathered up fresh ammunition. He saw Doralia crack the seal on the firewater and take a long swallow, but he said nothing. The scowl on her face as the drink went down was a rebuke he took to heart, though. He could not blame her for seeking what solace she may. It was his fault she was like this.

Jael Morgane watched the witch hunters readying themselves, strapping on their breastplates, pulling on their dusters and affixing their shoulder guards.

'How exciting it must be for you,' she said. She clasped her hands. 'Going on crusade, fighting the good fight! You hide your enthusiasm behind that gruff veneer, but I see it. You *live* for this, don't you?'

'I believe that is the only honest thing you have ever said,' he told her. 'And there's more truth in it than you can possibly understand. Our lives are lived in service to Sigmar's justice.'

He tucked his silver stakes into his belt and holstered his pistol. Doralia slung her crossbow over her shoulder and checked her own pistol, her knives, her sword. With a restrained flourish, she placed the wide-brimmed hat on her head. Father and daughter stood there in the centre of the austere room, unsmiling, armed to the teeth, and Jael Morgane's smile faltered just a little.

'Sigmar's justice, indeed,' she said.

CHAPTER SIXTEEN

WORD ON THE STREET

The streets were quiet as they cut through the Veins. They headed west towards the bastion gate, away from the marketplaces, the taverns, what remained of the public squares. The tenements gradually gave way to simpler wooden structures, empty lots smothered in weeds, alleyways unlit by torch or aether-lamp. Now and then a smashed gap in the buildings on their right revealed the ominous presence of the Spear of Mallus in the distance, chained in its berth by Excelsis Harbour. Over the centuries, the city had built up around it, drawing on its prophetic energies. To all intents and purposes it *was* the city, the source of all its power and prestige. The City of Secrets would be nothing without the Spear, and Sigmar alone knew what damage Briomedes could do if he managed to seize it.

Galen hurried on. A few months ago this would all have been a bustling thoroughfare, he knew – a rough-and-ready neighbourhood where hardworking folk tried to get by as best they could. On an evening like this, there would have been young mothers dandling their kids on their knees as they sat on their stoops, swapping the day's gossip. There would have been men and women trudging back from their shifts on building sites, or in the sewer patrols, or as butchers and weavers, watchmen and brewers, all of them looking forward to a plain hot meal and an ale or two. There would have been a hell of a lot of cursing and the odd fight, but there would have been laughter too. There would have been love, and life. Now, it was little better than a morgue. The skaven had boiled up from the sewers at the start of the siege, gnashing their way through the streets and tearing people apart with mouldering teeth and rusty blades. The flank of Kragnos' army had smashed its way through the edge of the district, sending a swarm of refugees heading for the dubious safety of the Trade Quarter. It had been too late for them, though. Any who had survived the fury of Kragnos then had to face the cruelty of Slaanesh, as the daemons began to manifest in the mirrored chambers of the Conclave Hall, spilling out into the streets in a sickening tide.

How many had died that day, he wondered, in just this one district alone? He wouldn't have been surprised at a figure of ten thousand. Now, each corpse lay there in its pit or in its grave, potential recruits for the army Briomedes would raise in pursuit of his insane scheme. If they were too late...

He stepped up his pace, Jael Morgane languidly striding alongside him. Pain uncoiled in his hips, like a hot wire in his bones, but he pushed it away. It sharpened him up, kept him going. Kept him angry.

'Not very talkative, are you?' the vampire said. If Galen barrelled through the streets like a hurricane, then Jael Morgane flowed through them like a sultry breeze. The evening was quiet, but everyone they passed recoiled in dread and horror when they saw her, making the sign of the comet against their chests, or even turning on their heels and running away. If he wasn't careful, Galen was going to be responsible for spreading a dozen dreadful rumours through the city by the time the night was over. There was no mistaking what she was. The black lace dress clung and drifted around her form, and in the simmering green light of the aether-lamps her skin looked as wax pale as a corpse.

She is *a corpse,* he thought. *Never forget that.*

'I've nothing to say to you, vampire,' he told her. 'Concentrate on the job in hand.'

'This is the job in hand, ven Denst,' she said. 'Don't you want more information on our quarry? Descriptions, intelligence and so on? I thought you were meant to be an investigator as well as an executioner? Think of it as me paying my way, demonstrating my use to you, so you don't feel tempted to use those stakes you have tucked in your belt.'

He was silent for a moment. Loath though he was to admit it, the vampire had a point. He was so appalled by the necessity of her presence beside him that the prospect of exchanging even the most innocuous words with her turned his stomach. But as Doralia had said back at their lodgings, they needed to work together. If the Order of Azyr had taught him anything in all the years he had been working for it, it was that personal emotions had no place in the execution of one's duty. No matter the task, no matter how distasteful or dangerous it might be, duty came first. He had ignored that once before, when he tracked Morgane down, blinding himself to the true threat against the city. Best not to do it a second time...

'The boy,' he said. The empty streets echoed with their footsteps. 'Tell me about the boy.'

'Timon? What do you want to know?' Jael asked. 'Like any other animated corpse, he seems below a beast in understanding. And yet, some things do seem to reach through to him. He fears fire, from what I've seen, and any tension or violence perturbs him to the smallest degree-'

'Damn you, monster,' he spat, 'tell me of the boy when he was alive! What was he like? Was he… was he a good lad, a loyal son? Did he know about his father's evil works?'

Jael began to laugh, but one look at Galen's face and the mirth died in her.

'He knew,' she said. 'Briomedes was going to train him in the arts of necromancy, but whether he had made any steps in that direction before the boy died, I don't know. Timon was quiet, studious. Shy, perhaps. He was his father's shadow, always trailing in his wake. I don't know what more I can say about him.'

'His father loved him, though?'

Jael smirked. 'As far as I understand these things…'

That had to be worth something. He cannot be all bad if he loved his child…

'Yet to inflict such monstrosities on the lad,' Galen muttered, as if to himself. 'The company of vampires and deadwalkers. To expose him to your kind, to corpses, to all the dead malice of necromancy…'

'And how did your daughter acquire her skills, I wonder?' Jael said sharply. 'By osmosis? Or because you took her in hand and trained her? How old was she when you armed her with a crossbow?'

He stopped dead and spun on his heel, his hand up to strike her. Jael's eyes burned in their sockets, her white teeth gleaming, her hands like claws.

'Damn you,' he hissed. 'It was *you* who put a crossbow in her hands for the first time! Your malice, your crimes!'

He reached for his sword as Jael hunched back, a snake preparing to strike. This was it – he had had enough of this sick pretence. Let her die now and be done with it. Let Excelsis die too if that was the cost!

The tramp of footsteps rang out at the other end of the street, the sharp, metallic clink of weapons and armour. He turned and saw a patrol of Freeguild soldiers, emerging from the dim light of the aether-lamps, as they passed through a weed-strewn patch of waste ground and crossed onto the cobblestones by the ruined shells of some burnt-out tenements. Judging by their green jackets, they were troops from the Iron Bulls. The lamplight cast their shadows against the high brick walls at the edge of the passage between the ruined buildings. As they came closer, Jael Morgane seemed to fade into the darkness like a gheist.

Galen hailed them as they drew near.

'I am Galen ven Denst, an agent of the Order of Azyr,' he said.

There were no more than twenty of them, heading no doubt to the bastion on the west gate. Their captain was a young woman, her head bare, her blonde hair tied back in a short ponytail. There was a hard cast to her face, the look of poise and confidence that only comes from experiencing combat.

'Captain Huber,' the young woman said, saluting as her patrol came to a halt. 'Do you need assistance, sir? Forgive me for saying it, but the presence of an agent rarely means good news.'

Galen looked the troopers over. Some wore tatty and faded uniforms, and their breastplates had seen better days. Few looked like hardened warriors. They weren't the most inspiring collection of soldiers he'd ever seen, but he knew the Freeguild had taken a beating in the siege. Recruits were hard to come by, and there was even talk of introducing conscription to bolster the ranks.

Nevertheless, he thought, thinking of Jael Morgane, *you fight with the weapons you have, not the weapons you would like...*

The captain's eyes slid over to where Morgane lurked in the shadows.

'Sigmar's blood!' she cried when she saw the vampire. She drew her sword, backing off, and the troops behind her cried out with shock. Galen grabbed the captain's wrist, staying her hand.

'She's with me,' he said urgently. 'I don't have time to explain, but you must trust me in this. I believe the city is on the brink of real danger.'

Captain Huber, wary and suspicious, slowly sheathed her blade and motioned to her troops to stand down. She turned to the witch hunter.

'Again, sir?' she said. 'We've hardly cleared up after the last time.'

Galen allowed himself a tight smile. He was warming to this young captain.

'Alas, we are cursed to live in such times,' he said, 'and few of us I am afraid can look forward to a peaceful death in our beds. Are you heading to the west bastion?'

'Yes, sir. Colonel Alicanthus is the commanding officer there.'

'I know of his reputation,' Galen said, grimacing.

A makeweight, content to offer the minimum of effort while his underlings covered for him. It was true, the best officers had fallen in the siege...

'Tell him to fortify his position and prepare for action,' he continued. 'I do not know when or where the blow may strike, but I fear before the night is out Excelsis will be put to the test once again.'

'Another siege?' Huber asked. She swallowed hard. 'I didn't think any of our foes had it in them to try again, sir. Not... not after last time. Sigmar's blood,' she said sharply, 'but we barely have the strength to resist as it is.'

'Whether the threat comes from without or within, I cannot say,' Galen said. He summoned the vampire and she emerged into the light of the aether-lamps again. She offered the captain a predator's grin. 'But make ready all the same. Trust in Sigmar, and the strength of your arms.'

Captain Huber saluted once more, giving another wary glance towards the vampire. Galen touched his forefinger to his temple as the soldiers hurried off down the narrow street, some of them glancing back with fear in their eyes to where Morgane stood, her arms folded, her cold and amused gaze following them back down the street. The soldiers' boots tramped hard on the cobblestones, and the echoes broke from the high brick walls of the shattered tenements. None of them looked thrilled by the information he'd just given them. If all went well, they would have a decent sleep in their barracks tonight. But if not...

'Come on, vampire,' he growled. 'The cemetery of St Solicus awaits.'

The Rusty Nail was, not to put too fine a point on it, a dump – but Doralia had got used to drinking in dumps over the last few months. The question was, had they got used to her?

She pushed through the creaking door and entered the dimly lit, low-ceilinged tavern, feet crunching on the fine grain of saw-dust on the ground. A smoky lamp fumed in a sconce on the right-hand wall, and there were a couple of candles sitting on the bar ahead of her in a puddle of melted wax. A drip from the ceiling went down the back of her collar as she crossed the room. She tried not to shudder.

Most taverns, you'd expect to hear a few lively conversations, see a couple of games of knucklebones or pinchpenny. You'd step in the door and be met by that rolling cacophony of people all talking at once; smell that ripe and enticing scent of fresh-brewed ale, sour wine and firewater. Here though, as she reached the bar and chapped her knuckles on the counter, the talk was more like a furtive mutter. It wasn't a big place, no more than twice the size of the parlour room back at her lodgings, but folk turned away as if they wanted to hide themselves in its shadows. Not that there were that many folk to begin with. Apart from the barman, there were a couple of shady characters with their heads together down by the lead-lined window on the other side of the room; a group of grimy-looking duardin draining their tankards in silence in the other corner; a scattering of cut-throats, drunks and pickpockets lined up against the bar.

'Ale,' she said, as the barman drew near. She thought of the big man back in Fortune all of a sudden, his soft, fleshy face, that drooping moustache. This one was his opposite: lean, hard look-ing, a rash of red stubble on his jaw. He spread his hands on the sticky wooden surface and looked her dead in the eye.

'Thought I barred you from here, witch hunter,' he said slowly.

It was almost imperceptible, but Doralia could feel the duardin over in the corner shifting their positions. On the other side of the room, she was sure one of the drunks had just slipped a hand into his coat. She took her hat off and laid it on the bar, and then drew back her own coat so they could see her knives, her pistol. The sword on her back would be useless. Not enough space to swing the damn thing in here, and of course the crossbow was out of the question.

'Barred?' she said. 'Up until this very moment I wasn't even sure that I'd been in here before. Figured I'd remember a place this fragrant. Care to tell me what for?'

'You know what for,' the barman said.

'Why don't you jog my memory.'

'*Affray*,' he said, after a moment's thought. 'That's what the city guard would call it, I'd wager. Some serious affray.'

She'd been in the Skaven's Head already this evening. The Arbi-ter's Choice. The Starbank. Nobody had heard or seen a thing about a necromancer and his dead son. No signs of corpses rising from their graves, no sense of anything amiss. Most people had nervously swallowed as soon as she entered the room and made a big show of being helpful. One old drunk in the Pot and Tankard had claimed he'd seen a bat as big as a dragon swooping over his house earlier that evening, but his hands shook so much and his eyes were so bloodshot that she didn't give it much credence. The Lock and Key was next on her list, a nice place on the edge of the Veins, near Stormstone Cross and the canal. Rebuilt, she'd heard, after the siege. New owners. An upmarket place. Thought she might see if they had any of that good zephyrwine she'd sampled back in Raven's Hollow while she was there... But first, she had to get through the Rusty Nail.

'Affray,' she said. 'Fancy word. If you mean things got a bit out of hand one night, maybe a touch rowdy, then I apologise. I didn't realise this was such a genteel establishment.'

'A touch *rowdy*?' he said. He showed her a mouthful of rotten teeth as he snickered out a laugh. 'That's what you call it? You damn near killed one of my customers, beat him half to death! Master Kharnick over there' – he cocked his head towards the group of duardin – 'you cut off his damn beard.'

The duardin shifted in their seats. One of them stood up, not more than five feet tall and just as wide, his thick, muscular arms folded. Doralia could see now that he did look a touch clean-shaven compared to the rest of his kin. She held up her hand. They could take it as a gesture of peace, or as a warning. Either was good for her.

'Barred or not,' she told them, 'I'm here now on official business.'

She looked round at them all, each in turn: the duardin, the pickpockets, the two younger men over by the window trying to keep their heads down.

'Official business,' she said again. 'You all know what that means...'

The fist came from somewhere behind her, caught her a solid blow to the kidneys. She felt a hand on the back of her neck, and then her head was slammed down onto the bar and all she could see were stars. She was on the ground all of a sudden and felt the boot go in, a decent kick, but not enough weight behind it to do too much damage. She thought she might be sick, but managed to keep it in. She took another kick while she waited for her head to clear, tried to make it all seem worse than it was.

That's the problem with this place, she thought, grunting. *Not enough room for a decent swing...*

'That jog your memory, witch hunter?' a voice laughed.

'Get her out the back, you morons,' she heard the barman hiss. 'Over the other side of the alley. Old Beckerson's pigs will feed well tonight...'

It was one of the drunks who had hit her and who was putting the boot in now, and he wasn't half as drunk as he had seemed before. She saw the three duardin advancing, keen to get in on the action.

She caught the foot as it came sailing in, twisting and throwing the drunk off balance. He was small but heavyset, with cropped hair, a couple of nasty, livid scars across his cheeks. She hoped she could add to his collection.

As the drunk skipped back on his left foot to keep his balance, Doralia kicked out at his knee and felt his leg break cleanly at the joint. He scrambled for a breath so he could scream, but before he could manage it, she leapt up and planted a solid punch right in his throat. Something crunched inside him – his hyoid bone, larynx maybe. He coughed blood and his eyes went vacant, and then she had her pistol out and pointing at the duardin. They backed off immediately, eyes wide. The drunk fell to the floor and twitched. His face was blue, blood bubbling from his lips.

'I'll shoot you if I have to,' she said to the duardin – and then something exploded past her ear and she was showered in plaster and stone from the ceiling.

'Sigmar's blood!' she muttered, hitting the ground. The duardin ran for the door and she had to make the call whether to shoot them or let them go. Lying on her back, she looked up at the bar and saw the barman fumbling the reload on some ancient, rusty black-powder firearm – a clockwork contraption that was all cogs and wheels. She was amazed it hadn't blown his hand off.

Lucky for the duardin he's got it, though, she thought.

She stood and aimed, sent a bullet popping straight through the barman's head in a great fan of blood and brains, hitting on a slight angle from his upper jaw to the back of his cranium. His arm spasmed as he fell, the firearm went flying, and her bullet shattered two bottles of firewater on the shelf behind him. The liquid splashed onto the candles and immediately ignited, a tongue of flame that leapt quickly along the surface of the bar like it was running a race and was in a real hurry to reach the finishing line.

'Sigmar's *blood…*' she sighed.

Doralia grabbed her hat and tried to whack the flames out, but she was just fanning them higher. They licked and lapped at the wooden beams that ran across the lintel above the bar.

Thirty seconds, she thought, *and this whole place is going to go up like a torch.*

The Rusty Nail's esteemed patrons had already fled the scene, barrelling into each other as they pushed through the door. In a district like this, a fire was one of the worst things that could happen. Wooden buildings, too far from any source of water. She'd come here trying to find information to save the city, and now it looked like she was going to be responsible for burning half of it down.

She was on the verge of running for the city guard when one of the young men from over by the window stepped up and flung a bucket of sand over the worst of the flames. They sputtered out immediately, a few tendrils escaping to whip across the last of the spilled firewater. Doralia beat them out easily with her hat. The brim was singed, and her head was still half spinning from being smacked down on the bar. Still, if a burnt hat and a few bruises were the worst she came away with, then she figured she'd got off lightly.

The man with the bucket of sand stood back, uncertain, the bucket held up in front of his chest like a shield. His friend was behind him, hands out at his side to show he was unarmed. They were both young, their hair neat and short, something in their bearing that suggested a military background, or at least a solid introduction to the soldierly arts. Doralia made a show of tucking away her pistol.

'You always make sure you leave the house with that?' she said.

'Sercken keeps a couple on hand,' the man said. He placed the empty bucket on the ground. 'Helps for cleaning up when someone pukes after a few too many.'

'Who's Sercken?'

'Man whose brains are all over the wall there,' he said. 'He runs this place. Ran, I guess.'

There was a stench in the air of burnt firewater and smoking wood. The drunkard she'd punched in the throat hissed once, like an inflated bladder losing air, and quietly died.

'Well,' she said, 'whoever takes over is going to have to redecorate.' She put her hat on her head, wrinkling her nose at the smell of singed leather. 'You two are deserters, aren't you? From the Iron Bulls I'd guess, given the nearest garrison at the west gate.'

The two men looked at each other, still with their hands at their sides. To be caught by a member of the Order of Azyr when you'd just left your regiment without permission was as good as a death sentence.

'You can do two things for me,' Doralia said, 'and I'll pretend I never saw you.' She uncorked a bottle from the bar and took a long swallow. 'First, information.'

'Anything we can do to help,' the second deserter offered. He couldn't be more than eighteen years old, she thought. Pale blue eyes, watery, as if he were on the verge of tears.

'I'm looking for a stranger round these parts – he'd be travelling with a child, a young boy. The boy seems unusual, like… Well, it might sound strange, but like he's dead. Can't tell you much more about the man, but he'd feel odd to you if you saw him, disturbing. Neither of them would seem right. Anything like that jog your memories?'

They looked at each other again, and she saw the understanding pass between them. Both looked scared for a moment, as if they'd glimpsed something awful behind a door they should never have opened. The first deserter nodded slowly. He ran a hand through his dark, close-cropped hair.

'Few nights back, when we were still with the regiment,' he said quietly, as if afraid someone would overhear. 'We were on duty as the gate was closing for the day. Trade caravan had just come in from Bilgeport along the Great Excelsis Road and we'd let them through. And then…'

The other one, with the blue eyes, joined in. 'Night began to fall and we were locking up the horse gate when we saw this figure in the distance, coming in from the wilds on the other side of the road. From where the grave pits were dug…'

Doralia looked up. 'You waited for him?' she asked. The first deserter nodded.

'Since the siege,' he said, 'everyone's jumpy, no one's got the time for charity or helping others. My mother was always a Sigmar-fearing woman, though,' he said, 'and she raised me right. We're only as strong as each other, so I thought I'd wait to let him in, do the right thing.' He looked to his comrade for reassurance. 'Why, if we locked him out overnight it'd be as good as if we killed him ourselves, Coast of Tusks being what it is.'

She smiled to herself. A pious deserter… Guess it took all sorts.

'But when he came near...' the first deserter said. He stared off into that dark memory, flinching away from it. 'He had the kind of face you forgot as soon as you looked at it, but the *boy*...'

'I didn't want to let him in,' Blue Eyes offered. 'Thought the boy might be ill, but then I saw his *eyes* and I knew... Sigmar save us, but he was already gone. The child was dead, and then he... he *looked* at me...'

So he's definitely here then, Doralia thought. *Days ahead of us, with all that time to prepare...*

She could feel it in the air, the sense of a storm about to break. The rain would fall before the night was through, and the winds would howl through the streets. The dead were coming...

'I think that was the moment we decided to desert,' the first one said. He set his jaw. He was still ashamed of the decision, she could tell. 'After the siege, it just felt like there wasn't much more we could take.'

'You took what you thought was the easy decision and ran,' she said. 'Turns out it was the harder one after all.'

The two men tensed. Deserters or no, she knew they'd defend themselves if they had to. She looked at the blood-spattered wall behind the bar. There would be plenty more killing to come before this was over. Hopefully, some of it would involve putting Jael Morgane in the ground for good, but for the moment she'd had her fill.

'You said two things,' the first deserter offered. 'Information was the first, what's the second?'

Doralia turned for the door. She needed to find her father as soon as possible.

'Old Beckerson and his pigs,' she said. 'You know where they are?'

'Might do,' Blue Eyes said. He looked sick at heart. The other deserter looked confused.

'I have the feeling he was a regular customer of Sercken's,' she said. 'Kill his pigs for me, and make sure he knows why.'

She looked around the dingy room, the low ceiling blasted by the barman's gun, the body on the floor, the overturned chairs where the duardin had been sitting.

'After that,' she said, 'I suppose you can call yourselves the proud new owners of the Rusty Nail.'

CHAPTER SEVENTEEN

HALLOWED GROUND

There were cemeteries up near the Noble Quarter that were grand, imposing places, with perfectly curated fields of marble mausoleums and tombstones behind their massive wrought iron gates. Teams of groundsmen and gardeners kept the grass tidy and the flowers growing, and for the richest families the quality of their ancestral resting places was a keen source of competitive pride. The better your position in death, the more you had gained in life.

The cemetery of St Solicus was quite different. A dark and tangled patch of land, not much more than a few acres wide, it was set up against the city walls on the other side of the Veins. The rusting iron fence was crooked with age, and the gate was locked only with a coiled length of old rope. Over the years, the statues and sarcophagi had been gnawed by the elements, their details obscured, and most of the headstones had long since collapsed into the grass. The footpaths between the avenues of the dead were muddy and overgrown. Here and there, dark trees reached dead branches to the blackened sky. Only a handful of the lamps along the footpaths had been lit. It was old ground, Galen knew, dating back to the city's first founding. Old, cold ground. One of the first things people did when they settled a new patch of land was to build a temple and set aside somewhere to bury their dead. As a native of the Amber Princedoms in Shyish, Galen knew that the dead were always with you one way or another.

Always more reassuring when they stay buried, though...

He stood at the gate and peered into the murky graveyard, listening to the rustle of the branches, the whisper of the grass, smelling the dead scent of rotting leaves and rich, loamy earth. On the other side of the cemetery, across a long strip of waste ground dotted with the shacks and huts of the city's poorest folk, the western walls of Excelsis stood before them. A rugged cliff face of black stormstone, the walls were gnarled with slights and fractures, and were propped up with buttresses and scaffolding.

'This is ancient ground,' Jael Morgane said beside him. 'I can tell. And the dead are buried deep.'

She laced her hands around the bars of the gate and inhaled. Even above the smell of the undergrowth, Galen could detect her dead-flower scent, the musty odour of the lace dress she had taken in Hollowcrest. He stepped away, revulsed, and unhooked the rope from the gate. Behind him, the twisted streets of the city brooded in their silence – a forest of gabled roofs, spires, blunt towers and black tenements.

'Wait...' the vampire said. Her brow was furrowed, and she placed a hand carefully against her stomach. 'There's something...'

'Briomedes?' he said. He reached for his sword.

Morgane faltered. She was afraid, he realised. If the necromancer had tortured her as thoroughly as she claimed, then even the most powerful need for vengeance had to break through the web of her fear, and there was probably no one in the Mortal Realms she feared right now as much as him. Galen stared through the gate onto the pathways of the graveyard. The clouds above slipped their shielding veil from the stars for just a moment, and those dark avenues were lined with silver. If Briomedes was here, then they could end this tonight, before it had even begun.

'Move, vampire,' he said. 'I would not be the author of your petty vengeance against him. If you want it, you must come and take it yourself.'

He pushed the gate open and entered, Morgane following reluctantly behind him.

'"Petty vengeance?"' she spat. 'Curse you, ven Denst! The pain Briomedes has caused me can only be paid in blood – you of all people should know that.'

'Indeed I do,' he muttered. 'And I mean to take my own when this is done, make no mistake.'

There was an old gatehouse on the right-hand side of the path as they entered the graveyard, a run-down and dilapidated cottage. The windows were dark, the walls smothered in ivy and bindweed, and by the side of the doorstep there was a Hysh-flower bush, the white petals open to the night, drinking in the light of the stars. The sight of them cheered him, somehow. A plant with all the cold beauty of that graceful realm, growing here in the dark ground of Excelsis as it brooded on the verge of mayhem. Perhaps he would see Hysh again, when this was over. He would travel there with Doralia, and they would both reacquaint themselves with the human city at Settler's Gain. They would renew themselves in the gentle benediction of its purifying light.

The cemetery stretched out before them, jumbled, dark, the sodden undergrowth pulling at their feet even as they walked along the avenues between the graves. Headstones blocked their paths from where age had toppled them, and the grass was pooled with deep shadows. Back and forth they stalked, the witch hunter and the vampire, examining the ground on either side of the pathways, until after the best part of twenty minutes Galen was forced to admit that there was nothing there. The earth was unbroken. The dead still slumbered undisturbed. Briomedes was not in St Solicus.

'Well?' he said to Jael. He stood with his hands on his hips in the centre of the cemetery, interrogating the shadows all around them. 'I thought you felt his presence here?'

The vampire was confused, the frown she had worn since they reached the cemetery still marring her alabaster skin. Her red eyes darted nervously to the graveyard's hidden corners.

'I did!' she protested. 'I do. It's faint, very faint, but... I can't explain it...'

'Try,' Galen growled.

'It's like he is here now, above us, below, all around...' She looked fearfully over her shoulder. 'But it's faint, a mere trace in the air and in the breeze. Wherever the dead are,' she said solemnly, 'there he is.'

He snorted and sheathed his sword. 'It strikes me,' he said, 'that you are our only witness to this man, if indeed he actually does exist in the first place. You have bought your life thus far by paying out information you claim to possess, but if you are lying to me, vampire, and have led us here on some poisonous whim, I swear–'

Morgane rounded on him, narrowing her eyes. 'Yes, yes, I understand perfectly well – my existence hangs by a thread! You know, you show remarkable confidence, ven Denst, threatening me at every turn when I could rip you in half without breaking my stride!' She flinched with revulsion. 'If I did not need your help as much as you need mine, I would have left you a mangled corpse in Hollowcrest, but to think that I have degraded myself by consorting with you and your offspring is almost more than I can bear.'

He allowed himself a smile. He patted the stakes in his belt.

'Just say the word,' he told her softly, 'and this sick farce can come to an end, right now.'

They each heard the scrape of soil at the same time, the sound of damp earth being turned over. Galen pulled his gun and took cover behind the crooked trunk of a thorn tree. Morgane seemed to melt into the shadows, a streak of ink, with only the red pinpricks of her dead eyes glowing in the darkness.

'Hello?' a tremulous voice called out. 'Who's there?'

Galen cocked his pistol. In the stillness of the cemetery the sound was as loud as a gunshot.

'Cemetery's closed for the night,' the voice said. 'Come back in the morning, if you're here paying your respects.'

'You can lower your weapon,' the vampire's cold voice whispered in Galen's ear. 'It's only the gravedigger.'

Galen stepped from the shadows behind the tree and crossed onto the cemetery's central path. At the other end, standing in the middle of a pool of light from the graveyard's solitary lamp, an old man stood with a shovel in his hand and a look of wary suspicion on his face. He had a cloth cap pushed back on his head, a straggly beard, and his overalls looked as though they'd never been washed.

'You don't look much like a mourner,' he said. He peered at Galen's coat, the breastplate, the lowered pistol in his hand. His eyes strayed to Jael Morgane and he staggered backwards. He gave a stifled gasp and made the sign of the comet.

'Hammer protect me!'

Galen could feel Morgane's pleasure radiating from her as they crossed over to meet the gravedigger, the quickening of her vampiric blood. She needed fear the way he needed his cigars or Doralia her firewater – a little jolt to get the system going. It was sickening.

'I am an agent of the Order of Azyr,' he said. 'Time is pressing and I don't have enough of it to explain. You are safe while you are with me, the vampire will not harm you.' He looked at Morgane. 'You have my word.'

If anything, the old man now looked even more afraid. He whipped off his cap and smoothed down the few errant hairs on his scalp.

'Anything to be of service, sir,' he mumbled. 'Sigmar protect me...'

'You live here, in the gatehouse?'

'Aye, sir, if it please you. Gravedigger here born and bred, all my life, sir.'

'Have you seen anything strange recently?' Galen pressed him. 'Anyone suspicious skulking around here? A man accompanied by a young boy?'

The gravedigger's face creased as he tried to think of the right answer. The eternal curse of the order, Galen thought. They had to inspire fear, but sometimes fear could be far less productive than trust.

'I couldn't rightly say, sir,' he quavered. 'Not that I've noticed particularly, but... well, as you see sir, I'm an old man, and...'

'Forget it, ven Denst,' Morgane said, dismissively. She eyed the gravedigger as if he were something she had scraped off her shoe. 'If this old fool had seen anything he would have remembered it.'

'Agreed,' Galen said. He dismissed the gravedigger, who bowed clumsily and scurried off deeper into the graveyard, no doubt to shut himself in his gatehouse and thank Sigmar on his knees for delivering him from Jael Morgane. 'Then we're back where we started, and no closer to the truth. Damn it!' he cried.

'He's here!' a voice shouted over the fence. 'Briomedes – he's here in the city!'

Galen turned and saw his daughter running for the gate, her coat billowing out behind her. She tore the coiled rope aside and came up to them. There was a furious-looking bruise across her forehead and flecks of dried blood spattered across her breastplate.

'What happened to your hat?' he asked her. It looked like she'd just pulled it from a fire.

'Long story.'

'And Briomedes?'

'He's been here a few days at least,' she panted as she gathered her breath. 'Two off-duty guardsmen from the Iron Bulls saw him coming in at the west gate, the boy with him. Seemed to think he'd been poking around the grave pits out there.'

'There you have it,' Morgane crowed. 'What did I say? And he has several days on us already. Too slow, old man.'

Doralia shrugged. 'Seems to be the case, there's no denying it. He's got the jump on us.'

'What do we do then, ven Denst?' Morgane demanded. 'Wait here, see if the dead rise inside the city? Or head out to the grave pits and hope he's there ahead of us?'

He stopped his hand from reaching for a cigar. He tried to think, but his thoughts were a roar of competing demands, possibilities, dangers.

The grave pits were the greater danger, he knew, but as long as the walls of Excelsis stood they would be hard-pressed to break through. If Briomedes raised the dead from the cemeteries as well, though, then the gates could easily fall from both sides – they could not defeat an enemy both without and within. It must be St Solicus, he thought, it must! But then Briomedes was not here, there was no denying it. And if he was not here, then there was only one other possibility…

He made his choice, and Sigmar help him if it was the wrong one.

'To the west gate,' he said.

* * *

The west bastion was a mile-wide square of demarcated land on the north edge of the Veins, a parade ground of beaten earth in the centre, barracks and armouries on the north flank. Under normal circumstances, the whole bastion would have been ringed by a low defensive wall with overlapping firing steps and squat, circular towers embedded in its span, but all that had been swept away during the violence of the siege. The inner wall was little more than rubble, most of the stone having been plundered to repair the defences on either side of the barbican, which was now only a shadow of its former self. The two tall flanking towers of black stormstone on either side of the city gate had once been perfect in their power and symmetry, each ten storeys high with arrow-slit windows and barbettes on the crown for a network of cannons, volley guns and rocket batteries. Now, the right-hand tower had been hewn down to its foundations. Although the left still stood to its former height, the walls on the city-facing side had been shorn completely away. It was like looking at a doll's house, or a hive of bees: Galen could see each floor open to the elements, the wooden stairs that connected each level, the adjutants flitting to guardrooms and stockades, bored soldiers on duty with their weapons shouldered as they shifted their weight from foot to foot.

A patrol of guardsmen from the Iron Bulls were just setting off along the Neck, the narrow road that ran around the inside of the city walls and passed through the two towers, but other than that the barbican looked woefully undermanned. On either side, the city walls were covered in scaffolding as the long, slow labour of repair went on.

This was one of the three main entrances to Excelsis by land, Galen thought, and it looked as if a stiff breeze would send it tumbling down.

The gate had been more forcefully repaired at least, and now stood there barring the entrance to the city with its two vast doors of reinforced Ghyranian ironoak, each portal set with thick brass bands and iron rivets. The horse gate in the centre of the right-hand door was open and was admitting a party of workmen as Galen, Doralia and Jael approached. They looked like gravediggers, he thought, bearing shovels and wheelbarrows, scarves tied around their mouths. The grave pits, a good mile from the city, were still being filled and maintained it seemed. Bodies bursting to the surface by the weight of their putrefaction, the slurry of decomposition staining the earth around them... Sometimes, when the wind blew softly from the west, the whole of the Veins could smell the dead. And the grave pits on this side of the city were only a fraction of what had been burned or buried in the aftermath of the siege. Freeguild troops and orruks alike, aelves and duardin and ogors – there was no sentiment in the wake of battle. Only the Stormcasts, Sigmar's blessed warriors, avoided the earthly contamination of death, their golden souls lancing back to the heavens on a spear point of lightning.

Galen looked to the sky, black and clouded, rolling like the deep. He was no hero. There would be no such journey for him when he died, he was quite sure. Too many questionable decisions, too many acts that in any other line of work would be considered crimes. No, his soul was blacker than most now.

There was a short flight of stone stairs leading up from the guardhouse to the Neck by the left-hand tower. Galen could see Captain Huber coming down them, the kind of bitterly harassed look on her face that only came from talking to a senior officer. He hailed her as they approached the gate.

'Agent ven Denst?' she said. Again, she glanced with fear and disgust at the vampire, although Galen could tell that she was enough of a career soldier to know not to ask questions where they weren't wanted. 'I passed on your information to the colonel, but, to put it mildly, he doesn't view the situation with the same urgency you do. He's aware we don't have the numbers here to properly defend against much of anything.'

'Damn the man,' Galen scorned. 'As if that would make our enemies draw off, rather than the opposite. Bring a few of your best soldiers,' he said. 'Decent handgunners if you have them.'

'But, sir, Colonel Alicanthus...' Captain Huber said.

Galen set his jaw. 'Here, captain, my authority is absolute.'

The captain nodded and hastened off to the temporary barracks at the base of the ruined right-hand tower. There was a snap of urgency in her step, Galen noted. No doubt she was bored with the menial duties of repair and craved something a little more interesting. Well, he would see what he could do...

Galen stepped back and looked up at the broken tower as it loomed above them, its open floors and chambers, the stairs and passageways, the ropes that had been strung across the empty spaces where the walls had been.

'Colonel Alicanthus!' he cried, his voice booming back from the stormstone city wall. He stood there on the rough parade ground with his hands on his hips, amongst the quarried stone that was being used to repair the bastion. Soldiers and workmen passing from the gate stopped and looked at him, the witch hunter in his leather duster, his breastplate gleaming, moustache bristling on his lip and the grizzled grey hair caught in the stinking breeze. Faces looked curiously down from the open spaces in the tower. From the chamber at the very top, Galen could see the tiny, pale face of the colonel peering over the edge.

'It's a commander's job to understand the conditions on the ground, colonel!' Galen shouted up at him. 'Not to hide aloof in his tower.' In the corner of his eye, he saw some of the gathered soldiers stifling a laugh. 'I will be taking some of your troops beyond the walls,' he said. 'Ready the remainder of your forces.'

'Damn your insolence, ven Denst!' the colonel shouted. His

voice, caught in the breeze, drifted weakly down. 'This is my regiment, my command!'

'This is Sigmar's regiment, and Sigmar's city,' Galen shouted. 'And my word carries Sigmar's weight when the city is threatened. Ready what troops you have, colonel. Send runners to every regiment in Excelsis. Prepare to fight, man!'

He gestured to Doralia and Huber. The captain had returned with a handful of her troops, four hard-looking men with well-maintained handguns and short swords on their hips. Jael Morgane stood off to the side and looked on them with barely disguised contempt.

'I suppose I should arm myself too,' she said, her languid voice unable to quite disguise her concern. 'If we have to refight the siege, then I'd rather not do it with my bare hands.'

'Sir?' Captain Huber said, glancing at Galen. 'Is that right? Are the forces of Kragnos coming again?'

'You could say that,' the vampire said, with a mocking laugh. 'Although perhaps not in quite the same state as when you last saw them...'

Morgane turned to one of the guardsmen Huber had volunteered and gave him an evil smile, her hand outstretched. Slowly, as if against his own will and with sweat beading on his forehead, the soldier drew his sword and passed it to her, hilt first. She gave it an exploratory swing.

'Cheap and mass-produced,' she sighed. 'No craftsmanship at all. The balance is appalling, and you'd have a hard time cutting a loaf of bread with this blade, let alone someone's throat. Still,' she grinned, glancing at Galen, 'you fight with the weapons you have, ven Denst, rather than the ones you would like. Isn't that right?'

CHAPTER EIGHTEEN

AFTERMATH OF WAR

They walked in silence, a mile from the city to the fields of the dead. The braziers arranged along the high walls of Excelsis cast down an eerie, flickering glow onto the scrubland before them as their boots crunched across the dirt. There was a sense beyond that ring of light of a vast and sultry darkness; of endless, dusty plains that stretched on and on until they met the wild, abandoned seas, and beyond them only storm and fury and a deeper darkness. All of Ghur lay before them, a mighty beast at rest, shivering with night-tremors, gripped by some insensate hunger it could barely understand.

Galen, carrying a torch to light their way, led them on. Captain Huber was by his side as they ranged out in front of the others. She knew the way to the grave pits, although any one of his odd patrol could have found them simply by following their nose.

He was impressed by the young officer, he had to admit. There was steel in her. She seemed tough and capable, ready to take on any task that befell her without complaint. If there were still leaders like this in Excelsis, then perhaps not all was lost.

'You saw action during the siege, then?' he asked her. The darkness kept his voice low.

'I joined the regiment afterwards, sir,' she said. 'But although I wasn't a soldier during it, I saw plenty of action all the same…'

'The struggle against Sigmar's enemies makes soldiers of us all, whether we wear a uniform or not,' he said solemnly.

'Had to barricade our house down near the harbour,' she said. 'When the ogor mercenaries turned against us…' Her voice faltered as she drew on those memories. With a visible effort she rallied herself. 'Made it through, though. So did my mother and father, I'm glad to say. After that, it just seemed common sense to get myself some proper training in case I needed to do it again. Which I've had to, and more than once. Our enemies never seem to sleep, do they, sir?'

'No, and I would be lying to you if I said your chances of even more fighting were slim,' he told her. 'It's a sad fact, but the benefits of peace will only be felt by those who gain a future from our actions now.'

'Always seems to be the case, sir,' Huber said. She rattled her sword in its scabbard. 'Peace has never been a gift freely given.'

Galen smiled. 'You have made your parents proud, captain, I'm quite sure.'

'I'd rather it was my colonel, sir.'

A faint track had been worked into the soil from the passage of the gravediggers, and he tried to follow it as best he could in the gloom. Behind him, he could see the diminishing prospect of Excelsis. On the other side of the city, the chained Spear of Mallus was wreathed in rippling blue energy, the tides of Excelsis Harbour washing around its base. He could see lights rising over there from the Kharadron's aether-berth, their frigates and ironclads slipping their moorings and heading out along their endless trade routes. The Floating Towers of the Collegiate Arcane flickered with corposant around the Spear, and he could even see the high spiral of the Grand Librarium, still standing after the siege, even though much of its precious stock had been destroyed in the fighting.

What the claws of ignorant orruks do not tear apart, the ravages of fire will soon see to...

The city, one of the greatest in the Mortal Realms, looked fragile to him all of a sudden, a faint ember that burned against the encroaching darkness. Every city he had travelled to in his long career was, in the end, no more than a candle flame in a hurricane, trying to stay lit. He would not be the one to see the fire go out. He swore it.

Doralia and Jael followed close behind, the four Iron Bulls handgunners spread out as they crossed over the darkened plain, their weapons drawn. The stench began to thicken around them. Ahead, on the very edge of the darkness, Galen could see a faint rise in the ground, the suggestion of broken earth. Before much longer, about a mile outside the city, they were all on the cusp of the grave pits. He took one of the cheroots from his pocket and hastily lit it.

'Doesn't seem like the most pleasant surroundings for a cigar,' Doralia said.

'It's for the smell,' Galen said, breathing out the rich, fragrant smoke. 'I can't think my cheroots will be doing my lungs any more damage than this charnel-reek.'

One of the handgunners turned to vomit, while the others covered their mouths. Only Jael Morgane was unconcerned. The effect on the others seemed to amuse her.

'You're all poor advertisements for mortality,' she laughed. 'Not for the first time, I'm glad I have no need to breathe.'

Calling them mere 'grave pits' did them a gross disservice. Such a phrase brought to mind a hastily dug hole in the ground, fit to sling a few corpses in, but these were lavish constructions, each one at least four hundred feet across. Only the duardin engineers of the Ironweld Arsenal knew how deep they were, but if Galen had been told they stretched down to the bowels of Ghur itself, he wouldn't have been surprised. There were three of them altogether, arranged in a rough semicircle. Vast earthen ramps had been built up at the side of each pit, the better to tip the bodies in, and he could see that a clever system of interconnected pathways had been marked out for the endless chain of barrows and carts bringing the dead from the city limits. Two of the pits had been filled in and covered over again, the earth forming a slight barrow above them, while the last was still open to the elements, its grotesque contents on plain display. As they approached, a trio of bone-vultures raggedly flapped up from the bodies on their greasy wings. They disappeared into the night, shrieking their outrage at being disturbed. Vultures of another kind picked amongst the leavings too, and Galen saw a few scavenger-folk scramble from the open pit and vanish into the darkness.

'Disgusting,' Captain Huber said. She gestured to one of the handgunners, who fired a quick warning shot into the air.

'Even the dead can have value, if you're poor enough,' Morgane said.

'You've suddenly developed a social conscience, have you?' Galen said. 'Your admirable concern for the poor aside, can you sense him here? Briomedes?'

'Yes…' she said, and even though the Ghurish night was warm and humid, the vampire seemed to shiver. She wrapped her arms around her chest. 'It's the same as at the cemetery. He has been here, or… or he's *still* here somehow. I can't explain it.'

Galen walked to the lip of the open pit and stared down at the jumbled corpses beneath him, holding up his torch to illuminate them. He took a long pull on his cigar and wreathed himself in its exhaled smoke. The level of the bodies was perhaps six feet down from the surface: plenty of space for more, and more were being dug out of the ruins in Excelsis every day. He could see the bloated, half-rotten forms of dead orruks, their armour stripped, those savage, pugnacious faces collapsed in on themselves with putrefaction. There in the slurry he could see the dank, matted fur of dead skaven; the burly corpses of ogors wrapped in rotten loincloths. There were even gargants in the mire – a massive protruding fist still clenched in a gesture of rage and destruction, each finger near five feet long; a slumped and empty face half buried in the bodies. He could see the cavern of its eye socket, the darkness within.

'No daemons at least,' Doralia said quietly at his side. 'They don't leave bodies behind when they die. If they do die.'

'They are things too foul and unnatural to leave earthly remains,' he said. 'A small consolation, but one we must take.'

'I wonder where they buried *our* dead,' she said. 'Not here, I hope.'

He sighed. The sight of all this had drained the energy from him. So much blood and treasure had been spent to put all these creatures in the ground, and still it wasn't enough. How much more must the city suffer?

He felt his daughter's hand on his shoulder. He wanted to reach up and take it, to squeeze her fingers and let her know that they would win through again, but he couldn't make the gesture. He cast the stub of his cigar into the pit, where it fizzled out in the slop of some dead ogor's guts. The night thrummed around them, febrile, mysterious.

Like a storm about to break, he thought. *If so, then let it break sooner rather than later. Anything is better than this waiting.*

Doralia, as if reading his thoughts, said, 'Show me the target and let me shoot, and I'm happy. This uncertainty bears down on the nerves, though. Standing here, waiting, on the strength of a vampire's word.'

Galen looked round at the others. Huber was examining the edges of the other pits, crouching now and then to run her fingers through the soil. Morgane stood alone, her arms folded, her head bowed and eyes closed. She was a shadow in the darkness, unmoving.

'I'm sorry,' he said.

'Father?'

'For putting you in this position. I...' He swallowed. 'I hope you can forgive me.'

Doralia squeezed his shoulder. She tried to smile.

'I never thought I'd be working alongside any vampire, let alone Jael Morgane, but we do what we have to do. You know that.'

He shook his head. He stared down at the corpses again, as if he would find his answers there in the muck.

'I don't just mean this, with Morgane. I mean the whole thing. The order, the horrors I have forced you into.' He saw her eyes go hard and he quickly took her hand. 'I regret what I said outside Hollowcrest, more than you can know. You're the best witch hunter I've ever seen, better than I ever was. Better than your mother, even. I only wish I had given you the chance for a normal life, away from...' He kicked a stone into the pit. 'Away from *this*.'

Doralia took his hand in both of hers. 'There is no such thing as a normal life, father,' she said. 'There's only life, or death. That's it. And you gave me life.'

Galen nodded, not trusting himself to speak. *Where there is life,* he thought, *there is always hope.*

'Agent ven Denst!' Captain Huber called suddenly. 'Come and see this!'

She was standing now at the edge of the furthermost pit. It stretched away from her into the darkness, a rucked sheet of beaten earth, distorted here and there by bubbles of corpse gas erupting from the soil. Galen and Doralia ran over. Huber pointed at the shadows, but Galen could see nothing.

'What is it?'

'The light, sir,' Huber said. 'Look, there! Running over the surface.'

He stared across the grave site, and slowly his eyes adjusted. He could see it, a faint trace of mist flickering across the soil, the colour of amethyst. The stench of corpses thickened in the air, and the ground began to tremble beneath him. This was it. Galen drew his sword.

'Fan out!' he cried. 'Find Briomedes before it's too late.'

He looked to Jael Morgane. Her fingers were tangled in her hair, her face distended by an awful, silent cry. She was shuddering, as if wracked by a fever.

'He's here!' she cried. 'He's here!'

'Where?' Galen demanded. 'Show me, damn you, and let me cut him down for his profanity!'

He whipped around to scan the shadows, saw Doralia running to the other side of the grave pits. She sprinted up the slope of the ramp by the open grave and stood there, panning her crossbow round, seeing nothing. Excelsis fumed in the distance, a blurred line of light and life hunkered on a brutal shore.

Morgane staggered over to the rising mist as it flowed around the grave pits. Her expression was numb, as if she weren't there at all and was strolling instead through the dark glades of her imagination. She reached out and let the purple mist run through her fingers. She turned to Galen. Her eyes were dim.

'See, ven Denst? He is here... He is right here...'

'What madness are you talking, vampire? Where is the necromancer? What is this?'

'This is what he's been doing,' she said. 'Every grave site beyond the city walls, every cemetery within it... He's laced some part of his essence into the earth, some element of his power, his soul. I don't know how he's done it' – she laughed, a brittle sound in the night that smothered them – 'but he doesn't need to be here in person. He *is* here. He's everywhere. Wherever the dead are, ven Denst... there is Briomedes.'

'Father!' Doralia cried. She ran back down the slope as if the dead already followed. 'They're rising!'

Galen sprinted to the open grave pit. He raised his torch, let its flickering light fall down onto that awful scene: a foul brew of rotting flesh, rancid bones and mouldering cloth, all lit now by that strange amethyst smoke.

The gargant's curled fist began to twitch. The fingers, grey with necrosis, slowly unfurled, the black nails cracked and flaking. The layer of bodies around it began to rise and fall, orruks and ogors and skaven shuddering together as if caught in some subterranean tide. Eyes that had been closed by arrow or sword suddenly flicked open. Mouths that had last screamed at the moment of their death began to writhe and champ.

'In the name of Sigmar...' Galen whispered. How many thousands in this pit alone? How many thousands in the others, in all the grave pits that ringed Excelsis? All of them beginning to stir...

'Agent ven Denst!' Captain Huber shouted.

There, at the furthest pit, the earth was shuddering. Dead hands and arms were thrust out from the depths, the lolling heads of corpses breaking through the soil. Dead orruks shambled from their graves, the slime of corruption dripping from their rotting bodies. The stench of death buffeted from the pits, so powerful now that Galen thought he might be sick.

By the other pit on the far left, Galen saw one of the handgunners being dragged to the ground, his leg caught by a rotting fist. His comrade, panicking, discharged his weapon and blew apart the soldier's knee. His scream tore across the night, so shrill they must have heard it all the way back in Excelsis. More hands lunged from the dirt, tearing at the handgunner, dragging him back into the boiling soil. Behind them, rising implacably from the earth, came a mouldering slop of corpses slowly gaining their feet.

'Help me!' the handgunner cried. Bodies flopped on top of him. Dead claws tore at his face. 'For Sigmar's sake, help!'

The other guardsman desperately tried to reload his weapon, but before he could do anything Captain Huber ran over and grabbed him by the collar.

'Leave him!' she shouted, pulling him back from the edge of the pit. 'There's nothing we can do.'

She drew her own pistol, her teeth bared, and with a trembling hand shot her screaming comrade in the head.

It was like fighting the sea as it smothered the shore. Galen threw his torch to the ground and wielded his blade two-handed, hacking down at the corpses as they dragged themselves from the open pit. He split skulls, chopped off gangling arms. Although a dozen bodies fell back, a thousand more were slowly rising to take their place. The gargant was hauling itself from the slop, corpses tumbling from its shoulders. It reached for the lip of the grave and drew itself to its feet, staggering onto the soil of the plains. He saw his daughter running from the slope on the other side, pivoting to slash the head from a lumbering orruk, its feet tangled in its own putrid entrails.

'We can't even begin to slow them down,' she cried as she drew near. 'We have to get back to the city now!'

She stared up at the gargant as it lurched forward. It looked at them without seeing, the hinge of its jaw lopsided and slack, its rotting mind intent only on the distant walls of Excelsis. The grey, distended flesh of its belly suddenly split open, unleashing a cloud of green corpse gas and a bubbling flood of putrefaction that splattered into the dirt. There, crawling and flopping in the spilled guts and stinking slime, he saw the half-digested remains of Freeguild soldiers, plucked from the streets during the siege, and now cruelly resurrected alongside the monster that had choked them down.

He felt acid in his throat, the surge of vomit. Doralia, grim-faced, took careful aim with her crossbow and shot a bolt through the gargant's glassy eye. The nullstone tore apart the chains of necromancy, the invisible web which kept its foul form together. The gargant's head slammed backwards; it tipped to the side, toppled, fell back into the grave pit to a ragged cheer from Captain Huber and her Iron Bulls. They backed off from the edge of the pits, their guns playing a discordant percussion. Bullets smashed through skulls and tore chunks of flesh from the bones of the dead, but it was like throwing pebbles into the ocean. He saw Jael Morgane striding through the line of corpses towards them, her blade slick with gore.

Gods, he thought, *but it almost looks like she's enjoying herself…*

Galen locked eyes with his daughter in silent agreement. 'Fall back!' he cried. 'Make for the city!'

They turned and ran, sprinting across the midnight scrubland, and there in the darkness behind them rolled the oncoming horde. Ahead, the lights of Excelsis seemed frail, faint things burning in the shadows, a wavering glow of sanctuary. He put his head down, the pain unshackling in his hips. He gritted his teeth, his sword heavy in his hand. How much heavier would it feel, he wondered, before the night was through?

CHAPTER NINETEEN

THE WEST GATE

The gates of Excelsis rose before them like a cliff face, black iron-wood painted in golden torchlight from the broken wall above. Candles flamed in the slitted windows of the remaining barbican tower. Lamps flickered on the battlements and on the scaffolding that held them up. There was something shivering and panicked about those lights, Doralia thought, her chest heaving after their run across the plain. A sense of confusion and disorder. As they approached, she could hear the clash of steel, the rising shouts of soldiers. There was a crackle of gunfire, a drawn-out, horrified scream. The horse gate was still open, but as they got closer an Iron Bulls trooper with blood smeared across his face scrambled to close it.

'Wait!' Captain Huber screamed. 'Hold that gate, soldier!'

The trooper fell to his knees. His eyes were hazy and he held one hand up to staunch a gash in his neck. Blood dribbled through his fingers, his green jacket soaked black with it. Huber ran to his side and pressed a handkerchief to the wound as Doralia pushed past. She stepped through the horse gate and down the short, sheltered corridor beneath the barbican, straight into a scene of madness.

'By the gods,' Galen muttered at her side. Quickly he reloaded his pistol. Doralia checked her quiver.

'Hardly twenty bolts left,' she said. 'And all the dead of St Solicus to deal with...'

Deadwalkers choked the parade ground in front of them, spilling from the Veins into the acre of beaten earth, smothering it from end to end. Doralia saw corpses tumbling over the ruined foundations of the defensive wall far on the other side, dead bodies lurching to their feet and staggering onwards towards the gates, hundreds more still pouring down the side streets on the northern edge. Screams rose from those streets, shouts of panic as the city's civilians realised what was walking in their midst. Some of the dead were so ancient they were little better than skeletons cloaked in musty grave shrouds. Others limped and shuffled, arms groping for those who still lived, their vacant eyes empty and unseeing. Most had been casualties of the siege, their bodies hewn by terrible wounds and broken down by implacable decay. Scraps of flesh fell from them as they stumbled across the parade ground, ropes of skin, the greasy stew of rotten organs. Some even wore the decaying uniforms of Freeguild regiments, defenders of the city who had been laid to rest with military honours, now risen to rend their comrades limb from limb.

The Iron Bulls, vastly outnumbered, scrambled to hold the dead back. A mob of guardsmen rushed out of the barracks on the far side of the broken tower to Doralia's left, only to disappear into the shambling mass of corpses. She saw a sword rise and fall, heard a faint, high-pitched scream that shrieked off into silence. Other troops emerged from the tower itself, hastily buckling on their breastplates, drawing their swords, snapping the wheel-lock mechanisms of their handguns. They backed off, waiting for orders, their faces frozen masks of horror. Gunshots popped erratically from the tower, from the troops who scurried back across the parade ground from the old bastion wall and from those who stood in the scaffolding by the city gates. Arrows lanced out of the darkness, falling with no effect into the deadwalkers' unfeeling flesh. Doralia snapped a bolt from her crossbow, straight into one deadwalker's skull not ten yards in front of her. The corpse fell to the ground, where it was trampled to pieces under the feet of the others. She may as well have thrown a stick or a stone for all the difference it made. She drew her sword and slung the strap of her crossbow over her head.

'Colonel Alicanthus!' Galen shouted up at the tower. Doralia saw the colonel's frightened pale face appear at the open wall of his chamber. 'Get down here at once, man! Lead your troops!' Galen turned away with a snort of disgust. 'Damn him,' he said. 'Bloody coward. He'd rather the city fell, as long as he was the last to die.'

'What do we do?' Doralia said. The dead were no more than twenty feet from them now, a buffeting stench preceding them. 'How do we find Briomedes when we have to fight through an army to get to him?'

Captain Huber ran past them and started roughly pushing the guardsmen into a defensive line. She beckoned others over from the barbican tower, handgunners in front, spearmen behind. She had no more than a hundred troops to work with, but Doralia could see what she was doing. It might be enough.

'Captain Huber!' Galen called. 'You have the command. Hold the dead off from the gate!' He looked up at the defences above the gate, the smashed and crenellated walls on either side, the flimsy scaffolding holding it all together. Some of the troops on the walkway up there had finally noticed the hordes lumbering in from the wastelands. Their panicked screams plucked at the courage of their comrades below. 'And get more troops on the walls!'

'What troops?' she cried. 'This is it, ven Denst!'

Doralia pulled her pistol, snapped out a shot at the cemetery dead. The two witch hunters retreated to take cover behind Huber's Freeguild. The handgunners in the front row began to fire nervously, while the spearmen at the back began to waver. On came the corpses, relentless, unstoppable.

'This is just one gate,' Doralia said. 'This could be happening at every side of the city, in every street. We need to find the necromancer *now*.'

Galen looked around. 'Where's that cursed vampire?' he muttered. 'Morgane, you scum! If you have more information to trade for your worthless life, then now is the time to do it!' He turned to Doralia. There was no doubt in him, she saw, no uncertainty. There was just the decision to be made, and the will to carry it through.

Morgane appeared on the edge of the torchlight behind them, her blade still in hand. Some of the troops in Huber's cobbled-together unit gave her a nervous glance and tried to shuffle away from her. More so even than the deadwalkers, there was something undeniably wrong about her, something malicious and unnatural radiating from her very being. Even now, after this long in her company, she made Doralia feel sick. Her fingers tightened on the trigger of her crossbow.

'Briomedes isn't here,' the vampire told them in a cold voice. 'He doesn't need to be, and my best guess is that he's already at the Spear.'

'How is he going to take it?' Galen demanded. 'What is his strategy here? Tell me, damn you!'

The vampire's eyes flashed with pleasure. 'Get me to the Spear and I'll tell you,' she drawled. 'Until then, don't presume to threaten me further.'

'Then go, now,' Galen said. 'Make yourself useful at last.' He looked up at the city walls behind them, the web of scaffolding, the handful of troops up on the battlements firing off a few ineffectual arrows into the scrubland beyond. He turned to Doralia. 'Go with her, find Briomedes. Kill him. Everything else is a mere holding action until Briomedes is dead.'

'What about you?' Doralia said.

Galen glanced around, a dour look on his face. 'I'll stay here. If we can hold the gate for even a few minutes more it might make a difference. A small difference, perhaps...'

'Wait!' Huber shouted to her troops. The dead shuffled closer, the contents of the cemetery regurgitated into the bastion. 'Wait, hold your fire...'

She chopped down with her arm. The front row disappeared in a cloud of gun smoke.

'Reload!' she cried. 'Rear rank, charge spears! Advance!'

The bristling line of spears came down and the guardsmen stepped nimbly through the gaps in the line of handgunners. The smoke cleared; there on the parade ground ahead of them were the splintered remains of a dozen corpses.

'Not nearly enough...' Huber said.

'We're going to have to do this the old-fashioned way, captain,' Galen said. He raised his sword and pointed at the dead. 'Doralia – hunt the necromancer down, and show no mercy. Any claims Briomedes could have made to clemency are gone now. He has unleashed hell on this city.'

Doralia nodded. She glanced at Morgane, who smiled luxuriantly at her. The undead didn't seem drawn to the vampire the same way they were drawn to the living, she had noticed. Did they see her as one of them? Or had they been instructed to avoid her? So much was being taken on trust here, and with one of the least trustworthy creatures in the realms, but what choice did she have now? Briomedes must be stopped.

'I will find you,' Galen said. He glanced at the meagre forces Captain Huber was trying to marshal. 'I know what I'm asking of you, daughter, but there aren't even a fraction of the troops needed to defend the gates here. One of us has to stay and help, and if the undead flood the city then it will be impossible to hunt the necromancer down. You'll be able to move faster than me – do not let yourself be turned aside for anything. Not for *anything*, do you understand?'

'Yes, father,' she said.

He gripped her shoulder. 'Be careful, my girl,' he said quietly. 'I do not know if you can trust Morgane, if her thirst for vengeance can overcome her thirst for blood, but do not forget what she is.'

'I won't,' Doralia said. She hefted her blade. 'I will see her dead as soon as the job is done.'

Galen nodded and looked away. The cold mask of duty fell back into place once more.

Doralia turned to go. This would be close work, she knew, and speed would be the only thing that would keep her alive. The whole city depended on how quickly she could reach the harbour, and how ruthlessly she could put the necromancer down.

She looked at the vampire, her red eyes, the blue veins under her perfect skin. There was a smear of blood on her mouth. She had fed this night, when no one was looking: a trooper, no doubt, snatched from the fringes of the action and dragged into the shadows to be devoured. Jael met her eyes and smiled, as if daring her to protest.

'Come then, dear girl,' she said. 'Let us make your father proud.'

CHAPTER TWENTY

THE BATTLE OF EXCELSIS

Captain Huber drew her sword as Galen pointed to the horde of the dead. He saw his daughter running with Morgane across the parade ground to the north, skirting the barracks and the mass of deadwalkers that milled about them, both of them hacking in with their swords to clear a path. He looked away; there was nothing he could do for her now. He had to trust in her skill at arms, her determination, as he now had to trust in his own.

'Sigmar watch over her,' he whispered. 'Captain?' he called. 'Send ten men back to reinforce the gate, or all this will be no more than a futile gesture.'

Huber gave a curt nod and called a few of her soldiers out of the formation. Galen could see some of the auxiliary troops at the gate frantically trying to bolster it with junk dragged from the lower floor of the barbican tower – tables and chairs, ammunition boxes, a bookcase even. Cooks and farriers, blacksmiths and tanners, everyone who could stand and hold a weapon was being pressed into the defence. And now the dead were almost upon them.

The corpses shuffled nearer, empty sockets and rotting eyes equally unseeing, their rotting limbs outstretched to tear them apart. Scraps of parchment-skin hung loosely from desiccated skulls. Others staggered in the greasy coils of their own guts, ropes of glistening intestine hanging down from their stomachs to entangle their feet. The stench was unbearable, the sight of this appalling army enough to twist anyone's mind into madness. One soldier leaned on his spear and spewed into the dirt, reeling as if he would faint. Galen saw Captain Huber step forward and pull him back into line with a firm instruction.

'One more volley, I think, Captain Huber!' Galen called. 'Point-blank should do it.'

Huber chopped her arm down again, the dead mere feet from them now, and the handgunners opened fire. Fifty firearms all shooting at once, the sound like a thunderclap, and when the smoke cleared another dozen deadwalkers lay in shuddering pieces on the beaten earth of the parade ground. Galen popped off a shot with his pistol, smashing the jaw from one corpse with a puff of bone dust.

'That's all that black powder can do for now,' he cried. 'Iron Bulls, into them!'

He charged forward, not even looking to see if he was being followed. Only a few bounding steps and then Galen was right in the midst of them, choking in the reek, swinging the great witch hunter's blade from a low guard and up into the first rank of the walking dead. Heads shattered under the impact, ribcages cracked open with a slop of putrefaction. He was spattered in slime but he kept swinging, using his blade as much as a cleaver or club as a weapon of finesse and subtlety. He hacked in great sweeping arcs until his arms felt like stone, smashing the corpses aside. Dead-walkers in the greying uniforms of Iron Bulls and Bronze Claws alike fell to his sword, and to each he muttered a small prayer to Sigmar to allay the torment of their souls. It was what his daughter would have done.

With a roar, the Iron Bulls charged in. Spears punched through the deadwalkers' bodies, lifting them from the ground until they jerked down the length of ironwood shafts. With a swift slash of a dagger or a short sword, heads were whipped from necks and the corpses cast aside. The handgunners, with less flair, hammered in with the butts of their guns. Skulls cracked, limbs were shattered. Galen saw Captain Huber lancing in with her sword, as lithe as if she were on the training ground, slicing off heads with a flick of her wrist. But still the dead kept coming.

'How's the gate looking, captain?' he called. He parried the scrabbling bony fist of a champing deadwalker, kicking out to send it sprawling on the ground where it was trampled by those that followed, a mangled wreck.

Huber risked a glance back. 'They've reinforced it as best they can. Can't see it's going to be enough for what's coming, though.'

'If we can slow them down, then we've done enough.'

He felt something scrabbling at his leg, looked down to see a corpse gnawing on his calf with a mouthful of rotten teeth. Galen grimaced and smashed its skull apart with the pommel of his sword.

Inexorably, they were being pushed back. The whole bastion was utterly overrun, from the ruined wall on the street side of the parade ground, to the grand city walls themselves. The tide of the dead surged up and over them, lapping against what remained of the barbican and the barricaded gate. This was more than the contents of one cemetery. The dead had arisen all over the city, and his stomach turned cold at the thought of this scene being played out at each bastion.

'There're too many!' Huber cried.

'Break out!' he yelled. 'Make for the stairs and the Neck, and then onto the walls!'

The corpses were behind them now, the rotting denizens of St Solicus pulling soldiers to the ground and ripping them apart. Galen saw one young lad, still alive, his face wrenched with horror, as two deadwalkers dabbled in his guts. By the edge of the barbican tower, a handgunner was swinging his weapon like a club, sweeping the corpses off their feet, still fighting as he went down and the dead began their grisly work.

They were surrounded now, and near half of Huber's command had fallen. Everywhere he looked, the deadwalkers shambled onwards, unstoppable. The dead of the grave pits were almost on the city from the other side, and Excelsis could muster no more than a few ragged regiments to oppose them. Even the Stormcasts might not be enough to make a difference, and their numbers were perilously low since the siege. A lesser man might have given in to despair then, but Galen ven Denst was not like lesser men. The odds against victory were meaningless. The prospect of success made no difference to the execution of duty. Where there was life, there was hope.

And where there is hate, there can be only vengeance.

Back to back with Captain Huber, the dead swarming around them in a stinking mob, Galen prepared to die. It did not take him long – it was something for which he had been preparing most of his life.

'It was an honour to fight by your side, captain,' he said. 'You know, you remind me of my daughter, and I can think of no higher praise.'

'The honour was mine, sir,' she said, her arm untiring as she hacked and slashed at the corpses. 'And if your daughter is half the fighter you are, I still hold out hope for victory.'

Galen laughed. 'Pity Sigmar's enemies when such warriors still oppose them.'

A high, pealing note suddenly blazed against the night, a brass chime that struck courage into the hearts of all those who heard it. The dead paid it no mind, but to the men and women of the Iron Bulls, it was the sound of liberation.

'The Palatine Guard!' Huber called. Galen cut through the dead behind them, trying to make for the stairs that led up onto the Neck. He took the first step and peered across the torchlit parade ground, the horde of corpses that mobbed and shuddered across it, the tattered bodies of dead Freeguild troops. He could see a thin line of soldiers charging in from the north-east of the Veins, vaulting the ruined bastion wall and pounding across the parade ground: tough, well-built troops in rich purple tunics and gold breastplates, their helmets topped with tall white-and-blue plumes. There was perhaps only a company of them, two hundred soldiers at most, but each wielded a polished halberd, and those weapons were far from ceremonial. As Galen watched, and as the Palatine Guard reached the horde of deadwalkers threatening the gate, they swung their halberds in a crisp and precise arc. Heads tumbled, limbs were scattered, the Guard sweeping into the deadwalkers with all the poise and military perfection of a regiment giving a display on the Festival of Sigmar's Tempest.

'They're a long way from the palace,' Huber called, as Galen reached for her hand. He dragged her up onto the steps and together they laid about them into the corpses that tried to follow. Galen split a deadwalker's skull in two, the grey brain matter splattering out onto the steps. The creature tipped to the side and fell into the throng that followed it. Behind the dead, the Palatine Guard were a thin, purple line slowly cutting its way towards them.

'Either it was a parade coming up the Pilgrim's Way, or the High Arbiter had realised what's happening – who knows, captain, but I'm not going to question it!'

Galen cut down and severed an arm that was reaching for his ankle. He pulled Huber further up the stairs, and together they ran for the scaffolding where the city stonemasons had been trying to repair the wall above the gate. The great network of platforms and struts stretched up a full ninety feet to the crenellated battlements, and in some places it was all that was keeping the wall in place. They had not had nearly enough time to restore it. Below them, at the gate itself, the few soldiers who had managed to barricade it were now fighting for their lives, desperately trying to hold off the zombies until the Palatine troops could reach them.

'Just hold on,' Galen muttered. 'Every minute counts now...'

They set foot to the first rungs of the ladders that led into the warren of scaffolding. Galen glanced up at the highest floor of the tower on his left, looming above them: a honeycomb of empty chambers and abandoned rooms, with every soldier bar one having hurried down to the defence. Colonel Alicanthus was nowhere to be seen, but Galen hoped the man had done the decent thing – a bottle of firewater and a pistol, and he could perhaps rescue a small scrap of his honour. If not, Galen had a bullet in his pouch for him, and he was more than willing to use it.

His heart clamoured for rest, and his legs felt like he was treading water. On he hiked, up the ramps and ladders, Captain Huber behind him. How much longer could he force himself onwards at this pace? Even the captain, a good thirty years his junior, looked blown out with exhaustion.

Be just my damned luck to drop dead from a heart attack before this is finished...

There was a hot, gravelly burn at the back of his throat, the faint taste of blood. Those black spots were back in front of his eyes. Galen shook his head clear and carried on, hand over hand, one rung at a time, one ramp and then another; and then finally they were at the top of the barbican wall – what remained of it, at any rate. Galen knew it should stretch at least another sixty feet higher, but most of it had been smashed down by the forces of Kragnos when they besieged Excelsis. This was as good as they had managed to repair in the time since, and it wasn't nearly good enough.

The night wind whipped clear, cold and sharp, and the clamour of violence far below was no more than the ringing of distant steel. The skies above broiled in the dark, a twisted whirlpool of black clouds streaked with midnight blue. Sconces lined the battlements at regular intervals, their torches fluttering in the breeze. Galen, hot from the climb, felt the sweat cooling against his face. There were a handful of soldiers up there, half a platoon at most. They stood on the walkway as if numb, rooted to the spot by what they could see approaching the city. Some had nocked arrows to their bows, but the bows hung slack in their hands. One young lad was crying, a stripling of sixteen at most, but nobody made a move to comfort him. Even the presence of Captain Huber, his commanding officer, didn't stop his tears. Galen rested against the wall, gasping for breath. He realised he had taken a cut across the face, and dried blood was caked against his cheek. Maybe not even his blood, who knew at this stage of the game? The walkway at the top of the battlements stretched on into the distance, where it curved around towards the southern bastion, but it was bare of troops. All that was left to defend the western wall of Excelsis were twenty raw soldiers, one of them in tears, and an old man.

'You don't like to take the easy jobs, do you?' Captain Huber said. She leaned against the broken wall, her sword in her hand, and stared off across the plains, the vast scrublands of Ghur stretching off into the limitless dark. 'I think your daughter might have had the simpler task.'

'Then you don't know what she's up against,' Galen said. 'Or who she has beside her.'

'The vampire?' Huber pointed her sword at the darkness beyond them. 'Reckon I'd take the vampire any day of the week, over *that...*'

Slowly, the dead of the grave pits were emerging from the shadows, stumbling into the light cast down onto the plains by the city. A silent, shambling horde with only one aim in what was left of their minds – kill that which lived. Leave nothing alive. Briomedes was going to flood Excelsis with the dead, forcing such a desperate fight on its overstretched defenders that no one would be able to stop him achieving his real aim.

He looked to the north, where the wall curved round into the misty dark. There the cold ocean battered the Coast of Tusks, and the harbour guarded the Spear of Mallus. He could see it, vast as a mountain, crackling with blue flame – ten miles away across the jagged peaks: the houses and temples, the spires of palaces and mansions, all the ruined architecture of Ghur's most powerful city. Were the dead pouring from other cemeteries, other grave pits, even now? Were the other gates on the verge of falling? Was his daughter running into a situation even more deadly than this one?

Galen turned to the west. The darkness fell away from the city like an ocean, and from that darkness came the living dead.

'It's more than I imagined,' Huber said. Her voice was shaking, but Galen didn't blame her. She rubbed a hand to her eye, pushed her hair out of her face. She gripped her sword. 'Much more.'

He could not have guessed at the numbers. Tens of thousands, at least. The horde, still perhaps a quarter of a mile from the city walls, stretched off so far to either side of the rucked scrubland that its flanks disappeared into the shadows. There were thousands of orruks, dead-eyed and slack-jawed, stripped of their armour. Few had weapons, but some still clutched crude swords and axes. Their skin was grey in the torchlight. In front of them, nimbler even in death, shuffled thousands of skaven, the ratmen's fur black with dried blood and grave slime. Ogors towered over the orruks, their thick, heavyset faces pulped with gunshot wounds, their massive, muscular limbs rent with sword thrust and axe blow. Towering even above the ogors were more gargants – Galen could see twenty of them, at least, their thick-legged strides crushing the corpses in their way and quickly leading them further out ahead of the horde. Vultures raggedly flapped to their shoulders and tore scraps of flesh from their bones. Though the corpses didn't make a sound, neither crying nor roaring with the lust for battle, the awful shuffling tread of so many deadwalkers was like a rolling, unsettled tide, sluggish with a pent-up rage.

'Aim for the gargants first!' Galen cried. He hastily reloaded his pistol and rested the barrel against his forearm. A few of the Iron Bulls were armed with handguns and they followed the witch hunter's lead, laying their weapons against the battlements. The archers, trembling with fear, drew back their bowstrings. 'Aim for the head. Even if we can only bring down one of them, we will have struck a blow for Sigmar.'

One of the archers dropped his bow and ran, wailing with terror, flinging himself down the scaffolding ladders a few rungs at a time. Huber cursed him and made to follow, but Galen held her back. The sounds of fighting down on the parade ground were as frantic as they had been before.

'Leave him,' he said. 'He'll find no safety down there. We must all choose our place.' He called out, so the other troops could hear. 'Where we fight, and where we die. That is the only choice left to you now!'

The gargants drew near, two hundred yards away now, the orruks and skaven and ogors shambling behind them.

One hundred yards.

The stench reached out like a malign hand to grip them all, the meagre defenders of the city.

'Make ready...' Galen called. He sighted along the barrel of his pistol. One shot, maybe two if he was lucky. That's all it came down to in the end. Make the shot, and make it count. 'Aim...'

The gargants lumbered on, some limping on mangled feet, others dragging their guts behind them. Their great jaws slowly opened and closed, as if their dead minds were lost in some remembered dream of gluttony. Their hands stretched out for the walls, each mighty fist big enough to crush a man to paste. Fifty yards now. Galen wiped the sweat from his forehead, sighted again down the length of the barrel.

'The one in the centre, everyone aim for it,' he shouted. 'We can take it down if we concentrate our fire.'

The gargant in question was a hideous thing, its skin spiralled in faded blue tattoos, a long Freeguild cannon hanging from its neck like a pendant. One half of its skull had been smashed in, and through a ragged tear in its cheek Galen could see its yellow champing teeth, each as big as his breastplate. He aimed carefully for its undamaged eye, a milky globe leaking fluid down its ruined face.

Twenty yards.

Huber was shaking beside him, sword drawn. The tallest of the gargants could easily reach the height of the barbican wall, so denuded had it been.

'Make the shot count...' Galen called.

The soldiers around him tensed to their guns, drew back the strings on their bows. He could feel them, poised, dreading the horror that approached them, waiting now only for the action to begin.

Sigmar guide my hand, Galen thought.

Ten yards.

'Fire!'

The crack of gunfire, the sharp whip of arrows striking true. A line of smoke ribboned off into the night and the gargant's head snapped back, the back of its skull blown out. Brains and blood lashed out into the breeze. The creature reached out a hand, the tree-trunk fingers with their blackened nails only a few inches from the top of the wall. The hand spasmed, some last reflex of the creature's former life sending it back to cup its shattered head. Galen stared down into the cavern of its open mouth as it began to fall, the jaw loose against its neck, the blunt tombstone teeth, the lolling tongue green with decay. It dribbled a sheet of black slime down its chest and reared slowly from the wall. Back it went, silently toppling to crash down into the line of the dead as they marched on Excelsis, crushing dozens of orruks beneath its lifeless body.

A loose cheer went up from the troops on the wall, but it soon faded. Three more gargants hobbled forward to take the place of the one that had fallen. The orruks and ogors had reached the gate, the undead skaven capering at their heels. As far as Galen could see across the scrubland, for miles in every direction, there was only the dead.

'Reload if you can!' he cried. 'Fight!'

It was too late. He slipped his pistol into his belt and drew his sword. The dead gargants reached up and took hold of the battlements, plucking stones from the walls with their giant hands. He saw Captain Huber hacking at their fingers, cutting deep into the dead flesh, but the gargants felt nothing. There was a great rending crash as huge sections of stone were torn away, then the scaffolding behind the wall began to tip, the simple wooden platforms and steel bars no match for the strength of the monsters.

Galen saw soldiers falling from the wall, screaming as they plunged into the mass of corpses. He fell to his knees and was pitched to the side. He reached for Captain Huber's hand, their eyes locking, her mouth open in a silent cry, but as the scaffolding buckled she slipped from his grasp. The platforms tipped further, the beams bent and cracked, and the whole edifice collapsed with a groan, back towards the maelstrom of the parade ground far below.

As the hordes of the dead hammered at the gates, Galen fell – and Excelsis fell with him.

It had taken a month to fill the grave pits to the north of the city, a task of such squalor and misery that no one could manage it for more than a day before they had to be replaced. The Freeguild and the engineers of the Ironweld Arsenal excavated the land a mile from the city walls, working day and night until four vast pits had been hewn from the earth, their sides reinforced with rubble taken from the city's shattered buildings. Horse-drawn carts, wheelbarrows, trolleys and gigs were all pressed into service to drag the corpses from the streets. They trundled endlessly from the northern bastion, day after day, tipping their putrid contents into the ground until each pit was filled to the brim. Duardin engineers, tough-minded characters more concerned with charts and mechanics than the horrors in front of them, oversaw the whole process. At last all four pits were sealed and flattened and covered with turf, becoming no more than vague undulations in the land that would in time take their place in the city's folklore.

It took a month to fill them, and less than an hour for the dead to claw their way free.

It was the same to the south and west. From the city walls, sentries caught their breath as the darkness revealed the dead, shuffling silently across the wasteland. Grave pits as big as some city neighbourhoods spewed their contents into the scrub, as if the earth itself were vomiting corpses, too nauseated to keep them down. The ravaged remains of gargants and orruk warbands, of skaven clans and ogor tribes, dragged their carcasses from the mire, caught in the necromantic snare of Briomedes' magic. In the city itself, an amethyst fume glistened in the cemeteries as the ground began to shudder. The soldiers of Freeguild regiments fumbled their way from the dirt and staggered through the ill-lit streets in search of their former comrades. Generations of people who had lived and died in Excelsis before most of its current citizens had been born, drew themselves from their drowsing sleep and emerged once more into the torchlit night. They lurched down the avenues and alleyways, slumped and mindless, roused only when their progress brought them into the path of some poor unfortunate – and then, with grotesque savagery, they would rend and tear until their victims were so much offal left lying in the street. Stirred by some strange instinct, they seemed to exist only to turn the living into the dead.

The northern gate fell quickly. A small retinue from the Knights Excelsior, their numbers thin, tried to hold back the tide. The white-armoured Stormcast warriors, singing praises to Sigmar, smashed corpses to pieces with hammer and sword, but they were soon pushed back, cast into scattered warbands that tried to fight their way back into the heart of the city. Most of the troops from a company of Bronze Claws, raw recruits who had yet to see combat, threw down their weapons and ran, seeking shelter in the warren of streets that led to the Prophesier's Guildhall. Too late, they were caught in the teeming throng of corpses that shambled from the Hennerdorf Necropolis and were torn to pieces.

Even drilled and cohesive units could do little against such numbers. Handgunners didn't have enough time to reload, spearmen were quickly overwhelmed before they could manage a second thrust. Platoons and companies broke up into ragged bands that sought shelter in the surrounding buildings, taking ineffectual potshots with arrow and bullet at the columns of the dead. At the bridge over the Palatine Brook, a lone Ironweld rocket battery kept up a punishing fire on the mouldering orruks that pressed against them, launching a stream of explosives that blew the corpses into a green, putrescent rain. When their ammunition was exhausted and the bridge was covered in a carpet of rotting flesh, the crew shook hands, drew their swords and charged the dead. They were never seen again.

The situation was equally dire at the southern bastion. A fine mist had rolled in from the distant Morruk Hills, masking the deadwalkers' progress from the grave pits and the cemeteries until it was too late to raise the alarm. Ironwood gates that had withstood the worst of the siege soon fell as they were attacked from both sides. Hardened soldiers faltered and fell back as they found themselves confronted by old friends and comrades, well-remembered faces broken down by decay into grotesque, oozing mockeries of those they had once known. Stormcast warriors from the Hammers of Sigmar, swept aside by the flood of corpses, formed ad hoc units and fought until their golden armour was drenched in slime. Shards of lightning leapt to the heavens as each hero fell, dragged down by numbers impossible to counter. Resurrected gargants, with as much brute power in death as they'd shown in life, punched the gates to kindling and shattered their fists on the stormstone walls. Into the gap poured the limitless dead – the defeated armies of the siege, returned once more to wreak a terrible vengeance on the city.

The promenades of Excelsis, so recently cleared of rubble and brought back to some rough approximation of their former glory, became stinking avenues of the dead. The cobbled streets were mephitic veins channelling poisoned blood into the heart of the city. Grand palaces and low hovels alike were no real refuge, hasty defences quickly thrown aside and trampled beneath the rotting feet of the mindless hordes. Glimmer addicts frantically crunched vials between their teeth even as the undead reached out their rotting hands for them, praying the drug would show them a way out. Palatial ballrooms in the mansions of the Noble Quarter and rickety garrets in the shanty towns of Squallside became the front line in the fight against the darkness. Across the city, lone acts of heroism went unheralded – a young woman defending her family with a broken chair leg until she was overwhelmed; an old man, grim-faced, holding a stairway with no more than his walking stick, fighting off the corpses of skaven and grots so his grandchildren could escape across the rooftops. In the arbitration chamber of the Grand Alchemist's and Philosopher's Disputation and Debating Society, Professor Haldar Vandestine mused on the nature of mortality as he drew the steel blade from his sword stick and tried to recall the fencing lessons of his distant youth. As the lolling hordes advanced into the chamber, slobbering through the broken windows and shuffling down the wood-panelled corridors of that most august institution, Vandestine thought with equanimity about his imminent demise. After all, he realised with satisfaction, at last he would be able to disprove that old fool Throndsen's ludicrous theories about the tripartite division of the soul after death…!

There was no coordination in the fight. Senior commanders, cut off from their regiments, tried to organise flying columns that could launch assaults wherever the enemy was strongest, but the undead seemed to have no real strategy or aim. Wherever the defenders gathered, there the corpse-hordes attacked, in numbers too vast to count. Soon, Excelsis became not a single battle site, but a multitude of desperate actions and chaotic last stands. Fires broke out and ravaged the tinder-dry districts of the Veins. Members of the Grand Conclave, the highest authorities in the city, downed bottles of the finest zephyrwine and threw themselves from their balconies, crazed with panic. Cut-throats and criminals sought refuge in the temples, trembling as they offered up remorseful prayers to Sigmar, begging for his intercession. At the Abbey of Remembered Souls, the High Theogonist capered on the steps of the chapel, tearing pages from *Intimations of the Comet* and sending them fluttering across the smoke-fumed air, laughing even as he was snatched from the ground by an undead gargant and crushed into a dribbling paste.

And in the far eastern quarter, deep in Excelsis Harbour, the Spear of Mallus rose from the waters, a shard of the World-that-Was chained in all its power and mystery to the realm itself. Ringed by the Floating Towers of the Collegiate Arcane, it loomed there over the city, a mountain wreathed in blue corposant – a flickering web of energy that, as the night advanced, slowly dimmed into the wildest purple, the rich amethyst that was the colour of necromancy: the colour of Death.

CHAPTER TWENTY-ONE

BROKEN CITY

The air was threaded with mist, a faint salt bite of the sea. Doralia could smell the harbour somewhere ahead, not far now: the saline tang of rotting seaweed, the foam and froth that gathered by the slipways, the greasy shingle and the rusting chains, caulking and boiled tar, the dusty smell of fresh canvas and the mouldy scent of ancient sail. The cobblestones underfoot were slippery and wet, and the black wooden walls of the thin harbourfront buildings on either side of the road glistened with moisture. Droplets gathered on the overhanging gables and dripped down onto the pavements, the roofs of the houses leaning over as if peering into the streets below them. Candles flickered and went out behind the diamond-shaped panes of the casement windows as they passed, the witch hunter and the vampire. Houses had been abandoned. Doors and windows had been nailed shut against the night. Word had spread like wildfire through Squallside: the dead were abroad.

The road ahead of them, a narrow and constricted passage striped with black shadow, twisted off to the right at the far end.

Doralia edged closer, hugging the wall, Jael Morgane behind her. Ten yards away, a lone lamp stood in a pool of green where the passage met the other end of Stellir Lane. She was glad of the shadows as she ducked into a doorway and drew her pistol. Under the hat brim, her eyes glittered with calculation – would it be better to try and break through here, or track back and find a quieter way? A diversion would take time that they didn't have, but trying to fight through could see them both killed. She remembered the black dog in the wilderness. The voice of a prophet, of Sigmar himself, if indeed that's what it was.

'A tide of the dead...' she muttered.

Ahead of them, a packed column of corpses ten abreast shuffled down Stellir Lane. Dead orruks dragged their fists along the paving stones, faces blank. Skaven lolloped beside them, dead rat eyes like white marble, yellow teeth in a chittering sneer. Humans also, dead soldiers, dead civilians, old men and women... Some of them still carried weapons, dragging their swords and axes behind them as if cleaving only to some faint memory of their purpose. The only sound they made came from their shuffling feet. The noise was like the whisper of rain falling on a rooftop. Nothing else, no voices, no cries of triumph or aggression. Just the march of the dead.

'They're heading for the harbour,' Jael whispered behind her. Doralia felt the hair rise up on the back of her neck and a shudder of revulsion passed through her. Easy to forget sometimes that the creature was there. Here in the shadows, amongst the living dead, she was in her natural habitat.

'That's where we need to be, but I don't think we're going to make it this way,' Doralia said. 'There must be... Gods, there must be thousands of them.'

'Luck has brought us this far, but I would not be keen to push it any further.'

'Luck,' Doralia said, gripping her blade in her other hand, 'and a strong right arm.'

They had hacked and dodged their way from the parade ground and into the tangled alleyways of the Veins two hours ago, darting through the district's northern quarter. Slipping down quiet side streets, hiding in doorways, cutting through lone bands of deadwalkers when they had to, they had navigated their way back and forth through the streets until they came to the wide avenues of the Pilgrim's Way: the ceremonial thoroughfare that led from the northern bastion to the Abbey of Remembered Souls in the heart of the city. The avenue, with its fine marble statues of saints and heroes from the city's storied past, its covered promenades, its theatres and gardens, was suffocated with corpses – a swarm of the dead, either shambling towards the bastion or milling uncertainly in the roadway as if awaiting further instruction. Everywhere she had looked, she had seen bodies lying in ragged pieces on the pavements, guts strewn about the road, scraps of flesh, the slime of decay. She had seen skirmishes and desperate actions where lone Stormcast warriors hewed left and right with sword and axe, or where small bands of troops held vital crossings and choke points with steely determination – until the sprawling waves of the dead proved too many to turn aside. She had sprinted with Jael through the ornamental gardens on the other side of the Pilgrim's Way, every instinct in her body screaming at her to turn around and fight.

But the real fight was not in the Pilgrim's Way, or in any other quarter of the city. It was here, at the harbour, where the Spear of Mallus plunged into the fuming waters of the bay, and now at last the harbour was almost in sight. The tall, sloped roofs of the houses around them blocked out any sight of the Spear from this angle, but Doralia could almost feel it: the low, electrical hum of its power, the sense of its immense weight slowly pulling on her body and pressing on her mind. They were close now, only a few streets away from the portside warehouses on the harbour's southern flank.

'If we can't go through,' Doralia said, glancing up at the roof-tops, 'we'll have to go over.'

They doubled back quickly, slipping along the alleyway until they came to the edge of the block, where a rickety, four-storey building leaned in close to its neighbour. The windows were broken and the front door had burst off its hinges, but there was no sign of the dead at this end. Looters perhaps, Doralia thought. There were always those who saw in a crisis only a means to their own ends. She looked up the side of the building, the wood dark with the moisture that floated thickly through the air around them. There was a black drainpipe leading up to the guttering on the edge of the roof.

'Come on,' she said. She tested the pipe, hooking her hands to the rusty metal and pulling her weight against it. The iron bands that clasped it to the wooden wall shrieked once, but they held. It would do.

They climbed swiftly, skittering like cats across the wet roof slates, pulling themselves up to the next building and darting between the chimney pots. Below them, the alleyway curved into Stellir Lane. The leaning rooftops were close enough for them to jump wildly from one side to the other, vaulting above the march-ing dead far below. She took a short run up and leapt, her coat billowing out behind her. She landed with a thump, her heel slip-ping out from under her and kicking a slate down to the street. She tumbled, rolled to the side, feet scrabbling out for the edge of the wet guttering. The dead thronged the road below, and the foul miasma of their stench drifted up to choke her. As she hit the rooftop, her crossbow clattered from her grip, skidding down the slates towards the edge, and in the split second before it fell she had time to wonder if she should dive after it. The fall might kill her – and even if it didn't, the dead would certainly do the job – but the crossbow was the most precious thing she owned: as a weapon, as a keepsake of her mother, as a symbol of everything she had gained and lost in her life. Losing it would be like losing her right arm or a shard of her soul.

She stretched, a desperate cry on her lips, but before she could reach it Jael Morgane had darted across the slates and snatched it from the air by its leather strap. Doralia tore it from her grip and cradled the weapon like a child. Jael stood there, a wavering silhouette balanced on the edge of the rooftop, backlit by the writhing purple energies of the distant Spear.

How easy it would be, Doralia thought, *to just pull this trigger now and send her damned soul winging back to the grave. Would my mother rest easy then, I wonder? Would my father? Would I?*

Morgane looked down at her, sprawled on the wet slates, as if she knew exactly what was going through her mind. She stood there, lithe and beautiful, her hands on her hips, the breeze dragging the weeds of her black hair back from her shoulders. The mouth, red-lipped, was turned in a sly smile.

'Why do I have the feeling,' the vampire said slowly, 'that I'm going to regret doing that?'

Doralia got to her feet, holding on to a chimney bracket for balance. She slipped the crossbow strap around her shoulder and nodded over at the Spear. The harbour was no more than a quarter of a mile from them now.

'Until that thing's safe,' she said, the words almost choking her, 'so are you.'

'I have your word, do I?' Jael sneered. 'The word of a witch hunter, most reliable I'm sure.'

'We're only here on the word of a vampire,' Doralia said. 'Turns out trusting that word was the right thing to do. Strange times.'

'Strange times indeed, my girl.'

'Call me "my girl" once more, though,' Doralia said, 'and you're smoke on the breeze, vampire. Understand?'

'Perfectly.' She laughed. 'You know, I think I like you even more than your father. He's grim all right, but you are something else, Doralia ven Denst. You have even more reason to despise me than he does, and yet you seem far more capable of putting that hatred aside than him.'

'The greater good outweighs my hatred,' Doralia said.

She almost believed it. Pressing against the edge of her mind was the realisation that her father was probably dead by now. She ignored it. Grief would come later, if there was time. Grief, and revenge, and the death of this disgusting creature whose very presence made her skin crawl.

'Does it now? And how far would you go for the greater good, I wonder?' Jael said. 'How much would you be willing to overlook until it was done?'

'Enough. I overlooked what you did to Caspar back at Hollowcrest. I overlooked whoever it was you killed at the bastion.'

'Oh, you saw that, did you?' Jael said. 'Well, it was only that young man who opened the gate for us. He was going to die regardless, it made no difference either way to him.'

'One way to rationalise it. I suppose all of us are going to die one way or the other.'

Jael sneered at her, as if Doralia had given her insult.

'I have no need to rationalise anything I do, witch hunter. I kill to survive. I will not apologise for wanting to live.'

'It's not living, vampire,' Doralia said. 'Whatever it is, it's as far from life as you can get.'

She thought of Caspar then, dying in the ruined temple at Hollowcrest. His body twisted on the floor, the vampire lapping at his wounds like a beast at a waterhole. Guilt, that's what she felt. Pure and simple. She wondered if, in some small way, this was what her father felt about inducting her into the order. He was responsible for whatever happened to her, in the same way she was responsible for what had happened to Caspar. But no, it wasn't that simple; it never was. She had chosen to stay, to fight. So had Caspar. He could have turned back after Raven's Hollow or run away while she slept. Hell, he could have stabbed her that first night after she rescued him from Fortune and that would have been the end of it. He had free will, he had made his choice. So had she. She wasn't like these corpses walking through the streets below them, leashed to the chain of Briomedes' will. And the choice she had made was to set her hatred aside, for the moment. Until this was done.

'Either way,' she said to the vampire, turning away, 'we don't have time for this. We need to move. The philosophical arguments can wait until after we're finished.'

And the moment we're finished, Morgane – so are you.

Flitting over the slate-grey, tumbledown roofs, they skirted the flank of Squallside and drew near to the harbour, the breeze kicking up a salt spray that lashed into their faces. The Spear of Mallus, that mountain of augury and portent, stabbed from the churning waters like the tooth of some colossal beast, too big to comprehend. Ripples of amethyst lanced and flickered around it, purple chains crackling with necromantic fire. Far above, the dark night sky was coiled like a whirlpool.

Doralia slumped against the salt-corroded brick of a chimney stack. They were atop what she was sure was the customs house next to the portside warehouses, where traders coming in by sea registered their goods if they didn't feel like paying the bribes. Off to their right, further south on the curve of the harbour as it hooked around the bay, was the tall tower of the Kharadron Overlords' aether-berth. It was capped by a wide, circular platform that glittered with the fumes of discharged aether-gold. A mile across the bay, high on a promontory on the other side, was a sullen pillar of stormstone: the Consecralium, the dread fortress of the Knights Excelsior. If any of them were left in there, Doralia thought, they would be too few to turn the tide now. She stared down at the harbourfront below them and said nothing.

'Well,' Jael said, 'it was perhaps too much to hope that this would get easier the closer we got to the Spear.'

The harbour was a scene of utter carnage. Corpses staggered at will, lurching from the radial streets to mass along the docks. Orruks and skaven, grots, ogors, gargants, even humans – every foul tribe and clan that had followed Kragnos in his maddened assault upon the city had returned now to finish his work. From the wide waters of the bay, a dozen ships of the Scourge Privateers fired cannons and crossbows, scouring the streets of the harbourfront in a brutal fusillade. Dockside taverns and doss-houses exploded as the cannons struck true, sending out a rain of burnt wood and shell fragments. Massive deck-mounted bolt throwers shot arrows six feet long to thud into the dead flesh of the gargants who were striding into the water from the quay-side. Far over on the other side of the docks, Doralia saw one gargant reel backwards with a flaming bolt sticking out of its face. It crashed into what must have been a munitions storehouse or magazine, because a split second later the harbour was lit with a blinding flash. A jet of fire and smoke ballooned up half a mile, the shockwave of the explosion lifting the lid of the water and scattering it like a scythe against the Privateers' ships. It shuddered across the bay, shaking the customs house where Doralia and Jael were perched. Buildings that had been constructed by some of the city's earliest settlers – strange, jagged halls and houses made from the bones of leviathans hauled from the bitter sea – blew apart in a burst of calcified shrapnel.

'Madness...' Doralia said. 'This is absolute madness...'

Still the Privateers fought on, but it made little difference. For every hundred corpses blown to pieces by their cannons, another thousand took their place. Doralia saw the ships hoisting their black sails to the masts, and she could hear the distant calls of their captains as they gave the orders to retreat. The waters of the bay were covered in a pearl-grey layer of cannon smoke, but she could still see the deadwalkers clambering out of the sea and up the ships' anchor chains, hauling themselves from the fumes and scrabbling up the sides of their hulls. They had walked across the seabed to reach them, mouldering orruks and gargants wading through the deeps. Even from here, half a mile away, she could see the chaos on deck as aelf fought zombie, as corpse-gargants dragged themselves from the waves and began smashing the ships to kindling. Sails crackled against the breeze, emblazoned with the proud devices of their crews; and then the ships' masts were falling, and the sails slumped into the littered sea. There was a stench in the air of black powder and burning hair, of the sea's viscous brine and the foul grave-reek of the dead.

This was going to be impossible. Doralia had no illusions, none. They didn't stand a chance.

She looked to where the Floating Towers of the Collegiate Arcane ringed the Spear of Mallus, a thousand feet up. Even those vast, esoteric devices had been caught in the web of Briomedes' power. Three of the towers, ornate amber spires of steeple and buttress wrapped in a vortex of arcane energy, hung at weird angles in the lowering sky. Lightning flashed from them, frenzied bursts of energy that sparked and dissipated against the clouds. Ribbons of crackling amethyst lanced out from one tower to spark against the other three, a snarling net that tore pieces from them, vast shards of marble and stone that fell crashing into the bay. The Eyrie itself, the gold-and-iron Stormkeep above the very tip of the Spear, blazed with that same withering fire. Smoke spewed from its arcane engines, tongues of flame. As they watched, it suddenly burst apart and scattered a ring of debris far out across the harbour.

'There,' Jael said, shielding her eyes. She leaned against the chimney and pointed up at the fourth tower, which hung far over the northern curve of the bay. 'That's where Briomedes is. He's seized the tower and he's using it to concentrate his energies, a locus for his ritual. It's... Gods, it must be strengthening his power a hundredfold!'

She could see tendrils of that energy lancing out from the fourth tower and surging down into the pinnacle of the Spear, ringing it like a vast corona. The Spear seemed to blaze with both heat and cold at the same time, and at its base, a mile out where it plunged into the ocean, she could see the water begin to boil. Nearby, disengaging from its floating wharfs and streaming from the hangars of the aether-berth, she saw the ironclads and frigates of the Kharadron Overlords heading east. They were leaving Excelsis to its fate. They had made their calculations, running the numbers from their ledgers through the mechanisms of their clockwork counting machines. There was no more profit in this, only loss. She wondered what the city looked like from up there. How bad must it seem, and how much more of it was still to fall?

Jael Morgane tried to give a cynical laugh, but there was something torn and frenzied in her tone. This close to her revenge, and she was watching it all fall apart.

'Even if we could get through these hordes, how are we supposed to get up to Briomedes? He's a thousand feet above the bay, and I doubt he'll be alone.'

She stood on the lip of the rooftop and looked down at the dockside three storeys below. The dead were breaking into the shops and houses along the wharf, dragging the living from their hiding places. Screams tore through the air, panicked cries for help or mercy. Two or three of the Privateer ships had managed to escape the harbour, striking their sails and making for the Clawing Sea. The rest were burning in the bay or were slowly capsizing as they succumbed to the appalling damage they had taken from the gargants.

'We don't stand a chance,' the vampire said bitterly. 'Davin, Ursula, my loves,' she whispered. 'I have failed you...'

'We never did stand a chance,' Doralia said. There was no pity in her voice; it was simple statement of fact. 'It was a fool's gamble that we could stop him once the dead began to rise.'

Doralia checked her weapons, drew down her tall, wide-brimmed hat on her head. She stood up from the sloped roof. The rain was still falling, a steady smirr that blurred the edges of things. It was getting cold. A bleak night, for the fall of a city. She wondered if she would live to see the dawn.

'Still,' she said, 'I've made more than a few fool's gambles in my time. The dead below us,' she asked Jael. 'Can you sense them?'

All the way through their headlong flight from the parade ground at the west bastion, Doralia had seen how the undead reacted to the vampire. As if she were one of them, just another corpse wandering through the streets. They recognised her as one of their own.

'Yes,' the vampire admitted. 'They're like moths batting against a window pane. I can feel them, but they're just vague shadows in my mind. Briomedes has them firmly in his grip.'

'You have some necromantic power of your own. Couldn't you move them out of the way, give us a clear run?'

Jael frowned and looked down from the edge of the roof.

'I don't have even a fraction of Briomedes' power,' she said. She struck her hand towards the hordes around the harbour. 'I could push a few out of our path if the need came to it, but I can't control all *this*.' She narrowed her blood-red eyes. 'Why?' she said, with suspicion. 'What are you going to do? A clear run at what?'

Doralia pointed to the Kharadron aether-berth, the high tower with its fan of wharfs and slipways, high above them on the southern curve of the docks. 'We make for that,' she said. 'We steal a Kharadron vessel, if there are any left, and we fly it into Briomedes' tower. We kill him, or we die trying.'

'Are you insane?' Jael scorned. She looked up at the chaos above them, the surge and flare of magics coruscating through the night, the sky itself writhing in agony as waves of necromantic force struck the monolithic hull of the Spear. 'It's sheer suicide!'

'Frightened, are you? Always pitied your kind, in a way,' she said. 'Doubt there's anyone more scared of death than an immortal.'

She gave the vampire a rare smile.

'You've got so much more to lose than the rest of us.'

CHAPTER TWENTY-TWO

BARRICADE

The sound of her screaming. The raw, red panic of her fear. She calls his name, crying for him to save her.

'I am coming!' he wants to say. 'Doralia, I'm here!'

He leans his head against the iron door, face twisted with anguish, fists clenched. He can hear her sobbing, and he can hear the slavering madness of the thing he has trapped in there with her.

He thinks of the burning corridor of their home, the sound of the vampire's laughter. He thinks of the moment he left that house for the last time, kissing Marie goodbye, ruffling Doralia's hair. Checking his weapons, following a lead, with no idea that Morgane was just waiting, waiting...

The man who left that house never came back. Another man returned in his stead. Someone else, the kind of man who could do something like this to his only child...

'Doralia,' he whispers at the door as his daughter screams for help. 'Forgive me.'

* * *

'*Forgive…*'

Light and flame broke against his face. Fire roared somewhere behind and above him. His face was wet. Tears, he thought, tears for his dead wife…

'Marie…?'

Steel striking steel somewhere. Screaming. There was a terrible weight on his chest, a pressure against his throat. He reached up and unlatched the gorget, letting it fall away. He stretched his fingers, tried to kick out with his legs.

'Galen!' a voice called from above. 'Galen, can you hear me?'

The weight against his chest began to shift. He could move his arm, he realised. That's all he wanted, in this moment: the strength to move his arm. He looked at the gloved hand before him, watched the fingers uncurl. It was his hand. It was strong enough to hold a sword. That was all that mattered. If he could hold a sword, he could fight. He could kill her, Morgane…

'Galen, please!'

'Doralia…' he said. He could see her… Face framed above him, staring down, his daughter. She had come back. She was going to save him. 'Forgive me,' he tried to say, but the words drifted off like smoke.

He could feel himself falling backwards, into the black. Shyish, he thought. The Amber Princedoms. Yes, at last… there to take up his sceptre in the Underworlds, the scion of an ancient name. It would be so peaceful there, so calm… It would be like coming home, and Marie would be there waiting for him, and together they would only have to wait a little longer for Doralia to join them too. She would come to them soon… At last they would be together again…

'Galen!'

The hard slap shocked him awake. Galen coughed, vision spiralling. Captain Huber stood above him, clawing at the rubble. She had a swollen welt on her forehead, her lip was smashed, and her face was covered in blood and dirt. Her uniform was filthy. He spat blood and cried out, and then Huber was dragging away a spur of wood, the metal poles of the scaffolding, the scattered rubble of the fallen wall. He rolled onto his front and pushed himself up with trembling arms. There was dried blood in his eye, and every time he took a breath something stabbed into his side.

Broken ribs, he thought. He tried to stand and made it to his feet without falling. His sword was on the ground beside him, and his pistol and silver stakes were still in his belt. *Nothing else broken, though…*

Through streaming eyes he stared up at the breach in the city wall.

Sigmar save us, he thought. *Lucky… lucky old man…*

They had fallen to the side as the wall came down, riding the scaffolding as it crashed and broke apart. It had pitched them off into the shadows beneath the flight of stone stairs that led up to the Neck at the edge of the barbican tower. The gates, those twenty-foot-tall ironwood symbols of the city's unyielding strength, were just twisted wreckage ahead of them, splintered wood roughly torn aside. Just beyond the gates was a breach so wide a regiment could have marched through ten abreast. Galen could see the open air of the wastelands beyond the walls. Excelsis was undefended.

Orruks still clad in the rusting armour of their tribes, skin grey with decay, dragged their feet across the beaten earth. Dead grots, hunched and twisted little things, scampered in their wake. Ogors with lank beards and wispy topknots, their slab-like muscles now dripping from their bones, left a festering trail of grave slime behind them. And soaring above them all, lumbering and rank with decay, their split bellies oozing a stream of putrefaction, came the undead gargants – creatures that would have dwarfed the gates even when they still stood.

Huber pulled him aside, deeper into the shadows behind the stairs. Everywhere Galen looked the corpses shambled unopposed, dragging the ropes of their guts across the parade ground, stumbling into the lower floors of the barbican tower behind them, or staggering on into the streets of the city, chained to the command of their dread master.

The west gate was down. The bastion had fallen.

'Have none of your men survived?' Galen asked her, keeping his voice low as they crouched in the darkness. Lamplight still flickered from the tower, from that honeycomb of empty chambers. Huber's face looked haunted.

'None that I can see,' she said. 'Although I think there's fighting over on the other side of the parade ground.' She peered out from behind the edge of the stairway, risking a glance. 'Over where the Bastion Road meets Grunndrak Street, looks like some of the Palatine Guard are still standing.'

Galen could hear it too – the clipped shouts of command, the regular punch of blades hacking into flesh. Huber thought for a moment. A shadow fell across them, the rolling progress of a gargant as it kicked its way through the broken gates, mere yards from where they were hiding. Galen reached for his pistol, but the gargant strode on, a rain of green slime dripping from its bloated skin.

'Grunndrak Street is part of the bastion's logistics chain,' Huber said. She gingerly probed the welt on her forehead, wincing. 'It leads down to some of the Ironweld munitions warehouses. There are stores there, maybe weapons we can use.'

'Then that's where we need to be. Anywhere but here.'

He took in the horrors that surrounded them, the parade ground packed with deadwalkers, the corpses that crawled and staggered through the breach. The shadows wouldn't hide them forever, and any moment he expected some reeling corpse to turn around and feel the dim understanding that something near it still lived. Someone was screaming from inside the barbican tower high above them on their left, the babbling fear of a man who hadn't made his peace with Sigmar before he died.

'Colonel Alicanthus...' Huber said. She swallowed and made the sign of the comet.

'It seems the regiment is yours, Captain Huber,' Galen said, his voice dry. 'What remains of it anyway.'

Huber grimaced. 'Story of my career,' she said. 'I only ever seem to get a promotion when everyone else around me is dead.'

'That tells me you're a survivor, at the very least.' He levered himself to his feet, sword in one hand and pistol in the other. He checked the firing mechanism, tried to ignore the stabbing pains in his ribs. 'Now, how are you as a sprinter?'

'Fast enough.' She gave him a bleak smile. 'Near a quarter of a mile across the parade ground, and I should know – I've marched it often enough. A quarter of a mile through all the dead of the siege...'

'If I fall,' Galen said solemnly, 'then don't stop for me. Keep going, save yourself.'

She shook her head. 'You have to make it, ven Denst. Find your daughter, help her save the city. If there's any city left...'

'Come on then, captain,' he said. 'Let's earn our pay.'

If the dead had one thing going for them as a foe, he thought as they cut through the parade ground, it was that at least they were slow. With a firm direction to aim for and some weight behind you, it was possible to barrel past even the resurrected orruks without too much trouble. A quick slash of the sword would clear a reasonable path, and as long as you didn't stop, there was a decent hope you might reach the other side. But if you did stop... then not a whole chamber of Stormcast Eternals could drag you from their murderous grip.

It was like trying to push your way through the crowds on market day, or at the height of some longed-for festival. Everywhere the dead lumbered and twitched, grasping out for them, reaching, desperate to tear them apart. Galen darted left, swung high, hacked the lopsided head from some greenskin brute. Captain Huber skewered a grot on the end of her blade, pausing only to kick it free and stamp on its putrid face with her heavy, regulation-issue boot. He drew his pistol, sent a nullstone bullet through the grey slop of an ogor's exposed brains. The creature spasmed and fell, and Galen leapt over its bloated body, barely pausing.

'Keep moving!' he shouted.

Huber, head down, sprinted onwards.

They were almost there, just a few more yards to go. He could see that the Palatine Guard had thrown up a barricade at the entrance to Grunndrak Street, a hastily stacked pile of smashed tables and chairs, ale barrels from the tavern on the corner. The street itself, stretching off behind the barricade, was bordered by low-rise functional houses, clapboard structures thrown up with a quick lick of paint. The Freeguild had commandeered them for officers' quarters while the bastion was being rebuilt. A few troops from the Iron Bulls, survivors from the assault on the gates, had joined the Palatines. They were reloading their handguns, taking well-aimed shots at the deadwalkers on the parade ground.

'They're trying to clear a path for us!' Huber called. She ducked and slashed out with her sword. Beside her, the head of a dead Freeguild trooper exploded, the corpse pitching down to the dirt. 'Damn things aren't accurate over a hundred yards, they should know that!'

'They seem accurate enough to me, captain!'

Two more deadwalkers fell, skulls smashed open by the handgunners' bullets. Galen smelled the clammy stench of the corpses all around him, the reek of decay and grave soil. He could feel their fingers clawing at his coat. Cutting them down was like scything wheat, but every moment he spent fighting only brought him closer to being swarmed. He stumbled over the soft bodies of dead soldiers beneath him, grabbed Huber's shoulder, propelled her forward through a gap in the mouldering crowd. They had a clear run at the barricade. Galen could see the Palatines' officer beckoning them onwards, even as he pushed all his weight against the barricade to stop the swarming dead from pushing it over.

There was a metallic taste in his mouth and his ribs were screaming fire, but Galen forced himself on. He felt rotting arms dragging at his feet, clawing at his elbow. Twisted jaws snapped and mumbled at him, broken fingernails tore at his breastplate. An orruk's head erupted in front of him, splattering him with gore. A moment later he heard the gunshot.

'Galen!' Captain Huber called.

He snapped his elbow into a fractured mouth, freed his arm, swung wide with his blade in both hands and cut himself a path – and then at last he was through, and the barricade was just before him. He slumped against the splintered wood as strong arms reached down to lift and drag him over, dropping him into the dust on the other side. Galen sprawled in the dirt until he caught his breath. A clean-cut young face looked down at him with concern, the dark hair above it slick with pomade, a fashion-able duelling scar running from one cheekbone to the edge of the mouth.

'Are you all right, grandfather?' the officer said. 'Can you hear me?'

Galen wiped his sleeve across his face and grabbed the young man's proffered hand.

'"Grandfather" me again, son, and I'll tan your damned hide,' he growled.

The officer looked nervously from Galen to Captain Huber and opted for a quick salute. Galen reloaded his pistol, taking in the scene. Dead Palatines lay slumped in the gutter, their faces clawed to ribbons. There were only a dozen left manning the barricade, plus the handful of Iron Bulls. Not much to hold back an army. The barricade itself was beginning to collapse against the weight of the deadwalkers behind it. He could see more gargants looming through the dust-fumed breach on the other side of the parade ground, vast unbalanced heads turned on twisted necks, black drool dripping from their open mouths. They had noticed this little obstruction, it seemed.

'What's your name, soldier?' He snapped the cap shut on his pistol.

'Lieutenant Oberon, sir,' the officer said. Galen could see him wondering about the salute again. 'We were sent to reinforce the north bastion by the High Arbiter himself, sir. There were strange tales, stories of huge bat-like things flying in from the wasteland outside the city. Then runners from the Bronze Claws brought the news of the attack, but by the time we were halfway down the Pilgrim's Way, it was too late. We were under attack, well... everywhere, sir. We couldn't even make it as far as the north gate.'

He looked mournfully at the remains of his command, the Palatine Guard struggling to hold the barricade up while they hacked and stabbed with their halberds.

'You've fought well, lieutenant, damned well,' Galen said.

He aimed and fired, smashing a flap of skull from a dead ogor as it tried to clamber over the barricade. It lurched and fell back into the horde. The tables and chairs began to creak, and the barrels were starting to tip.

'North, south and west, inside and outside the city, but the worst is at the harbour. We need to pull back, and after that it's everyone for themselves. Try and link up with others, hold back the deadwalkers wherever you can, but do not let yourself get swamped. Head for the palace,' Galen said, nodding as if he was thinking it over. 'Could be a good place for a last stand,' he mused. 'Fine place to die. Take a lot of these undead scum with you at least.'

'Yes, sir,' Oberon said. He looked sick.

'Galen!' Huber said. She pointed off down the road behind them. He turned, and for the first time in days allowed himself a smile.

'Oh,' he said, 'now *that's* a welcome sight indeed...'

Further down Grunndrak Street, a crew of Ironweld engineers were dragging three Hellblaster volley guns and a rocket battery from the munitions stores. They were led by a thickset duardin, his bald head flecked with old scars, his beard long and grizzled and tucked into his belt. A cigar fumed in the corner of his mouth. Galen caught its faint scent on the night breeze, even above the cloying stench of dead bodies, blood and rot.

Ghyranian cheroots... he thought. His heart lifted. He patted his pockets and drew out one of his own.

'I don't suppose you have a light, master duardin?' he called. He held up his cigar.

'I have more than one, witch hunter,' the duardin cackled. 'In truth, I have enough flame here for quite the party! Can you hold our friends there for just a short while longer, d'you think?'

'We'll do our best.'

Galen leapt to the barricade and put his shoulder to it, stabbing over the top with the point of his sword. The gargants were covering the parade ground in just a few strides. Dead skaven and grots, rancid sacks of slime and excrement, burst apart as they were crushed underfoot. The gargants' loose tattooed skin was sloughing from their bones, slipping down like rucked sheets to hang about their waists.

Risking a glance over his shoulder, he saw the engineers drag and pivot the guns into place at the other end of the street, spiking the carriage-trails down into the cobbles and snapping back the fuse mechanisms. When the barricade fell, they'd be firing at a distance of only twenty yards, virtually point-blank for such fearsome war engines.

'Ready when you are, lad!' the duardin called. 'I'd advise you to run along either side of the street there, if you don't want to get singed.' His bearded face was alight with glee as he capered around to the rear of the batteries.

The other engineers, experts all, checked the rocket tubes and the hammers on the volley guns. Satisfied with their work, they smartly stepped to the side of their machines and saluted.

'Ready, sir!' they cried.

'Now, if you please, witch hunter!' the duardin called.

Galen sprang back from the barricade, sweeping his arm at the others. The Palatine Guard turned and ran for the edge of the road, sprinting back towards the batteries. Huber waited until her own few Iron Bulls had discharged their weapons, then urged them back down the street. Galen followed her, turning to fire one more shot at the dead orruks as the barricade finally came down with a splintering crash. Behind them, too huge to seem real, framed in the grey smoke between the houses at the corner of Grunndrak Street, the dead gargants champed their teeth and lumbered over the broken barrier. The skin of their stinking feet split apart and leaked dark fluids onto the cobblestones.

'Fire, my beauties!' the duardin cried.

Galen threw himself to the ground and clamped his hands over his ears.

Fire and smoke, the whipcrack thunder of the guns. He felt the explosions hammering through his body, lifting him an inch from the cobblestones. He could hear the duardin's maniacal laughter, the snap of the clasps being thrown back, the smart click as the breech on the volley gun was set to fire once more.

'Fire again, boys!' the engineer cried. 'No respite! Elevate number one battery a degree, lad, let longshanks over there have a taste!'

Galen, still holding his hands over his ears, turned to watch. The other end of Grunndrak Street was like a cross between a butcher's yard and an ossuary, strewn with ruptured flesh and shattered bones. Smoke plumed in thick coils to the night sky. What was left of the barricade was on fire, and the gargant striding over it had been peppered from head to foot in shot from the volley gun. Rotten black blood poured from its wounds, and its massive left arm had been nearly sheared away, hanging there on a rope of tendons and clattering into the buildings beside it. The furthest rocket battery fizzed alarmingly as the engineers relit the fuses, and then with another searing flash of fire and smoke the missiles tore from their casings. Hurtling down the street, they struck the reeling gargant across the body in a deafening explosion, splitting it apart and sending a cascade of dead flesh far over the rooftops. The gargant's head shot away from its corpse like a cork from a bottle, tumbling off into the night. Only the legs were left standing there, two twisted, smoking tree trunks that slowly started to topple over.

'A good shot, master duardin,' Galen said as he got to his feet.

'Flint Kharacksson is the name,' the duardin said, holding out his rough, weather-beaten hand.

'Galen ven Denst.'

'I'm going to assume you have some idea what's going on here. You agents of the order usually have the inside track on these more… unusual situations. From the looks of things I already killed a few of these buggers during the siege, and I must admit, I resent having to do it all over again…'

'If I had time to explain, Kharacksson, you would be the first to know,' Galen said. 'In the meantime, and if you don't mind my amateur advice, I'd recommend bringing the buildings down on either side there, where Grunndrak Street meets the Bastion Road. Try and choke it off, prevent them getting any further.'

'Sound advice, witch hunter,' Kharacksson said. He looked around, to where the street rolled off behind them into the flickering shadows. 'Grunndrak Street's a thoroughfare down to the city barracks near the canal at the Cross Keys. If we can hold off these deadwalkers from both sides, we might have a chance at shoring up some kind of a defence.' He looked at the munitions stores, pondering. 'Plenty of ammunition at least.'

The dead, blown apart in their hundreds by the volley guns and the rocket battery, were beginning to mass once more. Through the drifting fumes, Galen could see lurching silhouettes, the press of bodies growing stronger every moment.

'Well,' Kharacksson shouted to the engine crews, 'hop to it, boys, we're not on parade here you know! Bring those buildings down, number one battery!'

As the guns cracked and flashed, Captain Huber drew Galen aside.

'You're going on to the harbour?' she said.

'I am,' he replied. He reloaded his pistol, wiped the gore from his blade. The broken ribs still stabbed in his side, but he would just have to put up with it. He didn't have any choice. 'If I'm lucky and Grunndrak Street's clear to the other end, then I can cut down to the canal, take the backstreets and alleyways, get over to the eastern quarter as quick as I can. If I'm not too late...'

He looked at her, her brown eyes flecked with green, the dark circles around them, her cropped blonde hair matted with sweat and blood. Her uniform was torn and her breastplate battered. She looked like she had taken a beating already, but she was still standing, still fighting.

'I'll come with you,' Huber said. 'You can't go alone through the city, it would be suicide.'

'You've already saved my life once, captain,' he said. 'Now your place is here, with your unit.'

'All three of them…' she said. 'We'll hold as long as we can, but afterwards…'

'Yes?'

Galen knew what she was going to say. He thought of Doralia. He saw again, unbidden, the iron box in that basement chamber.

'If you would have me, sir, I'd apply to join the order if I could.' She lowered her eyes. 'I've seen what we're up against, and we don't understand a fraction of it in the Freeguild. I want to make a difference, if I can.'

'Wherever you stand, you're making a difference, captain. The gates may have fallen, but as long as you're still here, you are the west bastion. The city needs you, and there are many ways to serve yet.'

'You're turning me down,' she said. She gave a sardonic smile, but she couldn't disguise her bitterness. 'I don't have what it takes.'

Galen took her hand. With all the sincerity he could muster, he said, 'You have proved yourself more than capable. You would be an asset to the order, I have no doubt. But what we do, the way we live, the dangers we face… I would not inflict that on anyone, not now. The cost is too great. When this is over you may well have peace, for a while,' he said. 'But for Doralia and I it will only be a short respite from further horror.'

The guns boomed, the rockets spat their flame, and the walls of the buildings began to tumble into the street. Kharacksson laughed to see the corpses buried for a second time.

'Funny how we do twice the work, but only ever seem to get paid the once!' he cried.

'Your reward cannot be counted in coin, Master Kharacksson,' Galen said. He held Huber's hand a moment longer, and then turned to go.

'Good luck,' he called over his shoulder. 'When the fighting is done, I hope we can meet again – Colonel Huber.'

CHAPTER TWENTY-THREE

THE FLIGHT
OF THE GARAZ-GOR

The platform of the Kharadron Overlords' tower fanned out high above the harbour. Like some vast toadstool at the tip of a spindly stalk, it shed spores of aether-gold into the raging night. The flank of the tower was constructed of reinforced ironwood and leviathan bones dredged from the bay, all of them riveted and augmented by the Kharadron's mechanical skills. Above, three hundred feet high, the slipways and berths were still thronged with their airships, all of them slowly disengaging and gaining height as they fled the city. Great ironclads and frigates, bristling with guns, swayed off into the night. Their aether-endrins thrummed, casting out their vibrations across the air, the ships' klaxons blaring and trumpeting as they pulled away.

'Come on,' Doralia said as they ran across the cobbles of the harbourfront. 'With any luck they'll have left something behind.'

'Duardin leave behind something valuable?' Jael sneered. 'I'd like to see *that*.'

There was a jostle of corpses up ahead, a knot of dead sailors and fishermen by the looks of them. Doralia sidestepped and swung her sword, splitting one of them in two. A gaggle of undead grots scuttled towards her across the wharf, loping between the hawsers. They ignored Jael, giving her ample time to step behind them and hack them to pieces. She laughed as she did so.

'Takes some of the fun out of it, when they don't even know you're there,' she said. 'Not that I'd waste my time on grots, if I didn't have to.'

Doralia glanced over her shoulder. The dockside was as crowded as when the fishing fleet came in: thousands of walking corpses milling back and forth, some of them still stumbling into the water even though the Privateer ships had long since sailed away, others mashing the broken bodies of those they had already killed. The crooked buildings and warehouses that stretched along the quayside glistened in the night air, their windows broken, many splintered ruins after the attentions of the Privateers' guns. High above the harbour as the madness went on, the Spear of Mallus groaned and crackled with power, a whipping amethyst wind surging faster and faster around it. The water shook and simmered, a great cloud of steam slowly rising to smother the bay.

'Get moving,' Doralia said, 'or we'll be joining those grots.'

There was a brass door at the base of the Kharadron tower. A few spilled crates of cargo were scattered across the cobblestones beside it, next to the customs officials' desk. Slumped in the doorway of the tower was a dead duardin, his aeronautical uniform half ripped from his body, his skull smashed to a pulp. More Kharadron corpses were spilled across the cobblestones, and as they drew near Doralia saw a few bobbing face down in the oily black water of the harbour. At the side of the tower, hidden in the flickering shadows, a resurrected ogor was busily tearing another duardin in half. Eight feet of rotting muscle, plates of rusting armour still strapped to its body, the ogor stuffed chunks of the dead duardin in its mouth, only to see them tumble from the ruin of its exposed belly.

Their feet ringing on the cobblestones, Doralia and Jael came to a skidding stop as the creature swivelled its head towards them. Strips of flesh dangled from its broken jaw. Its face was sunken and crumpled with decay, its body punctured with old wounds that must have been earned during the siege. It dropped the dead duardin and slowly shuffled towards them, arms extended, the great bludgeoning hands grasping at the air.

Doralia looked over her shoulder again. Their mad, headlong dash from the alleyway had been noticed, and more of the dead were now lumbering down the wharf towards them. She turned to the vampire. 'Now's your moment, Morgane. Make it count!'

Jael's eyes, those blood-red pinprick pupils, began to glow. Her lips split to show the rack of fangs in her mouth, and slowly she extended her hand towards the dead ogor. For the briefest and most disorientating flash, Doralia saw something else overlaid against the face of the cold and beautiful young woman before her: something ancient and foul, the leathery mask of a malicious creature with a leering snout, grinning in its cave. Instinctively she drew up her sword, but then the illusion was gone – or, better to say, the illusion had reasserted itself, and Jael Morgane once more stood before her as deathless as she always was, as smooth and uncorrupted as a porcelain doll.

The ogor lurched to the side, slobbering past them and dragging its grave-stink with it. Doralia, her sword still on guard, watched it stagger into the mob of orruks and humans that followed them, rending them to bits, ripping off arms and crushing heads. The dead tore into the dead, a silent maelstrom of butchery and horror.

'If you can keep that up,' Doralia said, 'we might actually make it out of this alive. Well...' She glanced at the vampire. 'I might, anyway.'

Jael dropped her hand and staggered backwards, swooning. Her face was wrenched with pain. Doralia caught her arm.

'What is it?'

'Briomedes...' the vampire murmured. She shook her head. 'If he didn't know I was here before, he does now. I just tore something from his control, and he won't take that kindly.'

Doralia looked up at the Floating Tower high above them, the amethyst afterburn of lightning imprinting itself against the night sky. She clutched her crossbow, checked the quiver on her hip for bolts. Still a dozen or so left. She only needed one good shot.

They broached the brass doors, stepping from the carnage of the dockside to the turmoil of the aether-berth. The deadwalkers had broken in here too, and the Kharadron were hard-pressed to hold them back. Far across the polished metal floor, Doralia saw a scrum of walking corpses being cut to pieces by the disciplined volleys of a Kharadron unit. Their faces were hidden behind their stylised metal helmets, pistols bucking in their hands as they blasted the deadwalkers apart. Pipes and tubes crossed the ceiling like vines, hissing with steam. There was a breach in the wood-and-brass plates of the far wall, on the other side of the ground floor. More deadwalkers were slopping through it, gangling things that staggered into the aether-berth and walked clean into the duardin's murderous fire as they pivoted smartly to meet them. Doralia saw a gargant's rotting hand probing through the breach, writhing with maggots. It snatched up duardin and deadwalkers alike and dragged them back into the open air.

They were an organised, methodical race, the Kharadron Overlords, who set their store in charts and figures. Not for them the wilder shores of faith or magic, or an enemy that couldn't even be bargained with. Doralia didn't think she'd ever seen two such contrasting enemies as the tough and unbending duardin, and the blank-faced, inscrutable dead.

Aethershot streaked above their heads. A pipe exploded in a gout of steam, scalding one duardin as he ran past, trailing blood from a severed arm. Somewhere a scream shrieked higher and higher until it was abruptly cut off. Kharadron and corpses alike staggered back and forth across the ground floor of the aether-berth, grappling with each other. Doralia ducked as a greenskin with half its face missing swung its simian arms at her. She hacked a leg off at the knee, swung down to take its head from its shoulders.

'There!' Jael shouted. She pointed to the other side of the berth, thirty feet away, where a brass staircase spiralled up towards the higher floors.

They ran for the stairs, skidding past skirmishing knots of duardin and deadwalkers, struggling and gouging at each other. Guns blasted around them, and the high, acrid stink of the Kharadron's aethershot weapons was heavy in the air. The metal floor, emblazoned with a proud rune in meticulously crafted gold leaf, was slick with blood and offal. As they reached the stairs, Jael just ahead of Doralia, the vampire slammed into a Kharadron crewman who was coming down them at the same time. He clanged back onto his brass backpack, rubber boots sliding on the metal steps, and before either of them could say anything he aimed his pistol and shot the vampire through the chest.

Jael soared backwards from the force of the shot, blood arcing from the wound. She hit the metal floor, skidded, rolled, and came up hissing with a look of unbridled savagery on her face.

'You stunted little scum!' she roared. 'I'm going to peel you from that suit and rip your entrails out through your mouth!'

The duardin struggled to his feet and aimed again, but with a swift kick Doralia knocked the gun from his hand. She grabbed the back of his helmet and tossed him head over heels down the last few stairs, where he scurried after his pistol and disappeared into the maelstrom. Jael clutched her chest and limped over, but even as she crossed the last few feet towards the stairs, Doralia could see that the wound was already starting to heal.

'Hurts, does it?' she said. She couldn't help smiling.

'Don't think that just because I am of the undead, I can't feel pain, witch hunter!'

'Rather you than me.'

'Why don't I take a moment to convert you,' the vampire sneered. 'It might help you live longer.'

'Like my mother, you mean,' Doralia said.

Jael flicked a nervous glimpse at her; just for a moment, there was the smallest grain of anxiety in her face. Doralia noted it. She would see that expression again before the night was through, she promised herself.

Jael pushed past her, saying nothing, and took the stairs three at a time. Doralia girded herself and followed.

The stairs twisted round and round, reaching ever upwards – floor after floor, stretching up to the wharfs and jetties where the Kharadron ships were at harbour. The stairs were slick with blood and the ichor of the grave, and now and then they met more duardin running down the steps, charging their weapons and preparing to join the fight. The presence of the witch hunter seemed to confuse them long enough not to put a bullet in Jael until they were past. Doralia grabbed the brass rail, her legs like rubber after the climb, and hauled herself onwards. Reflexively she patted her pocket for the firewater, but the bottle was gone.

'Damn it!' she muttered. 'Must have slipped out when we were on the rooftops. As if this night could get any worse…'

At last they came out into the middle of the hangar at the top, the wide disc of jetties and berths where cargo boats and warships alike flew in to dock. It was a vast circular space perhaps a thousand feet across, more like a ship's engine room than anything else. Red and green lamps flickered on the walls. Fuel pipes and aether-ports were arrayed around the hall, with coiled rubber tubes snaking across the floor. There were great brass containers with steaming valves by each berth, and raised walkways crossing the space above them. The jetties stretched out through wide apertures into the open air above the harbour, each aperture taller than the doors to the Great Cathedral of Sigmar in the centre of the city. A cold wind whipped through them, and she could see the spark and flare of Briomedes' necromancy lashing across the night sky outside.

The dead had managed to drag their foul presence even here. Gunshots sparked through the air, the hiss of aether-weapons, the battle cries of Kharadron deck crews fighting them off. Most of the berths were empty, but there were still a handful of smaller Kharadron ships moored in place. As they staggered out onto the hangar floor, Doralia saw one of the ships, a frigate as far as she knew, tipping wildly from its berth. Deadwalkers, a motley collection of dead aelves, orruks, humans and grots, mobbed the deck and flung themselves at the Kharadron crew as they desperately tried to take off. Metal screamed against metal as the frigate ripped free of its moorings. The boat pitched with a great rending flash of light, and then smoke was belching from its portholes. She saw duardin and deadwalker alike tumble from the deck, the Kharadron crewmen screaming as they fell down through the aperture towards the harbour far below. The air thrummed with the crash of gunfire and explosions, the pounding havoc of the aether-ships' engines. The lamps flickered and went dark, and from somewhere a blazing klaxon gave a distorted bark.

'I don't think your plan was quite the stroke of genius you assumed!' Jael cried.

She stumbled as an explosion far below shook the tower to its foundations. Doralia grabbed her arm and dragged her towards a jetty near the harbour-side edge of the platform. There were corpses scattered about the floor, tattered rags cut down by aethershot or the Kharadron crews' brutal pikes and cutters. Locked into the berth was a smaller, two-seater ship, its purple hull connected to a large brass dirigible by a pair of double struts. One seat was for the pilot, the other for a gunner, but there was no other space for crew or cargo. There was a heavy-gauge sky cannon protruding from the front of the hull, a smaller aethershot carbine in front of the pilot's seat. This was a warship, nothing less – one of the Kharadron's agile little gunhaulers, designed to harry the enemy and protect the larger boats from harm.

Doralia kicked the restraining hook and the boat bobbed as the dirigible took its weight. The craft's name was printed in duardin script on its side: *Garaz-Gor*, she deciphered. She didn't know what it meant, but she hoped it was a good omen.

'Get in,' she shouted at Jael. Aethershot cracked somewhere above them, raining sparks down on their heads.

'You truly have tired of life, haven't you, witch hunter?' The vampire was incredulous. 'Do you even have the first clue how to fly one of these things?'

'How hard can it be?' Doralia replied with a shrug.

She crammed herself into the cockpit while Jael leapt into the gunner's seat. Neither woman was particularly tall, but the ship had been built to duardin specifications and it was a tight fit. Doralia grasped the twin flying sticks, one on each side, and gave them a tentative pull. The ship lurched to the side as it disengaged from the berth, and for a moment Doralia remembered the raft across the river near Raven's Hollow. She thought of Caspar clutching the rail, trying not to be sick.

Expect you'd have some choice words to say about this, she thought.

Slowly, in sudden fits and lurching starts, the boat slipped its mooring and floated erratically from the dock. The jetty fell away behind them, the sounds of gunfire and screaming faded, and then with one last quick surge of speed they were suddenly out there, weaving through the midnight dark, floating higher and higher. The spheres of the cosmos planed smoothly across the night sky above them, close enough, it seemed, to touch. Far ahead the searing ropes of amethyst burst like a thunderstorm across the black. The city burned below, a patchwork spread of flickering light and drifting smoke, while the Floating Towers flared madly, like fireworks, spewing out streams of iridescent vapour as they toppled and pitched further to the side. Higher and higher they floated, until the Spear was booming beneath them, groaning in agony.

Doralia's breath was snatched away. It was extraordinary. No wonder the Kharadron looked down on other races. When you lived up in the very heights, then the world beneath, and all the people in it, must seem suddenly very small.

Jael clutched the gunner's wheel, her hands like claws. She shrieked and laughed, her hair lashing back from her head, blacker than the night. 'Gods above and below, witch hunter, this is a sight wasted on those stunted little duardin, is it not?'

Doralia's wide-brimmed hat was plucked from her head by the wind, and she took a moment to curse the loss. Her eyes were streaming with the cold air. The boat bucked and swayed beneath her, buffeted by the wind, shifting erratically from side to side as she tried to figure out the steering. There were pedals at her feet, and she soon discovered that if she pulled one stick and kicked the opposite pedal she could spin the boat round and still keep it on a steady plane. She had lost all sense of direction, but as she looked about wildly she soon saw the quartet of Floating Towers some way ahead and above them. She felt as queasy as if she were in the middle of a raging storm.

'How does the damn thing go higher?' she shouted. She pulled both sticks at once and the boat tipped backwards, nose pointing straight up. Jael screamed again. Doralia quite liked the sound. She tucked the sticks back, gently, trying to feel the weight and power of the machine around her, and soon they were making a steady climb towards the first tower. It belched amber light, a smeared halo of fire and smoke. Beyond it, hazed by amethyst flames, the tower that Briomedes had seized glowered in the night sky. She slipped the gunhauler out of the arc of purple flame that leapt and scattered from the first of the towers as it sailed past on their right, the hull shuddering underneath her, the whipping wind screaming through the metal struts. She could see tiny figures falling from the burning structure as it toppled sideways in the sky, ants dropping from a disturbed nest. Some, caught in the flames, fell like fireflies to extinguish themselves in the cold water of the bay. Her stomach turned as she watched them fall.

'We're not alone,' Jael cried beside her. She gripped the wheel and spun it round, cranking the carbine in its housing. Doralia scanned the night air as Briomedes' tower blazed nearer, but she couldn't see anything. The vampire pointed, her night vision more perfectly attuned. 'Flying creatures of some kind,' she said. She peered intently. 'Oh, perfect,' she muttered. 'He's resurrected dead thunderwyrms...'

She saw them then, faint, bat-like things cutting across the purple backwash of Briomedes' tower. As they drew closer she tried to gain height, turning the craft so it could approach the open hangar at a more oblique angle. The thunderwyrms were circling the tower, at least ten of them: foul serpentine creatures with great leathery wings, their heads like monstrous bats. All of them were dead creatures brought back to life by the necromancer's art, some of them putrid sacks of rotting meat, others near skeletal, and still held aloft on the tattered membranes of their wings. These things had provided the bones for Raven's Hollow, she remembered. Well, they were a long way from Raven's Hollow now.

'Explains how he got up here,' Doralia shouted. 'Must have swarmed the tower with the wyrms when the dead began to rise. They didn't stand a chance.'

Her voice was snatched away by the wind. Her face felt numb, it was so cold. No wonder the duardin encased themselves in those helmets and pressure suits.

The thunderwyrms undulated through the sky, like eels cutting through deep water, and as the craft came dipping in from the west, their attention was suddenly hooked. Swooping through the air, gliding and lifting on the currents of the burning city, they planed around and launched their attack.

Doralia would have expected shrieks and screams, the roars of animals preparing to bring down their prey, but the dead creatures were silent as they approached. The only sound was the ragged beating of their wings.

'Morgane,' Doralia said. 'Blow them out of the sky.'

The heavy gun seemed to rear in its mount as Jael scrabbled at the controls, and there was the satisfyingly mechanical sound of the ammunition ratcheting into place. The sky cannon roared, a solid burst of flame that scorched across the night. Doralia had a split-second glimpse of the shot erupting against one of the wyrms, and then the creature was just tattered rags drifting to the harbour far below. She engaged the carbine, chopping another wyrm to pieces. Two more of the creatures came sailing in, riding the thermals, a rank stench buffeting around them. Doralia saw rotten jaws, rows of broken teeth, a black tongue. She pushed the steering columns and the gunship dropped, then pulled them back almost immediately to take them into a vertical climb. The thunderwyrms cut past them, wings hissing against the brass aether-dome. The Floating Tower sent out crackling whips of energy around them, and then suddenly it was filling their sight, looming closer, far larger than Doralia had imagined. It was like a temple, like the nave of the Great Cathedral, all buttresses and spires and sweeping golden turrets. A thrashing cable of energy gushed from it, coiling down into the crown of the Spear far below. Ahead and below them as she struggled with the controls, Doralia could see the wide crescent of the tower's anchorage shooting towards them. She felt a dark shadow move across her, and then the gunhauler was shuddering chaotically in the air, a mad cacophony of bells and klaxons ringing from the machine's control panel.

Closer the tower came. They were speeding towards it, veering around in the air as if caught in a gale. The instruments screamed, and Morgane was laughing, and the stink of death and rot was heavy in her nose. Doralia looked up, staring into the rotting scales of a thunderwyrm's belly as it crouched on the aether-dome, jaws silently opening and closing. She tried to reach for her pistol, tried to hang on to the steering columns as they were ripped from her grasp. The craft was spinning wildly now, the tower haring towards them, the vast chamber of the anchorage aflame with purple fire. Smoke belched from the gunhauler's engine, something else crashed into them from below with a juddering shriek, and then they were plummeting into the guts of the tower, flames lashing up the sides of the hull.

She was blinded by a whirlwind of red and black, her head filled only with the screaming of metal, and then Doralia was flung to the side and saw nothing.

CHAPTER TWENTY-FOUR

BRIOMEDES

In the dream she was sitting on the edge of her bed, trying to pull her boots off. She'd had too much to drink, couldn't get a damn grip on the things, kept falling off the bed onto the floor. Thumping across the boards, head reeling, the taste of vomit in her mouth. *The hell with it*, she thought. *Sleep with my boots on then...*

She lay down on the bed, looked up at the bare whitewashed ceiling of her room as it shuddered and spun around. Except it wasn't her ceiling, she realised. It wasn't bare whitewash, but gold leaf and polished steel. She tried to reach up, to brush her fingers against it...

She opened her eyes. She was in a cathedral, and it was on fire. The great bones of the rafters high above, the vaulted ceiling, frail smoke drifting across the frescoes. She saw the Judgement of Sigmar on Mount Celestian, the Slaying of the Lode-Griffon, the Freeing of Grungni. Threads of arcane energy sputtered through the air. There was a smell of ozone, burning hair. A smell of refined

magic, like a winter's day in Hysh at the highest point of the year…
that year when she had stayed with her father at Settler's Gain, a
long season while they trained and readied their weapons, where
she had designed and crafted the nullstone bolts for her crossbow,
the bullets for their guns… And there was her father, his hand on
her shoulder, standing there proud as she was accepted into the
order by the Grandmaster in Shyish…

Something tugged at her foot again. Doralia shook her head
clear and tried to turn onto her side. A thunderwyrm, half its
face sheared off and its wings aflame, was gnawing at her boot.
Its head was as big as her body, and although its teeth were just
broken stumps it was only the tough boot leather that was keeping
her whole foot from being bitten off.

'Sigmar's blood…' She pulled her pistol and shot it through
the head.

The creature rattled to the side, all bone and dry sinew, the nullstone sending it back to silence. She dragged her foot from its
mouth and checked herself for injuries. She still had her crossbow
over her shoulder, and her sword was still strapped to her back.
She reached for her hat and then remembered the wind snatching it from her head. Blood was caked to the back of her neck
and there was a sharp, stabbing pain in her knee when she got to
her feet, but other than that she'd had a lucky escape.

Still in one piece, she thought. *Still able to fight…*

The open air at the mouth of the anchorage was like a black
sheet streaked with flame. Tongues of purple fire spasmed across
the night. The whole structure of the tower was trembling, as if the
night itself were a monstrous beast and was savaging it in its jaws.

She looked around, dwarfed by the great golden hall where
aether-craft were anchored on slipways and berths in the heights
above her, connected by a fan of gantries and walkways to a
vast imperial staircase far over on the other side. Ornate pillars

and beams soared up to the vaulted ceiling, where the intricate beauty of the frescoes glared down at her. Gods and heroes of ages past, philosophers and wizards of the Collegiate Arcane, silently witnessing the destruction of one of their greatest engines.

The Floating Tower shuddered once more as Doralia reloaded her gun. She looked at the wreckage of the Kharadron gunhauler, crumpled against the wall. The aether-dome was leaking gold vapour, and there were claw marks torn down the outside of the hull. It had scorched a trench into the golden marble of the tower's deck, and there were tattered scraps of thunderwyrm carcass still hanging from its twisted struts. She touched the chain of the pendant around her neck. Sigmar's comet; her mother had given it to her, to keep her safe when Morgane burst into their house.

Morgane...

The vampire was howling with laughter on the other side of the anchorage. Deadwalkers lumbered near her, resurrected Collegiate wizards and their apprentices, their skin grey but otherwise unmarked, arcane robes singed and burned as if struck by lightning. Doralia watched as Jael punched her fist through one wizard's chest, reaching in, both her hands red up to the elbows, tearing and pulling until he was ripped in half. The golden floor at her feet, decorated with intricate runes and the flowing cursive script of ancient spells and prayers, was as bloody as a field hospital. The vampire tossed the body parts aside and reached for the next one, another dead wizard with a lavish silver beard, who seemed utterly unaware that she was there. She took a firm grip of his head under the chin, her other hand cupping the back of his neck. With inhuman strength she twisted and pulled, and with a horrible shucking gasp the head came free, trailing a tail of spinal column. Jael threw it over her shoulder, the head tumbling over the floor until it reached Doralia's feet.

'So you're alive then,' Jael called. 'I wasn't sure for a minute.

Thought I might have to do all this myself, but I have to confess it's an ordeal I find I'm quite enjoying. I don't know, ever since I freed myself from Briomedes I find I have a particular hatred of the arcane. Stealing that Kharadron ship was a masterstroke, ven Denst, I've no idea how we would have got up here without it.'

The deck of the anchorage was as wide as the meeting chamber in the Conclave Hall, a huge, ornate space that was empty of anyone apart from the handful of dead wizards that opposed them. As Doralia drew near, they started lurching towards her, pulled at last by their desire to tear apart the living. Jael, as if sharing a treat, stepped aside and watched as Doralia cut them down.

Some of the finest minds in the Mortal Realms, great seekers of truth and power, reduced to this stumbling wreckage; it was disgusting. How Briomedes must have laughed to see them brought so low.

The chamber shuddered again, and the tower groaned. A cascade of energy bubbled from the walls behind them. There was a strange pressure building up in the air, and she felt almost porous, as if something were leaking into her mind from outside. She looked back at the open mouth of the anchorage, the wild night air, the glinting stars, the glow of flames from the burning city below. The tide of amethyst buckled through the black.

'What is it?' Jael asked her. 'You look odd, witch hunter. More so than usual.'

'Don't you feel it?' Doralia said. She reached out her hand…

…and then her father was standing there, his arms crossed, his face lit by flames… Watching something burn, the pain and sorrow on his face… the resolution.

'Can't you see him?'

Jael narrowed her eyes. 'It's the ritual,' she said, 'the arcane backlash from the Spear. Briomedes must be almost finished.'

'What do you mean?'

'The Spear is a thing of raw, unbridled prophecy, and it's being twisted by his necromantic magics. The air is thick with foresight and prediction, more than mortal minds can comprehend. You're seeing what will come to pass, what has happened, what will be. Everything is in flux. Yes, witch hunter, this is certainly going to be… *interesting*.'

Doralia squeezed her eyes shut and tried to focus. Under her shirt she could feel the pendant warm against her skin. She tried to concentrate on it, to fix herself in place.

'"Interesting" is what I'd call the advertisements in the *Excelsis Examiner*,' she said. 'This is something a little different.'

They ran on, crossing the golden marble of the anchorage hall, passing the majestic imperial staircase with its red velvet carpet as it stretched up towards the gantries and walkways of the aether-berths. There were scorch marks across the marble, the smell of burning flesh and the aether-stench of magic. Great blackened holes had been blasted from the walls, and everywhere she looked Doralia could see weird kaleidoscopes of colours drifting like tendrils of mist: the burnt residue of powerful spells. Far over on the other side of the hall they came to a grand avenue of silver flagstones and statuary niches, with floating crystal aether-lamps drifting around the ceiling twenty feet above their heads. The avenue curved off to the right, dipping down on a gentle slope as it headed into the bowels of the tower.

'This way,' Jael said. Her voice was rough and pained. 'We're close, we're… I feel him pressing there, against…' She winced and clutched her head. 'We only have moments, the ritual is nearly complete!'

They hurried on, Doralia limping on her sprained knee, her crossbow ready in her arms. She couldn't begin to comprehend what would happen to the city if Briomedes was successful. Was it even possible, could he truly harness the power of the Spear and bend reality to his will? Wrench the flow of time out of its proper channel, hurl it backwards into a place more pleasing to him, where his son was still alive and all the grief and failure of the present was just a warning sign of what he had to avoid?

She understood the motive only too well. If someone could give her the chance to go back to when her mother was still alive, and all her grim victories in the order were only so many idle dreams and fancies, would she take it? Would she spare herself all that pain, even if it meant causing untold pain to others?

No, she thought. *The pain is mine, for good or ill. It is part of who I am, and there's no going back now. Everything else is nothing but cheap nostalgia.*

Further into the depths of the tower they went, cutting their way through the wandering dead. The deeper they went, running through the corridors into the swirling turbulence at the heart of the structure, the more evidence they found of the Collegiate's ferocious defence. Spells had melted steel, had transmuted gold into boiling steam that crackled across the ceiling. Deadwalkers had been blasted to pieces or transformed to brittle statues of crystal and glass. They soon found evidence of Briomedes' more formidable weapons as well, though – massive Ironjawz orruks, their glazed eyes dripping down their rotten faces; corpulent ogors, their bellies swollen with corpse gas. Briomedes must have used the thunderwyrms to carry them all up to the Floating Towers, Doralia realised, sending them to quickly flood the defences while he seized control. No matter how hard the Collegiate mages had tried to defend themselves, the numbers of the dead had been overwhelming. Everyone who fell in the attack was then pressed into service, jerked back into a ceaseless unlife by Briomedes' power.

Jael was able to turn the deadwalkers aside, briefly, long enough for Doralia to sever their heads or put nullstone bolts into their brains. Soon they had left a trail of butchered corpses behind them, but the closer they got to the centre of the tower, charging down corridors of lit crystal and decorative glass, passing opulent debating chambers and laboratories, the more the vibrant backlash of the necromancer's ritual destabilised reality around them. The walls spat and flickered with energy. Bursts of amaranthine magic erupted from the ground behind them, shattering the flagstones. The tower was on the very edge of destruction.

They came out at last into a monumental chamber low in the inner workings of the tower. The ribbed ceiling burned with the flash of blue corposant, and the air seemed to stick to them as they forced their way onwards. There was a sharp, abrasive edge to it. Doralia could feel it scratching at her mind, paring away at her skin. She gritted her teeth, concentrated on the sullen throb of her sprained knee, the feel of the crossbow in her hands, the dried blood flaking off the back of her neck. Ahead of them, in the middle of the chamber, were two huge glowing spheres floating a few feet off the ground and slowly rotating around each other. Like Penumbral Engines, they were each clasped in two gyrating circles of charged gold, so bright that it was painful to look on them. The spheres dominated the room, each twice as big as the aether-dome that had powered the gunhauler Doralia had stolen from the Kharadron berth. Inside the spheres rolled balls of gas and light, pale blue and vibrant green, the aether through which they moved stained now with tendrils of necromantic magic. These were the arcane engines that kept the tower afloat, Doralia knew, leashed by Briomedes to his own fell purposes. Between the spheres there was a shuddering wave of energy, passing back and forth as they crossed each other's path, circling round and round and throwing off a trail of vapour that smothered the ground underfoot. There was a deep, bass hum droning through the chamber – Doralia could feel it in her chest, so low and persistent it almost made her want to be sick. She staggered, a wave of nausea passing over her.

'There he is!' Jael Morgane hissed in her ear. 'Shoot him, damn you! Shoot him!'

Standing in the midst of the shivering wave as it lapped and spun between the two spheres was a tall figure dressed in black robes. His back was to them, but Doralia knew immediately that he was aware of their presence. His arms were outstretched, his head thrown back, and he was chanting in a language that was more colour than sound: a drab weave of midnight blue and grave-yard grey, of blackened purples and bottle greens. The colours seemed to stretch and break apart in the air around him, thread-ing their sickly currents into the roiling aether inside the spheres.

Next to him there was a smaller figure, half hidden in the folds of his robes, clutching at the necromancer's leg. A young boy, Doralia could see: Timon, his son. The boy was dressed in a loose black doublet, black breeches, black buckled shoes. He looked slowly around at her, and the crossbow felt like a spur of iron in her hands, heavier than she could possibly hold.

Her arms began to tremble. The boy's face was thin and wan, a drained grey colour, the eyes like black pits carved out of candle wax. His jaw hung loose and his hair was like lank weeds strewn across his scalp. The boy gulped, and from the black tunnel of his mouth came an awful lowing sound, a groan dredged up from the very depths of despair. His arm jerked upwards. His finger uncurled, stiff, near skeletal. Agitated, shaking and groaning, the black sockets of his dead eyes like holes torn into the void beyond, the boy pulled at his father's robes. Briomedes did not even turn around.

'Your tenacity is admirable, witch hunter,' he said. Even as he spoke, the chanting of his ritual seemed to continue around him.

'And yet, it is futile in the end. I will not let you stop me, not now. You have suffered much, to no end.'

Jael was hunched over, her face a mask of confusion, her eyes staring into the otherworld of memory or dreams. Her hand reached out for something that wasn't there. 'Davin...?' she said, her voice trembling. 'Davin, my child... Ursula...! My love, I am sorry! Please, I'm so sorry... Soon, I promise... soon.'

Shoot it, Doralia!

Her father, screaming in the Conclave Hall. The mirror in a monstrous hand, Sentanus, the Talon and the Voice.

The stench of those butterflies, the whipcrack of expanding magic as the mirror breaks apart.

Shoot it! Shoot her, your mother, shoot her!

Jael sobbed and hid her face in her hands. Doralia staggered and almost fell. She tried to step forward, tried to raise the crossbow to shoot, but the mad vortex of bleak colour seemed to leach all the strength from her body. Suddenly she could see her father and Jael Morgane, the vampire savaging her teeth into her father's throat. He was dying. Around him there was only flame, a terrible burning. The image began to fray at the edges, fading into a picture of her mother. She saw herself as a child, and her mother's mouth stretching open, impossibly wide, the slavering fangs. Doralia recoiled as she was caught in her grip – and then the fangs were descending, and her mother's mouth kissed the fragile skin of her neck, the teeth sinking deep into muscle and vein... Behind that dreadful image she saw herself once more as a child, but as a child transformed into something unutterably evil and grotesque – a vampire sick with bloodlust, with her vampire mother at her side. Her skin was so pale it was almost transparent, and the veins beneath thrummed with unholy power.

'No...' she said.

Her voice was only a hoarse whisper. She tried to push the image away but it would not move, hanging there in the firmament that had enveloped her, a mocking possibility of what her life could have been. She saw her father, emaciated, half dead, leashed on a chain in some squalid basement, dragged out only to be fed upon and tortured...

'I have plucked many an image from Morgane's mind,' Briomedes said. He turned towards them now, his arms still raised, the weave of his spell still threading through the aether of the spheres on either side. There was a softness to his face that was surprising, an affable sense of entitlement to the way he looked at them. 'But these images of your mother's death are particularly interesting,' he continued. 'You have my sympathies, witch hunter, to have suffered such a loss at such a young age, and at the hands of such a monster. I must confess, vampires have always sickened me. Pathetic half-things, preying on the lives of others. They think themselves great aristocrats of undeath, heirs of an ancient nobility, but I find that there is a certain grubby sense of pollution to them, don't you agree? An impurity, a contamination. Those that have truly died have completed their journey and are ready to be pressed into a new service. There is a cleanliness to death, an order to it. The vampire, on the other hand...'

He looked at Jael with scorn. She was on her knees now, her eyes unfocused, her hands clasped together as if she were praying.

'Morgane's facsimile of life and will is no more than the echo of her departed soul. Look at her, witch hunter. Do you not feel both pity and disgust comingled? It makes you wonder what she must have been like in her former life. I would venture that she was equally cruel and malicious as she is now, and the curse of her vampiric blood only emphasises the qualities that already existed in her... It would be a not particularly onerous task for me to resurrect your mother, you realise?' he said then. 'It is merely a question of uniting that which has been severed, the body and the soul. Although of course, she had already been turned by Morgane at the point of her death, and so the question would be which version of your mother would be returned to you...'

He seemed to ponder this for a moment. Doralia could see the amused smile on his lips, the professional curiosity.

'Yes,' he said, 'it would be most interesting indeed...'

Doralia dropped the crossbow. All the strength was gone from her. In the corner of her eye, more vivid than what was right there in front of her, she could see herself and her vampire mother preying on the weak, tormenting the strong, indulging the very worst of their most perverted desires. She reeled, fighting down the urge to vomit.

'I'd rather die a thousand times over,' she groaned, 'than see her memory so profaned!'

'Well, let us not get ahead of ourselves,' Briomedes chuckled. 'It is striking what even the undead will do if the lives of their loved ones sit in the balance. Morgane has told you of these "children" of hers?' he went on. 'Davin and Ursula, they were called. Her sentimental attachment to them was most fascinating, and I confess it was not something I expected. Vicious little creatures, but she did seem to care for them in her way. At least, she gave the impression of genuine distress when I flayed them in front of her, taking them apart piece by piece. I wondered then if her emotions were real, and to this day, I confess I am not quite sure.'

Beside the necromancer, the dead boy howled. He tugged at his father's robes, head jerking on his bony neck, hands twitching and grasping. Briomedes stooped to him, gathering him close.

'Peace, Timon,' he said. His voice was soothing and gentle, and he stroked the child's lank hair. 'Quieten yourself, my boy, it is nearly done.'

Doralia dropped to her knees. It felt like all the weight of her every last memory was pushing against the inside of her skull – every mistake she had ever made, every moment when a decision could have gone one way instead of another. It was as if she were on the cusp of each of those moments, and her choices branched out into a million different directions. She felt the pendant glowing against her chest, burning, as hot as fire. The crossbow was right there in front of her. All she had to do was pick it up.

'Alas, time is not something I have under my control yet,' Briomedes said. 'You are, however, witch hunter. Under normal circumstances, I would be happy for you to kill the author of all your pain, to stake that monstrous creature through the heart and be free of her forever. You would be performing a valuable service to the realm at large, I'm quite sure.'

Briomedes stood up. He looked Doralia in the eye, and his expression was one of strange pity.

'But I am afraid these are not normal circumstances.' He placed his hand on his son's head. 'Life demands life. A soul demands another soul in return, and the vampire has told me how strong the bond is between you and your father. Strong enough, I think, for the sacrifice I need. A daughter will die so that a son might live, and the world can be made anew...'

He nodded and turned back to his ritual.

'Morgane,' he said. 'Kill her.'

The blow was like being struck by a hammer. Doralia felt her breastplate crumple, all the breath knocked from her lungs as she flew across the chamber floor. She crashed into the curved walls on the other side, and when her vision cleared she could see Jael Morgane stalking towards her, hands like claws, her face twisted and fierce. There was nothing behind her eyes, nothing but hate.

'Jael...wait!' she managed to cry, but then the vampire was on her again. She felt the inhuman strength in the creature's hands as Morgane lifted her from the ground, slamming her up against the wall, drawing her hand back for the fatal blow. As the vampire's fist came sailing in, Doralia dodged to the side and Morgane punched through a solid foot of steel and stone. She dropped to the ground, tried to run, but the vampire grabbed her collar and spun her around, sinking her fist into Doralia's stomach, raking a claw across her face. She was clubbed to the ground and retched blood onto the floor.

'Fight it!' she groaned. She kicked her heels against the polished marble to push herself backwards as the vampire advanced. 'He's in your head, Morgane, fight him!'

The air around her fluttered with bleak colours. The great churning hum of the tower's arcane engines roared and sputtered as Briomedes continued his ritual. The walls of the chamber were shaking, the rafters beginning to split apart. Dust rained down onto them. She reached for her pistol, aimed and fired, hand shaking, but the bullet only skimmed across Morgane's shoulder with a puff of blood. Doralia threw the gun at her, still backing off, pushing herself along the floor.

'You don't understand, witch hunter...' Jael moaned. Slaver dripped from her teeth, her red eyes burning in her head. 'I have to do this if I want them to live again. He'll bring them back, don't you see? Davin and Ursula, he has promised them to me. I drew you out of the city so Briomedes could act unopposed, and I have brought you back to him so your sacrifice can power his ritual. When your corpse is no more than an empty husk on the ground I will have my children back!'

Quick as lightning, she reached down and grabbed Doralia's throat, lifting her from the ground with one hand, the other drawn back like a dagger. Through clouded vision, choking, she saw the vampire's nails as sharp as claws aimed right at her face. She clutched her arm, tried to prise the fingers from her throat, but the grip was stronger than stone. She fumbled for a dagger, dropped it, heard it clatter to the ground.

She thought of her mother – and then she could see her, standing there just behind Morgane's shoulder, reaching out. Smiling, so sad… but it was going to be all right now… they would be together again, at last.

And then her mother shook her head and dropped her hand, and slowly turned away…

Doralia tried to call her back, but all the breath was gone in her. Her vision was black, and beyond the black was only a cold, empty light. She felt the pendant against her skin, reached to hook her fingers into the chain.

With the last ounce of her strength, she pulled out the pendant and pressed it hard against the vampire's cheek. Sigmar's comet, the last thing her mother had given her.

Just superstition, she thought. *Doesn't do a damn thing to them…*

There was a scorching reek of burnt flesh. Morgane screamed and threw her to the ground, both hands up to cover the bleeding scar on her face. She bent double, howling, smoke twisting out between her fingers. The pendant clattered to the ground, charred black. Doralia flopped across the marble floor, dragging herself forward on her elbows, kicking and retching, sucking air down into lungs that burned like fire. She saw Briomedes turn and glance disdainfully over his shoulder, the great spheres swinging around him, the aether now as dark and corrupted as the grave. And then she saw her crossbow, just out of reach.

'You scum!' Morgane screamed. 'I'm going to pluck both your eyes out and make you eat them before I'm done with you!'

'Morgane,' Briomedes called. 'Enough of this nonsense. Finish her, if you want to see your gutter rat children again.'

Doralia dived, hands outstretched. Fingertips on the stock, hands curling to the trigger. She saw Briomedes turn back to the ritual, Timon groaning and trembling beside him. She heard the savage howl of Morgane's approach; glanced back, saw the madness in her face, the hatred, the thirst. The spheres moved on, paths crossing, Briomedes a streak of black amongst the weave of magics. She could feel the Spear far below them, like a creature moaning in agony. Reality itself was starting to fray and unravel, the skeins of fate boiling around them. Timon crying at his father's side. Her mother, baring those teeth, sinking them into her neck...

One shot.

She aimed. The spheres rolled onwards. Her hands were shaking. She could smell Jael Morgane behind her, the stink of blood, the burnt skin, the hatred rising off her.

Shoot it...

Doralia pulled the trigger, and the sphere exploded.

CHAPTER TWENTY-FIVE

BROKEN TOWER

It was not over, not yet. No matter how quick and brutal the assault, how weakened the defences, Excelsis had not succumbed.

Where there is life... he thought.

Everywhere Galen looked as he tore through the streets, he saw evidence of the city's reckless courage. In doorways and in lonely courtyards he saw ordinary citizens fight with as much bravery as the most experienced Freeguild soldier, defending their homes with every last ounce of their strength, sacrificing themselves so that others might live. He saw ad hoc units of troops, led by junior officers who had scarcely earned their commissions, fight skilful withdrawals and launch devastating ambushes against the throng of deadwalkers. Small pockets of Stormcast Eternals, Sigmar's holy warriors, were bulwarks against the tide of corpses. Knights Excelsior and Hammers of Sigmar planted themselves in plazas and avenues and would not move, no matter how vast the numbers thrown against them, or how ferocious the attack. Every minute of the night felt etched onto his soul, and his body was now beyond exhaustion, but as he cut down side streets and alleyways, clambered over walls, sprinted through backyards and dodged the thickest knots of fighting, he saw much to gladden his heart and put steel in his sinews.

Fight on, he thought. *Until the very end, and beyond. Never give up. Never!*

Briomedes' legions seemed inexhaustible. Every cadaver slung into the pits outside the city now wandered freely through its streets, the vanguard and the dregs alike of the army Kragnos had led to Excelsis. The teeming skaven, which had flooded out of the sewers before the siege, now crept and skittered in their rotting thousands, paws still clutching their rusty blades. Orruks, subdued by death but no less deadly, lumbered in their warbands ready to rend and tear the living, and everywhere the Sons of Behemat, dread gargants of the Ghurish mountains, stomped and smashed everything that crossed their path. The scrapings of the cemeteries joined those who they would have despised in life, and everywhere the living were hard-pressed against the dead.

He had avoided combat as much as possible, and although it had sickened him to do so, he had turned and run on many an occasion. He could not afford to lose any time caught up in street fights or bloody skirmishes, but his blade was still stained with gore by the time he reached the harbour, the barrel of his pistol scorched with powder burns. On he ran, his boots clattering against the cobblestones, the echo beating back to him from the slanted roofs and slate-grey walls of the rickety hovels near the harbourfront.

Soon the harbour itself was in sight, the vast half circle of Excelsis Bay, the seething sea beyond. Fires raged amongst the warehouses and the customs buildings, the low market stores, the tanneries and gutting sheds. A great plume of smoke hung heavy over the quayside, and there was a stench in the air of burning corpses. Boats smouldered on the water, wrecked spars pointing like admonishing fingers towards the quartet of blazing towers high above the Spear of Mallus. That colossus of ancient rock, planted deep in the waters, seemed withered in the purple flames that coruscated down its sides. Galen could feel the grinding, subsonic hum of its distress. There was no sign of Doralia, no sign even of Morgane. They had been too late.

He stared up into the night sky, now almost as bright as day. Up there, three of the Floating Towers were on fire, voiding great ribbons of aether and arcane energy. They looked like galleons capsizing in a raging sea. There were spots of light falling from them, drifting down into the harbour water, and it took him a moment to realise that they were people caught up in the conflagration. Burning bodies, people so tormented by the flames that they sought the refuge of the open air rather than the hell behind them… Faint screams reached him from a thousand feet up, desperate, agonised. He covered his mouth with the back of his hand; it was too grotesque.

A fourth tower flared mightily, a twisting column of amaranthine energy ripping down from it to strike the Spear's crown. Ragged black shapes swirled and planed around it – creatures of some kind, as big as wyverns. Further flares of magic lanced out from the tower to burst against the others, a punishing arcane fusillade that harried them as they tipped and sank. He had to shield his eyes against the dazzle, it was so bright. Raw magic, untamed, tore across the sky. There was a howling roar, as if the realm itself were being ripped asunder. Light seemed to bend and fracture around him. He looked on the burning buildings further down the harbourfront, and for a moment he saw long green fields in their place, a headland blistered by the salt wind. He squeezed his eyes shut, feeling suddenly nauseous, and instead of the fields he saw tall spires reaching impossibly high into the air, gleaming metal lit by a thousand lamp lights, the hiss of engines cutting across the sky between them.

Galen shook his head. He thought he was going to be sick. It was prophecy, he knew, the unfiltered prophetic magics of the Spear bleeding out into reality all around him. The world slid back from him, and overlaying it was a brief glimpse of a time before human feet had ever trodden the earth here; and then reality slipped once more and he was looking at some unimaginably distant future, when Excelsis itself had been transformed out of all recognition.

He gripped his sword, closed his eyes against the swirling nausea, the sick feeling that he was sliding off the skin of the world. He felt the old pain pulse in his legs and he tried to hang on to it, an anchor to keep himself desperately in place. Pain, his oldest friend, his most constant companion... the pain that got him up in the morning, that sent him out every day to fight the worst the realms could muster. Until the end, until the last breath...

'In Sigmar's name...' he gasped.

He opened his eyes, saw the warehouses burning on the far northern curve of the harbour. Saw the swelling ranks of the dead, stumbling along the quayside towards him. High above, flitting like black sheets, the swooping forms of vast and ragged bat-like creatures. He held up his sword.

'Come on then!' he cried. 'Damn you all, but there's one blade left in Excelsis still to drink its fill! Come on!'

Three orruks, mangled by decay, turned from a wrecked warehouse further up the quayside ahead of him, where they were tearing chunks of flesh from the bodies of those they had killed. They limped towards him, their ape-like arms hanging to the ground. Galen held up his sword in a mocking salute.

He sidestepped, swung, hacked the jaw from the first orruk.

Pivoting, drawing the sword into a great cleaving backhand swipe, he cut the creature in half. Pistol out, he aimed, fired, saw the bullet smash the brains of the second orruk out onto the street.

'Fight, scum!' he cried. 'Is this all you have?'

The third orruk made a grasping lunge for him, but he stabbed his blade up under its chin and wrenched it to the side, taking off half its head.

Skaven next, scurrying between the hawsers by the lip of the wharf. Near-skeletal things, the matted fur dripping from their bones, their faces as dried and twisted as tree roots. He kicked one in the muzzle, felt the neck snap, cut in low and took its leg off with one blow. He stamped on its skull and shattered it, kicking the rotten sludge of its brains across the cobblestones. The next two died quickly, but three more rattled up towards him, trailing their broken swords across the ground. Behind them, more orruks, grots as well, all drawn by his bellowed cries and by the clash of his blade. He paid them no mind, concentrated only on what was in front of him. Cutting, hacking, swinging the sword left to right, up and under. They tried to swarm him, but always he moved out of reach, backing off, keeping some empty space behind him so that he wasn't cornered. He was screaming, he realised. Battle madness, the lust of combat – something he hadn't felt in an age. It was like he was watching himself from outside, a grizzled old veteran using every trick he knew to take as many of the bastards down with him before he fell. And the toll he was taking was immense.

Bodies littered the harbourfront. Lank strings of intestine were scattered like rope against the ground. Some of the corpses, still locked in their unlife, tried to drag themselves across the stones with shattered limbs. Others, rendered into pieces, were no more threat. As the remaining corpses shuffled towards him, they tripped over the bodies of the fallen, sprawling out onto the oily cobblestones, where he gave them no mercy. His muscles ached with fatigue, his sword was notched in a dozen places and his coat was spattered with gore, but he did not stop. He wielded his empty pistol like a club, caving in faces, breaking skulls, shattering bones. His breath was a fire in his lungs. Black spots swam before his eyes. The sky above was a field of glowing flame, and the Spear was cracking into pieces. It would not be long now.

He heard shouting then, the clipped call of command. There was a rattle of musketry, the sharp whine of arrows in flight. Galen staggered back and looked up the quayside, to the north where the warehouses were burning. There he could see soldiers running, backlit by the flames, perhaps a quarter of a mile away, their polished weapons and armour gleaming. More rifles spat, and the deadwalkers that advanced on him, their attention dimly snared by the greater pickings behind, began to turn and stumble off.

He fell to his knees. He rested on his sword, sucking air into his lungs, wiping the cold sweat from his face. Bodies stank around him, a swamp of hewn corpses. He heard the soldiers further up the harbour, shooting, pinning the deadwalkers with their spears. He heard the water slapping against the harbour wall, the groan of the broken ships, the distant crackle of flames. He could even hear a sign creaking above a shopfront somewhere behind him, a sad and homely sound, and from somewhere far off across the city the tolling of a single bell.

He wondered if his daughter was dead. The thought was like a sword sliding into his heart.

Too slow, every step of the way. Galen raised his eyes to the heavens. Did Sigmar see him now? Would he forgive him, for what he had failed to do? Grief and vengeance had been his calling, not duty, and now he had condemned an entire city to death. He had condemned his daughter to death. Their defeat was absolute.

Galen looked up at the Floating Tower overhead, poised on its column of amethyst fire.

And then the night was lit by a burning sun.

A low, distorted howl rent the air. Spars of steel and jagged chunks of marble rained down into the waters. Caught in the explosion, the flying wyvern-like creatures were immolated and fell as burning scraps of flame. Galen blinked the afterburn away from his eyes and picked himself up from where he had thrown himself to the ground. Contrails of gold and purple ripped across the sky from the explosion, the Floating Tower vomiting arcane fire from the shattered buttresses around its base. As ornate as any cathedral nave, the whole structure began to tip to the side, drifting off true. It rolled and fell, trailing a great fume of energy like a comet's tail as it collapsed slowly towards the harbour far below. He watched it, as if in some suspended slow motion, crash into the flank of the Spear of Mallus with a shuddering roar, shedding a cascade of wreckage that threw up great plumes of water from the harbour. Fireballs spat across the sky and slammed into the rickety backstreets behind the harbourfront. Debris clattered around him, smacking across the cobblestones. Shielding his head, he ran to the dubious safety of a fishmonger's doorway, the patterned glass shattered and the counter of the unfortunate fishmonger smeared with blood from where he had been ripped to pieces by a dead-walker mob.

And still the Floating Tower fell. One of the wonders of the city, a symbol of the Collegiate Arcane's unparalleled mastery of the mystical arts, the tower broke apart like a flimsy skiff scraping against a hidden sandbank. It tipped end over end as it slammed down the length of the Spear, with a shriek that had Galen covering his ears. Plunging into the water tip first, the structure keeled over to smash down into the harbour. Hunched in the doorway, arms wrapped around his head, he peered around just in time to see a ten-foot wave of displaced water as it slammed across the quayside towards him.

The wave gripped him, unyielding, an oily sludge that plucked him from the doorway and hauled him off into the bay. Galen fell into the water and tumbled to the deeps, choking, eyes bulging, above him the rippled light of the burning city just out of reach. He kicked and thrashed his arms, the heavy coat dragging him down, the weight of his armour. With numb fingers he unbuckled the breastplate and let it fall, unstrapped the pauldrons on his shoulders. The water, caught in the tide of the tower's collapse, sucked him back further from the harbour wall, turning him over. He spun, felt the quagmire of mud on the sea bottom under his feet, kicked out again, grasped madly for the air just above his head. He dropped his blade, shrugged out of the coat, fingers reaching, the last breath of air like a pocket of fire in his lungs...

A hand grabbed his wrist. Clear air kissed his face, the rush of oxygen. He retched and coughed, spewing up the foul black water of the bay. There was a spar of wood in front of him, an oily plank from one of the wrecked ships further out on the ocean-side of the harbour. He hooked his arms around it and felt the fatigue wash over him. He drifted on the very edge of unconsciousness.

'Not the most pleasant place for a swim,' his daughter said.

'Doralia!' Galen opened his eyes and saw her, resting on the spar beside him. He sobbed once before he could master himself and clutched her hand. Her face was a mass of bruises and cuts, two claw marks dragged down from her forehead to her chin. Most of the hair on the right-hand side of her head was scorched away. If it was any consolation, he was sure he didn't look much better. 'Gods above and below, you were in the tower?'

'For my sins,' she said. They both held on to the spar and kicked out through the water, covering the short distance to the flight of stone stairs near the slipway further down. 'I was aiming for Briomedes but couldn't trust the shot. Damn hands were shaking too much after the beating Morgane gave me, so I hit one of the aether-spheres instead. Briomedes was corrupting it with his ritual, feeding the energy down into the Spear, drawing it off the other towers too. Whole thing went up like one of the Collegiate's grand illuminations on Gods-Mourning Night. Near blinded me.'

'Morgane attacked you?'

'She was working for the necromancer all along. He'd promised to resurrect her children, Davin and Ursula, if she lured us out of the city, and if she offered me up as a sacrifice. Needed a soul for the ritual, felt mine would be the best fit.' She coughed, spewing up seawater. 'I had time for one shot only, the sphere or Morgane, so I chose the sphere. Kind of wish I'd picked the other though, I have to admit.'

She raised her hand and held up one of her nullstone bolts.

'Crossbow's at the bottom of the harbour, but I've still got this. I'll stake it through her heart if she's survived. That I promise you.'

Galen felt under the water for his ammunition belt around his waist. It was still there, and the silver stakes were still slotted in their pouches.

'Not if I do it first. Curse her,' he muttered, his voice thick with hate. 'Every step of the way she has mocked us, and her treachery knows no bounds!'

They reached the slipway and dragged themselves from the water. Even though there were flames racing through the harbour, he still felt the shock of the cold air. Scattered fires crackled along the length of the quayside, smouldering in the deeper streets behind. The water of the bay was like a ship's graveyard, littered with broken rubbish, sodden sails, drifting lengths of rope. Dead bodies floated face down – aelves from the Scourge Privateers, the blackened corpses of wizards who had fallen from the burning towers. The wrecked tower itself squatted there beside the Spear of Mallus, fifty yards across the water, the waves lapping at its fractured base. It looked like some ancient temple drowned by the passage of time and broken by the elements, hidden in a glade or swamp far from human sight. Purple fire and golden flame licked across its shattered walls and cast a lurid light against the Spear behind it.

Galen clambered out onto the quayside, crawling on his hands and knees. He could see the troops clashing with the deadwalkers far over on the northern spur of the harbourfront. Pinning them with spears and peppering them with black-powder shot, the soldiers were trying to funnel them into the water where a slick of oil had caught fire.

'If the deadwalkers are still active,' Doralia said, 'then that means Briomedes is still alive.' She hunched down on the cobblestones and stared out across the choppy water. 'Out there maybe, still in the depths of the tower. Sigmar alone knows how I managed to get free. All I remember was the explosion, then the next thing I know I'm hitting the water like a cannonball.'

'I saw the tower fall,' he said. He coughed again, spat water to the stone. 'The explosion must have lit the sky all along the Coast of Tusks. Didn't think anything could have survived that.'

Doralia stiffened beside him. She pointed to the southern quarter of the harbour, where the Kharadron aether-berth speared up into the burning sky.

'More than you might think,' she said. 'Look!'

Galen, still on his knees, turned. There, much further down the long curve of the quayside, where the older wooden jetties and slipways stretched out into the bay, he could see a young man in black robes dragging something from the water. A child, he realised. A dead child, who yet lived.

'Briomedes…' he hissed.

Doralia drew her sword. Galen got to his feet, and then their eyes met – the witch hunters and the necromancer, through all the smoky wreckage of Excelsis Harbour. Briomedes gave an inarticulate howl and dragged his son to his feet, and together they turned and ran.

'After them!' Galen cried. 'Until he's in the ground, none of this will be over!'

Doralia leapt forward, but as she did so, the water on their left erupted in a spray of foam. Something launched itself from the lip of the quayside, crashing into her and sending her sprawling to the ground. Galen, on reflex, pulled one of his silver stakes. His sword was at the bottom of the harbour, his pistol just kindling, lost somewhere on the cobblestones; and before him now stood Jael Morgane, her lace dress a straggled wreck, her black hair like dripping weeds. Her face was as cruel and malicious as he had ever seen it. The mask she had worn all the way from Hollowcrest had been thrown aside. Once more she was the monster that had killed his wife.

Doralia rolled as she hit the ground, sword up.

'I'm almost glad you survived the explosion,' she said. 'Too easy a way for you to die.'

Galen thought fast. 'No, Doralia,' he said. 'Go after Briomedes, now! We don't have time.' He looked at Morgane as she prowled the cobbles, a twisted half-smile on her face. 'I will deal with this, as I should have dealt with it twenty years ago...'

Doralia looked at him. He could see the pain in her eyes, the fear. He nodded once and she threw her sword to him. He snatched it from the air. And then she turned and ran, without looking back, deep into the warren of cramped passageways and rubbish-strewn alleys where Briomedes had disappeared.

'Alone at last, ven Denst,' Morgane mocked him. 'When I have finished with you then your daughter will be next, I swear. I fancy she would make a good vampire herself, you know. Like her mother...'

Galen did not take the bait. He held up the sword in one hand, the stake in the other, and backed off, away from the edge of the harbour wall.

'This is the necromancer in your head, Morgane, dabbling his fingers in what's left of your wizened soul. You could still fight this. You could help us track him down and kill him, as you promised in Hollowcrest. You could be free of him, take revenge for what he has done to you.'

She laughed then, long and clear, a sound like winter ice breaking underfoot.

'No, witch hunter,' she said. 'I don't think I will ever be free of him... You were fools to think he could ever be stopped.'

'And yet we have stopped him. The ritual has been broken. He is on the run, alone, and my daughter is on his trail. And I promise you, she is the greatest tracker I have ever met – she will not let him get away.'

The vampire stepped carefully towards him, first to one side and then to the other, her eyes never leaving him. The teeth behind those dark red lips were sharp as razors. Her hands hung ready at her sides, her sharp nails ready to rend and tear.

'No, she will die too, ven Denst,' she said. 'That I promise you. But you will be first, and it will not be pleasant. Twenty years I have waited for this. I have few regrets in my long life but allowing you to live was my greatest mistake.'

The winds of prophecy leaking from the Spear had slackened and died away now, no longer conjured by the necromancer's spell. But still, as Galen stood there on the burning harbourfront, the smoke drifting like a fine mist around them, he seemed to see Marie and Doralia as they had been back then. His wife, his daughter. His failure.

No, he thought. Doralia was not his failure. She had gone further and fought harder than he would have ever believed possible. She would never give up. She was his greatest triumph.

He smiled, and he was pleased to see a small flicker of concern in the vampire's eyes.

'Two decades is a mere blink of the eye to one cursed with immortality,' he said. In his voice was all the bitterness and rage of every single one of those years. 'But imagine what it is to me, vampire. A third of my life. Twenty years that I have spent refining my hatred of you. You are a child, Jael Morgane, an *amateur*, when it comes to regret.'

He raised his sword.

'And now you will see how pure my hatred really is.'

CHAPTER TWENTY-SIX

VENGEANCE AND GRIEF

The pain in her knee sang with every step. The gash in her face from the vampire's claws burned like fire. She clutched the crossbow bolt in her hand and ran, threading her way through the tight passages of the harbour slums, cutting down grim little streets with ancient, rickety old houses dark on either side, their peaked roofs like arrowheads aimed at the brooding sky. Broken glass littered the streets. Bodies were slumped in doorways, on tumbledown stoops, choking the mouths of alleyways like so much refuse. Now and then, a rangy crow gave a tattered shriek and flapped up to the rooftops, leaving its feast behind. The glow of flames across the district lit the clouds and cast down a shimmering light onto the streets.

She gulped air, coughed, felt the weight of this endless night lying heavy against her shoulders. Her head was pounding, her mouth parched. She tried not to think of her father and his fight against Morgane. For so long now she had worried about him. Ever since the siege he had seemed a broken man to her, frail, lost in gloom and depression. But it had all been just his concern for her, his fear that she was condemned to the same pain and violence that had marked his life. And if he now seemed as imperishable as he had before the siege, then she hoped the same was true of her. Both of them needed only to dig a little deeper; just a little more, and it would be over. One way or another, all this would be done.

She could hear the necromancer hurrying on ahead of her – the rustle of his robes against the flagstones, the erratic shuffle of his son as he dragged him on. Every corner she turned, she expected to see him. She passed through a slender yard at the back of a block of shacks, a patch of waste ground drenched in shadows, and saw Briomedes hauling Timon through a wooden gate at the other end. From the Floating Towers above Excelsis, to the backstreets of its slums – this night had taken them both from the heights to the very depths.

'You can't keep running!' Doralia shouted.

She slammed through the gate and came out into a narrow earthen lane, with drying greens and outhouses on either side. There was a stench of raw sewage in the air, and as she reached the end of the lane she saw the necromancer crossing the bleak stew of a canal over a humpbacked stone bridge. He was limping just as badly as she was, and his robes were stained and torn. He held his arm tight around the boy's shoulders, stooping down to drag him on.

'Briomedes!' she called. 'It's over!'

The brown sludge of the water bubbled underneath her as she took the bridge. Rats darted away and flopped into the canal. She saw the necromancer hobble across an obscure little backstreet square, bordered on two sides by the backs of those tall fishermen's lodgings for which the district was known. She saw a few scattered ale barrels on the right-hand side of the square; they must be at the back of a tavern, she thought. What she wouldn't give for a drink right about now...

There was a tangle of corpses at the other end, about half a dozen Freeguild troops by the looks of it. Bronze Claws, from what Doralia could see of their uniforms. Briomedes stopped in front of them and spun around with a look of triumph. One of his eyes had been burned shut, she saw, and the pale, youthful face was scorched and bleeding. Given he had been caught in the very middle of the explosion when she had shot the sphere, it was a miracle he was still alive.

'Curse you, witch hunter,' he mumbled. His jaw seemed broken. He grimaced with pain and hugged his son tight. Timon, blank-faced, the dead hollows of his eyes seeing nothing, moaned softly. 'You and your vampire pet. I was so close... don't you understand! Another few moments and all of us could have been living in a better time. A better world!'

He sneered and raised his hand, palm upwards, fingers curled like a claw. Behind him, the dead Freeguild soldiers wrenched themselves up from the ground. Heads flopped forward on broken necks. Savaged limbs jerked up as if still holding their weapons.

'But I would not expect you to understand,' he said. 'You are just another mindless lackey of Sigmar, witch hunter, nothing more.' He spat blood to the flagstones and turned away. 'No better in your way than the mindless dead I turn to my own purposes.'

Every cut he made, she healed in moments. The vampire stood there as if deriding his efforts, turning aside the sweep of his blade as she darted from its edge. Galen slashed her across the forearm, dragging the sword back and trying to thrust it upwards into her chest, but she was too quick for him and neatly stepped away. With a desultory backhand she knocked him to the ground. He felt his cheekbone crack. He could hear the sound of fighting far away, the Freeguild soldiers still trying to sweep the harbour clear of the dead over at the northern spur.

Too far to make a difference, he thought. *I'll be long dead before they get here…*

'A poor effort, old man,' she sighed with mock solemnity. 'Your years are telling on you, I fear. So long spent on the trail of monsters…' She held up her arm and before his eyes the bloody rent knitted back together. 'I suppose you've always known that one day the monsters would be the death of you.'

Galen said nothing, swept the sword out at her legs and hauled himself up as she jumped back. He stabbed in with the blade again, a one-handed lunge, and tried to knife his silver stake into her neck. The point grazed her jaw, drawing a hiss from her. Morgane snapped out a punch to his stomach and kicked him back from the dockside, crashing him through the doors of a ropemaker's yard. He sprawled across the brick floor, a mess of fibre, twine and tackle blocks. His sword went skittering off under a rusty loom. Dust rained down from the rafters above.

As Morgane stepped in through the splintered door, he snatched up a length of ship's cable and whipped it hard at her head. Heavy, tar-caulked rope, the cable smashed her full in the face and sent her stumbling to the side. He darted back, deeper into the yard, slipping past looms and hatchels, the stake still in his hand. Somewhere behind him, the vampire cried out a litany of foul curses. He saved his breath and didn't reply.

She was too fast for him. He had no advantage here, none. His weapons were gone, and all he had to defend himself was a single stake. Crouching in the darkness, hidden behind the long wooden benches where the hatchellers stretched out the hemp fibres, Galen knew his only real chance was to lead her towards the Freeguild troops and hope they had a sufficient weight of fire to pin her down. Put enough holes in her and she might pause long enough for him to get in there with the stake. But then if that plan failed, he would be putting those soldiers at an inexcusable risk. Morgane would tear through them like a hurricane, and it would all be his fault.

'So we're playing fox and rabbit now, are we, ven Denst?' the vampire called. 'The little rabbit hiding safe in its burrow, while the fox hunts for it… Safe in your burrow, little rabbit, but not for long…'

Galen fingered the point of the stake. He could hear the vampire somewhere near the harbour side of the yard, tearing up the coiled bales of rope, smashing equipment as she searched the shadows for him. Carefully he slipped back from under the table, crept through the lines of benches until he reached the wall at the rear of the yard. His ribs were grinding in his side, and he could only suck in shallow breaths. He couldn't take much more of this. He was running on pure adrenaline now, nothing more.

'Where are you?' she sang.

He crawled along the side of the wall until he came to a door. Through the dimpled glass he could see the vague outline of an alleyway at the back of the yard. He tried the handle, reaching up and gently twisting it with his left hand, as silently as he could.

'There you are, rabbit!'

Morgane lashed out and grabbed his hand, crushing his fingers against the door handle. Galen cried out, and then she prised his hand loose and twisted until the bones in his wrist snapped with a dull click.

'Now,' she hissed. 'The fox is hungry after her hunt…'

Doralia darted back and snatched up a length of wood from a broken crate beside the ale barrels, swung it round like she was trying to fell a tree. The plank smashed into the dead soldier's face, caving in his cheekbone, popping an eyeball from its socket. She snapped its thigh with a well-aimed kick and then the corpse was on the ground. The next one lumbered towards her, a big man in life, a slack pot belly bursting from his tunic. She slammed the end of the plank into his throat, pushed him back until he stumbled and fell over onto two of the others. After that, it was easy enough to hammer down on their skulls until they shattered.

She lured the other three back down the square towards the canal, dodging past them once they were within an arm's length and using the plank like a shield to push them all into the stagnant water. As the corpses splashed and staggered through the rank stew, she saw the rats begin swimming towards them, eager to feast.

Back in the square, she snatched up a blade from the fallen troops, a brace of pistols. She tucked the nullstone bolt and the pistols in her belt and ran on, the pain in her knee just a dull, admonishing ache now. Across the square, past another patch of waste ground where the torn remains of another young soldier were scattered in the grass and an undead orruk writhed on the spear point that pinned him to a gnarled tree. She saw Briomedes ahead, twenty yards away, limping badly and dragging his son by the hand as they came to the dead end of an alleyway. The necromancer roared with frustration, turned, saw Doralia staggering towards him. His face held a hunted look, a wild abandon that, she guessed, he had never felt before in his life. He had always been the master, in absolute control. Now he was the prey, run to ground in these dingy backstreets, with no hope of escape. Beside him, Timon groaned and howled, as mournful a sound as Doralia had ever heard. It wrenched her heart, but she pulled the pistol all the same.

'Briomedes!'

She fired, the bullet skimming the side of his head and taking off most of his ear. The necromancer screamed, his eyes like purple fire. He stabbed his fingers at her, and Doralia took an involuntary step back.

There was something in the air, a low, threatening rumble that she could almost feel. She paused, tossed the empty pistol to the ground and drew the other. It was getting closer. The rumble began to separate out into different sounds: a steady, loping tread; a thin, erratic shuffle; the scrape of steel on stone. The wet slobbering sound of open wounds and trailing intestines.

Every corpse in Excelsis was heading straight for her.

Briomedes doubled back down the alleyway, shouldered his way through a door on his left with a splintering of wood. She sprinted forward and followed, pistol out. She reached the doorway, the back entrance to some run-down tenement, and emerged into a stained and derelict hallway. A lone lamp sputtered on the wall, and the whitewashed plaster was flaking from the ceiling. The floor was a mass of oily puddles.

Briomedes darted through the shadows just up ahead, crashed through a ramshackle door, dragging Timon with him. Doralia snapped off another shot and the bullet caught the necromancer in the thigh. He screamed again and fell forwards, collapsing into a low and ill-lit room, stained dirty windows leaking in a little light from the street outside. There was a smell in the air of boiled cabbage, sweat and burnt candle wax. She stood in the doorway, sword up. Timon was sprawled on the floorboards at her feet, Briomedes just beyond, staggering up on his wounded leg and trying to reach the window latch. There were three children huddled together under a table in the corner of the room, two boys and a girl, their dirty faces peering with terror at the witch hunter standing in their doorway, a dead boy at her feet. One of the children, a lad no more than four or five years old, started to cry.

Doralia threw the pistol to the floor. She could feel it all around her now, the shaking of the dead. The tenement trembled with it. Thousands, tens of thousands of corpses converging on a single space, tramping down every street and avenue until they reached their master.

Glass broke in the alleyway outside. Somebody screamed, far off over the rooftops. The groans of the gathering dead were like a bleak wind harrying an empty forest.

Doralia stood over Timon as the boy writhed on the floor. He moaned softly. The smell coming off him was sickening: camphor and rot, brackish water, the grave.

'Briomedes,' she said softly. She held her sword above the boy, ready to strike. The necromancer turned on his ruined leg. He held the table edge for balance and sobbed when he saw his son. His face was caked with blood from where she had shot him in the alleyway. 'Submit,' she said. 'There is nowhere else for you to run. It's over.'

'Put your sword down!' Briomedes cried. He held out a trembling hand. 'Please...' He swallowed. 'He is my son. Everything I have done is for my son, don't you understand? I want him back... back as he was, before...'

'I understand,' she said. 'I know what grief is, believe me. I know what it's like to lose someone close to you.' She thought of her father, the iron box and the basement chamber. 'I know how grief can derange you.'

'Then I am begging you, let us go. Give him back to me, and we shall leave Excelsis. I will hide us away deep in the realm where no one will find us and we shall be no trouble to anyone ever again, I promise you this. Please! Just let Timon live.'

'I can't do that,' she said. She held the sword steady. 'Didn't you ever stop to think how many people in this city would lose sons of their own? Daughters, mothers, sisters? Fathers...'

The tramp of the dead was insistent, an earthquake approaching.

Something wrenched and broke in the tenement behind her, the crush of corpses pushing into the hallway. The rickety building shook, bursting at the seams with the resurrected slain. The street outside was packed with them. She heard scattered gunfire, the clash of swords. Screams, more and more screams.

'You must understand, witch hunter,' Briomedes begged her. 'You are in no position to be making demands of any kind! In moments they will be upon you, the hordes of my deadwalkers. They will tear you to pieces and not harm a hair on my or Timon's head.'

The children under the table sobbed, terrified. Briomedes snatched the youngest boy up by the hair and dragged him screaming into the centre of the room. He brandished the boy like a shield.

'They will kill these youngsters too, is that what you want? With your last breath you would see them mangled and destroyed, their heads ripped from their shoulders, skin torn from their bones and their guts strewn like offal around this filthy room! Would you spend your last moments as witness to such crimes? Now,' he screamed, 'damn you, witch hunter, give me my son!'

He stabbed the stake into her thigh, snatched back his broken wrist. He could hardly breathe, the pain was so bad. The vampire groaned at the silver burning in her leg, but she plucked the stake free and tossed it into the shadows.

'Naughty rabbit,' she snarled. 'That hurt!'

She picked him up by the hair and smashed his face into the glass panel of the door. Galen slumped to the ground, bleeding from a dozen cuts, but Morgane would give him no peace yet.

'Enough of these games now, Galen,' she said.

She hooked her claws to the collar of his tunic, dragged him up and sent him crashing through the doorway into the alley beyond. He tried to break his fall as he hit the ground, but then the vampire was on him again, pitching him forwards to tumble head first into a mass of scaffolding by a broken wall on the other side. He crumpled into one of the iron poles, pitched it over, tried to cover his head as planks and slats of wood came slamming down on top of him.

Gods, he thought, *Sigmar, please, just end it now. Just let me die...*

Jael hunched over him as he lay there, his sight as clouded as the night sky above. He could smell her, that strange scent of blood and withered flowers, the husky touch of her breath against his cheek, the feel of her body writhing on top of him. She stroked a fingertip along the side of his throat.

'Will you taste like her, I wonder?' she whispered. 'Like Marie, your dear wife? Hmm, Galen? Haven't you wondered what this moment would be like? Here,' she said, so softly. 'Let me show you the true *ecstasy* of pain...'

She bared her teeth and sank them into his flesh.

The smell of them, a tidal wave of grave-stench vomited from the ground. The stink of rot and putrescence. She could feel them, moments away now, the corridor behind her thick with corpses. Hands reaching for her, the children screaming, the boy in the necromancer's grip crying at her to save him. Dead fingertips scrabbled at the window glass. Doralia gripped her sword in both hands. Timon moaned softly at her feet.

'Now!' Briomedes screamed. 'Your life and the life of everyone left in this city hangs in the balance, witch hunter! What is it to be! Death? Or duty?'

She closed her eyes. The stench was heavy in her nose, the shuffling reek of the zombies as they pressed into the room. There were hands reaching for her, the dead hands of grots and orruks, of soldiers and civilians, men and women, children. The dead of Excelsis. Cold fingers brushed at her hair, grasped her shoulder...

She thought of her mother.

The sword tumbled from her grip.

Briomedes cried in triumph, dropping the child he had snatched, darting forward towards his son; and before he could take another step Doralia plucked the nullstone bolt from her belt and sent it spinning across the room.

'Duty,' she said.

The necromancer choked, hands flying up to his throat, fingers scrabbling at the shaft as blood bubbled between his fingers. Shrieking, a strangulated whine, he tried to pluck the bolt free.

Doralia snatched her blade from the ground, stepped forward and calmly plunged it straight through his black heart.

The vampire screamed as if she had swallowed fire. She reared up, staggered on the rubble of the scaffolding and fell backwards onto the dirty flagstones of the alleyway. Her face was twisted in pain and confusion, her hands shaking, feet kicking as if she were having a fit.

Galen pulled himself up, groaning, one hand staunching the blood as it dripped from his wounded throat. He picked up a spar of scaffolding pole, a solid two-foot length of iron.

Morgane stilled herself, her red eyes clearing, her breath coming in a dreamy flutter. She tried to sit up.

'Briomedes,' she whispered. 'He's dead, ven Denst... She did it, Doralia... He's dead... I'm... I'm free...'

Galen swung the pole with every last reserve of strength he had and caved in the side of her head.

'You're a long way from free, vampire,' he said.

She slammed to the ground, face spasming in shock. He hit her again, same place. Then he hit her again, and then again. He didn't stop hitting her until her skull was a cracked shambles against the stone, and even as he watched, he saw it slowly bubble back together. Like mycelium creeping across a rotting log, the bones and brains wove their sinews slowly into shape.

He looked at the ropemaker's yard across the alleyway.

He smiled. And then he hit her again.

The dead lay all around her. Stacked in piles, sprawled across the floorboards of the bare little backstreet room. Through the dirty window she could see corpses in the alleyway, some with their hands still reaching for the glass. An orruk's fist was curled around her ankle. A Freeguild guardsman with half his face blown off was slumped against her leg. The corridor behind her was so crushed with bodies that they were still standing up, all crammed together in that narrow, constricted space. The last of the dark magic that had made them walk had faded away. They were all still, at last. They were all at peace.

The children cried quietly to themselves under the table. Briomedes lay on the ground at her feet, one eye still twitching, the sword quivering in his chest as his heart wrenched and thumped a final time. Doralia drew the sword free, and with a final gasp of bloody breath, the name of his son on his lips, the necromancer died. He slipped away, falling into that thing he had spent his whole life bending to his control.

She knelt by the boy, Timon. She drew her hand across his eyes to close them. There was something serene about his face, she thought. It was as if a great burden had been taken away from him. At last he had been allowed to lie down and rest.

Out there, the city was silent. No more the clash of arms, the screams of the dying, the barked commands of soldiers desperately fighting back. After a moment, from somewhere very far away, a bell began to peal. She picked Timon up and carried him over to Briomedes, laying him down in his father's arms.

'It's all over,' she said to the children as they huddled together under the table. She swallowed, her voice flat. 'You're safe now. I promise.'

The eldest, the girl, clutched her brother fiercely. 'Are you okay?' she said.

Doralia nodded. She tried to smile. 'Don't worry about me,' she said. She cleared her throat and closed her eyes. 'It's all in a day's work...'

EPILOGUE

The sun was on its long decline as the vampire opened her eyes. Spears of light lanced down from the far horizon and stabbed into the plain. The afternoon drowsed into dusk, coloured by all the bold shades of Ghur: purple and scarlet, orange and gold. It would be a dark and sultry night, but she would not live to see it.

She tried to move her arms but they were bound tightly behind her back. Her feet were lashed together, and there was a rope coiled around her throat. Other ropes, like thick ship's cables, tied her to the stake. Beneath her was a mound of kindling, packed high and tight.

She laughed, a sharp and sudden sound, harsh and unfeeling. The breeze carried it away, back across the plain towards the vast walls of the city behind her. Her head felt fragile, as if something were broken deep inside it. Something was missing, something very important... She searched her mind, plunging through her dark and humid memories, and then after a moment she realised what it was.

He was gone.

She could not feel him any more. Not as a lodestone burning on the far horizon, or as a sickness coiled deep inside her very sinews. Briomedes was gone.

She struggled against the ropes but they held her fast. She laughed again, but soon the laughter turned into a spluttering rage. The breeze faltered, caressing the dusty scrubland. The sound of the city trembled behind her, the sound of people and life. The kindling shifted slightly under her weight. She strained against her confines. She could smell something like naphtha or leviathan oil. Her dress was drenched in it, she realised.

'Ven Denst!' she cried. 'Witch hunters! Show yourselves!'

She saw them then, two silhouettes backlit by the dying sun, standing just a little way off. One tall, bareheaded, a long black coat dusting the ground at his feet. The other shorter, in a similar coat and with a tall, wide-brimmed hat. The taller figure held a burning torch aloft.

'Wait!' the vampire said. 'Galen, Doralia... you must listen to me! Briomedes, at the end, in the Floating Tower – Doralia, he took control of my mind, you know that! It wasn't my fault, it was his!'

The taller figure passed the torch to the shorter.

'I helped you find him, I helped – Doralia, for the sake of all the gods, you know how much I helped you! I don't deserve this,' she cried.

The shorter figure removed her wide-brimmed hat and strode forward with the torch. As she got closer, the vampire looked at her, and the look in the witch hunter's eyes chilled all the blood that lay dormant in her undead veins.

'Doralia, don't make me beg for clemency. I will not do it, you know that. You killed Briomedes, Excelsis is saved and all the dead fallen back into their long sleep – is that not enough? Must you take your vengeance to the very end?'

The witch hunter pressed the torch to the kindling, and with a sudden breath of flame the fire caught. It lashed up the stacked wood and flickered across the vampire's dress. It threw its hot caress against her midnight-black hair.

'Galen, stop her, please!' she screamed. 'Galen! Doralia! Curse your very bones, you bastards, you monsters! Have you no mercy? Have you no mercy at all!'

She screamed again as the fire rolled across her skin. Her eyes blistered. She could feel the flames burrowing into her flesh, searing along her veins, burning like ice. She screamed until the sounds that came from her mouth were not screams at all, but the daemonic howls of something dragged down into the very pits of oblivion, where there was no mercy or torment, no blame or forgiveness – where there was only the long, cold extinction of death.

They stood and watched until the fire smouldered low, just a scattering of embers in a ring of black stones. Night was falling true now. Excelsis was a welcome glow just beyond the curve of the road to Izalend.

Galen reached into his pocket with his good hand. The other was bandaged and strapped to his chest. He took out a handful of Ghyranian cheroots and tossed them into the white ashes. They flared and smoked, crisping up into nothing.

Doralia took a bottle of firewater from her pocket and cracked the seal. She offered the bottle to her father but he shook his head. She nodded, pushed the cork back into the neck. After a moment's thought she threw it onto the dying flames.

They walked back to the city, ten minutes across the scrub. They said nothing to each other. The night moved around them like a body of warm water, and the walls of Excelsis were like a safe harbour in a raging sea. The sound of hammers tapping, the scrape and rend of scaffolding going up, of stonemasons cutting new blocks for the walls. The work of rebuilding, once again.

'Heard some rumours,' Galen said, gruffly, after a moment.

'That so?'

'Nullstone Brotherhood,' he said. 'Could be there's some pockets of them in the sewers still. Just rumours, maybe. Maybe not.'

'Well,' Doralia said. She pulled down the brim of her hat. 'Guess we'd better take a look then.'

ABOUT THE AUTHOR

Richard Strachan is a writer and editor who lives
with his partner and two children in Edinburgh, UK.
Despite his best efforts, both children stubbornly
refuse to be interested in tabletop wargaming. His first
story for Black Library, 'The Widow Tide', appeared in
the Warhammer Horror anthology *Maledictions*, and
he has since written 'Blood of the Flayer', 'Tesserae',
the Warcry Catacombs novel *Blood of the Everchosen*
and the Age of Sigmar novel *The End
of Enlightenment*.

YOUR
NEXT READ

KRAGNOS: AVATAR OF DESTRUCTION
by David Guymer

In the savage depths of Ghur, an ancient deity stirs, and the drumbeat of war has whipped the forces of Destruction into a deadly fervor. Generals Ellisior Seraphine Lisandr and Casius Braun set out on a suicidal march to conquer new land, testing the forces of Order like never before.